PRAISE FOR AMANDA PROWSE

'Amanda Prowse is the queen of family drama'

Daily Mail

'A deeply emotional, unputdownable read'

Red

'Heartbreaking and heartwarming in equal measure'

The Lady

'Amanda Prowse is the queen of heartbreak fiction'

MailOnline

'Captivating, heartbreaking and superbly written'

Closer

'Uplifting and positive but you may still need a box of tissues'

Cosmopolitan

'You'll fall in love with this'

Cosmopolitan

'Powerful and emotional drama that packs a real punch'

Heat

'Warmly accessible but subtle . . . moving and inspiring'

Daily Mail

'Magical'

Now

All
Good
Things

ALSO BY AMANDA PROWSE
Novels

Novellas

The Game
Something Quite Beautiful
A Christmas Wish
Ten Pound Ticket
Imogen's Baby
Miss Potterton's Birthday Tea
Mr Portobello's Morning Paper
I Wish . . .
A Whole Heap of Wishes

Memoirs

The Boy Between: A Mother and Son's Journey From a World Gone Grey
(with Josiah Hartley)
Women Like Us

All
Good
Things

Amanda
Prowse

LAKE UNION

PUBLISHING

Text copyright © 2023 by Lionhead Media Ltd.
All rights reserved.

Published by Lake Union Publishing, Seattle

www.apub.com

Amazon, the Amazon logo, and Lake Union Publishing are trademarks of Amazon.com, Inc., or its affiliates.

ISBN-13: 9781542024822
eISBN: 9781542024839

Cover design by Emma Rogers
Cover image: ©Design PRESENT / Shutterstock; ©ONYXprj / Shutterstock; ©Inspiring / Shutterstock

Printed in the United States of America

This book is dedicated to the memory of Annie Powell. An inspiration to everyone she met, and who lived each and every day to the fullest. Annie managed to fit 100 years of living into just 54. She will remain in the hearts of her family and friends forever . . .

CHAPTER ONE

Daisy Harrop

Daisy Harrop stepped over the 'Welcome' mat in the hallway, with an ironic twist to her mouth. The mat, thick with dust, covered in clumps of mud and bald in places, was not really that welcoming. She picked up the hand-delivered letter addressed to her parents from the floor, admiring the official-looking council crest before placing it on top of the old cool box in the corner – that being the spot where mail was left for collection and recycling items nested until they were grabbed and plopped in the appropriate bins.

Popping her soft mustard-coloured beret on her head at a jaunty angle and tying her cotton scarf in a natty knot, she opened the front door. The sky was blue, even as the day crawled towards night.

'See you later!' she called out to whoever might be listening and wasn't surprised to receive no response. She did this: found a jolly voice that wouldn't be amiss in an advert or movie, as if saying things in this particular way might make *her* life more like an advert or movie. So far, as a strategy, it had proved unsuccessful. There was no bashful yet keen boyfriend on the scene, no lovely apartment with a balcony and a view, no spare cash, no happy ending where she got to laugh with her good-looking friends as catchy music played and she danced off into the sunset. Instead, the house remained silent. It was no surprise; she knew her mum would be napping on the sofa before supper, her dad would be napping in the chair post his shift at the sorting office and her older brother Jake would be in bed having an after-school nap. They napped a lot, the other three Harrops.

Wheeling her bike from the porch, she looked over the fence towards the Kelleways' house, as was her habit. This she did just in case he might be visiting his grandparents – Cassian, the boy who filled her thoughts. Only this morning she had seen the local florist amble up their driveway with an armful of red roses.

'It's our anniversary!' she had heard Mrs Kelleway, Cassian's gran, exclaim, as she took the vast bunch of flowers into her arms. 'Can you believe he still does this after forty years married?' She laughed. 'I am one lucky lady!'

Daisy couldn't imagine her dad buying her mum flowers at any stage; maybe that was what was wrong with them. She pictured him arriving home with a handful of daffs and her mum busting out a happy dance before slipping into his arms . . .

'Nope!' She shook her head, knowing it would take more than a fancy bouquet to thaw out her frosty parents. They hadn't always been this way. She could recall pockets of laughter coming from them on the sofa and had even caught them kissing one Sunday in the kitchen. She remembered the way they'd sprung apart, blushing and laughing like teens . . . It had made her feel inexplicably happy, safe. But for the last three or four years, this coolness had been the norm. It felt as if the cracks had appeared overnight, or maybe that was simply her awareness of them, like looking up one day to find it raining, realising only then that the roof was gone.

Not that the state of their marriage was the only thing at the front of her mind. Daisy worried deeply about her mother. Watching her hide from the world each day was, without trying to sound ironic, a little depressing. She knew enough biology to wonder if her decision to withdraw from life so suddenly might be connected to the peri-menopause – the age certainly fit. But surely their doctor would be aware of the possibility? Broaching it with her mum was a whole other thing, though. It felt too personal, invasive. Instead, she showed her kindness and did chores where and when she could. This, she felt, was the best way to help them all get through it. Because get through it they must – what was the alternative?

Not that it didn't directly affect her. It did. First, it had altered her life, changed their once sunny home where music played and food was cooked from scratch and the garden was pretty, into one covered in a quiet shade, punctuated by the ping of the microwave. And second, she dreaded the same happening to her if this was her genes. It wasn't easy living in a house where someone had depression. It threw its cloak over them all, and it was shocking how quickly their home life had disintegrated once one of the four pillars had crumbled, leaving her, Jake and their dad listing, tilted and clinging on, wary of the fall. So no, with so much to worry about, her parents' less than convivial marriage didn't upset her per se, not anymore. Like every other aspect of her life, it was just how it was.

She paused on the doorstep and studied the four oaks that stood at the top of the road and gave this area of town its name. These trees were markers – grand, wide-trunked sentinels – the sight of which, as she approached from any direction, meant home. If she lay at a particular angle and squinted through her bedroom window, she could see the tops of them from her bed. They stood in a perfect square, wide enough apart to allow their road to be built right through the middle. One thing was for sure, whoever had been around when they were no more than sprouting acorns

3

wouldn't recognise the place; they now had a Lidl and were within a short drive of a multiplex cinema.

She liked the fact that her gran would have navigated by the mighty oaks too, as had her mother. They were part of her history, part of all their histories. Solid, immovable things in a world that could at times feel a little fragile, a little flimsy. Privately, she called them Nan and Gramps, Papa and Nanny, as, having been without grandparents for the longest time now, she liked to think they watched over her, provided shelter in the same way her living kin would. How she loved these towering woody elder substitutes – aside from the fact she'd much prefer the real thing to be on hand to offer her out-of-date butterscotch sweets and buy her vouchers as birthday and Christmas gifts.

The street bore the after-effects of a warm day. There wasn't much activity. Cats sat lazily on steps, windows were thrown open, the pavements were dry and pale. It looked to be quiet over at the Kelleways'. This she noted with equal measures of relief and disappointment. No sign of anyone in the uniform front garden where the gravel was raked, litter-free, neat, and dotted with pots that provided year-round colourful blooms to draw the eye. They certainly drew hers. Flowers were her absolute favourite! She vowed that when she had her own garden, outside space or window box, she would fill it with fragrant herbs and plants, tending to them like they were babies.

Not that she could see that happening anytime soon, what with house prices going so crazy. Even rental costs felt unattainable for someone like her who, instead of beavering away for a deposit, planned on being a student long after she finished school. The financial world for her generation was a harsh and daunting one and there was a lot to contend with: student debt, the soaring cost of living, interest rate hikes and competition for jobs, to name but a few. She swallowed the bitter thought that she might actually be living at home forever! Oh God, she'd *never* have sex! How could she if she was under her parents' roof with her mum usually in the room next door?

'Urgh!' She shuddered at the thought.

With no sign of Cassian next door, she let her stomach relax, vowing to cut down on pasta and eat more salad, determined in that moment to get the kind of body that a boy like Cassian might desire. Lawrence, Cassian's dad, often parked his shiny Mercedes in the driveway, next to his dad's fancy electric Audi. The only other time she saw cars this pristine was in the window of the showrooms on the outskirts of town, but this was the Kelleways all over. Everything they owned and the way they did things was perfect and shiny.

Hoicking her leg over her rusty steed, she glanced at the windows of her parents' house. It was certainly the shabbiest in the road and no doubt the one everyone discussed at the Christmas drinks parties to which they were no longer invited. And she understood, figuring people feared that what ailed her mum might be contagious or, at best, that she'd have nothing to say, having been in bed for the best part of three years. On the latter point they might be right.

Lisa was her mum and yet sometimes even she found they had nothing to say to each other. This fact alone sent shivers of sorrow through her limbs. How she hated those moments when her mum would stare at her, silently pleading, as if she needed something urgently. And yet their words were calm and predictable.

'You okay, Mum?'

'Yep.' Her whispered response.

They'd then stare at each other for a beat or two, both entirely helpless, mute, and floundering. Daisy didn't know what it was her mum needed, didn't know how to make it better, and her mum, it seemed, felt the same. In these situations, she often imagined how much easier it would be if her mum's peril were more apparent.

She's fallen in . . . throw her a life preserver!

She's on the very edge . . . secure her with a rope!
Fire! Fire! I need a bucket of water over here right now!

But it was not apparent, and this was why they engaged in the silent, desperate dance of stillness that left Daisy feeling sometimes like *she* might be on the very edge and in need of securing with a rope.

Every street had a dwelling like theirs. One in the grip of decay or decorated with questionable taste. How she hated that it was their house. She often wondered if there was a correlation between her not having friends and the state of their home. I mean, how could she invite people in or have a sleepover?

It wasn't that she was ashamed of it or even angry about it, but more that it made her unbearably sad. The state of the place was indicative of the fractured relationships and broken marriage that lived inside its walls.

When her gran died, her dad had gone to town, rubbing down banisters, plugging holes in the roof, knocking up a bin store out of old planks he found in the shed, and whistling while he did all three. This industry had come to a dramatic halt a few years ago, along with his whistling. It was as if some unseen force had pulled a plug on the family. They used to play boardgames: Scrabble, Cluedo and Monopoly, holding tournaments and leaving the game set up on the kitchen table so they could continue after work/school. They'd lovingly bicker, debate and jest, wildly celebrating wins, and were not above bribery and coercion if it meant moving forward. Daisy wasn't sure she'd recognise that family now.

Yes, theirs was a sad building where paint clung in thin strips of pale lemon, the front door let wind and leaves whistle through a gap at the bottom and the original wooden garage doors hung off-centre to the right. This allowed sight of the oil-stained floor and brick walls of the room that was a haven for cobwebs and things that scuttled in the dark. It was a space too small for modern cars and which the Kelleways had long ago cleverly converted into a study on their side of the fence – of course they had. No doubt a study from where Mr Kelleway ran his linen business, supplying hotels and restaurants as far north as Wolverhampton, apparently.

Her dad gave a calm yet constant running commentary on all the things the perfect Kelleways did or acquired that annoyed him. Their shiny replacement windows, the fancy hot tub nestling in its own little open shed in the corner of the garden and the grand kitchen extension with lantern roof.

'Here we go again!' he'd huff as Mrs Kelleway greeted builders with trays of tea and bacon sandwiches before they'd so much as lifted a hammer. He seemed to particularly obsess over their ostentatious barbecue sitting under a wooden bandstand structure that was artfully strung with fairy lights, and from where the tinkle of glassware, the subtle rise of communal laughter and the waft of good meat filtered over the fence and through their windows. He disliked it all.

Of course, he didn't dislike any of it, not really. What he disliked was living in his deceased mother-in-law's house with his wife, Lisa, son Jake and her, Daisy, watching helplessly as the roof leaked, the fence rotted, weeds popped up between the cracks on the uneven crazy paving and the kitchen clock ticked ever louder. And so she'd verbally agree with his huff-laden observations, offered with a rasp of disappointment to his voice, as he peered from behind the curtain.

'*Another* delivery! Can you believe it? What could they possibly need now? Place must be bursting at the seams!'

But she didn't agree, not deep down, and would lie beneath the duvet at night wondering what it might feel like to be a Kelleway just for a day . . . She'd sit in that hot tub for a start and then Zoom her whole class from the marble work surface in the kitchen, the installation of which Mrs Kelleway had told her all about. And Daisy would do this with a fancy latte in her hand and Cassian in the background. In his underwear. He was a bit of a legend around school, what with having lived in Australia and everything. Picking up speed, she pedalled fast, her legs moving automatically and rhythmically, the handlebars tilting and turning as if her bike knew the way, while her thoughts stayed firmly in that hot tub . . . She could but dream.

As ever, she arrived at the back of the restaurant on the high street without remembering the ride. The heady aroma of garlic and fresh herbs wafted from the building, making her mouth water. No matter what was going on at home, this food, free when she was working, filled her with joy.

With her transport locked and propped up in the alleyway, she removed her beret and cotton scarf, both to be placed in the bottom of her locker at the back of the restaurant next to the staff bathroom. It wasn't that it was cold, far from it. Dusk, mid-June, and the weather was clement with a sun that seemed reluctant to retire for the evening. No, she wasn't cold, but preferred to hide as much of her body and face as possible. A hat and scarf helped shield her a little from view. She wanted so badly to be attractive and popular but was, in her own rather diminished view, without the traits that might give her a fighting chance.

Her hair was thin with a cow's lick on the top that prevented her from perfecting nearly all the styles she favoured. Her skin was greasy, prone to breakouts, her breasts non-existent and her knees were one of her most hated body parts. Great clumping lumps of bone that drew the eye, meaning minis, shorts, swimming costumes and any item that might reveal her 'wrestler's knees', as Jake had once described them, were not an option. Having spent more time than she was willing to admit googling medical interventions that might make her knees presentable, she was convinced surgery was not an option. In fact, just the memory of the images she'd seen in her quest to discover how to achieve the perfect knee was enough to make her feel queasy.

She was also smart. Seriously smart, and yet most of the boys she liked the look of were pretty and dumb. Her intelligence, she figured, might be less than alluring. Who wanted to go out with a wannabe astrophysicist when girls like Julianna Norton and Katie Priest were all bouncy curls, white teeth, fits of giggles and normal knees? Not that it would bother her, going out with a stupid boy. Not in the least.

Unbidden, and not that he was especially stupid, a picture of Cassian flew into her mind, as it did when she first woke up, again on the bus to school, during lessons, break time, over lunch, on the journey home and right before she fell asleep, when, for good measure, her dreams were peppered with delicious stomach-warming images of the two of them. Sometimes they were entwined on a beach or bed, or walking hand in hand, but always with him staring at her with a look of such intensity it caused the words to stutter in her throat and made her shiver with a longing that she carried with her for much of the following day. *Cassian . . .*

It was mental self-flagellation of sorts. There were boys in her class who had flattered her with praise, but they barely ignited a flicker of want. If anything, their nasal braying, scrupulous note-taking in lectures, and encyclopaedic knowledge of *Star Wars* disgusted her. It just wasn't what she desired. She had attempted to rail against her most basic wants, but there seemed to be no way to justify or temper it.

It wasn't as if she hadn't *tried* to feel attraction for boys like Dylan Roper, who was tall with enviably thick, long hair. Dylan was in fact sweet, smart and nice. He paid her attention, and she appreciated it, even when he over-laughed at her jokes and popped

9

breath mints before sitting next to her in chemistry. But he was no Cassian Kelleway.

She understood that life might be easier if only she could figure out how to stay in her lane. But alas, her misery was only intensified when she understood that it was nothing more than basic biology, and there wasn't a whole lot she could do about it. It seemed her loins only jumped and her stomach only folded for a lithe, blond boy who moved in a pack and whom she doubted had ever noticed her. He knew her, of course he did – she was Jake's little sister, and Jake was his best friend – but *notice* her? No, that was a different thing entirely.

It was her fate to be a background girl. Wallpaper. If only Cassian would give her a chance! She wasn't interested in his opinion on cubism with a specific focus on Cézanne, whether he could mentally resolve complex quadratic equations or his thoughts on alternative energy sources. It didn't even matter if he didn't share her passion for botany – all topics she held in fascination. No, she just wanted to kiss him and for him to kiss her back. And not just a peck, but the kind of kissing that led to other stuff. The other stuff she imagined as she dawdled home from school or when she was in the library where, with a weighty textbook in her hand, she elevated her mind to the dizziest of heights, while stealing glimpses at him and any other athletes who roamed the halls in vests and shorts, her thoughts very much in the gutter.

'Evening, Daisy.'

'Hi, Gia.'

Walking into the kitchen, she greeted the co-owner and chef, who stood with her lustrous dark hair piled on the top of her head and a piping bag in her big hands. How Daisy envied the woman her hair and her ample bosom which jiggled as she worked. Twisting the top of the piping bag, Gianna released fat ribbons of her delicious mascarpone mix, which she speedily and expertly laid in a delicate pattern of waves over the top of the coffee-soaked sponge.

Daisy knew it was a smell that would always make her mouth water and one that she was certain in years to come would transport her right back to this kitchen of the Italian restaurant where she had worked for the last two years, graduating from pot washer to waitress when Piero had left. And now, with business not quite as brisk and their opening hours pared down a little, it was just the four of them who kept the cogs turning and the machine of the restaurant oiled – an older lady, Nancy, worked the shifts Daisy didn't. And Doug, who lived upstairs, came in to wash dishes on the rare occasion they were super busy.

The money was better waiting tables, but there had been something gloriously rudimentary about spending hours with her hands submerged in the murky water of the sink where a constant stack of dishes waited to be rinsed and loaded into the dishwasher. It was freedom of sorts; no happy face required, but somewhere Daisy could simply be lost to the handling of heavy pots where the crust of charred meat clung and pale-coloured licks of sauces sat like tide marks inside them, waiting to feel the heavy swipe of a scouring pad and a sluice of lemony scented bubbles. A place where she could order her thoughts and breathe . . .

'Did you get your essay back?' Gianna asked without looking up from the task in hand.

'Yep.' She stashed her scarf and hat, happy that the woman took this interest in her, remembered things like the return of her essay. 'I did okay.' It felt easier than confessing to the red-ringed A+ on her paper, putting her at the top of the class for her year group.

'Clever girl.' Gianna smiled. 'There's lasagne in the oven or I can make you a salad. Or would you like both?'

The way Gianna fussed over her was one of the very best parts of her day. Daisy ran her hand over her stomach; the scent from the oven was way too tempting . . .

'Lasagne will be lovely, thank you, Gia.'

'My pleasure!'

Daisy fastened the apron around her waist and pulled her inadequate hair into a ponytail as she walked through the half louvre doors into the dimly lit thirty-cover restaurant.

'Fully booked!' Carlo clapped his hands, as he did when he was happy. His happiness, it seemed, was entirely dependent on the amount of money they were going to make.

'Great.' She smiled; they would all rather be busy. Not only did this make the hours fly, but it meant tips were better.

'Gia set up after lunch, so we're all good. We have a table of eight in at seven o'clock! It's a wedding anniversary. The daughter is bringing a cake.'

Oh no! She felt her stomach drop.

'A wedding anniversary?' she asked, her mouth dry.

'Yes.' Carlo ran his finger under the booking in the diary which sat open on the table by the napkin and cutlery station. It was also where the phone lurked, allowing them to jot down bookings and take the odd pizza order. These had been a little thin on the ground since a fancy, cheap, sourdough place had opened up in town – they delivered, and their trendy brand was appealing to people just like her. Oh, and their pizzas were *incredible*! Not that she'd ever share this with Carlo. Or admit to feasting on them, eating quickly and greedily within the confines of her bedroom, feeling all at once disloyal and in complete raptures over the beauty of their bubbly, blackened, divine, soft, salty dough.

'Mr and Mrs Kelleway. You know the Kelleways, they come in a lot. The old man likes to splash the cash.'

Kelleway . . . She spoke the word in her head as Carlo drew her back to the present. She nodded, and her ugly, bulky knees went a little soft.

'I don't . . .' she began, trying to calm her flustered pulse and think logically of how she could get out of there quickly. 'I don't feel too well.' She pulled open the neck of her shirt as if, in some cartoonesque fashion, to let off steam. The thought of serving Cassian, of him seeing her here at work! It was mortifying. Not that she was ashamed of her job – no, siree – she was embarrassed to see him anywhere! But the thought of being trapped here, in such close proximity . . .

'Daisy' – Carlo put his podgy fingers over his mouth – 'don't do this to me! We have a busy night! Have a drink of water and put off being ill until your shift ends.' His eyes crinkled into the smile that made her love working for him and his wife. They were lovely people who paid her well, treated her kindly and sent her family a boxed panettone and six bottles of red wine each Christmas. 'I'm half joking. Are you sick?' He took a step towards her, his concerned expression almost more than she could stand.

'No, I'm not sick, I'm . . .' How to describe it? *Dreading it! Wishing I could fall through the floor! Wondering if I can hide in the cupboard? Wear a disguise?* 'I'm fine.'

'*Grazie Dio!*' He held his hands up.

Daisy walked to the long table in the window and ran her hand over the back of a chair, trying to swallow down her nausea. But suddenly the desire to vomit overcame her and she rushed to the loo and retched until she spat. *Dammit!* Taking her time to wash her hands thoroughly, she braced her arms on the sink, looking directly into the mirror, trying to steady her trembling limbs. Nerves always had the power to get the better of her.

Loping back into the kitchen, Gianna stared at her, concerned. 'Carlo said you're not feeling well. Your lasagne is ready, but maybe

I can make you something different, darling? Some green tea?' she asked, as she wrapped the ciabatta slathered with herby garlic butter in foil, before reaching for the wooden brush doused in olive oil, which she let dance over the fat focaccia studded with sweet roasted onions and olives, and sprinkled with flakes of sea salt.

'I'm okay, Gia. I might eat later, it's just . . .' She liked her boss, found her easy to talk to – far easier than her own mum who was more than a little preoccupied, what with her napping and all. Daisy could joke about it mentally, but the truth was she missed her mum, missed her being present, missed squabbling over the Monopoly board. 'I *know* the family that are coming in tonight. The Kelleways.'

'Yes, of course, they're regulars.'

'And they're my next-door neighbours.'

'Yes, I knew that, and it's great!' Gianna nodded with a forced smile. Daisy wondered if she was tired. 'Like a party! It makes it easier to work on a Friday night instead of being out with your friends! Or something like that. I don't know, what can I say that will make it seem better?'

Daisy felt the creep of tears. 'It's not so great.' She sighed.

Gianna's words had only exacerbated her sadness; she didn't go out on a Friday night. She didn't have friends to speak of. I mean, yes, there were acquaintances at school, a couple of girls she could chat to at chess club, but the kind of mates you could call on and make plans, talk about boys and go dancing with, text any random or funny thoughts? No, not that kind. She didn't really know why but she'd always found it hard to find her gang. Girls in her classes were in the minority and those she studied with were as socially awkward as her.

There had been a couple of girls – Melodie and Fiona, who lived in the neighbouring street – who she'd hung out with a couple of times, watching DVDs while their mum, who was friends with her own mother, drank wine in the kitchen. It proved to be a glue of sorts, but her mother's wine-drinking kitchen catch-ups had been non-existent for the last few years and by default so had her friendship with Melodie and Fiona. Not that she missed them. Melodie's hobby was eating *all* the snacks and Fiona's hobby was whining that her sister had eaten all the snacks.

'Daisy, Daisy! This is not like you!' Abandoning her brush, Gianna wiped her hands on her apron and reached for her, holding her in a warm hug. 'You're not happy? I want you to be happy! Why don't you go out with that nice boy who hangs around outside sometimes on his bike? What's his name? He has a nice face, long hair!'

Daisy closed her eyes briefly, wondering what it might feel like if Gianna was her mum, knowing she could only benefit from contact like this, concern like this. She felt a lance of betrayal that she could even consider such a thing. But how she hated how her mum's depression had stolen the woman she loved away. She wished she knew how to steal her back.

'It's Dylan. Dylan with the nice face and the long hair. But he's just someone in my class.'

'You should give him a chance. Things like attraction and love are not always instant – this is real life, not a movie.'

'Don't I know it!' Daisy sighed, kind of wishing that it was.

'Sometimes things need a gentle prod.' Gianna smiled.

'Did you have to give Carlo a gentle prod before you fell in love?' She loved to hear stories of how things started for couples, wondering what her own story might be and when it might begin.

'Carlo . . .' Gianna laughed softly and bit her lip in memory. 'I was so unsure, even when we were standing in front of the church doors, me in white and he with hair oil holding back his thick, dark locks, and everyone we loved throwing rice at us. We didn't know what was ahead – who does? But we've woven a story. I'm no longer that girl who stood blushing on the church steps in front of

Father Alberti. I mean, look at me, Daisy, my waist is thicker, hair thinner, bosom bigger, bottom wider.'

Daisy smiled at the woman who was still, despite her dire self-assessment, beautiful.

'But I gave him a chance and here we are, and it's not all been sunshine and roses. We never got to be parents and that broke my heart, but there came a day when we decided enough was enough and folded away the baby clothes, dismantled the crib, wrapped up the hand-knitted blankets and gave away the soft toys. It was never going to happen for us. And that was that. The point is . . .' She coughed to clear her throat. 'I guess what I'm saying is, you need to find someone who gets you, who likes you and who you like in return.'

'And love.' She pointed out the obvious.

'That too is very useful, but liking is, I think, just as important. I want you to be happy.'

'And I am happy most of the time. It's just that the Kelleways are' – how best to describe them? – 'perfect.'

'No one is perfect,' Gianna boomed, her tone knowing. 'Trust me. No one!'

Daisy stepped back and smiled at her boss. 'But they are! Literally perfect. They're good-looking. They're quite rich. They drive nice cars. They love each other. They laugh, a lot. They even have a holiday villa, and they go there together and post pictures of themselves all tanned and happy by their pool, holding up drinks with little umbrellas in them. Some of them used to live in *Australia*! Their house is extended, smart. And . . .' She took a breath.

'And what, *bambina*?' Gianna coaxed while her expression was a little pained, as if she doubted any family could be this flawless. But Daisy knew best – they were, after all, her next-door neighbours.

'And I can't imagine being part of a family like that and to me they are like a mirror in which I see my own family reflected,

16

and we don't compare that well.' She thought about her mum, wrapped in her fleecy blanket on the sofa, and her dad, working too hard, eating and drinking too much, and in recent years being too wound-up about all that went on next door. 'Let's just say, I'm not proud of feeling envious of them, but I guess I am a bit.'

'I think your envy is misplaced. You're a wonderful girl. A smart, wonderful girl and you will lead a magnificent life! It is all waiting for you, Daisy. This' – Gianna waved her hand in the air – 'this is the first rung of your ladder. It might be my last, but it's your first.'

'Do you really think so?' She wanted so badly to believe that good things lay ahead. Wanted to think that maybe, just maybe, she might after all get to dance off into the sunset.

'I don't think so, I *know* so. Those grades you get, the way you work so hard, but mostly your beautiful heart, they will all bring you the life you want. All good things come to those who wait. Just you wait and see.' The way Gianna enthused made Daisy wonder if she was waiting for good things to come her way too.

All good things come to those who wait . . . God she hoped so.

'Am I paying you two to stand and chat?' Carlo called through the doors, his tone jovial but with something sincere in his words. He was always a little antsy when they were fully booked, a bit like pre-show nerves.

'I can't remember the last time you paid me anything!' Gianna shouted, wanting to make Daisy laugh, she suspected.

'Feeling a bit better, Daisy?' he asked with a look of concern.

'Much,' she lied.

'Good, good.' He breathed a sigh of relief. 'Because it's going to be one helluva night!'

CHAPTER TWO

WINNIE KELLEWAY

Winnie Kelleway sat perched on the velvet stool in front of the triptych of gilt-edged mirrors and pulled up her chin, running her hand over the crepe of her neck, rubbing in where she had dotted the thick moisturising cream that she hoped might help keep the years at bay. And actually, she liked what she saw. There was none of this negative self-hate she knew dogged some women; if anything she was the opposite, brimming with satisfaction. Sure, her hair was greying, although a monthly visit to her hairdresser put paid to that. And to the woman on TV who had said that a face lift was the best gift anyone in their fifties could give themself, well, Winnie certainly owed her a drink! *Everyone* said she looked twenty years younger.

'Oh, stop it, you!' She'd bat away their words, while joy at the compliment pinged in her veins. Aware of their flattery, she knew it was more like ten, but hey, she'd take it!

Dressing impeccably had always been important to her and this standard was as vital as ever now her seventies lurked on the horizon. Only this afternoon she'd spent the best part of half an hour deciding which wrap to place about her shoulders this evening – the sage, the mocha, the plum. All colours that worked with her dress, but which complemented her skin and jewellery the best? The dusky rose linen, drop-waisted frock with bias cut hem hung on the front of the wardrobe; she'd pair it with her tan sandals and lots of chunky beaded jewellery – pieces she'd picked up over the years on their excursions overseas. Her whole ensemble looked like she hadn't bothered at all, as if she'd just plunged her hand into the wardrobe and flung on whatever her fingers grazed, but in fact her clothes for all events were planned days, if not weeks, in advance.

Winnie Kelleway was a woman who liked a plan.

It was nearly time to leave for the restaurant. Having earlier taken two of the roses from her glorious bouquet and placed them in a crystal bud vase, they now sat reflected in the glass, adding a small fragranced scent to her dressing area. The sight of them made her smile. Yes, she was one lucky, lucky lady.

It wasn't without a certain smugness that she had woken on this the morning of her anniversary. It felt a lot like winning when she thought about the countless couples – acquaintances, neighbours, and friends – whose marriages had disintegrated. There were some she knew whose thinly disguised hatred lubricated their vowels when addressing their spouse. To live like that was, she believed, enforced misery of the worst order. For others, divorce had clearly felt like the best option, even if it was a decision made in haste. Those same friends now lived in a state of barely hidden resentment, quietly seething at the fact that, unlike them, she didn't have to forgo every other Christmas with her children and grandchildren or worry about cold feet in her twilight years, not with Bernie's plump calves to rest her soles on as sleep beckoned.

She was proud of their longevity, their history; proud of her close-knit family, all living within walking distance, and wanted everyone to see it, acknowledge it. This, she figured, somehow made them even stronger – if everyone could *see* their happiness . . .

The secret to her long and happy marriage had been using her smarts, her cunning. Sex had always been on tap for her husband, whenever, wherever. She fed his sexual appetite, knowing that when it came to asking for more cash, a holiday, an addition to the house, she only had to bat her lashes or unbutton the top button of her blouse and he'd agree to almost anything. It seemed simple to her. A trade, if you like. She didn't have to enjoy it as much as he did, although she often did, didn't even have to pay heed to the grunts, groans, thrusts, and meandering hands that got him so riled. No, instead, she could plan supper, remind herself to water her seedlings, even dissect the news stories of the day, as long as outwardly she gave the occasional murmur or offered a word of encouragement.

He, of course, believed she was as lost to the raptures of physical connection as he. It was a neat trick and one that meant she and Bernie lived happily. How could they not? Her husband enjoyed the benefits of a gorgeous house, supper on the table, a willing wife and all the material comforts that came with the success of their business. Winnie was confident in the knowledge that she was definitely 'steak at home'.

Four decades married! How was that even possible? Time seemed to be going faster. *Forty years* . . . and she wouldn't have traded a single one of them. Checking her phone, she did the mental maths, wondering what the time might be in Portland, Oregon and whether her sister Patricia would be awake yet. Yep, plenty of time for her to have texted or called with her words of congratulations. Jealousy was, she thought, a most unbecoming trait. In truth, she pitied her sister a little.

Winnie was both cursed and blessed with an extraordinary memory. Her sibling's sneer when Winnie had announced one Sunday evening over tea that she and Bernard were engaged had stuck with her. As did the accompanying words of derision.

'Bernie Kelleway? Good Lord, Win, he's not got two brass far-things to rub together.'

'And who are we, the Rockefellers?' she had cut in.

'No, but we are *pretty* and that's currency,' Pattie had reasoned. 'He's got a very big nose and rumour has it was born the wrong side of the sheets, if you get my meaning. That's what everyone at church always says.'

'Well' – she had splayed her fingers and marvelled at the nar-row gold band with no more than a chip of a diamond on it – 'I reckon people should worry less about rumours and more about what goes on in their own backyard, especially if they are the good, churchgoing type.'

That had shut her sister up.

With her hairbrush now raised, she smiled at the sparkling 2.4 carat rock that had long since replaced that little diamond chip. She wondered where that had got to. It had been years since she'd seen it.

'Oh, Pattie . . .' She shook her head. Try as she might not to dwell on it, it rankled that she hadn't made contact. Her *only* sister who, in her early forties, had given up sweater sets and the stability of her job as a senior librarian and set off on her great life adventure – or mid-life crisis, depending on your viewpoint. Pattie, who one day announced she wanted to be a 'better citizen of the planet', if you can believe such a thing. And who currently resided in the wilds of Oregon with her latest beau, running an organic vegan food truck in the evenings. What did that even *mean*? Winnie could only picture lentils, dirty fingernails and cabbage. And with this night-time employment, she wondered how Pattie spent her days. No doubt running barefoot over the forest floor with her long, grey hair flowing.

'Urgh.' Just the thought of such a life among all that tofu, pan-pipe music and nature made her skin crawl. She'd take a decently disinfected surface, Nespresso machine and a good air-con unit any day of the week.

She might not have been bookish like her sister but had been wise enough to see the spark inside the Kelleway boy whose eyes shone with a fierce determination to do more, have more, be more. She'd observed him for weeks from across the street while he waited at the bus stop. It would have been hard to say what first drew her to him. Physical attraction, certainly. And young Winnie was no stranger to physical attraction, having tested the waters with a few boys – all gorgeous – for a short while until their gloss wore off, which happened far too quickly for her liking. They were all the same: mad for her, breathing heavily enough to fog up car windows as they grappled with the hook and eye of her corset, scratching desperately at her thighs with inept fingers to release her suspenders from her stockings. It was thrilling, a power of sorts and one she wielded quite carelessly, until she spied Bernard Kelleway from across the street and instinct told her that he had the makings of something solid. She liked his height and those long, long legs, quite unable to see herself with a short man. And it was as a born-again virgin that she plotted her move.

Her childhood poverty made her uncomfortable in wealthy circles, aware that she lacked the nuances that money gave you. No, what she wanted was a boy with whom she could rise up the social ranks, someone she could learn the ropes with, working alongside him without worrying about making a misstep because he would be like her, starting on the bottom rung . . . Yes, she had wanted a boy like that. A boy like Bernard Kelleway.

Hiding her face behind a magazine, she had sat in the window of the local cafe on her reconnaissance mission. She'd spied him pulling the cheap fabric of his suit taut, as if it needed a good press, saw the way his head followed the shiniest cars that whizzed by and noted the way his fingers balled into fists and his neck corded, as if riven with the desire to have the same, to be the one driving past in such a vehicle, and not standing there under the inadequate shelter, waiting for the number seventy-four in all weathers. And she understood, because she was the same. She bided her time, not willing to chase him exactly, but also not wanting to let the boy with determination in his eyes slip through her fingers. It was all about timing. When the moment was right, she finished her cup of tea, put down the magazine and sauntered across the street, ready to make her move. And the rest, as they say, was history.

Quite unlike her sniping sister, pre her 'love the world/save the world' epiphany. Her parents had always been lovely, their home bland, basic, cool and neat. She and Patricia never went hungry, as daily their mother ladled hot, beige food on to chipped plates that had once belonged to her grandma. Yet no matter how lovely, Winnie could never shake the feeling that there was a greater life to be lived, one with more material comfort. It wasn't the only thing she craved, of course: she wanted children, travel and opportunity. But a very nice house was at the top of her list. Deep pillows, thick carpet, soft towels and an array of pretty things lining her shelves all danced on her mental wish list. One thing she hated most about her childhood home was the sparseness of it, the hard tread of floorboards beneath her bare feet, the scratchy towels that inadequately soaked up the tepid water of her weekly bath, and patched curtains that let the light shine through.

Having watched her parents struggle, she saw how a lack of finances pulled even the most dedicated of love thin. How even the fieriest sunset could turn grey when bills went unpaid, and how pitiful it was when anything made of fabric was darned and mended until it disintegrated under the lightest touch. She figured life would be infinitely more comfortable if she lived it with a cushion of cash to soften the blows she would inevitably be dealt. She wanted a more substantial life.

Almost by reflex, her hand shot to the locket in which sat the only two pictures of Louis: one taken of him in her arms – she could still recall the skin-to-skin contact if she closed her eyes – and the other of his face, close up, tiny fists curled at his face, born sleeping . . .

'Leaving in ten, darling!' Bernie called up the stairs.

'Nearly ready!' she shouted over her shoulder.

This was one of the bits she enjoyed the most: the excited antic- ipation of the evening ahead. How she loved to have her family all together, on show. Wherever they gathered, they stood out like bright beacons among the gloom. Not that it was intentional, they just knew how to dress, what cologne to wear and how much, the right level of conversation and oh, the laughter! This evening, as she always did, Winnie would imagine how they looked and sounded as a group, as if she were on the outside looking in, and knew without doubt that she would be impressed. This was very, very important – especially tonight.

Cassian and Domino, her grandchildren, were extremely hand- some, and she took pride in the fact. As if it was all part of her masterplan – to have good-looking kids who had good-looking kids. Julie, her son's wife, was slim, sure, but beautiful? Not so much. She had one of those faces that when you first met her and she was heavily made-up, might pass as such, but with time and age, in her view, Julie looked a little homely. Would it kill the woman to get a facial and a decent hair cut? Winnie had no idea how anyone could live with crispy ends to their locks. Her son Lawrence was a different matter altogether. He was always neat, well turned-out and incredibly good-looking. Everyone had always said so. For this, too, she took credit, as if it was her genes alone that shone from his handsome face.

It was ironic, however, that whilst her son was so blessed, her daughter Cleo, who she loved very much, most definitely took after her father, especially in the nose department. Not that she didn't dress well and keep her weight down – thankfully she did both. But Cleo was without the natural attributes that made a face stand out: no razor-sharp cheekbones, no large eyes with luscious lashes and no full lips that hid white, straight teeth. Instead, she was rather a doughy-looking girl, pale and with the mousy/auburn hair of her absent aunt Pattie. Winnie had been gently suggesting since her daughter was a teenager that a quick rinse with a bottle of blonde would lift her whole look, but to no avail; Cleo refused point blank to dye her hair. Her daughter's reluctance mystified her.

Winnie knew every parent had a favourite and to say otherwise was a lie. Her son Lawrence was hers. Did it make her a bad parent? No. It made her an honest one. Not that her daughter would ever know this, nor was she aware, and that was absolutely right. But it was a fact nonetheless that Lawrence was and always had been the child that made her heart swell with pride.

Cleo was kind, no doubt, but her appearance, lack of ambition and the fact that she had married the rather hapless van driver Georgie cemented her middle ranking when it came to life. But, as Bernie had reminded her many, many times, as long as Cleo was happy, wasn't that what life was all about? Winnie had smiled sweetly and nodded as, yes, he was no doubt right, but still it irked her. But *Georgie*. For the love of God! He had been a friend of Lawrence's from school and Winnie felt it was that familiarity that made Cleo comfortable in dating him. In this regard she half-blamed herself, thinking of all the times she'd made Georgie a glass of squash or invited him to stay for supper. If she'd known how things were going to turn out and could turn back time, she'd have shooed him out the door and hunted down a better prospect.

What she hadn't told her husband, or anyone for that matter, was that she had actually found a perfect partner for Cleo – the rather lovely Mr Portland of Portland and Portland, the local estate agents. He co-owned the business with his older brother and had only recently been seen in a shiny new blue Porsche 911. He was about the same age as Cleo, single, and although a snappy dresser, was not exactly Hollywood handsome, meaning the competition wouldn't be too fierce and equally that *he* couldn't afford to be too picky. Judging by the way he kept his gaze and voice low, he was a man more than aware of his limitations. Yes, he and Cleo would be smashing together. Winnie could also tell that he liked her and Bernie, always waving heartily and smiling brightly when he drove past them on the high street; clearly, he would have no aversion to joining the Kelleway gang. She'd even mentioned to Mr Portland in passing that Lawrence had a place up on Newman Road, knowing that he, more than most, would be aware of the average selling price and plot size which were the highest and biggest in the postcode. Yes, Four Oaks was without doubt the most desirable area for schools and amenities, but Newman Road was in a class of its own. All she had to do was wait until Georgie either messed up spectacularly, as she had no doubt he would, or Cleo came to her senses, finally tiring of the mediocrity of life in their new-build in Swallow Drive and plodding about in slippers on her laminate floor.

'Cleo Portland,' she tested the moniker under her breath. It sounded good.

With her dress on and her hair sprayed, she fastened the strappy sandals on to her feet and stood to admire herself in the full-length mirror. She ran her hand over her stomach, liking the feel of it, slender and flat, a woman who knew how to look after herself.

Bernie's whistle from the doorway made her giggle like a teen.

'Oh, stop it, you!' She batted away his whistled compliment.

'You look knock-out!' He breathed heavily, walking forward with that look in his eye that told her if time were not so pressing and her dress not so expertly ironed, he would lower her down on the bed right there and then. And with his tanned skin looking good against his white shirt, she'd let him.

'Seriously,' he whispered against her neck, holding her against him, 'you do something to me . . . you always have, and I have to admit, knowing I'm the only man who has ever known the delight of you, Winnie, it's a very attractive thing.' He gently bit her shoulder.

'How lucky are we, Bernie? After all these years . . .' She let the thought trail.

'I don't know what I'd do without you, Win.'

'You don't have to worry about that. I'm not going anywhere.' She kissed his cheek. 'Now come on, Cleo's picking us up any minute and we need to lock up.'

'Hope she's okay.' He pulled away. 'I keep thinking about when you had our kids and it was hard to watch and not be able to help more.'

'Oh, you poor thing, was it hard for you having to observe all that?' she gently mocked, running her hand over his face. 'You weren't even at the business end!'

'You know what I mean.' He caught her wrist. 'When the woman you love is in distress or pain, you feel so helpless.' He shook his head.

'Long time ago.' She reached for her wrap and raffia bag from the chair and popped her lipstick and scent into it. 'Long time ago.'

'I've put the cake by the front door – we can't forget it!'

'No, of course, good thinking. Did I mention the woman who made it had a cake on *Gardeners' World*? She's practically famous.' Winnie liked to think her cake was good enough to be presented on the BBC.

'You did.' He smiled.

The sound of three horn beeps could be heard from the driveway. She rolled her eyes. 'Even the way he beeps the horn irritates me.'

'He's a good man, and he's Cleo's choice. Soon to be father of your grandchild.' He kissed her lightly.

Thanks for reminding me . . . This she kept to herself as she followed him out of the bedroom door.

Bernie turned back to face her, halting on the landing, 'Did you see the letter from the council about the tree?'

'What letter about what tree?'

'I'll take that as a no.' He continued down the stairs. 'Hand-delivered. I only skimmed it, but they're saying they might need to take down one of the four oaks. Decay apparently, dangerous or something, but someone's assessed it as in risk of falling. Can you imagine? That'd do some damage! You wouldn't want to be underneath it when it went.'

Winnie faltered on the stair and held the banister. 'They can't do that! They absolutely cannot do that!' Her thoughts tumbled, as her heart rate rose rapidly. They would become a laughing stock! How could you boast of living in Four Oaks when there were only three? The very idea! Not to mention what it would do to house prices. Four Oaks without its landmark, its mascots? The idea left her cold.

'Let's not worry about it tonight. Anyway, I'm sure it won't come to that.' Bernie waited for her at the bottom of the stairs and reached for her hand.

She nodded, hoping to God he was right.

CHAPTER THREE

CASSIAN KELLEWAY

Cassian Kelleway, seated in the back of his dad's Mercedes, studied his hands. His fingers were overly long, but his skin smooth and nails a good shape. His dad's hands, in contrast, were scarred, with veins bulging on the back, unsightly clumps of hair sprouting above his knuckles – and there was an indent in his thumb, the result of a bike chain incident in his youth, the telling of which had made Cassian feel a little sick. He might grow old and ugly, but he hoped his hands would stay this way. After all, they would touch the skin of someone he loved, shake hands with strangers, make a home, paint pictures, hold babies . . . who knew what else? Not that he could paint. He smiled now at the thought of his crappy child-like artwork being hung anywhere.

His sister, watching him with a sideways stare, sighed loudly, and he curled his fingers away. His phone beeped and he flicked off the volume button, putting it face down on his leg. It might be another girl sliding into his DMs. It happened daily, either girls from school or randoms who simply liked the look of him on social media. He cringed on their behalf, finding it hard to feel flattered. He never responded and was quite bemused by the fact they seemed to believe a compliment about his hair, face or body might be enough to lead to something more. It was, in his view, a little clichéd, a little sad, a little desperate. Although a small part of him admired their confidence. He should be so bold.

They stop-started in the traffic. How he hated the weighted silence inside the car. Other than the fan of the air conditioning humming loudly, there was nothing. He swallowed the lump that rose in his throat, keeping it all at bay. Unsure how to mourn all they had lost. He thought about the journeys they had taken in and around Melbourne, different people in a different time. Quite unrecognisable now. His parents in their sunnies, the radio tuned to Gold, roof down, laughing at everything and anything, making stupid jokes, singing along, planning what they'd do when they got to St Kilda, what they'd eat when they got home . . . It was like they lived in a bubble of happiness, a permanent holiday, and he had thought that was the way it would always be.

His distress at having to leave the country he loved was exacerbated not only by all that he would miss, but at the very fact that he had not seen it coming. Remembering even now, over three years later, the sensation in his gut that he was spinning, confused, scared. It had been, and still was, a shock.

'It's green, you old arsehole!' His dad's words drew him sharply from his thoughts, shattering the quiet, but not in any way that Cassian had hoped. 'What're you waiting for, a written invitation? Go! Go! Go! You moron!' He then made a shooing motion with his hands, calling and gesturing to the car in front who had slowed a little. His dad's words and volume made Cassian's stomach shrink.

His dad was now breathing loudly through his nose and his mum stared out of the side window with her precious handbag on her lap and her fingers over her mouth, as if deep in thought. Which was probably accurate. He knew they had a lot to think about. His musings, however, were now quite straightforward as his stomach growled, prompting a more immediate consideration.

Chicken Parmigiana or lasagne, not sure what I'll order. I like both . . . Did I have breakfast? Can't remember. What have I eaten today? Tuna and sweetcorn sandwich for lunch, not much else. I won't have dessert, but I might have garlic bread and there's bound to be cake . . . Yes, I'll have some cake; Nan will want me to taste it. I hope she doesn't start going on about Gardeners' World *again and just lets us enjoy it – as if anyone cares! God, I'm starving . . . I'll see Jake later. Do I have any chewing gum? I can't go socialising if I stink of garlic!*

'Did you see who might be signing for Spurs?'

He became aware of his dad's question and sat up straight. 'Yeah, I got an alert on my phone.'

'Idiots, paying all that money. It's ridiculous. He's already running on old legs as it is.' His dad shook his head. 'Fans won't like it, I'll tell you that for nothing.'

'Yep.' It was all he felt he could add. He didn't care about football, never had, but knew that to say as much would be like a knife in his dad's gut, as well as entirely incomprehensible. Cricket was Cassian's sport, Melbourne Stars his team. No matter how hard he tried, he couldn't find the same enthusiasm for Spurs. Domino stared at him.

'What?' he mouthed.

Domino turned away, closing her eyes in a dismissive way, ignoring him. Not that it bothered him; they had very little in common, thank God. He wished, however, that he did have more of an interest in the things his dad liked. He figured that if they found it easier to talk about all the things that didn't matter, it might just help them talk about the one thing that did. But what did he know? He was eighteen and, according to Jake, knew lickety shit about life. Maybe he was right. Not that he was sure Jake knew that much more, being as his whole life had been spent in Four Oaks, walking to and from school, and playing nerd games that baffled Cassian on his computer until the early hours.

'You and Jake off out later?'

'Think so.' He nodded. His dad winked in the rear-view mirror.

'Course you are. Good-looking boy like you, out with your wingman on a Friday night.'

'For God's sake, Loz.' His mum's tone was disapproving, judgemental.

He echoed her words inside his head.

For God's sake, Dad! Is that all you can think of? Is that all you've got to say to me?

'What now?' He banged the steering wheel. 'Exactly what is wrong with saying that to my son?'

'Nothing. Nothing at all. You carry on.' Having poked the bear, she gave a long sigh before turning to speak through the gap between the front seats. He noted her manicure was less than perfect. Things like that bothered him. The small examples of decline and indifference – he noticed them. Little indicators of a life that was out of kilter, a life where the timing was off. He watched her closely as she found a smile. 'We're going to have a nice evening.' It sounded like an order or a reminder. 'Forty years is some achievement.'

'Get less for murder, eh, Cass?' His dad laughed.

'Yep.'

He couldn't imagine being married for forty years. Couldn't imagine being married full stop, although maybe one day. But *forty years* . . . that was such a long, long time. Forty was old! So old. When he got to forty, he'd have had his whole life over again plus four years. It was unthinkable. It was odd to him how people of that age, like his parents, still went out, had holidays, danced. What was the point when you were that ancient? Surely it couldn't be any fun when you were wrinkly and unfashionable. He figured that at that age, he'd probably just live quietly. Do jigsaw puzzles, learn Spanish, take up golf . . . Was it possible that any attraction he felt right now could last for forty years? He shook his head almost imperceptibly; the weight of the thought was too much right now. Not that he was thinking too far ahead. It was all he could do not to worry about his A-level results that were due in a few weeks.

Good grades would mean he got a place at his university of choice: Oxford Brookes to study sports coaching for three years.

Pleeeease . . . He threw the silent prayer out into the ether, wanting nothing more than to move away, shed skin and start over, so he could choose what and who he would take with him from this chapter in his life. It wasn't that he didn't love his family, he did. It was more that he was waiting for his life to start, and living here with his mum, dad and younger sister felt a lot like he was wearing something too small, as if he had a scarf wound tightly at his neck and all he wanted to do was fling it off and breathe!

He knew they meant well, as did his grandparents. He knew he was loved, but what he couldn't reconcile was how little he had in common with any of them. They might have been his flesh and blood, but if it wasn't for the fact that the same red stuff travelled through their veins, what did he actually have in connection with these people?

It hadn't always been this way, far from it, but life in Melbourne was no more than a distant memory, out of reach. And what Cassian was still trying to figure out was which set of parents was the impostor? The laughing ones who threw steak on the barbecue and jumped into the pool in their clothes just because, or these sullen, bickering, disappointed people? It was impossible to tell, but he knew which he preferred.

It wasn't only his family; he felt quite disconnected from his peers, teammates, everyone, certain he was the only one ever to have felt this way. He didn't share the history his peers did – kids who had lived in and around the Four Oaks area since they were babies. He was marked as different, a novelty, but also an outsider. In more ways than one.

He had now been at his 'new' school for just over three years and was still trying to fit in, learn the lingo, follow the often bizarre rules that made absolutely no sense to him. Why did it matter if he took two bread rolls at lunchtime and not one, if he was willing to pay for them? And who decided his bladder could only be emptied at ten forty-five, twelve thirty and two forty-five? The whole school experience was so different to his schooling in Melbourne, and despite the time that had passed, he was still learning the ropes.

Thank goodness for Jake, who made him feel less odd, less like he was in freefall, figuring out life one day at a time. Yes, he missed a lot about his old life: the weather, of course, playing different sports that weren't going to get called off due to rain, but mainly the way they had felt like a family. It had been such a happy time, he and Domino contentedly unaware that the foundation for the future they thought was solid was in fact a crumbling bridge on which they teetered. Ignorance most certainly had been bliss. His dad's energy and his mum's enthusiasm had been infectious. It made him believe anything was possible if he just worked hard enough. But things had been very different since they'd arrived here. *Home.* That's what his parents had said. '*We're going home . . .*' But it didn't feel like home, not at all. The three years in Australia had shown him what home felt like and it wasn't this.

His dad parked in the layby in front of his Auntie Cleo and Uncle Georgie's car. His nan and grandad waved furiously from the back seat and even after he'd given them a wave they kept on waving! He wished they could be calm, cool, and not quite so . . . showy. But hey, it was their ruby wedding anniversary, and they could celebrate it however they saw fit. His mum was right, it really was some achievement.

He watched his dad jump out of the car and paint on a smile. A smile that he guessed would have been much appreciated by the older man who had slowed a little at the traffic lights earlier.

'Here he is!' his nan shouted, as she was wont to do.

His dad put his arms around her and she kissed his cheek, he then threw his arms around his dad, Grandad Bernie, and there the three stood on the pavement, greeting each other as if it had been months not hours since they'd last been together. Cassian noticed how his Auntie Cleo watched the spectacle as she climbed out of the car. Her stomach was huge! Absolutely massive! He tried not to stare at it, wondering what it must feel like to have to carry that big thing around inside you. A baby! A little human sucking up all your nutrition and swimming around inside your gut. He had to admit he could only think of scenes from *Alien* and the whole idea made him feel a little queasy.

'Hungry?'

He hadn't heard Georgie approach, lost in his thoughts of parasites and childbirth.

'Yep.' He smiled. He liked Georgie, who always spoke to him like he was a regular person and not Loz's little boy.

'Have you been here before? They do smashing food. We come for pizza sometimes. We prefer it to that trendy place that's opened up – you know the one, all organic sourdough and organic this and that. Do you know what organic means?'

'Not really.' Cassian was sure he did know but was aware enough to understand that if Georgie was asking it was because he wanted to give him the answer.

His uncle leaned in. 'The difference between an organic vegetable and a non-organic vegetable is that the organic one has had a bit of shit rubbed on it and is three times the price.'

Cassian stared at the man, unsure if he was joking and therefore awkward about laughing.

'Plus, the tiramisu here is the best I've had.' Georgie clapped his big hands, rubbing them as if in anticipation of that very dessert.

'Listen to you banging on about tiramisu.' Cleo laughed, having overheard. 'Are you auditioning for *MasterChef*?' She slipped her arm through her husband's. 'I bet you're looking forward to tonight, Cass.' Cleo stared at him with laughter about her eyes.

'I'm sure there's nowhere else an eighteen-year-old would rather be than in the local Italian with his ageing relatives on a Friday night.'

He laughed. 'I'm looking forward to the food.' He spoke honestly as his stomach rumbled.

'I hear ya; the food but not the company. I feel about the same,' she whispered and winked at him. Her admission, he was sure, was meant to be inclusive, a revelation she figured might be common to them both, but again he only felt awkward. 'Don't forget to get the cake out of the boot, Georgie.'

'What are you lot whispering about?' His dad stood next to them and placed his hand on his back.

'We were just saying how much we're looking forward to celebrating. Forty years!' Georgie papered over their chat. 'It's quite something.'

'I said to Cass earlier, you'd get less for murder, didn't I, Cass? You'd get less for murder!' he repeated.

His nan roared her laughter. 'Did you hear that, Bernie? Loz said you'd get less for murder, the little devil!'

Everyone roared, although personally he didn't find it that funny, especially at the third time of telling. This evening, however, was not about him, it was about his nan and grandad having the best time possible. He would make the most of it, smile when needed, chat when required and get through it. He turned to face his mum, ready to walk her in, offer his arm, make sure she was accompanied. The look on her face was serious as she stared at the laughing Kelleways as if she was part of it, but not part of it.

And as they made their way en masse into the Italian restaurant, he understood.

CHAPTER FOUR

Daisy Harrop

Daisy swept the floor, filled the salt and pepper pots on the tables and wiped dust from the neck of some of the wine bottles that were for display only behind the narrow, dark-wood bar. She closed her eyes and tried to control her nerves. She owed Gianna and Carlo more than to be some dithering wreck all evening. And just like that the bell above the door rang and in they walked: the perfect Kelleways.

As if it was a movie clip, they entered in slo-mo, the whole crew: Mr Bernie Kelleway and his bouquet-receiving wife, Winnie, who had known Daisy since before she was born – as the woman was fond of reminding her. Their son Lawrence and his wife Julie. Lawrence's younger sister Cleo and her husband Georgie, who was carrying a stunning, ornately decorated cake which Carlo carefully took from him and placed on the bar. Finally, Lawrence and Julie's children. Their pretty daughter Domino was in the year below her at school and seemed to rarely speak. Daisy had heard whispers in the lunch queue that the girl had a reputation as a bit of a rebel, a party girl, but she very much doubted the accuracy of this information. To her she seemed a little timid, a little unsure, and Daisy hated how the rumour mill, often churning out misinformation, could malign someone in this way. And then came their son . . . their son, who happened to be her brother Jake's best friend as well as the object of her desire. *Cassian*.

'Daisy!' Mrs Kelleway called loudly, her smile wide as she waved. 'Hello, lovey! We were hoping you'd be on tonight. I said to Bernie, "I do hope it's our Daisy's night," and here you are!'

'She's working, Winnie, don't distract her.' Mr Kelleway tutted and smiled at her. Lovely Mr Kelleway who she liked to watch in the garden from her bedroom window, taking his time, snipping the dead leaves and heads from his rose bush one cut at a time as he chatted on his phone. His patience and precision fascinated her, as well as his love for his flowers, which she totally understood. Hours were spent ogling the garden next door from her bedroom window, not only in case she caught sight of Cassian, but peering at their flower beds and lawn was the closest she was going to get to having her own lovely garden.

Their own back yard was a little threadbare. The grass was sparse, flowerbeds devoid of flowers and groaning with weeds. The dirt was clotted, crumbly and dry, and the patio littered with broken flowerpots, empty planters, Jake's old roller-skates, a bucket or two and a long-since dumped basin that she had no recollection of seeing inside the house. Sometimes in dreams she recalled the way the garden used to be – dotted with flowers, never grand, ornate or immaculate, but pretty enough, pleasant to sit in. To open her curtains and face the reality was jarring. Caring for the garden had also come to a halt when her mum stopped caring for herself. Daisy was reluctant to step in and take the task over. It had always been her mum's space and while she was keen to help, what she really wanted was for her mum to find her spark and get back out there.

'I can't help it; I'm pleased to see her!' Mrs Kelleway beamed and shrugged her arms from her silk wrap, which she threw on to a chair. She treated it carelessly, obviously it was something she'd just grabbed to ward off the chill, but its plum tone set off her tan and perfectly matched the beads of her necklace. She looked lovely, glamorous.

'I've known her since she was a baby, haven't I, Daisy? Her gran was my neighbour for years!'

'That's right.' She smiled at Lawrence and Julie, who acknowledged her and took seats at the back of the table. Cleo, with her big round pregnant tummy, sidled on to the bench and Georgie, her husband, plonked down beside her.

'Look!' Mrs Kelleway yelled. 'Look at us all! This is what we do, we take over! There's so many of us, always feels like an invasion when the Kelleways turn up; all these kids and grandchildren, and another on the way.' She tutted, but the woman's volume, directed towards the back of the restaurant, and expression left Daisy in no doubt that it was a state that delighted her.

'Can you get in there all right, Georgie?' Lawrence teased Georgie, as his brother-in-law placed his hand on his tum, which was not far off the dimensions of his wife's, and took up his seat. 'Do you want me to pull the table out a bit?'

'I can manage.' Georgie shook his head. 'Do you want me to pull it out on my side so you can get your ego and your big gob in?'

Lawrence laughed loudly, as Julie raised her eyebrows at Cleo. Daisy watched, fascinated, noting the interactions, the abundant love, the affection, the ribbing, and all of it wrapped in the shining beauty that the Kelleway collective possessed.

Domino waved at her. A small, hesitant, closed-fingered wave from a young girl who was yet to understand the power in her beauty. Domino certainly seemed sweet, naïve, and Daisy waved back, aware of the heartache that growing up would bring to her door. Not that she herself had lived, exactly, but at a full year older, no doubt she had the upper hand when it came to life and experience.

As if to prove the point, Cassian briefly put his hand on Daisy's arm as he made to take his seat. It was fireworks! It was lava! It was his touch on her skin! She gasped and prayed she had done so silently. She could smell his cologne, which was intoxicating and floral. A little lightheaded, she prayed she wouldn't fall down right there on the floor. She could only imagine lying there like a goldfish out of water, and worse still, her knees might be exposed . . .

'Jake at home?'

'Yhaaaarh.' It wasn't a word, let alone a response. She could still feel the heat of his hand, which radiated up along her arm and sent a blush of discomfort across her chest. 'Uh huh.' She managed to nod.

'Cool. I'll see him after this. We're going back to my nan's so they can open their presents.' He thumbed in the direction of his family, not that she could take her eyes from his face.

'Mmm hmm.' Again, all that she was able to produce were these sounds. It was that or risk opening her mouth fully and letting long and well-rehearsed lamentations of love and lust spill from her lips.

The evening was passing quickly. Their service was a well-rehearsed dance that saw Gianna dishing up the food, dressing the plates, and she and Carlo delivering it, while serving wine, pouring drinks, offering menu options, and encouraging dessert. The restaurant might have been busy with couples holding hands next to the guttering tea lights with stomachs full of sauce-coated pasta and the mellow house red, but Daisy could only hear the burble of conversation that hung in an enticing cloud over the Kelleways. They were for her a fascination.

'Look at him, he's so handsome!' Mrs Kelleway pointed at Cassian, who slunk down in his chair, closing his eyes as if praying she would be quiet. Daisy thought it was sweet.

'Leave him alone, Mum.' She liked how Lawrence stood up for his son.

'Leave him alone? I'm only saying how handsome he is. I bet you've got all the girls chasing after you, haven't you, Cass?'

Daisy felt the air rush from her lungs. She held her breath, her finger poised over the computer, about to print the bill for table nine, but she was paralysed, wanting more than anything to hear Cassian's response, and feeling like she might throw up again, as a cold film of sweat doused her.

'Not really,' came his inadequate response.

'Course you 'ave! Like your dad, I bet. He was always popular, weren't you, Loz?' Winnie's rounded vowels slipped away with each sip of wine, revealing the voice of her childhood.

'I don't remember it quite like that.' He pulled a face at Julie, who closed her eyes lovingly.

'Yeah, you were! They all wanted you.' The woman wasn't done. 'What with you being picked up to play for Tottenham Colts, all the girls were interested in you. A professional footballer! I've never been so proud. Never.'

'Careful, Winnie, we'll never get his head in the car!' Julie leaned over, put her cheek on her husband's shoulder. Daisy liked the gesture; it was full of love, supportive and kind. She wished her mum and dad would behave in a similar way, show love to each other, give love to each other. It would be nice to spend time in an atmosphere where this radiated.

'Yeah, and look how that dream turned out. Can we talk about something else?' Lawrence tried to shake off the topic. Daisy saw him roll his ankle under the table, as if mention of his career-ending injury was enough to cause him physical pain.

'You got nothing to regret! Absolutely nothing!' Mrs Kelleway spoke loudly. 'You had a wonderful life in Australia, all that time by the beach, and now you've got a beautiful house, lovely Mercedes, two fantastic kids, brand-new sofa, your own business. You've done as well as any footballer and it's marvellous!'

Cassian snorted.

Lawrence looked down and shook his head, clearly embarrassed to be so publicly reminded of his success.

'Your mum's right. It is marvellous.' Georgie raised his glass. 'I've already told Daisy you'll be picking up the tab tonight, Mr Moneybags, haven't I, Daisy?' he called over to her. 'I mean, there's no point shoving it under my nose; I drive a van for a living. I can just about afford the starter!'

'You do more than all right.' Cleo reached up and kissed her husband's face. 'Ignore him, Daisy!'

'Sorry?' Daisy felt her face blush scarlet as she pretended she hadn't been earwigging intently to every word.

'I said can we have some champagne? Loz is buying!' Georgie quipped.

Cleo laughed, as Julie, she noted, looked down into her lap, arranging and rearranging her napkin as if she were a little embarrassed or maybe she just felt a little awkward about the topic. It can't have been nice to have their wealth so publicly dissected and discussed. Not that Daisy would mind; it felt like a small price to pay to drive that fancy car and live in a big old house on Newman Road. There were harder things to deal with, this much she knew.

'I'm only teasing him. He knows that.' Georgie turned to his brother-in-law. 'It's only right everyone's so proud of you, bruv.' His tone was sincere. 'It's true. What you've achieved, it is brilliant, and I know more than most how gutted you were to have to hang up your football boots. It's all you used to talk about at school. But just look at you now. I love you, mate.'

Lawrence raised his glass to his friend, who had married his sister. This, too, Daisy knew because her mum had been at school with both men.

'Oh, boys! Now look what you've done.' Mrs Kelleway took the edge of her napkin and ran it under her eyes where a smudge of tears and mascara lurked. 'Family! My wonderful family!' she shouted.

'Come on then, Daisy, more wine over here!' Mr Kelleway slapped the table, as she popped the bill on table nine and twirled back to the bar.

'Did you hear about the tree?' Mrs Kelleway called across the table so all could hear. 'They're going to take down one of the oaks.'

'Which oaks?' Georgie asked.

Daisy was tuned in as she gathered bottles from the cold wine fridge.

'One of *the* oaks, Georgie, one of the four oaks!' Mr Kelleway filled him in.

Daisy paused in her task. Surely not! They couldn't do that. She felt a little stunned and swallowed the urge to bombard the customers with questions. Why? Why would they do that? She loved those trees. Loved them! They were part of her family history! Markers that guided her home. They were her grandparents!

'We got a letter from the council,' Mr Kelleway continued, and she remembered the mail she had popped on the cool box. 'If it's a dangerous tree it needs to come down. Folk might not like it—'

'I don't like it!' Winnie cut in and Daisy loved her in that moment for taking the side of the tree.

'Yes, but you'd like it a lot less if it came crashing down on your car or your house or your kids who happened to be walking past!'

Mrs Kelleway bit her lip, seemingly she had no answer for that.

'They'll have to rename your area, Winnie!' Georgie chuckled. 'Three Oaks! Doesn't have quite the same ring, does it? People will be sitting in care homes saying, "I remember the good old days when there was four of them!"' He reached for another slice of garlic bread that had long ago gone cool, and stuffed it into his mouth. 'Everyone will no doubt get their knickers in a twist over it, but they'll soon get used to it, like everything. A shock at first but it quickly becomes the norm. Like contactless credit cards and self-serve tills; we recoil at the thought until we find ourselves going with the flow.'

Having unloaded two more bottles on to the table with a shaking hand, keen to get home and read the communiqué that waited in the porch, Daisy had to admit that her knickers were most definitely in a twist. She tried to picture a trio of trees, and even imagining the lack of symmetry made the hairs on the back of her neck stand up.

Gathering up empty plates, she tried not to stare at Cassian, who looked a little lost in thought. She wondered if he too felt an inexplicable sense of sadness at the prospect of losing a tree. She liked to think so. Kindred spirits.

On his plate, she noted a couple of discarded breaded mozzarella chunks and honestly considered eating them when she was safely out of sight in the kitchen. It was enlivening, the thought of putting her fingers on food he'd touched, the half-bitten piece that had touched his lips that she would place on her own . . .

For the love of God, get a grip, girl! She focused. Gianna had been right; it wasn't so bad serving the family next door and was actually a bit like being at a party. Her anxiety over the evening melted away.

'Thank you, Daisy.' Mr Kelleway grinned at her. 'I think they're trying to bankrupt me, this family of mine!' He reached for a fresh bottle and topped up his glass.

She bit the inside of her cheek to subdue her grin, unsure if she should be having this much fun and wanting to look as cool as possible in front of Cassian as she plodded to and from the kitchen with laden trays, dishes of olives, platters of warm breads, and bowls of steaming pasta, all containing enough garlic to ensure they were vampire-free for the coming months.

'Bankrupt you? I think you'll find I'm costing you very little tonight.' Cleo, who had overheard, rubbed her baby bump. 'Apart from my very large bowl of Fettucine Alfredo, which I could eat again right now. I think I'm addicted!'

'You're my only girl. And you're having our new grandchild. You can cost me as much as you like, sweetheart.' Mr Kelleway beamed.

'Cleo, tell Daisy when you're due!' Mrs Kelleway smiled.

'Any day.' Cleo nodded at her husband, who nodded back and bit his lip as if the emotion that threatened was more than he could handle.

'Can you believe it?' Mrs Kelleway held her clasped hands under her chin, as if her prayers had been answered. 'Any day! Any minute! Hope you've got some clean towels and hot water out the back there!'

'That's . . . lovely.' She didn't know how to respond and was also ridiculously over-aware of the fact that they were talking about sex and babies and all within earshot of Cassian, with whom she had fantasised about both topics. That and she dreaded the thought of Cleo going into labour there and then. She could only imagine the mess and the screaming – if it was anything like she'd seen on TV.

'It's actually due on my grandad's birthday, tomorrow,' Georgie announced, but it seemed no one heard him.

'What I want to know,' Lawrence chimed, 'is what event there was nine months before now that was a cause for celebration for you and Georgie?'

'And my great-grandparents!' Georgie added, but again his voice was lost in the back and forth.

'For the love of God, Loz!' Cleo rolled her eyes, as Domino and Julie pulled faces of disgust.

'What?' He chuckled as Georgie balled a napkin and threw it at his brother-in-law's head. Cassian reached for his phone and her heart flexed with the desire to know who and what he was texting. Wishing beyond wish that her phone might beep in her locker.

'You boys.' Mrs Kelleway gave her a knowing look, as if they were talking about the misbehaviour of little kids and not the jesting of two grown men.

Daisy felt the lance of envy go through her core. What must it feel like to be part of a family like this? A family who ate in restaurants together, who laughed and loved together. She tried to imagine her dad and his older brother Keith engaging in this way. Weird Keith who collected bird books and counted his carrots before he ate them. Then she thought of her mum, whose every syllable dripped with sadness as she whispered from within the confines of her fleecy blanket, seeming to feel the cold even on a sun-filled June day like today.

She hoped Gianna was right. She prayed that her future was something shiny and glorious, imagining in that moment being coupled with Cassian, which would mean that she was part of this glorious unit, a Kelleway . . . If only. Suddenly thoughts of her and him in that hot tub filled her mind.

With dusk now having given way to the dark of evening, only one other table was still occupied and Daisy noted that her tips were low. She wasn't surprised. After all, who wanted to dine like a support act while all attention and the whole room was dominated by the perfect Kelleways? She felt a little guilty, not that there was a whole lot she could do about it now.

It was post-dessert. Gianna's tiramisu had been eaten quickly and greedily and everyone had admired the prettily iced cake that honoured their special celebration. With wine sloshing in their veins, three of the Kelleways grew louder, their words somewhat slurred, and they slumped a little in their seats. Pregnant Cleo, the upright Julie, Georgie who sat as if he were on high alert, sweet little Domino, and Cassian, all stood out like sentinels dotted around the table. Like guardians of the drunken elders, watching closely in case they were needed to mop up any fallout from the drink-fuelled antics.

'Speech! Speech!' Lawrence suddenly called out, banging the table with the flat of his hand.

'No, no – no speeches!' Mr Kelleway shook his head and reached for his wine. 'Definitely not.'

'You have to, Dad!' Cleo pleaded. 'It's your anniversary!'

'It's all right, I'll do one.' Mrs Kelleway made to stand, and this was when her husband stood, as if the thought were enough to goad him into action. He placed his hand on her shoulder and kissed the top of her head. The family clapped and stomped their feet, and all assembled had no choice other than to listen.

'Come on, Bernie, you got this!' Georgie called his encouragement.

Mr Kelleway took his time, gripping the wineglass under his tanned chin like it was a microphone. Daisy stood in front of the bar, feeling simultaneously fascinated and like an interloper. As a hush fell over the room, Gianna and Carlo stood by her side. The three leaned on the bar behind them, all, it seemed, interested in what Mr Kelleway had to say.

'I hadn't intended on speaking,' he began. 'I naïvely thought anything I might want to say would be done in the privacy of our home, just the two of us.' He smiled awkwardly in Winnie's direction and Daisy felt her neighbour's embarrassment. It was sweet to see. 'Please, Mr and Mrs Bianchi, don't feel the need to stand and listen to my drivel!' He pointed towards the kitchen.

'It's fine, my friend! You go ahead.' Carlo nodded, his chest out. 'We are Italian! Emotion and family are to us like breathing!'

Daisy hoped her expression told him that he had nothing to fear; no one was going to think any less of him for showing his feelings tonight of all nights. She felt Gianna shift and sigh next to her, knowing her boss must be tired, as she often was towards the end of a shift.

'Come on, Dad!' Cleo encouraged. 'There'll never be another moment like this. Forty years!' She clapped.

'All right then. I feel obligated, but all right then.' He spoke slowly, sincerely and it was moving.

'I don't know where to start.' He took a deep breath and blushed.

'The beginning?' Lawrence suggested.

'Yes.' Mr Kelleway coughed. 'The beginning. I guess all I want to say is that I got lucky the day I met Winnie.'

Mrs Kelleway reached up and took his hand, running the back of his knuckles over her cheek with her head cocked to one side. Daisy knew that if nothing else, she wanted to be like this when she was old, still reaching for the man she loved. It was so beautiful to see. She stole a glance at Cassian.

'We met quite by chance, fate if you like. There was me standing at the bus stop on an ordinary day. I was a streak of a lad, nothing to recommend me, counting the coins in my palm, and wondering how far twelve pence would take me. And she walked straight up to me with this big smile and a clear, confident voice: "Is it late again? Oh well, might be quicker to walk!" That's what she said, that's all she said. And I can see you nodding as this is not a new story for you, but the point is, I knew by those few words that her nature was wonderful, not only was she beautiful—'

'Was?' Mrs Kelleway tutted and gave a mock sulk, flashing a glimpse of her perfect porcelain gnashers.

'Is!' Her husband brought their joined hands to his lips and kissed. 'You *are* beautiful. Of course, you are. But it was more than that: with those words you told me that you were the kind of girl who, if the bus was late or didn't show up at all, was happy to walk. I knew then that you'd look for a way to get over obstacles in life. And you did, and we have.' He paused and let go of her hand to wipe his eyes. 'You took a chance on me, Winnifred Wallace. You didn't laugh when I told you about my idea to buy linen and hire it out, returning it to hotels and restaurants neatly washed and folded, saving them the job. You didn't laugh. You had faith in me. You loved me.' He looked into her eyes. 'And all those hours with little ones running around your feet, tired, so tired, endlessly washing and ironing tablecloths, napkins and sheets, but you did it – we did it.' He looked around at his children, his family, and Daisy felt the weight of his words. 'And it paid off. We grew our business, bought the laundries until we supplied linens as far north as Wolverhampton and someone else did all that washing and ironing, and what a wonderful life we've had.'

'We have,' his wife chimed. 'We have.'

'But the greatest gift you ever gave me was our beautiful kids.' His voice cracked, and Lawrence sniffed. Cleo let her tears flow and Georgie handed her a handkerchief. 'Loz, our oldest, then our Louis, who was too precious an angel to stick around.' He looked up and crossed his chest. 'And then came little Cleo, and now our grandchildren, Cass and sweet Dom and another on the way. I thought I was lucky that day at the bus stop, couldn't believe you happened to be walking by, but forty years later, I can tell you that I am the luckiest man on the planet. Here's to the next forty, my love!' He raised his glass as his family stood.

'The next forty!' they chorused, before sipping champagne and moving around the table to hold each other, kiss each other and lay their arms across each other's backs.

Daisy looked up to the sound of Gianna crying and she understood. It was moving and it was rare, the kind of sentiment you usually only saw in movies.

Lawrence stepped away from the table and came towards her. She felt her heart race in advance of the interaction.

'Daisy, you have made tonight for us. Thank you for working so hard.' He reached out and placed some paper in her hand. It felt like money, but she didn't dare look down as that would seem rude and a bit grabby.

'Thank you, Mr Kelleway.' She felt the blush of awkwardness and slipped the notes into the front of her apron.

'You're very welcome.' He smiled. 'And please call me Lawrence. Your mum and I go way back – we're practically family.'

That's what he said! That she was practically a Kelleway! Her heart soared at the thought.

'Right!' He turned back to the table and shouted loudly. 'Mum and Dad, let's head home and get your gifts open!'

Mr Kelleway beckoned to Carlo, who took the envelope he passed him; cash, it seemed, was the order of the day. The two men shook hands.

'You okay, Gia?' she asked, as her boss cried openly.

'I am. It's just that sometimes life . . .' She ran out of words.

Daisy watched as Cassian walked out of the restaurant without giving her so much as a second glance. Her stomach sank with disappointment, although she wasn't entirely sure what she had hoped for.

'Yep, life.' She concurred, as the two women walked back into the kitchen. Reaching into her apron pocket, she scanned the notes in her hand. Her mouth flew open. 'Oh my God! You're kidding me! He's given me a hundred and fifty quid! I can't believe it!' She jumped on the spot. It was a wonderful surprise.

'I'm so happy for you, darling girl.'

'Gia,' let me go halves with you, we can—'

'No! No, don't be daft.' Gianna was still mopping at her residual tears. It really was some speech. 'Your tips are always your tips, Daisy Daisy. We wouldn't have it any other way.'

'I don't know what to say. Thank you, Gia!' She threw her arms around her boss and gave her a tight hug. 'Oh, my goodness, thank you! I can't believe it. A hundred and fifty pounds!' Again, she counted the cash to make sure. 'Do you think it's a mistake? Should I chase after him?'

'It's no mistake,' Gianna reassured her. 'He likes to tip big, and he can afford to, so why not?'

'So why not!' Daisy twirled on the spot.

'Go and do something fun while you are young! All *I* want is to get my throbbing feet out of these clogs, to soak my aching back in a bath and sit in the dark until my headache has passed.'

'Can I get you anything?' Daisy returned the kind concern Gianna had shown her earlier.

'No, sweet girl, no one can fix what ails me.' She spoke with a faraway look in her eye that was a little unnerving. 'But thank you.'

'Are you sure you're okay, Gia?'

The woman rallied a little and took her time in answering.

'Ignore me.' She forced a smile. 'I'm just a little tired. It's one of those nights where the evening has rumbled on longer than I would have wished. It's like this sometimes, isn't it? The minutes ticking by so slowly that you start to feel a little resentful towards the customers still hanging around. That's not fair, of course. It's their night out and I'm grateful they choose us to share it with.'

'Can I make you some tea?'

'Actually, that would be lovely, Daisy, thank you.'

She reached for one of the mismatched mugs reserved for staff and lobbed a teabag into it before filling the kettle.

'Sorry, Daisy, I shouldn't be so morose, especially after your big tip. We should be celebrating! But I don't know . . .' Gianna took a slow breath. 'It feels like, recently, I just want to finish up and get home earlier and earlier. I can't help it; they bug me, the lingerers, the lurkers, the drinkers, even the loud ones who want to shout out their next long story. Do they not have homes to go to, soft beds with clean sheets, warm showers where they can wash away the dirt of the day? I know I do . . .'

It was rare to hear Gianna quite so reflective and it bothered her.

'I still like it when we get quiet couples on first dates. Do you remember that man last month who dropped his cutlery and then stuttered his order – I felt so sorry for him!' Daisy pictured the sweaty, hapless chap.

'Yes, and we were betting on him and his date's chances of success. I don't think he scored very well.'

'He didn't!' she confirmed.

'Ah, but you never can tell by looking, Daisy. Sometimes even the most mismatched of pairs can be blissfully happy and those who are all smiles and vino . . . Well, you don't know what happens behind closed doors.'

'I guess that's true.'

'It is.'

Daisy squeezed the teabag against the inside of the mug and added a splash of milk until the tea turned the colour of dark toffee, just the way Gianna liked it. She handed her the cup.

'Thank you, dear. Or maybe I'm just an old cynic. What do you think?'

'I think everything feels hard when you're tired. I know . . .' She paused; it was rare for her to talk about home. Wary that to do so here might in some way dilute her haven. This and the fact that she didn't want pity, never that. 'I know my mum finds things difficult; she's tired a lot.'

'Well, she's lucky to have you, we all are.' Gianna's eyes smiled at her as she sipped her tea.

'Who's lucky to have who?' Carlo came into the kitchen with empty bowls stacked on his upturned wrist and a clutch of dirty napkins in his hand.

'We are lucky to have Daisy,' Gianna said.

'We are.' He nodded, as he threw the napkins in the dirty linen basket and popped the bowls in the sink. 'Not much longer. The last table have finished their liqueur and they look about ready to go. Is that tea?' Carlo sniffed the air.

'Would you like one?' Daisy reached for a mug.

'I really would.' Carlo winked at her. She liked that she could do this one small thing for them at the end of a long day. 'Back in a mo.'

He whisked back out to the restaurant and in no time she heard the bell ring above the door and the sound of the bolt being shot as the last of the customers left. It fascinated her, the way Gianna and Carlo, in a well-rehearsed routine, closed the restaurant for the night. Switching off lights, turning off power, flicking switches, closing doors. There was something captivating and intimate about it. The place never felt so cosy as it did at times like this when they'd worked hard, laughter and emotion still coated the walls, and the dining room now slumbered in semi-darkness. She liked it. Carlo stood by the sink and sipped the hot tea as if it was nectar.

'I used to have nice hands.' Gianna flexed her fingers. 'But now I've got these veins that bulge like fat worms.' She nodded at the back of her hands. 'They're a mess, look!'

It was true, Gianna's fingers were etched with scars and burns, the slip of a blade wielded by a distracted hand, and the scald of steam had left angry red streaks. Calluses had formed where the heavy wooden handle of her favourite knives had toughened the once soft skin with the repeated action. Daisy guessed this was just collateral damage of a life lived in service to these four walls and the thousands and thousands of suppers, lunches and snacks she had prepared for the paying customers. It was as unexpected as it was awkward when Gianna started crying again.

'Hey! Why tears?' Carlo put down his tea and walked over to his wife.

'I'd better . . .' Daisy walked over to her locker to retrieve her hat, scarf and bike lock, trying not to listen, wishing she were somewhere else. It felt intrusive and embarrassing all at once.

Carlo placed his arms around his wife. 'Don't cry, *bella*.'

He spoke with such sweet concern it was like a knife to her heart. She could only imagine someone talking to her in that way.

'I think . . . I think I'm tired,' Gianna stuttered.

'It's been a long month. A busy one. We're up fifteen per cent on this time last year.' He nodded, as if this fact alone should be enough to lift his wife's mood.

Daisy understood a while back that whilst Carlo was motivated by the rise in their bank balance, it didn't seem to be the same for Gianna, whose face lit up not at the sound of the till, but at the wows and gasps of delight that filtered back into the kitchen when food was presented and tasted.

'I'm a little emotional. I was just thinking, Carlo, about the day we might stop, about when it will be the right time to shut up shop and go home.'

'We are going home!' He rattled the keys in his hand and laughed at her tired mumbling. Daisy thought it was both placatory and a little condescending. 'We'd be there a lot quicker if we weren't stood here chatting.'

Gianna shook her head. 'No, I mean *home.*'

Daisy tried not to listen, tried to open the fiddly padlock on her locker that often took a while to budge, tried to merge into the background, hum . . .

'I know my mother has been dead for decades, but just the memory of her kitchen with her in it . . . I can't explain, but it makes me so sad!' This recollection was apparently enough to encourage the next bout of tears. 'Sometimes it's as if I lost her only yesterday and not all those years ago.'

Daisy could understand that; she too found that despite the situation she lived with, sometimes just the thought of her mother's depression was enough to pull the rug from under her. And each time it caught her off guard, this torrent of grief and loss for the life they once lived had the power to knock the wind from her lungs. She wondered if it would ever stop, hoping in some way it would, and yet taking solace from the strength of feeling which meant she still cared deeply for the woman who was in there somewhere.

Gianna continued, 'I'm . . . I'm thinking a lot about sitting in the sun, growing our own food, taking slow walks, afternoon naps – all the things we've spoken about for so long. I feel like it's time.'

'Don't cry, *tesoro mio*, don't cry!' Carlo leaned on the stainless-steel countertop and folded his arms across his chest. 'Wouldn't you miss the restaurant?' He looked around and Daisy knew he spoke for himself.

Finally, Daisy's locker sprang open, she grabbed her scarf and hat and slammed it shut, wondering if maybe Gianna had forgotten that she was there.

'I'd miss some of it.'

'Daisy.' He smiled. 'You'd miss her.'

They both looked over at her and Daisy felt her heart sink a little at the thought of them not being around . . .

'Oh yes, I'd miss you, our little Daisy Daisy.'

I'd miss you too. Please don't go anywhere, she thought, as saying it out loud felt like too much, as if acknowledging it might make it possible.

'But the swollen feet, aching back, varicose veins and tired bones? No, I wouldn't miss any of that. I think I'd like a rest. I think we've earned it. I mean, wouldn't you like a change, Carlo? Aren't you tired?'

Daisy felt conflicted; she desperately wanted to dash out and hurry home, but to leave them in the midst of such a discussion felt a little rude. She watched Carlo look around at the racks stuffed with pots and pans, the ten-litre bottles of olive oil, the bread baskets, shiny fridges, and the vast burner hob on which his wife created magic. His reply was slow in coming.

'I too am sometimes tired, but then I try to imagine who I might hand the place over to, who would hold the keys after us, or maybe it would close altogether, become something different entirely, and then I think about all the years and all the hours and how hard we have worked to get to this point and my heart breaks that it will come to an end.'

Daisy knew it would break her heart too.

'Yes.' Gianna followed his gaze, and Daisy could see how it felt easier somehow to talk about anything in the half light. 'But if we always look at it like that, we will never stop. Never. We'll keep working all the hours God sends until I collapse at the stove, and you carry me out in my apron, or you fall down in the restaurant with a tray of tiramisu in your hand!'

'Would that be such a bad thing?' His short snort of laughter told her that he spoke only half in jest. Gianna, however, didn't laugh.

'It would be a bad thing for me. It would mean I never made it back, and we always said' – Gianna swallowed the catch in her throat – 'we always said we'd work hard, save up, make a life, and then go home. Go home to sit in the sun, to spend time with our families! That was the plan.'

'We did.' He nodded. 'But plans can change.'

'They can. *I* know that better than most,' she answered a little sharply, and Daisy, not for the first time felt a little intrusive.

'I'd better get going.' She tied her scarf around her neck and pointed towards the door.

'Yes, of course. Go home, darling. It's Friday evening. Kitchen's closed and we have all had quite a night. You don't want to stand and listen to the ramblings of an old woman.'

'You're not old, Gianna.'

'Well, I feel it.'

'If you're sure there's nothing else you want me to do?' She bit her lip, knowing how very lucky she was to work here and still lit within at the glorious night that had passed, topped off by an extraordinary act of generosity, which had been the icing on the cake.

'I'm sure.' Gianna's eyes crinkled in a fleeting smile. It seemed that Mr Kelleway's speech had really got to her, made her think. And Daisy got it, feeling more than a little emotional herself. She knew tonight she would ask the universe to please, please not let anyone chop down one of her beloved trees and also not to let Gianna and Carlo close up the restaurant and go home to Italy. Of course, she wanted them to be happy, but for her, it would be the very worst thing.

'How about I grab us a nice Brunello red,' Carlo boomed, 'and we go home, kick off our shoes, sit in the garden and open it? Just the two of us. How about that, Gianna? I will rub your feet and put a blanket over your shoulders.'

Gianna nodded. 'Let's do that.'

Having unshackled her bike, Daisy headed for home, happy and with a satisfied ache to her limbs that she welcomed after a hard evening's work. Sparks of joy fizzed in her veins every time she pictured the big fat tip given to her by Mr Moneybags – 'call me Lawrence' – nestling in her pocket.

Cycling so quickly that her turns at roundabouts and junctions were a little risky, she sped along, feeling alive! The wind hit her in the face and the onset of the evening chill made her shiver with something close to delight. She couldn't wait to burst through the door and tell her family about her big, big tip.

With her bike safely stashed in the porch for the night, she opened the front door and walked into the quiet house.

There was no one to tell. No one was waiting for her.

Her mum was no doubt sleeping. Her dad too, and Jake was of course ensconced behind his bedroom door. Her immediate feeling was one of sadness. The house was too quiet; loneliness prodded her in the ribs and whispered in her ear. She leaned on the wall and listened very carefully, able to make out the faint sound of music and she was sure she heard laughter. Standing in the silent gloom, she wondered again what it might feel like to live in the house next door where laughter and love was their glue and they had so much money they could fling a tip like that at their scrawny waitress. Their scrawny waitress with overly large knees.

Standing on the first stair, the letter from the council caught her eye, now propped up on the hallstand opposite – a relic from her gran. She could see that it had been opened and her heart beat quickly. It felt a little as if things were unravelling. First, one of her beloved oaks could be lost and now Gianna and Carlo too . . . She closed her eyes and felt her way up the stairs, thinking that if she could block out the thoughts, they might not trouble her.

CHAPTER FIVE

Julie Kelleway

It was a relief for Julie to be outside in the mild June night air. The menopause, sitting like a growling shadow in the background, had begun to play havoc with her internal thermometer. She closed her eyes, letting the subtle breeze lift her hair and cool her brow. Pinching her loose floral blouse at the front, she wafted it back and forth to send shivers of cold air over her body. It had been quite a night. But no less than she had expected: a little boisterous, a little loud, a little too much consumed by them all. Standard, really, for any Kelleway celebration, where it seemed that if it wasn't done to excess it could hardly be considered a celebration.

'Come on, you.' She spoke softly to Cassian as she gathered her Mulberry handbag to her chest, still after seven years of ownership loving the feel of it against her skin. Its delicate ivory tone perfect for all seasons and the brass logo plate still gave her a shudder of delight when she ran her thumb over it. It had been a present for her birthday – a total surprise – and she smiled now to think of that glorious day when Lawrence had presented her with the fancy parcel, tied with a wide ribbon.

'What is it?' She'd held her breath, excited.

'Something beautiful for my beautiful wife . . .' His words only cementing the perfect point in their wonderful life.

A quick shake of her head shifted the memory, which right now was almost too painful to consider.

It's okay, Jules, keep it together, keep smiling, keep walking, it's all going to be okay . . . She did this, repeated small reminders, keeping her interior monologue as supportive and positive as possible. It helped.

She placed her hand on her son's shoulder, knowing how he hated the spectacle of walking along with his family en masse. And she understood, a little. Like any bauble-decked herd, as they left the restaurant, they took up a lot of space and made more noise than was comfortable: a fanfare, an exhibition. She was aware of the stares of passers-by and the glimpses from drivers making their way up the high street as they clogged the pavement. It certainly wasn't her way, the showiness of it.

Jake's younger sister – what was her name? Darcy? – the little waitress seemed nice enough, but looked like a rabbit caught in the headlights. The girl's expression had kind of summed up how Julie had felt in those early days when newly hitched and still figuring out how to be a Kelleway. It had been an exhausting time, trying to make Winnie like her, wanting Bernie to befriend her but not so much that it might irritate Winnie. Wanting to look at ease and not entirely thrown by the opulence of their get-togethers, whilst almost paralysed with anxiety about doing or saying the wrong thing.

It was another world! The sheer abundance of . . . everything, and the way the family interacted; the constant planning for the next event, the next holiday, the next anniversary, the swapping of dates, the high jinks, the brunches, the lunches, the restaurant dates, the big, big cakes for each and every celebration for everything from birthdays to driving tests. The giving of gifts, the receiving of gifts, the wrapping of gifts, the gift lists shared on WhatsApp, and the expectancy and pressure to keep up and under no circumstances could they ever, ever be late. There was not a reason or excuse in the land that could justify tardiness. Even if Winnie smiled and batted away a late arrival as if it were of no consequence, her eyes always told a very different tale. Julie had quickly learned that there was no event considered too small to celebrate with the opening of a bottle of fizz, a slack handful of crisps in a crystal bowl and the gathering in the family home that held them all fast like a magnet.

It was all so very different from her own quiet upbringing on the other side of town. There had been a lot to take in. But she was more than used to it now, a little less fearful of it – the overly loud laughter, the ribbing, the same jokes told in any number of variants, yes, she got it: Georgie was a little podgy, Lawrence was good-looking, Domino quiet, Cassian a good boy . . . Sometimes, watching everyone play their part, she wanted to scream! It wasn't always easy, toeing the line, remembering who she was talking to and what inside knowledge she had. Cleo, for example, was her friend and Julie knew that in Winnie and Bernie's view, she had 'settled' when she'd married Georgie.

And then there was her husband, Lawrence: the golden boy, who wrapped his barbed comments in jest and threw them at anyone close enough for them to land. She saw through this, of course, his affability, his easy-going nature, witness as she was to his bouts of anger and introspection, his manic planning, his wild and elaborate schemes that could become his sole occupation until another took its place. Yes, she saw through him, all right. Not that it would ever be the case for Winnie or Bernie, who literally thought the sun shined out of his bum hole.

She ran her hand over Cassian's back, understanding that loving that much made it easy to be blind. She hoped, however, that she was more realistic when it came to loving *her* complex son.

Cassian seemed, at the moment, to keep more in than he let out. She wished he'd open up to her more, but also wanted to respect his privacy and his boundaries. The truth was that after leaving Melbourne, it felt a little like the trust they'd shared had been eroded. Not that she blamed him; it wasn't as if life was easy for any of them. Her own mother reminded her that her brother had been the same, and that eighteen was an awkward age – technically an adult, but really still no more than a child, filled with teenage angst, stumbling and flailing in the unfamiliar wilderness between boy and man. She hoped he knew that when he stumbled and if he fell, she would catch him. Always.

'See you back at ours!' Winnie shouted to no one in particular as she climbed into Georgie's saloon.

Julie felt her gut bunch at the volume of her mother-in-law's holler. Maybe she wasn't as used to it as she'd thought, even after nearly two decades tethered to this family.

Raising her hand in a wave, she felt happy that, yes, she loved Cassian in a more realistic way, and that open and honest communication was the pillar on which their love stood strong. Cassian could tell her and his dad anything, ask them anything, and that was something Lawrence could only dream of. Oh no, as the oldest Kelleway and only boy, he had to continue with the illusion, polish the façade, hoping and praying that he could hold things together long enough to avoid watching his parents fold, crushed with disappointment at any perceived failure.

For Winnie and Bernie to learn that their boy made of gold was actually only dusted with the thinnest veneer, which was rapidly wearing to reveal his dull, unshiny interior, would be too much. Their son. Her husband. The man who grew up with his sights on the Premier League and had ended up hauling bricks and eventually building houses, including some as grand as their own palatial pile on Newman Road.

Not that she saw anything wrong in hauling bricks for a living, far from it. It was just a shame Lawrence didn't feel the same. She knew that whatever he achieved, wherever they lived or what car he drove, it would never, could never, come close to putting on the number ten jersey for Spurs, and that was something he couldn't seem to get over.

In the early days, it had been her belief that with enough love and reassurance she could take away that feeling of failure, help him see what really mattered in life and that it wasn't kicking a football. Not that any of it mattered now; they had so many bigger things to worry about.

'You okay, Dom?' she asked her daughter, who walked a little behind them, tapping away into her phone.

'Just arranging to meet Rubes once we get this over and done with. It's Friday night.' Her girl's terse reply.

'I know, but it's also Nan and Grandad's anniversary. Please just—'

Domino tutted. 'For God's sake, Mother, I knowah!'

Julie felt the sting of her daughter's dismissal and tried to imagine talking to her own mother at sixteen, indeed at any age, in a similar manner. It was unthinkable. But then there was much that was unthinkable about her life. It was a lot like living in a play, where the audience believed what they saw, and only the players on the stage knew the reality. In truth, she often wanted to exit stage left and shatter the façade.

'What's wrong with you?' Lawrence toyed with his car keys, asking Domino face to face with no mention of the attitude she had directed at her mother.

'What's wrong with me is that it's Friday night, I'm stuck here with you lot and when I do go out later, I'll be wearing this shit I found at the back of my wardrobe!' She clutched at the sheer blouse that perfectly skimmed her slender waist. 'And I want to be back in Melbourne! That's what's wrong.'

It was the same refrain Julie had heard in so many variants since the plane had ascended the runway in Tullamarine. This was one of the reasons Julie went easy on her daughter, let her get away with more than she knew to be wise, because she felt guilty that loading her family on to the plane with such urgency had been partly her fault; she had allowed it, been too compliant, too trusting to rail against it. Her daughter's appalling lack of respect was, she knew, only one of the consequences of her inaction.

'I think you look beautiful.' Lawrence spoke softly, missing the point entirely that his role in that moment was not to bolster their daughter's already strong self-esteem, but to remind her how lucky she was, how much she had, and how it was only stuff, only clothes . . . Julie could well imagine how that speech might have gone down. He had always done this; let guilt steer his parenting choices, while giving in to their daughter's material demands.

But did she really have a right to judge? Was she any different? Was going easy on Domino not as bad? It was as if her husband thought showing love meant the showering of gifts, the providing of things, and she could hardly blame him, having seen this very theory at play from his parents. This, too, she had thought she could erase, show him another way. Again, she nestled her bag to her chest.

Domino ignored her dad and shook her head with obvious irritation. Her lips narrowed and pressed together, an expression which in Julie's view took away a little of her beauty, but not nearly as much as using such a tone at her tender age or the absolute disdain in which she held the life of privilege they had both worked so hard to provide did. In truth, Julie had grown weary of fighting with her daughter, and had almost thrown in the towel. It was hard enough to find the energy to keep bailing in a ship that was, if not sinking, then certainly listing, without trying to tackle her daughter's attitude, again. What would she think if she were an outsider looking in? *Lazy parenting . . . defeatist . . . spoiled brat . . . weak . . .* Yes, to all the above. Awareness of this didn't make her feel good. But to those outsiders she would say, 'Try walking in my shoes for a day and you too would find it hard to summon the energy when your heart is sad and your head is full of what comes next. It is harder than you know . . .'

Domino went back to her phone, no doubt planning with Ruby Powell, who lived on the Merrigo estate where Julie herself had grown up. The council estate where she had lived wrapped in love and where she would lie awake at night on the bottom bunk, happy, safe, and warm. Without full realisation of just how glorious and nurturing her young life was, she would wonder what it would be like to one day travel and then return to live in one of the big houses up on Newman Road.

Well, now she knew. Her mouth twisted into a wry smile. She sometimes wished she could go back, alter her aspirations, knowing with certainty that if she hadn't believed the route to happiness and satisfaction was in the acquiring of things, owning a spare bedroom or two, then she probably wouldn't have been so enamoured with a boy like Lawrence Kelleway . . . or maybe that was unfair. Looking now at her two beautiful kids, she knew she would make the same choices all over again if it meant she got them.

Without discussion, in a familiar pre-arrangement, Lawrence, who as per his MO had enjoyed more than the odd glass, handed her the keys to his beloved Merc. She opened the doors and, popping the boot, she placed her precious handbag inside. Domino and Cassian took up their places on the back seat and buckled up, while she climbed in and adjusted the mirrors. She knew this bothered her husband but couldn't face explaining yet again that no matter how much it might piss him off having to make minor adjustments to the mirrors when it was his turn to drive, it was far better than crashing in a ball of flames because she couldn't see a bloody thing!

She watched him clamber into the leather passenger seat of their luxurious car and let his head loll backwards.

'Did you all have a nice time? Food was lovely, wasn't it? I've eaten far more than I should.' She spoke to the kids in the rear-view mirror, trying to stoke the embers of conversation.

Cassian nodded.

'Thought you were a little quiet, love.' She smiled at him as the engine roared into life. 'Was it all a bit much? I heard Nan teasing you *again*.' This she spoke loudly, reminding Lawrence that it was his mother and that maybe he should have another word with Winnie about her outdated and sometimes dangerous interior monologue that she liked to spill whenever the fancy took her.

'*Cass, you're so handsome, you don't need to worry about grades! Who wouldn't give you a job?*'

'*Domino, you're too skinny, you've not been making yourself sick after eating, have you? I know it's all the rage, but you honestly don't need to do that! You're perfect just as you are!*'

'I'm okay.' Cassian kept his gaze beyond the window. Georgie pulled out and slid past them. Everyone waved and they all waved back. For the love of God! It felt never-ending, the pantomime.

'There he goes, Georgie boy in his saloooooon.' Lawrence snorted laughter and waved at his family as they passed.

'Don't be mean.' She spoke as she popped her glasses on and indicated.

'I'm just saying, does the man not have any shame? Driving around in that old lady car? And my poor sister, knowing that's the best she can hope for!' He tutted.

'Why's it an old lady car?' This had seemingly caught Domino's attention.

'Because it's a car for carrying cat baskets to the vets. A car for loading up with prunes, biscuits, soup and other horrible food that old people eat. And it's dusty and I bet a pound to a pinch of shit that he's got ketchup and mayonnaise sachets in the glove box and a few dozen McDonald's sauces for just in case. In fact' – he twisted to face their daughter – 'there's probably half a dozen old chicken nuggets under the passenger seat and sweets in the drink holders.'

Domino sucked in her cheeks; Julie could see she was trying not to laugh. It made her uncomfortable, the unkind name-calling, the backbiting – and the fact that Domino was on board bothered her even more. Lawrence, however, wasn't done.

'You know when you read about those people who get stranded in the bush or up a mountain track in the snow and they have to live off dew and fingernails just to survive? Well, that could never happen to Georgie; he's probably got enough calories lurking in that vehicle to keep him going for months!'

Domino laughed out loud. Cassian ignored him.

'At least he *owns* his car.' Julie knew this was a match to kindling but couldn't help it. It just slipped out.

'What's that supposed to mean?' Lawrence, sobering a little, turned to face her.

'Nothing.' She glanced in the rear-view mirror, and then at her husband, meeting his gaze, trying to indicate that she didn't want to have this row, not tonight and not in front of their children. Even though it was she who had started it.

'No, come on, Jules, what d'you mean by that? You can't just say something like that and then stay schtum.'

She could smell the acrid tang of wine on his breath and knew he was not going to let it go. The best she could hope for now was to put the topic to bed before they arrived at her in-laws for more gaiety. What did she have to lose?

'I guess what I mean is that you might not approve of his car or think he's a suitable match for your sister, but no one can take his car away from him. He'll be ferrying his little baby around when it arrives, and Cleo can sleep at night knowing they're safe.'

'You think I don't keep my family safe?' he asked. The crack in his voice was like a knife to her gut.

Julie shook her head. 'No, you keep us safe, you just don't . . .' She bit her lip, wanting to get the words right, and again wishing the kids weren't within earshot, but what did it matter? It wasn't as if they were ignorant of their current situation. The sham that was their high life.

'Don't what?' He coughed to clear his throat and the emotion it suggested tore at her heart.

'I sometimes think that you don't know what's important.' There. She had said it.

He exhaled as if someone had punched his gut.

'I don't know what's important?' He rubbed his fingers over his stubbled chin. 'You think I don't lie awake at night, tossing and turning, trying to figure out ways to hang on to what's important?' Again, he laughed and shook his head. The tension in the car rose and she gripped the steering wheel as her heart raced. How she hated the predictability and futility of their rows. It was utterly exhausting. This in part because she knew there was no neat solution, no moment of reconciliation and harmony. Instead, just this endless hot ember being passed back and forth, back and forth between the two of them. It was impossible for either of them to avoid getting burned.

'No, I think you do lie awake at night. In fact, I know you do as you disturb me with all your tossing and turning, but that's kind of my point; you don't need to worry about hanging on to anything, it would be better for us all if you could let things go.'

'I can't win!' he yelled.

'Here we go.' Domino spoke to her brother but loud enough for them all to hear.

'No, I'm sorry, Dom, but your mother can't be saying things like that and not expect me to respond. Explain to me exactly what you mean by I "don't know what's important"?'

Taking her foot off the accelerator, Julie let the car slow, wanting to give them as much time to clear the air and settle down before they arrived at Winnie and Bernie's. Not wanting to walk into the home of her in-laws with words of discord spiralling above their heads like halos of discontent.

She drew breath, took her time. Where to begin?

'I guess there was a horrible moment when Bernie was giving his speech, that I thought you were going to offer to buy the champagne for the table.' She glanced over at her husband, who stared out of the window, his eyes avoiding hers.

'Nope. That was never going to happen. You misjudge me. So I guess there's not much more to say about it.'

'Jesus Christ,' she sighed. He had asked her to elaborate, and this was his response! She now wanted *him* to shut up! Wanted the talking to stop! So sick of the words they chased around on an endless bickering loop, making her want to pull her hair out. This was her life, treading water, trying to keep her head above the rising flood while all they had worked for floated away and all she could do was watch and offer platitudes, trying to reassure her kids that it would all be okay, if they could only just hang on for a little bit longer . . .

'Jesus Christ? You think he's going to help?' Lawrence whipped around to face her and just like that they were off again.

'Oh, Loz, I know he can't help. I've been asking him for help for the last eighteen months and it turns out both he and I are fresh out of ideas.' She gripped the steering wheel, worried as ever about rowing in front of the kids, but also relishing the chance to clear the air, to discuss their current situation at all, when more often than not her husband was either absent or evasive.

Domino put her ear buds in and closed her eyes. Julie could just make out the tinny echo of the music as she nodded her head. She envied her daughter the escape.

'Can't we leave it, just for one night?' Lawrence raised his voice. 'Can't you just get off my case?'

'Sure. Let's do that.' She felt the pulse in her neck. She *hadn't* been on his case, but this was always his defence, a deflection, with the focus on her *nagging*, her *madness*, her *selfish* nature, her *fault* . . . She knew it was all utter bollocks, but it didn't make having to take it on the chin any easier. She concentrated now on the road ahead, wending her way to her in-laws, where Winnie would no doubt be in full shout mode and Bernie would be weeping with joy, and quietly mumbling clichés that she had long since felt to be irritating and verging on the insincere. It was as if the old man figured he could use his words as sticking plasters to hold together all that was fragile and all that threatened to fall apart.

Some hope . . .

She parked the car in the driveway next to Georgie's and, taking a moment to compose herself and find a smile, she followed her children as the four of them trod the neat gravel which crunched underfoot. Lawrence opened the wide front door.

'There you are! I was beginning to worry. Come on in!' Winnie called accusatorily from the spacious kitchen, as if she'd been waiting for hours.

Julie knew they could only have arrived minutes ahead. She watched as Winnie placed two varieties of grapes on a vast olive wood board that groaned under the weight of various cheeses, fresh figs, an assortment of crackers and bowls of jewel-coloured chutneys and spicy jams. It was quite the display. This, too, all absolutely standard: the overt show of wealth, the mountain of food, the inevitable waste.

'Will you have some cheese, Jules?' Her mother-in-law beamed.

'Oh, I couldn't! I'm so full, but it looks lovely.' She smiled.

'I'll give you a plate in case you change your mind.' Winnie nodded as she shoved the gold-rimmed side plate into her hand with a napkin folded on top, her expression indicating she hoped her daughter-in-law would succumb.

'Thanks.'

'I think everyone's on the terrace. I'll be out in a mo. Bernie's got the ice buckets out – it's going to be a long night!' Winnie trilled.

Julie walked across the plush pale-blue carpet and out on to the terrace where the family had sunk down into the soft cushions of the grey rattan furniture and now clutched glasses of fizz to their chests. Lawrence was chatting to Georgie, and her kids were either side of their grandad; Cleo patted a space on the sofa next to her.

'Wasn't that a fabulous meal?' Bernie greeted her. 'Great food for my beautiful, incredible family, and such a milestone. Forty years!' He shook his head as tears beckoned.

'It really was.' She took the seat next to Cleo, who looked tired.

'How you doing?' She spoke softly to her sister-in-law. Cleo was kind and unassuming and Julie knew that even had they met in any other circumstances they would still be friends. It was nice. An ally of sorts.

'I'm tired.' Cleo let her head fall forward. 'Do I look tired?'

'No! You look glowy and wonderful,' she lied.

'I don't feel particularly glowy.' Cleo rubbed the thin paisley print cotton tunic that clung to her bump.

'I know you'll be sick of people asking, I remember it felt like a pressure, but anything happening?' She squeezed Cleo's hand. It was wonderful and exciting that this baby was nearly here. Julie couldn't wait to meet her new niece or nephew. There was something about holding a newborn in her arms that set the whole world right. It reminded her of a time when hers had been tiny, and the future for them all had looked so rosy.

'Hard to tell.' Cleo ran her hand under and over her swollen stomach. 'I've felt a bit achy for days, I can't sleep, obviously, peeing non-stop. I'm . . . heavy and the heaviness is low.' Again she cradled the base of her tummy. 'There's the odd cramp, but how do you know if you've not experienced it before whether this is "it" or whether it's just regular end-of-pregnancy grumbles?'

'You don't, I guess, and with my two, each pregnancy was entirely different so just because I'd been through it, I was none the wiser.'

'Were you scared?' Cleo rubbed her palms together.

'Little bit. Are you?'

'More than a little bit.' She sucked air through her teeth.

'Don't be. Just remember that the maternity team have delivered thousands and thousands of babies. It's what they do all day, every day and they have seen every eventuality and have a plan for it. So even though it's all new and scary for you, for them it's like shelling peas.'

'Shelling peas.' Cleo exhaled. 'I know you're right. I guess because this little one has been so hard fought for.' It was no secret, the battle she and Georgie had had to get pregnant. 'And the thought of it going wrong at this point, after we've come so far . . .' Cleo stopped talking, as if even to voice the words felt too much.

'It won't. You've got this.'

'I know.' Cleo looked over at Winnie. 'I guess I'm super-aware. I've heard what happened to Louis and it feels weird to know that Mum's pregnancy was perfect, just perfect, and then just like that it wasn't. It scares me.'

'Yeah, but from what I understand, Louis was poorly and nowadays that would have been picked up on the scan so at least your mum and dad could have mentally prepared for what might happen, but it was different then, I guess.'

'I guess.'

Julie could tell from Cleo's tone that her words offered little comfort. She remembered the day she went into labour with Domino, Lawrence rushing home from the site out of town, where they were converting an industrial warehouse into flats. He was so excited, they all were, even Cassian who had helped paint the nursery and chosen a big stuffed panda as her first soft toy. The memory of that beautiful, carefree time made tears gather at the back of her throat. A very different time. A very different life.

'You okay, Jules?'

'Mmm . . . Just thinking about when they were little.' She nodded towards her kids. Cassian was chatting to Bernie while Domino was sitting quietly, taking it all in. 'It felt like everything was possible.'

'Everything *is* possible! For you guys at least. I said to Georgie, "There'll be Cass and Dom driving around the town in Ferraris while our little one waits at the bus stop like Dad when Mum came along. Hope they stop and give him or her a lift, especially if it's bloody raining!"'

'Why do you say things like that?' Julie hadn't meant to snap.

'I . . . I don't know, I just . . .' Cleo blushed as a cloak of unease descended over them, which Julie instantly regretted.

'Sorry, Cleo. It's not you. I just hate the bloody obsession with cars and cash and all the other rubbish that goes with it. Is it all anyone talks about?'

'I was only joking.' Cleo spoke softly. 'It's what we do! Joke about Mr Moneybags!'

'Well, how about we try doing something different?'

There was an awkward second of silence while the two friends let the dust of their unfamiliar exchange settle.

'I shouldn't have snapped at you like that.' Julie tucked her hair behind her ears, a slippery coating of guilt making her feel uncomfortable.

'I'm worried about you.' Cleo kept her voice low as she spoke the words that were at once concerned and forgiving.

I'm worried about me too . . . There were moments when the predicament her family found themselves in felt more than a little overwhelming. This was one of them. She knew it was their reputation – flash, rich, big spenders – but if and when that all disappeared, what would be left? What would people say then?

'I'm fine!' She spoke with an overeager tone that would have made Winnie proud. 'There's just a lot going on right now.'

'A lot how?' Cleo studied her face, and Julie looked away, not sure what or how to tell Cleo that she and Lawrence were in trouble. Big trouble. And even if she had known the words, she had promised her husband that they would keep things to themselves. *Least said soonest mended . . .* But this mantra was getting harder and harder to observe. Even Cleo, who was staring at her earnestly, was starting to see the cracks.

'You can talk to me, Jules.' Her friend thumbed the back of her hand. 'You know that. You can talk to me anytime.'

'I know, it's just that . . .' What to say that would both placate her sister-in-law and keep her husband's confidences? 'It's just that—'

'Cheese!' Winnie's booming voice interrupted her. Immediately all eyes and focus were on the matriarch and her tray of sumptuous dairy. 'I've got Danish blue, goat's cheese, Emmental, a warmed Brie, fresh figs, home-made chutney, crackers, and a ton of grapes. Come on! All dig in! Dig in!' She placed the large wooden tray in the centre of the outside dining table and went back for plates and cheese knives for those who didn't have them.

'This baby is already doggie paddling around in fettuccine and tiramisu, I can't shove cheese in there too. I might explode!' Cleo filled her cheeks with air.

'You all right, babe?' Georgie called across the table. Julie caught the loving look the two exchanged.

'Uh-huh.' Cleo closed her eyes briefly at her husband and rubbed her tum.

'If you want to get home and rest up . . . ?' he offered courageously in front of everyone, fearless and seemingly not in the least concerned about what Winnie and Bernie might want, knowing as well as her that they would baulk at an early exit.

'I'm fine for a bit longer.' Cleo reached for a grape and placed it in her mouth; apparently there was still wriggle room for a grape among all that pasta.

'How about a little bit of cheese, Dom, make your nana happy?'

Julie watched as Winnie dangled a piece of Brie in her daughter's direction.

'Thank you, Nan. Just a little bit.' Domino smiled sweetly.

'Such a good girl! So polite!' Winnie handed her granddaughter a hefty wedge of the cheese. 'We are so lucky!'

Julie felt an unattractive stab of jealousy, wondering why her daughter couldn't show her the same level of courtesy, before remembering the sweet girl who had stroked her hair on the sofa while they watched TV and who liked to surprise her with a cup of tea while she did chores. But never since they'd returned to the UK, not one hair stroke, not one cuppa. Domino's lack of kindness was, she figured, punishment of sorts and, again, she understood.

'Oh no!' Winnie shouted and placed a hand on her forehead. 'Oh, I'm such an idiot!'

'What's the matter, Mum? What is it?' Lawrence stood, concerned and ready to act, to fix whatever the problem might be. Everyone stared at the matriarch whose composure was a little rattled; whatever had popped into her thoughts must be something pretty big . . .

'I've forgotten to get the chocolates!'

'Don't worry about it, Winnie. I don't think anyone could manage chocolates on top of the cheese,' Georgie placated.

'Come off it, Georgie, you could manage chocolates at any time!' Lawrence snickered and Bernie joined in. Cleo, she noted, pushed out her bottom lip in the direction of her husband, as if this might make him feel better, supported, a sign.

'I can't serve coffee without chocolates, not tonight.' Winnie looked downward, as if the sky was about to fall in, and still it amazed Julie that this was the case; the small details, the tiny touches upon which her mother-in-law's happiness or displeasure were hung.

'I'll go pick some up.' Lawrence clapped. 'No problem. Won't take me a minute.'

'No.' Julie stood, reminding her husband that he'd had a drink and couldn't drive and relishing the thought of escaping the family for a wee while. 'I'll go.'

'Are you sure, Jules?' Winnie cocked her head to one side.

'Absolutely.'

'Precious girl.' Winnie smiled at her.

'Yup.' Julie grabbed her bag and fished in it for the keys before closing the front door and not for the first time that night, breathing in the cooling night air. She took a moment as she sat in the car, appreciating the quiet, the solitude. A quick glance in the rear-view mirror and she ran her finger along the dark shadows of fatigue that sat beneath her eyes, as if proof of her insomnia were needed.

'What are you going to do, Jules?' she whispered. 'What the hell are you going to do?'

It was an easy drive to the parade of shops a couple of roads away. Having parked the car, she went inside the convenience store, grabbing a basket, into which she put a carton of milk and Cassian's favourite sugary cereal, knowing they were low on both. The box of chocolates she lobbed on top and went to the till.

The girl behind the counter chewed gum and had the look of disdain that Julie recognised as the one her daughter used, suspecting that this young lady, too, resented working on a Friday night.

'D'you need a bag?' the girl asked as she scanned the three items.

'No, thank you.' Julie held her phone case in her hand, in which her credit and bank cards were secreted. No matter how relieved she'd been to get out of the house, the errand still irritated her a little.

'Eight pounds sixty-three.' The girl chewed her gum and looked into the middle distance.

Without too much thought, Julie held out her credit card to the contactless pay machine. Nothing happened. The girl picked up the terminal and held it out. 'Could you try again, please?'

Again, she held the card against the reader and this time it beeped.

'Your card's been rejected.' The girl stared at her.

'Oh.' Julie felt the hot swarm of embarrassment snake over her. She had suspected this might happen one day, but not yet and certainly not tonight. She'd believed Lawrence when he'd told her that things were in hand and that she didn't have to worry. To worry hadn't entered her head, so distracted was she by the whole anniversary palaver. 'Sorry, it's probably me. I'll try this one.' She gave a small laugh, trying to defuse the situation, and held up her bank card, which also failed to make the payment.

'Maybe try inserting it? Maybe it's the contactless thing playing up?' The girl vigorously rattled the terminal, which, whilst Julie was not an IT expert, she suspected might do more harm than good. The girl's tone suggested more than a whiff of impatience.

Julie put her card into the terminal and bashed in her PIN with a sinking feeling in her gut that fed a rising state of panic.

'I'm sorry. Your card has been refused; it says you need to contact your bank.' She popped gum against the roof of her mouth.

'I . . . I don't know why that is.' She felt the spread of humiliation, aware now of the two or three people behind her in the queue who seemed to be equal parts impatient and captivated.

'I'll pay cash, that'll be easier! Technology and I are not good together!' She shook her head and felt her gut roll as she pulled her purse from the depths of her ivory-coloured Mulberry bag and reached for the emergency stash of money she had hidden there for just such an occurrence. Turning to the small gathering behind her she painted on a big smile. 'I'm so sorry to keep you all waiting!'

They ignored her, apart from one guy who jutted his chin and shook his head, but the fact that he was holding only beer eased her guilt. He could wait.

As quickly as she was able, she unzipped the purse and felt her stomach drop to her boots. It was empty. That couldn't be right! She put her fingers inside it and wiggled them around, despite knowing that any notes could not hide.

'Oh!' She felt the breath leave her lungs. *He's taken the cash. He's taken the bloody cash . . .*

'I'm so sorry. I'll have to, erm, I'll have to pop back with my other purse.' She spoke through lips sticky with nerves. 'Would you like me to put these things back on the shelf?' she offered, wanting nothing more than to leave as quickly as possible and with zero intention of returning. Ever.

'No, you're okay. I'll do it later.' The girl shoved the items out of sight behind the counter and yelled, 'Next!'

Her feet felt leaden, as she took the heavy, slow steps from the shop with what felt like all eyes on her back. Her desire to cry was strong, but she would not. Not here. With trembling fingers, she pulled out the car keys and climbed into the leather driver's seat. *He took my cash . . .* The thought rattled around her head. *He took my bloody cash . . .*

'Eh, love!' The beer man she recognised from the queue yelled through the window. 'You must have a spare couple of quid laying around in that Mercedes, eh?' He chuckled, and she clamped her teeth together. The temptation to wind down the window and shout at him was strong, but what would she say?

'No, mate, no cash in here. It's a flash car, that's true, but it's leased, and we owe money on it. In fact, we are about to lose our house. We're flat broke! I can't even buy a pint of fucking milk and a box of chocolates! Not that we can admit to my husband's family that we are in this shitty position again! Oh yes, we've been here before. Had to run away from Australia where we loved life, just to avoid my husband's debts catching up with us! And we were only there because we were running away from debt here! It's laughable really. And you know what? I envy someone that drives a shitty saloon that he owns outright, because in a few weeks, he will still have his shitty saloon and we won't have a car at all!

It was a moment of reckoning. She knew they could not carry on like this, knew *she* could not carry on like this! Having the notes rolled inside the purse had felt a little like sanctuary, the thinnest and most insubstantial of safety blankets, and Lawrence had invaded that.

So, what needed to happen? Counselling? An intervention of some sort? Yes, and yes, but how to broach it when she had failed so miserably at being open about how she was feeling prior to his action? This, however, felt like the right time. To try to get things on track, to rewrite the rules, reset the boundaries when it came to how they as a family communicated. They needed to face up to the dire mess they were in, and this was no longer a wish but had to become their reality or else she could not see a future. This thought alone meant her breathing came in stuttered bursts, as it did of late, with the feeling that she was only one tiny papercut away from a panic attack.

Her phone beeped. She looked at the message, an alert from eBay – one of her listed items had sold.

Used – Mulberry handbag. Ivory-coloured leather. Good condition . . .

Running her hand over the soft leather she felt the threat of tears again. This bag, the nicest thing he'd ever bought her, and he'd given it with promises of a rosy future. And here she was, sitting in a layby outside the shop, wondering how she was going to return to her in-laws and explain her lack of chocolates, how she was going to calmly look Lawrence in the eye and not scream at him there and then, '*One hundred and fifty quid! My last one hundred and fifty quid! What in the world did you need it for that was more important than food for our family, you fucking idiot?*'

But of course she wouldn't, because they were the Kelleways. She was married to the golden boy, Mr Moneybags. And ultimately, she didn't want to make a fuss that might upset her kids, wanting to keep the true desperation of their situation from them. Yes, this she would do until she had absolutely no choice other than to bring a hammer down on all they thought was solid and secure, shattering it into fragments that she knew would never again fit back together in quite the same way.

And this she knew because this was what had happened when they left Australia. They were, as a family, changed in shape: chipped, cracked and less robust, fragile almost.

Instead, she'd walk into the house where the family, mid-celebration, waited for her, make up some excuse about being ditzy, and, in an attempt to keep her controlling mother-in-law happy, eat some bloody cheese . . .

CHAPTER SIX

CLEO RICHARDSON

Cleo Richardson was both intrigued and perturbed by Julie's odd behaviour. Her friend and sister-in-law had seemed a little 'off' all night. She wondered if her mum was right when she'd whispered that Julie's nose might be a little out of joint at the thought of another baby on the way, seeing as her status as the only one to have provided grandchildren in the family was about to be demolished. Cleo didn't think it possible, didn't *want* to think it was possible; Julie and Lawrence knew all about their IVF journey and just how much they had longed and prayed for this baby. The miracle child they had long ago given up hope of ever having. Yet it would explain how Julie had acted. Especially after she'd returned from the shop with some very odd story about not being able to park the car and then forgetting the chocolates, before stuffing her face with Brie. Her mum had sidled up to her and whispered, 'How much cheese is she going to scoff? So rude!'

Cleo knew enough to nod and say nothing. Her mum did this, provided enough food to sink a ship and then made cutting comments about anyone who overindulged. Plus, she nearly always had something negative to say about Julie, whose crime had been no greater than to snare Lawrence, give birth to Cassian and Domino, and then whisk them all off to Australia, as if the woman had strong-armed Lawrence into it and he'd been frog-marched to Heathrow against his will.

On the day they had left, her mother had taken to her bed, bereft and full of blame and foul words for 'that girl' who had clearly, in her view, insisted they pack up and haul their belongings to the other side of the world. Cleo had never said as much, but if this *had* been the case, she'd have understood. Her mum could be hard work.

Winnie had stayed in bed for a week, mourning the absence of her only son. It had made Cleo question whether her presence was any consolation at all. She knew Lawrence was her mother's favourite, always had, even if she'd denied it, but it was obvious in a thousand small ways. Going right back to her childhood, Cleo could picture the way her mum's whole demeanour lit up when he came out of school, quite unaware that she was being watched, her face beaming at the sight of him, whereas Cleo would have to tug her coat to make her aware of her presence. It had hurt then, it hurt now.

'Oh, hello, Cleo. How was your day?' she'd ask flatly, while her eyes sought out her boy across the playground and her hand waved furiously to get his attention.

It had taken her a few weeks, but her mother had soon bounced back to life with a new set of highlights in her hair and a plan to remodel the kitchen. It had been a golden time for Cleo; with her brother away, she became the sole recipient of their mother's attention. Winnie invited her out to lunch, they went shopping and her mum would buy her endless little gifts like soft socks, glossy magazines and flowers. It had been lovely, gluing together some of the fissures that had run through their relationship for the longest time.

To find out four years later that the golden son was returning from the land down under had sent Winnie into a spin. She again dropped Cleo like a hot potato and organised a welcome home party, had a banner printed, and stocked up the freezer with all the things she thought her son might like to eat. It smarted to be so quickly and obviously relegated, but Cleo didn't dwell on it – what would be the point? She had Georgie and he was more than adequate compensation for all her mother's failings.

And now here they all were, celebrating her parents' anniversary. One big, happy family.

She watched quietly as her mum tore the wrapping paper to reveal the fancy gold-framed oil painting Lawrence and Julie had bought, and smiled warmly at the voucher Cleo had got them for John Lewis. Then, just after her mother had read aloud every word from every card that had plopped through their letterbox, informing them all loudly that their aunty Pattie hadn't bothered to get in touch and that they should all remember that when it came to sending Christmas cards, Cleo felt a very real and sudden cramp in her lower abdomen, immediately followed by a rippling ache that was new, different. Her breathing increased in excited and nervous anticipation. Looking over the table towards her man, she called out softly, 'Georgie? I think I'm ready to call it a night. I'm very tired.' She spoke wide-eyed and deliberately, knowing he'd understand that she was trying subtly to say more.

Putting down his can of Coke, he stood quickly, and she loved him for it. This was what he did, put her first, did everything in his power to make her happy and comfortable. Always. He loved her in a million small ways that made the biggest difference. He gave her the window seat when they travelled, offered her the most perfect slice of whatever they were sharing and he let her sleep like a Swiss roll, entombed in their duvet while he shivered, rather than wake her. It felt wonderful to have this man in her life who prioritised her and adored her as much as she did him. There was no having to weigh up her options, no second guessing or censoring her words; she and Georgie just worked, and always had. They were great mates as well as husband and wife. Her life was infinitely better because he was in it.

'Off already, Cleo? Anything going on we need to know about?' Winnie yelled, clasping her hands at her chest, watching her daughter rise and reach for her cardigan.

Cleo shook her head. 'No, just tired, Mum. Thank you for such a lovely evening and happy anniversary. And you can't keep asking me if there's anything happening – I've told you already, it could be another couple of weeks! Due dates are no guarantee.'

'Oh, darling!' Winnie took her into her arms and held her tight, whispering in her ear, 'Apparently eating curry, driving over bumpy roads and having sex can bring things on.'

'All at once?' She pulled a face, trying to ignore the fact her mum was annoyingly prying. This was nothing new, but Cleo had never freely given information to her mother, deciding long ago that Winnie couldn't have it both ways: she couldn't give Cleo a second-rank position and then expect her to open up. Where her mother was concerned, she felt it was safer, nicer, better to keep a certain distance. Self-protection, if you like. 'I'd give it a go, but I worry I'd spill my jalfrezi.'

Her mother ignored her.

With the whole family ritually kissed goodbye and after being waved off from the driveway, she clambered into their car and sank back into the passenger seat. Closing her eyes, she enjoyed the quiet as Georgie pulled out on to the road.

'How are you feeling, my little love?' He reached across and ran his hand over her leg.

'I didn't want to say anything back there and create a big hullaballoo, but I think there might be something happening,

Georgie.' She bit her lip, smiling at the man she loved, who exhaled slowly.

'I knew it. What do you want me to do?' he gabbled. 'Should we go straight to the hospital or go home? We've got your bag in the boot. Tell me what to do!' His fast speech caused her pulse to quicken.

'What you need to do is calm down, love. Nothing is happening right now, and it might be a false alarm; the midwife said that was possible. We need to save the drama for when it's actually needed. So just breathe. Please.'

'Gotcha.' He nodded and took a deep breath in through his mouth and out through his nose.

'Just take me home.' It was her favourite place in the whole wide world, their little house in Swallow Drive, where they had chosen everything in it together – the paint colours, the sofa, the bed linen – and it was where she liked to be. 'All I want right now is a warm bath and a cup of tea and then if things start moving, we can go to the hospital. Is that okay?' She tried to erase the flicker of nerves at the thought of what lay ahead. Keeping calm for Georgie was one thing but the prospect of giving birth thrilled and petrified her in equal measure.

'Of course, it's okay. I'm excited but shitting myself as well.'

'I know that feeling.' She laughed.

'I love you,' he told her for the millionth time that day.

'And I love you.'

'Do you think we should call your mum or Jules? Do you want them with you?' He drove with increasing caution, slow enough to irritate whoever was behind them. And it made her smile, as if he was aware more than ever of the precious cargo they carried.

'No, I don't want you to call anyone. I only need you with me, only want you with me.'

He nodded, his eyes firmly on the road. 'I want to make this the best for you that it can possibly be and so at any point, whatever you need or whoever you need, you just let me know and I will do all I can to make it happen. I love you, Cleo.'

'And I love you.' She felt the familiar flush of warmth at the words and chuckled, wondering if he was aware of how, when nervous, he told her this on repeat . . .

What she and Georgie shared was special and rare. Having seen her parents' marriage up close, where they filled any holes with wine, laughter and cake, and Lawrence and Julie's too, where their smiles were sometimes a little too fixed and their interactions a little stilted, she understood that the friendship and mutual admiration she and Georgie shared was a precious thing.

Images of the evening just past filled her mind. She'd seen Lawrence hand Daisy Harrop a wad of cash for a tip. It was typical of him, making a big splash, going overboard so it all became about him. It bothered her on so many levels, not least when they were saving every penny for this baby to have the very best start, when a handful of cash like that, which might have been small fry to him, would have made the biggest difference to her and Georgie. It wasn't that she was jealous – she didn't begrudge Daisy a penny, she was a sweet girl, who Cleo knew didn't have the easiest of times at home – but it was more that his whole easy come, easy go attitude to money irritated her when she and Georgie worked so hard for so much less. Was that jealousy? She hoped not.

'Can't we just keep driving, Georgie . . . can't we go far, far away from them all? Change our names and live a quiet life on the coast, just the three of us . . . We could go to Ilfracombe, paddle in the sea when the sun shone and gather shells on the beach at dusk. We'd have picnics in the cove and grow sunflowers in our garden.' She let the image form in her mind.

It felt tempting, the idyllic life away from the noise of her family, away from the pressure she felt to show up and fit in when her mother put out the call, knowing that no matter how often she was on time, how many times she gave them lifts, whatever gift she got them, she would only ever come a close second to Lawrence. She looked across at her husband's handsome face in the orangey glow of the streetlamps, the man who always put her first, knowing she needed no more than him and their soon-to-arrive baby.

'If it made you happy, I'd go anywhere.' His tone told her he wasn't joking.

'Seriously?' She felt the excited bloom of anticipation at the prospect of starting over somewhere new without the weight of Kelleway expectation dragging her down . . . 'Can you imagine, a life without Mum shouting and force-feeding us bloody cheese. Evenings out without Lawrence rubbing his success in our faces at every opportunity. And don't get me started on the way he teases you . . .' It angered her as much now as it always had. She felt the flare of irritation in her veins, but also the comforting thought that escape might be possible.

'He doesn't mean it.' Georgie, her sweet, sweet man, who now made the familiar excuse for his friend. 'It's always been that way. I remember when he was playing football and all the boys in our year wanted to be his mate – literally everyone. It was like he was already famous. And then when he injured himself and couldn't play anymore, they all dropped away one by one and I was the last one standing.'

'And yet instead of thanking you for still being there, he treats you like shite.'

Georgie narrowed his eyes, as if her words wounded and she wished she could rephrase them; the last thing in the world she wanted was to upset her guy.

'Can you imagine what it was like for him?' He licked his top lip. 'He was golden. He had it all. He believed all the hype, he listened to what his coaches and teachers told him lay ahead, and he was ready for it. He could see the future they painted for him . . .

And then he was nothing, not even a contender. It was all gone in the very second he heard that snap. All of it taken away from him in a heartbeat. He was only a kid. So, yes, he might have a dig at me, but there's two things to remember: first, he does it because he doesn't know how to be any different, doesn't know how else to express his affection, so he does it by teasing me. It's a legacy of the walls he felt he had to build.'

She didn't believe this for a second, but loved so much that Georgie was the kind of person who did. 'And the second thing?'

'The second thing is that he can call me what he likes, he can treat me how he likes – I couldn't care less because he introduced me to you. If it wasn't for him, I wouldn't be here now with you, the most beautiful woman I've ever seen, and the sexiest.' He nodded at this truth. 'And so I forgive him the whole world because he gave me mine.'

She felt the threat of tears at the back of her nose; it must be all those pregnancy hormones throwing her off course.

'And I thought Dad was going to be awarded Speech of the Night.'

'I mean it, Cleo. Loz struggles in his own way, but I get him. And if you think about it, he could be off mixing with millionaires, people who shop in Waitrose and who like golf and boats like he does, but he doesn't; he hangs around with us. He's my mate, no matter what. He'd die for our family and he's my best friend. What he needs is kindness and understanding.'

'If you say so.' She had never really shared the same closeness to her brother that Georgie had.

'I do.' Again he reached for her leg, and she knew it was pointless to debate further on the topic.

'Do you really think I'm the sexiest woman you've ever seen?' She ran her fingernail up and down his arm.

'I wouldn't say it if I didn't think it was true.'

'It's just that I might have heard that sex can hurry things along in situations like this.' She giggled.

'I think, Cleo, that we have more sex than anyone else on the planet.'

'I think you're right.' She smiled, knowing this glorious bond they shared, which every magazine article and story had suggested would wane once they were wed, was just as strong now as it had been a little over fourteen years ago when they had walked down the aisle hand in hand. And they were just as connected sexually as they had always been.

'Do you think we'll have as much sex when the baby is here? How will we fit it all in?' he asked with mock concern.

'We'll find a way, my gorgeous, sexy beast, we'll find a way. And who knows where we might be having it, where would we go, Georgie, if we could go anywhere, live anywhere?'

'You still thinking about that?'

'I am. I'm thinking north Devon. A little cottage in Fore Street.' Moving her foot to get comfortable, she felt a bump under the sole of her Converse. 'What's that?' Bending forward as best she could, she reached her hand down and grabbed at what lay in the footwell of the passenger seat. Pulling it up into view, she saw the fur-covered chicken nugget. 'Georgie! You have chicken nuggets under the seat!'

'You should see what's in the glove box!' He laughed.

'Ooh!' It was a visceral reaction to a sharp, low pain that took her breath away. She dropped the offending fowl and put her hand on her belly.

'You all right?'

She heard the alarm in his question and nodded until the sensation passed. 'That was a bit cheeky!' She tried to lighten the atmosphere and quell her own concern.

'Are you sure you still want to head home? We could double back here and take a left.' He pointed ahead. 'I could have you at the hospital in—'

'No, no.' She was adamant. 'Let's go home.'

'Really?' He glanced at her repeatedly, trying to do that and keep his eyes on the road.

'Yes, please, babe.' She settled back in the seat. 'I hope if we have a little girl, she's as sweet as Domino. She really is a lovely little thing.'

'She is,' he agreed. 'Just sits there taking it all in. Say what you want about Lawrence, but he's a bloody good dad. They're kind, respectful kids. There aren't many teens who would be happy to spend the whole of their Friday night with their grandparents instead of going out with their mates. They're a credit to their parents.'

'They are.' She hoped one day someone would say something similar about her little one.

'Just think, Georgie, very soon there'll be a baby in its seat travelling with us. Can you imagine? An extra passenger after all these years.'

'I can take them out with me in the van when they get older.' He beamed. 'Show them how their old dad makes a living.'

'Oh, they'll love that! A day out with their daddy, dropping off building supplies and stopping off for hamburgers on the way.' She pictured waving them off from the doorstep.

'I want them to be proud of me, Cleo.'

'How could they not be?' She twisted to face him. 'How could they not see that you are the most wonderful, generous and kindest man ever! They will love you and they will be proud of you. As am I.'

The ache in her stomach grumbled and she felt a new stir of anxiety. A nice bath, cup of tea and then off to the hospital . . . It sounded like a plan.

CHAPTER SEVEN

DOMINO KELLEWAY

Domino Kelleway hugged her nan tightly.

'I don't know, first Aunty Cleo and now you, Dom. My guests are dropping like flies! I thought we'd be dancing till dawn!'

'Sorry, Nan,' Domino whispered.

'You don't have to be sorry, my darling. I don't know many young girls who would study this late on a Friday night. Don't overdo it, and don't go to bed too late. Your sleep is important.'

'I won't, I promise.'

Her nan pulled away and searched her face. 'You make us all so proud.'

'You really do,' her grandad chimed. 'Now, I know you're not a baby' – he winked – 'but your nan's right, you make us all so proud. Can we give you some sweetie money?' He reached into his pocket where his slim brown folded wallet lived and peeled out two twenty-pound notes.

'Blimey, Dad, that's a lot of sweeties!' Lawrence joked.

'You don't have to do that, Grandad.' Domino looked at the floor and let her hair fall over her face.

'I know we don't have to, but we want to. You're our only granddaughter!' Winnie linked arms with her husband.

'For now.' Domino smiled and raised her shoulders, excited. 'Aunty Cleo might have a little girl.'

'Oh, Dom! Won't it be lovely, another little baby running around?' Her nan lay her head on her grandad's shoulder. 'It feels like only minutes ago we were chasing you around on your fat little legs. Look at you now! A proper stunner. Not an ounce of fat on you.'

'Here you go, darling.' Her grandad pushed the notes into the palm of her hand.

'Are you sure, Grandad?' she asked softly. He was always generous, and she loved him for it.

'Of course! You treat yourself.' He smiled.

'Thank you.' Domino put the cash into her micro bag and threw her arms around his neck. 'Love you.'

'And we love you.' He patted her back.

Her phone beeped. She read the text from Ruby.

'That's my friend who's come to pick me up.'

'Do they want to come in for a hot chocolate or some cheese?' Winnie indicated the cheese board that was still heavily laden. Cassian sat between their mum and dad, picking at the crackers.

'I don't think so. She's really shy.'

'Like you then,' her nan observed. 'It's nice you've found friends you get on with, and you should be more confident, you know, Dom. You've got the lot, darling: brains and beauty. I hope you realise that one day and speak up.'

'Well, I won't be very brainy if I don't hit those books. Night night, everyone!'

'Call me when you want picking up tomorrow!' her dad yelled, and her mum gave a small nod as the two exchanged a look.

Her mum had been quiet all evening. Well, she was not going to let her mother's bad mood spoil her Friday night. What was it with old people who didn't know how to live? She was never, ever, ever going to be like that.

She gave a final small wave and walked slowly from the garden, through the overdone house – where a lack of taste had never stopped her grandparents from making endless home improvements – and across the gravelled driveway. From the corner of her eye, she saw the sway of net curtain from the side window of the house next door where Jake and his loser sister Daisy lived. Daisy was a proper weirdo. Domino had watched her earlier in the evening, waiting their table and gazing at them as if they were superstars. It wouldn't surprise her if right now she was ogling them through the window. She shivered. The thought made her cringe. Poor Jake. Imagine being saddled with a sibling like that. She might think Cassian was a boring prick, but at least he was popular.

The little red car parked on the corner opposite flashed its lights. Her ride had arrived. The passenger door opened and she climbed in. Ruby was in the back seat and their friend Essie was driving. Closing the door, she buckled up.

'For fuck's sake, someone give me a cigarette before I die!' She put her fingers in her hair. 'I've just had the worst fucking evening of my entire life! Soooo boring. At one point I actually considered stabbing myself in the face with a fucking cheese knife! God, I hate my family! How can one group of people be so dull! Urgh!'

'You're such a drama queen.' Ruby laughed and handed her a lit, half-smoked cigarette which Domino drew on like it was fresh air.

'You don't have to live with them,' she responded.

'Yeah, it must be hell being driven around by your hot dad in his flash car, worrying that the hot tub might not be the right temperature and which pair of Choos to wear out.'

'Shut the fuck up, Ruby, it's nothing like that!' she fired, knowing that her parents rowed a lot about money and guessing that they might be in trouble once more. The thought of having to up sticks and move out yet again was more than she could handle. Not that she wanted to elaborate for her friends or indeed let such thoughts ruin her Friday night. Speaking with the cigarette resting on her bottom lip, she removed her jacket and threw it on to the back seat before unbuttoning two buttons on her blouse to ensure the lacy cups of her push-up bra were visible. 'God, I need a drink. Where are we thinking? Shiskas or The Race Club?'

'Both!' Essie yelled and Ruby drummed the back of her seat while she stamped her feet.

The stereo jumped into life and Domino felt the rise in her gut of good, excited energy, as her chest pulsed with the beat. As the car pulled around the corner, past the four oaks – one of which was apparently under threat, not that she gave a shit about some old tree – and out on to the main road, she turned to her friend on the backseat.

'Did you just say my dad was hot?' she screamed.

'He is though!' Ruby squealed, swigging from a half-bottle of vodka that she passed to Domino. 'Face it, you have a hot dad!'

'That's disgusting. You're such a desperate tart!' She took a mouthful of the booze and let it slip down her throat before shuddering as the warmth radiated within her. 'Besides, he's too old for you!' She laughed.

'Too old for her? I have two words—' Essie shouted over the din of the techno thumping through the car.

'Don't you dare!' Domino screamed, trying to put her hand over Essie's mouth, who ducked out of the way. The car swerved a little to the right before Essie steered it back on course.

'One . . . two . . . three!' Ruby counted before she and Essie both yelled in unison, 'Micky Tate!'

'You're a couple of bitches! Both of you! Complete bitches!' Domino roared and flicked her hair over her shoulder as she took another long swig and the vodka started to work its magic.

Micky Tate . . . She wondered if he was going to be out tonight. God she hoped so! It was something that had sustained her all week; any dull moment during the blandest of days could be made magical at the thought that Micky might be interested in her. Because she was certainly interested in him. Removing her lip gloss from her bag, she slathered her lips and pouted into the little mirror in the sun visor, very much liking what she saw. She was in the zone and ready to go!

'Can't this fucking old rust bucket go any faster?' she yelled, as Essie and Ruby laughed loudly. How could it be this much fun just driving along with the girls? But it was. The freedom she felt at being out of the house, away from her family, was intoxicating!

Domino loved Shiskas. The fact that it was a club slightly out of town and they had to drive there made it feel like an adventure. It gave her a buzz knowing that they went there regularly; it felt like their place, one where she knew the layout, the best spot to sit, which loo cubicle they could all fit into for catching up and drinking smuggled-in booze, who behind the bar would give them free drinks, and which DJ played the best set.

It made her feel smug to eye the nervous girls in their best weekend clothes, pressed items probably bought for the occasion, and tonight this was the only thing she envied about them; again she plucked at the front of her blouse. Yes, she'd watch the shiny girls, who were always much older than her, clinging to the wall or huddling in a herd, scared to be noticed while desperately wanting just that. She thought they were a little pathetic. Not that she, Essie, and Ruby had to worry about being underage for the place, knowing with confidence that the security team would wave them in without checking their fake ID. Especially if Andrea was on the door – he was a total sweetie. A bald, muscled, tattooed sweetie, but a sweetie, nonetheless.

It was one of the perks of being pretty and having a fantastic rack. Her mum banged on and on about grades and how they were her key to a great future, blah blah blah . . . Domino, however, knew otherwise, and with these pert puppies resting inside her shirt, figured she could do better than hot-footing it country to country in the wake of a fucking loser like her dad. Oh yes, she could do much better. She had her sights set on a footballer. And she wasn't thinking of a local lad who knocked about in a Sunday league with his mates before retiring to the pub to drink warm pints of beer and talk tactics, and who might, if she was very lucky, provide her with a new build on a grim housing estate. Like the grotty little place Cleo and Georgie lived in. No, thank you! Her sights were set a little higher. She was determined to bag a bloke who played in the Premier League and that's where a nightclub like Shiskas played its part.

When they arrived, she did a quick scan of the car park and counted three Lambos, a couple of Porsches, a souped-up Range Rover and finally there it was! Her eyes widened at the sight of the teal McLaren 720S with the personalised plate. *Micky* . . . Micky Tate, who was good-looking, rich and a very successful footballer. And who also happened to be twenty-seven. But age was just a number, right? Besides, she always went for older boys. They seemed to like her and that was good because she certainly liked them. The last time she'd been here, Micky had done a double-take as she walked past and had winked at her as she swung her leather jacket over her shoulder when she left.

'We are going to have a good night, girls!' she screeched and reached again for the vodka bottle. 'I can feel it in my bones!'

Essie parked her little red car at the side of the club where the ground was uneven and the more mundane cars were abandoned in pure shame. The three leaped out in a cloud of laughter and with so much energy, Domino was sure they gave off sparks. It felt good knowing they were 'those girls' – the ones the other girls were intimidated by and the ones the boys wanted to take home. As if she'd swap this feeling, this high for good grades.

What did Julie know, bless her, with her split ends and her dated clothes? The woman didn't even have the sense to get Botox! Her mother might have been a lost cause, but Domino's life was going to be very different. Never was she going to have to pack up in the middle of the night to run away, scrabbling around for cash because her man couldn't support her properly, kept her living on a knife edge of uncertainty. She'd make sure of it. When she was an adult, she never wanted to feel the nervous swirl in her gut, the feeling that she was standing on shaky ground, waiting for the earthquake, to see the ground open up beneath her and suck her down and down, taking everything she held dear too. Swallowing her up and dragging her into the dark space below where nothing but sadness and uncertainty lurked. A dark space where she found it hard to take a deep breath, wondering if she would ever again rise up into the sunshine.

No, she would not live like that. She simply refused, having had more than enough of living like that as a child. The answer to her was clear and obvious: find a wealthy man and hold on to him tightly. A man who, unlike her dad, was able to make it as a pro footballer. A man who, unlike her dad, would not let his family down.

Dancing as they walked through the door was kind of their thing. It was what they did: they made an entrance, announced their arrival, catching the eye of anyone who was watching and inviting those who weren't to start watching. It was a calling card of sorts, letting the likes of Micky Tate know that they were in the house. Domino sashayed with her arms raised over her head, caring little that her blouse had ridden up to just under her bra to show off her flat, tanned stomach. I mean, why not? If you've got it, flaunt it! And she intended to do just that.

Clicking her fingers and with her eyes half closed, she made her way to the dance floor where the three girls moved together in a dozen well-choreographed moves, mere inches away from each other. Dancing almost skin to skin, mouth to mouth. It was a performance, and Domino was in no doubt that she was the star.

Looking up she saw a gaggle of men staring at them, mouths slack, unable, it seemed, to look away. It was thrilling to recognise one of them as Micky Tate. At the sight of his face, his white teeth picked out in the UV light that shone from the ceiling, a surge of want fired right through her. He downed his drink and turned to walk to the bar, looking over his shoulder with his gaze lingering over her. Domino kissed Ruby hard on the lips, and followed him, dancing slowly as she went. The group of transfixed men seemed to part as she approached, leaving a path right to the footballer who rested on a bar stool with his long legs stretched out in front of him.

'That was quite a display.' He chuckled.

'I don't know what you're talking about.' She pouted, just like she did for her Insta, getting the look just right: the slightly open lips, the tip of her tongue on the side of her mouth, eyes down, looking up, stomach sucked in, chest out, leg forward to elongate the line of her silhouette . . . It took a lot of practice.

'Sure you don't.' He looked skyward and shook his head. 'You're sensational.' The top of his lip curled as if he were hungry and she were meat, and she felt the power in being able to make a man like Micky Tate – a rich man, a successful man – feel that way. Her giggle burbled from her. Yes, yes, she *was* sensational . . .

Clicking his fingers, the guy behind the bar ran over. 'What're you having?' Micky pointed to the optics.

'Champagne,' she answered, her eyes never leaving his face.

'Champagne?' He shook his head and gave a small laugh. 'A woman of expensive tastes.'

Flicking her long hair over her shoulder, she smiled at the fact that he had called her a woman.

'I guess it's what I'm used to.' She held his eyeline and the tension between them was palpable.

'They only have the cheap stuff here.' He pulled a face. 'And I think someone like you deserves only the very best.'

'I would have to agree.' She sucked her finger. 'And where would we find the very best?' She ran the wet tip of her finger down over her collarbone, edging towards her cleavage.

'My pool house has a fridge full of the stuff.'

'Your pool house?' She laughed loudly, amused and intoxicated not only by his attention but the fact that he had a frickin' pool house! This was more like it. 'I like nothing more than a warm pool on a dark night. Trouble is, I don't have my bathers.' She clicked her tongue against the roof of her mouth and folded her arms under her bust, making sure to lift her bosom to its best advantage. Domino was no stranger to using her body to get what she wanted. It was a power she had employed with her ex-flings, who had yielded expensive dinners, a nice bracelet, lifts to anywhere at any time. They, however, had been mere practice. It was Micky Tate who was the big prize. She viewed him now through her vodka-tinged filter, and he looked good.

'I'm sure we can work something out.' He reached out and put his hand on her waist, drawing her to him.

That first skin-to-skin contact was electric and she shivered as his palm grazed the soft space where her tight jeans met her hip bone. Coming to rest in the space where his legs parted, she let him run his fingers over her ribs. Her eyes took in the labels: D&G jeans, simple black Dior t-shirt, Nike Air Yeezys and the chunky Breitling nestling on his wrist. It was important to recognise the labels, to know what to look for. She thought of it as a bit like shopping; not being able to identify such things would be like going into a supermarket and searching for an artichoke but without having ever seen or eaten one – it would make life tricky to say the least. So she made it her business to know a designer label when she saw it; studying them was a bit like homework. And whilst she might not have read the recommended text by Jane Austen, had no idea about improper fractions, and had yet to start her coursework on detailed glacial motion – in label identification, she was guaranteed a straight A.

There was something about being seen with this man who was rich and famous, something about being seen to be *desired* by this man who was rich and famous, that made her feel both lightheaded and deliriously happy! It was almost impossible not to let her thoughts race ahead to a place where she could see herself on his arm, sharing moments, staring at sunsets from expensive hotel beaches and even . . . yes, even walking down the aisle . . . in Vera Wang. Her stomach bunched in excitement at the prospect. Looking towards her friends on the dance floor, she saw Ruby turn and put her hand over her mouth, as if to stifle a yell, before turning to Essie and whispering into her ear. Her mates laughed, winked, and gave subtle signs of approval, whilst trying to look cool and continue dancing. She knew they'd be happy for her. She had set her sights, made her move and she had scored! It was the dream.

'Shall we get out of here?' he whispered into her ear. She could feel the warmth of his breath on her neck. It sent goosebumps along her back.

'Sure, I just need to tell my friends.' She pointed towards the dance floor where the girls danced with their heads rolling to the beat, lost to the pull of the music that drew them in and held them fast.

'No need, I'm only five minutes away. I can drop you back, after . . .' He let this hang and her stomach flipped at the word. *After . . .* This was happening.

With her hand in his, she liked the way everyone – the security guys, Andrea the sweetie included – almost lowered their heads in reverence when he passed. Micky Tate was a big deal, and it was her who held his hand and was about to climb into his McLaren and head off to his pool house. Excitement pinged around her gut like fireflies. It made her feel like a big deal too. And she liked it.

The car lit up as they drew close. It was low to the ground and yet wonderfully comfortable once she had managed to manoeuvre inside the pale tan leather seat. It smelled of money. It *felt* like money. Not the kind of money that meant her dad got to drive a flash rented Merc, but serious money.

'You really live just five minutes away?' she asked, her heart fluttering with nerves as he pumped the accelerator and the engine roared.

'It is if I drive like this.' He laughed as he pulled out of the parking lot, quickly picking up speed along the lanes. With his arms out straight, gripping the leather steering wheel, and his chunky watch glinting when it caught the light, he twisted the car to the left and right, and the vehicle glided as if it was on rails. She gasped. Micky clearly saw this as an indicator of joy and went faster and faster. There was no way he could know what was coming the other way around the blind bends, and it was at this point that she felt the first flicker of fear that they might crash. Yet there was something about his recklessness that was a little thrilling. The swaying, winding motion at such speed, however, she found a lot less thrilling.

Without warning, her head flew back against the headrest, and what started as a low-level suggestion of nausea quickly developed into an instant and most pressing need to vomit.

'Stop the car!' she yelled with urgency, the back of her head pinned to the headrest; she banged the door with the flat of her hand.

'What do you mean, "stop the car"? I promise you I've got as much champagne as you can—'

'I'm going to be—'

Domino never got to finish the sentence. Whether it was the gut-churning combination of garlic bread, fresh creamy carbonara, a healthy slice of anniversary cake, three chunky slices of Brie, the generous slosh of vodka, topped off with cigarette smoke, or whether it was simply the potent mix of nerves and speed was neither here nor there. Either way, the result was the same.

She tried her best to stem the vomit that flew from her mouth by placing her fingers over her lips. Sadly, this only served to act as a fan and directed thin lines of pale-coloured sick on to the dashboard and underside of the windscreen.

'What the fuck?' Micky actually screamed and slammed on the brakes. 'My fucking car!' he screamed again. 'Just stop it!'

But she couldn't stop it. She couldn't speak, she couldn't cry, apologise or do anything other than continue to hose the interior of this man's very expensive sports car with the soupy contents of her stomach. He wound down the windows as the car slowed to a stop and it would only be in hindsight that she would feel shame at the horrendous stench of the dairy- and garlic-infused fluid. And more shame at the thought that where her sick had splashed the windows and he had wound them down, her vodka-soaked Italian supper was now inside the car window mechanism.

Micky jumped out of the car and ran around to the passenger side. Yanking open the door, he pulled her forcibly by the arm. 'Get out! Get out!' he yelled, his tone urgent, angry.

She felt her body fall sideways as he manhandled her from the soiled leather interior, and she collapsed on the verge with sick clinging to her hair, all over her hands and dripping from her mouth down the front of the shitty blouse she'd found at the back of her wardrobe. There was also a rind of Brie sitting in her perky cleavage.

'I'm sorr—'

'Don't! Just don't!' He held up his hand to stop her talking before marching back and forth around the car with his hands on his hips. 'What the fuck?' he yelled, snorting through his nose, as if he could not comprehend what she had done.

'You were going so fast, and I've been out for—'

'I said don't.' He almost growled, pointing at her. 'Don't speak! There is nothing you can do or say! Look at the state of my fucking car!' He sounded like he might cry.

'Shall we go back to the club and get some paper towels and—'

'Paper towels?' He stared at her as if she were stupid and she felt her insides shrink. Bringing her knees up to her chest, she wrapped her arms around her shins to try to stem the tremor to her limbs that being so very sick had created.

'If you think you're setting foot inside my car or that you will ever be able to show your face inside that club again, you are more of a fucking idiot than I thought.' He walked to the driver's side and opened the door. 'God, it stinks! That smell!' He banged the roof, clearly furious, and she felt the beginnings of fear.

'What are you going to do, leave me here?' She looked up and down the lane into the darkness and her heart jumped at the prospect. 'You can't leave me here on my own.' Her voice cracked as her tears gathered. 'I haven't got my phone!'

'Jesus Christ!' he yelled again into the night sky. He walked briskly towards her and handed her his phone. 'One call! And make it brief.'

With trembling fingers, she took his phone and saw the way he winced as her vomit-covered hand reached out. Domino didn't know who to call. Her dad? She began to punch in his number before deciding this was a bad idea – he thought she was studying with Ruby – when something odd happened. She put in the final digits but didn't put the call through, deciding it would be better to call Ruby or Essie, when the name 'Kelleway' popped up on Micky's screen.

'Why have you got my dad's number in your phone?' She stared at it, trying to figure the connection.

'What are you talking about?' he spat.

'This is my dad's number.' She held out the phone, which he grabbed and stared at the name Kelleway. His laugh when it came was mocking, nasty, and not for the first time, Domino felt the shiver of fear.

'I don't fucking believe it! Perfect.' He kicked at the ground and let out a guttural yell, scuffing the toe of his immaculate trainer. 'Fucking perfect!'

'I . . . I still need to make a call.' She spoke in a quiet voice, almost afraid to raise it and wary of asking again about how he knew her dad when his reaction had been so strange.

Breathing heavily through his nose, he seemed to consider this and made a call.

'Andrea, it's me. Look, I need a favour. I've had to fly tip a dozy tart and I need it collecting.' He laughed but it was a mean snort that rendered her silent. She knew she would never forget being described in that way; this was what he thought of her. No more than *rubbish . . . trash . . . waste . . .* It made her feel small, less than. It made her feel like the kind of girl who would not get picked to live a life of shared moments, staring at sunsets from expensive hotel beaches and not the kind of girl who could waltz into a lucky, lucky life by walking down the aisle . . . in Vera Wang.

'Where from? Er . . . I'm sending the location. Give it to her slag mates.'

It horrified her to hear her friends described in this way, but riven with shame and reflection, edged now with fear, she said nothing. And the fact that she felt unable to speak out was something that would bother her for the longest time: learning how quickly she could be subdued, reduced, made invisible. She pictured her mum packing up the car and painting on a smile and in that moment longed to feel her mother's arms around her, the woman who made things feel better.

She watched him send a message, end the call, and without so much as a glance in her direction, he climbed into his flashy car. The one she had so admired.

Shouting now through the open window, he revved the engine. 'The little tarts you arrived with are coming to pick you up. And I can't believe you were so worried about your lift when you should be worried about my fucking car! Have you any idea the damage you've done to the leather? Do you know what it's going to cost to get that stench out? What a fucking family! What a shambles of a fucking family!'

Fat tears trickled down her face. It was a hard thing to hear. She shook her head, wishing in that moment that she was still in her nan's back garden, picking at cheese and sitting on the comfy sofa. What was it Grandad Bernie had said? *Your nan's right, you make us all so proud . . .* She wondered how proud he would be right now. Or if not there, she'd like to be at home in Newman Road with her mum and dad, or better still, in her bedroom in their house in Melbourne, when life had been good, the sun warm, her friends sweet and her life had felt in control.

It had been a good life, where she *had* worried about her grades, read books, played netball for her school, eaten ice cream in the park, and just the thought of not handing in a piece of coursework on glacial drift would have kept her awake with the sheer worry of it. A treat was a sleepover where her mum packed her off to her friend's house with a packet of peanut butter Tim Tams and where, for a midnight feast, she and her schoolfriends had greedily eaten delicious, melted-cheese Jaffles.

How had she arrived here in just three years? How had things spiralled so quickly until she felt empty like this – empty and hopeless, sitting here in the dark with this arsehole as she tried to carve a life that meant security. It occurred to her then that this type of security came at a heavy price. But surely anything – anything – would be better than listening out for every sound in the early hours, every bump in the night, in case it meant they were on the move again, that bags had to be quickly packed as they were given the green light to go, go, go!

'Do you want to take a rain check?' she asked, flicking the Brie from her cleavage. 'I could come out to your place, we could—'

'You've got to be fucking joking! Listen to yourself. A *rain check*? You're a stupid little girl who's seen one too many movies. I don't even know your first name and that suits me just fine. It's enough to know you are a Kelleway – of course you are! I see you have your dad's gift of fucking up everything you go near. If I never set eyes on you again that'll be too soon!'

The taillights of the car were gone in a second and the lane was suddenly dark. She shivered, partly in fear because there were noises all around that sounded like something or someone was present, but that could have been her imagination.

Being so sick had left her feeling wretched, but more than that, she was aware of a cold kernel of something that felt a lot like grief that had taken root in her stomach. Was she really like her dad? Was her life to be similar? It was as she felt this small icy kernel of self-doubt embed itself in her chest that her sorrow came in earnest. Thick ribbons of snot and tears streaked her face, and the remnants of her mascara found their way on to her cheeks. She wished she had her coat, which had her phone in the pocket, both of which she had flung on to the back seat of Essie's car.

But even if she did have her phone, who would she honestly call? Not her parents. Her grandparents? They'd only think it a hoax – their little Domino would never find herself in such a situation. Cassian? Yes, yes, she could call Cassian, her big brother. This thought provided a small blanket of comfort. She didn't really dislike him. Truth was, she didn't really know him; he was quiet and had never opened up to her. But she knew he was kind. Unlike her, who didn't really give a shit about anyone or anything.

Not that she had always been this way. In Melbourne she'd cared about everyone and everything, but being wrenched from there with little notice and having to give up her school, her home, her friends, her whole beautiful life . . . Well, it had changed her. And now here she was, sitting on a grass verge in the dark, cold, scared and covered in sick. The thought summoned a new batch of tears.

She wasn't sure how long she sat there – ten minutes, twenty? But enough time for her to stop crying and become strangely calm. Resigned, almost. She recognised the knocking engine of the little red runaround, and her relief was sweet when Essie pulled up, and both she and Ruby jumped out.

'Oh my God!'

'What the actual fuck?'

'Why are you out here on your own?'

'Did he hurt you?'

'Are you hurt, baby?'

'Talk to us!'

'God, you smell bad!'

Their questions and observations came thick and fast and were fired in such quick succession, it gave her no time to answer.

'I'm okay,' she managed, gratefully accepting the pairs of arms that held her tightly, taking both warmth and comfort from them.

'We've been chucked out the club and they told us never to go back,' Essie sighed.

'We're barred!' Ruby echoed in disbelief. 'Can you believe that?'

For some reason their horror at something so seemingly minor in comparison to the shitstorm that was her life struck her as funny and a small giggle stuttered from her before building into laughter that Essie and Ruby matched. Pretty soon, all three howled their laughter, wiping tears and clinging to each other as they fell back on to the damp grass of the verge.

'It's Friday night!' Essie yelled between their laughter. 'And we're lying in a ditch!'

This set them all off again.

Eventually Domino sat up and wiped her face with the back of her palm. Enough. Enough tears, enough sadness. Essie was right. It was Friday night, they were young and pretty, and life was for living! This was far better than letting any deep-seated worries over her family situation drag her down. She would bury her melancholy under a neat padding of vodka, laughter and music.

'Will someone please give me some booze and a fucking cigarette!' she boomed into the night sky.

CHAPTER EIGHT

LISA HARROP

Lisa Harrop glanced at the clock on the bedside table; it had just gone eleven o'clock. She had listened to Daisy climb the stairs and felt her shoulders slump against the pillows, resting easier knowing her daughter was home safely. It worried her, her little girl travelling about on the roads on that rickety old bike. She had read some terrible stories in recent years about cyclists sideswiped and crushed under lorries or injured when they fell and hit their heads.

The TV was on in the bedroom, it was company for her of sorts; a visual machine that helped eat up the seconds, minutes, hours of time that she was keen to kill. She liked the flickering blue of the lights, even though the sound was turned off and she had no idea what she was watching – a cop show of some description, but whether real or fiction it was hard to tell.

Lying back on the mattress she looked up at the ceiling where a water splat from the leaking header tank some months ago had formed an image that she thought looked similar to a map. It was her favourite thing to do: stare at the watermark until her eyes closed, transporting herself to a hot country where she would live a beach life, eat well, throw on shorts and walk outdoors. A place far away from this house and this life that held her in its grip like a fly caught in a treacle pot trap of her own making.

No, that was unfair. Marty, Jake and Daisy had not trapped her; more like she had fallen into the treacle pot and didn't know how to climb out. This thought alone was enough to encourage tears to fall across her temple, travelling over her sore eyes, railing against the constant trickle of salt on her skin. It was so very tiring, being this low.

Her bedroom door creaked open, and she recognised the outline of her daughter, standing in silhouette.

'Mum? Are you awake?'

'Yes.' She sat up and tucked her hair behind her ears. 'Everything okay?' It was unusual for her girl to disturb her, to enter her room like this. Realisation of this was like a punch to her throat. How far they had slipped off course, to the point where for her daughter to simply enter her room felt like a big deal. This thought ladled guilt on to her already fractured self-esteem. It felt like a mere blink ago that young Daisy, Jake too, would bound in and jump up on to the bed, snuggling next to her, their little heads – mussed and fresh from sleep – close to hers on the pillow. They were nearly always clutching books or soft toys, wanting stories or to chat about nothing much in their sweet burbling tones . . . How she missed it. How she wished she could go back to then.

'Yes, everything's okay.' Daisy walked further in and sat on the end of the bed.

Lisa smiled. She could see the outline of Daisy's nose, reminding her so powerfully of her dad it made her heart jump.

'I just wanted to tell you something,' her little girl whispered, almost in reverence of the dark and late hour.

'What is it, my love? Is it about the tree? Because I already know. Read the letter when I nipped downstairs for a glass of water. I knew you'd be upset. But not sure there's a whole lot we can do about it. I guess we could write a letter, complain, get involved, but more often than not it seems that once the council have made a decision . . .'

'It wasn't about the tree, but yes, that has made me really sad. I can't think they'll actually do it, Mum. Can't believe they'd chop something down that's so old and so beautiful. What would Four Oaks look like without one of the trees?'

Lisa noted the way her daughter's chest rose and fell. 'Don't worry about it, darling. There's no point worrying about anything until you have to.' Oh, the irony! It was so easy to give this advice and yet she worried about *everything* before it happened, playing out the very worst scenario based on no more than what ifs . . . Her words made her a hypocrite, and this too only served to take her mood lower and add to her feelings of worthlessness.

'I guess.' Daisy picked at the quilt cover. 'But I think we *should* write a letter, complain and get involved. If everyone did, it might make them reconsider what's best for the tree, the area, everything.'

'It might. Let's have a think about it,' was the best she could manage, wary of yet again making false promises that she knew could only further damage the trust between them. It can't have been easy for her kids, knowing she would let them down.

Daisy sat up straight and smiled. 'What I wanted to tell you was that I got a huge tip tonight, the biggest I've ever had! Like, enough to get my bike done up, probably get a new bike! Not a new new one, but you know.'

Lisa could hear the joy in her voice and loved that her girl was so grounded that with spare cash, the best she could think of was to upgrade her bike.

'That's brilliant! I'm sure you deserved it. You work hard for Gia and Carlo, they're lucky to have you.'

'I kind of feel lucky to have them. Guess how much it was.'

She didn't want to embark on a guessing game, felt wiped out at the prospect, but this was Daisy and she loved her and the least she could do was play along. 'Oh, I don't know, twenty pounds?'

'More!' Her daughter sounded excited.

'More? Okay, fifty pounds?' She raised her hands and let them fall on to her blanket.

'Much more, Mum. I got a hundred and fifty pounds! A hundred and fifty pounds on top of the money for my shift. Can you believe it?'

'Oh, my goodness!' It was a huge amount and Lisa felt a rare flicker of joy on behalf of her daughter. 'I've never heard anything like it.'

'It was from Mr and Mrs Kelleway. They came in to celebrate their ruby wedding anniversary and the whole night was like a party. I'd probably have worked for free just to be there! And then as they were leaving, Lawrence – and I'm not being rude, he said "Call me Lawrence" – came over to say thank you and he put the cash in my hand.'

To hear his name in her daughter's mouth made her wince. The thought of Lawrence being flash and handing out the money raised a grim image. The boy next door who had always believed he could fix just about any problem, smooth anything over, with enough money to throw at it. He had always been that way.

'I shoved it in my apron pocket and didn't count it till they'd gone. I was freaking out, like it must have been a mistake or something. I thought about running after him, but Gia said I'd earned it and it's not as if he can't afford it, is it? They were calling him Mr Moneybags and now I'm Miss Moneybags!' she squealed with delight.

'I'm happy for you, Daisy. I really am.' She spoke with a tightening in her throat, feeling discomfort at how impressed her daughter seemed with the Kelleways. Lisa knew there was so much more to life than the acquisition of stuff, and having seen the family next door at close quarters for most of her life, she knew that what lay beneath the shiny exterior wasn't always what it seemed. Her mother used to call Winnie 'smiler' on account of the fact that she always grinned when she stepped over her threshold to face the world, as if everything was always perfect. Lisa knew more than most that this was not real life; perfection did not exist, no matter how hard Winnie tried to convince the neighbourhood otherwise.

'Anyway, it's late. I just wanted to let you know, Mum.'

'Thank you, darling. I love you.' She meant it; the words, as ever, filled her throat with a flood of emotion. How she loved her! How she loved them all and how wretched she felt that she didn't show them more.

'Love you too. I'm going to bed – not that I can sleep right now. I'm too excited! One hundred and fifty pounds! I can't believe it!' she repeated. 'It's brilliant, isn't it?'

'It is, darling. Have you seen Dad?' She wondered if Marty had been similarly regaled with the news.

'The telly's on in the front room; he's probably asleep on the sofa.' She spoke matter-of-factly and it tore at Lisa's heart that this was the norm. Her husband, too, finding it difficult to bound into the room, jump on to the bed, relax in her presence. This thought that she held the whole household in the grip of her sadness was as debilitating as it was a pressure. She wished she could smash her way out, throw off the blanket and let air into the place! Knowing that her family, like her, just needed to breathe . . .

'And Jake's in his room. Shock horror!' Daisy came over and kissed her sweetly on the cheek. Her small kindness and show of affection again almost moved her to tears – it was far, far more than she deserved.

'Night night, my sweet girl. Maybe . . . maybe tomorrow we can go into the garden and pull up some of those weeds. Maybe we could plant some of the flowers you talk about and try to get the garden straight.' She did this often, her mouth writing cheques her body knew she had no hope of cashing, but it felt necessary to do so, as if she believed that if she made them often enough, one day, they might come true. 'And maybe you're right: we should write that letter, complain about the threat to the tree, get involved. If everyone wrote, it *might* make them reconsider chopping it down.'

'Maybe.' Daisy's tone told her that she didn't believe a word of it, and it wounded her, ladling guilt on to the low self-esteem that living this half-life fed.

I'm sorry, my darling girl. I am so, so sorry. I want to be better . . . but it's like living on a knife edge . . . waiting for my whole world to come crashing down . . .

She heard Daisy's bedroom door close as Jake's opened and she listened to the rhythmical padding of his feet on the wooden stairs. Sometimes she considered that it might be better to have a turnstile fitted instead of a front door; there was always someone coming in or going out. Everyone, it seemed, lived their life behind closed doors, nipping out when they needed air, light, sustenance or inter-action. Holding secret lives close to their chests. Keeping emotions in check. Doing what they had to do to get through the day. One child in, one child out. Husband leaving for work, husband back from work. Daisy off to her shift at the restaurant, Daisy home. And Jake, her lovely, quiet boy . . . God only knew where he slunk off to in the early hours or just before sunup.

These were the markers in her existence, the interludes to her long, dull days; the squeak of a bedroom door hinge, the creak of the stair tread, the rattle of the letterbox as the front door closed, and the key in the lock when it opened. The click of the kettle, the chink of the china mugs. The ping of the microwave. The flush of the loo, the sound of water hitting the tray in the shower. She waited for them, was alerted by them, and knew that as long as they continued to bash out the symphony of life all round her, then that was good enough. It meant the engine of family life went on, even if she had stalled. The truth was she often lost track of where everyone was and on some days would hear the front door and think Marty was heading off to start the day when a quick look at the clock told her it was nearly teatime.

She didn't want to live like this. Who would? This hidden existence where she preferred the feel of a blanket up to her chin to anything else. A life devoid of hope and enthusiasm for whatever lay ahead. A life lived in fear. Because that was the truth: she was very, very afraid of things over which she had no control. It was rotten, like living with someone else holding the reins, steering her life, and she woke every day drenched in guilt that if this was how it was for her, what must it be like for her kids? Having to tiptoe past her sleeping form, make their own supper, wash their own clothes . . . This thought was enough for her to pull the blanket over her head, unsure what she was hiding from. She wanted to be better for them, wanted better for herself, but goodness, the pull of the mattress and the lure of a darkened room was, at that point in time, far stronger than she.

One hundred and fifty pounds . . .

The air in the bedroom was a little stale. Aware that the bed linen hadn't been changed for a couple of weeks, she vowed, again, to do it tomorrow. Embarrassed that her daughter had visited and had to endure this less than fragrant space. It was easy, making suggestions and promises in the dark, suggesting they start the weeding, get planting, write letters to the council to try to save the tree. And in the moment she voiced them, all these things felt possible, edged with something close to excitement. But in the cold light of day the same ideas would sit like rocks tethered to her body, trailing behind her, tying her down, weighting her spirit and making even standing up feel like too much.

It was hot. The air a little stifling. Discarding the blanket, she slowly shuffled off the mattress and walked to the window where blobs of dark mould gathered in the corners of the ancient, once white UPVC. What would her lovely mum, who had had a strict routine of daily, weekly, and monthly chores, have to say about the state of her once pristine home?

'I'm sorry, Mum.' She closed her eyes at the familiar lament.

Pulling the drapes, she opened the window wide and let the cool night air wash over her face. It was a nice feeling, instantly uplifting, contact of sorts with the world outside her house, which had in the last three years become both her home and her prison. With her eyes closed, she became aware of the sound of laughter and her heart jumped. The Kelleways, of course. Outside and making merry on this June night. Celebrating a ruby wedding and flinging vast tips at Daisy as if the paper were no more than confetti.

'It's all out there, waiting . . . waiting for us. A big wide world and we can grab as much of it as we want!' She shivered at the memory despite the warmth of the evening.

Something caught her eye on the side path and as her gaze adjusted to the dull outside light, she became aware of a shadowy figure standing next to the fence, staring up. Staring at her.

'Oh God, no!' Her heart raced as she jumped behind the curtain.

It was him. And he was in their spot. She would know him anywhere: his shape, the exact space he took up in the world, a form that used to fit so perfectly against her own it was like they were one.

'Lee!' he called, and her hand shot over her mouth, as if she might be able to mentally convey her will for him to be silent, that and she feared she might scream.

'Lee!' he called again. He wasn't going to give up. She had no choice other than to act.

Drawing a sharp breath and with a mouth dry with nerves, she steadied herself on the windowsill and looked down, trying to make out detail, features that the darkness denied her. This was both a disappointment and a relief, figuring if she couldn't see him too clearly then he couldn't see her. Her limbs trembled and yet her stomach jumped with something that mimicked excitement. *No!* It was more than she could handle.

'Come down!' he called. 'Please! Come here!' He could obviously see her. This fired a bolt of exposure right through her that made her feel weak.

His voice! Oh, his voice! It was a beacon, a code that punched life into her soul. It sparked joy, fear, lust, and longing – yes, just those few words enough to remind her of what he had meant to her. And she to him.

'Shut up! Just be quiet!' This she spoke out loud to silence the voice that haunted her dreams, to quieten her interior monologue and to prevent Daisy in the room next door or Marty who slept in the front room from hearing his call.

'Come down! I need to talk to you!' he half whispered, half yelled, and her heart felt like it might jump right out of her chest.

This man standing in the shadows had the power to blow up her whole life right now! The very thing she had spent the last three years dreading, he could do it – this very second! The thought was more than she could stand. Knowing every nuance of his tone, she could tell he'd been drinking and knew she needed to make him stop talking before he did or said something stupid. She needed him to go away.

'Go away! Just go away!' she pleaded.

'If you're not coming down, I'll come over to you then!' he called back with an undertone of amusement in his voice as he lifted his leg as if to hightail it over the fence.

'Okay! Okay.' He had won. Again.

It felt like she had little choice other than to do his bidding. A thin film of cold sweat covered her.

Running her hand over her face, she tried as best as she could to smooth her thick, wavy hair, which was a little matted at the back, a little greasy and flat on the top. Taking a tentative step out on to the landing, she checked that Daisy hadn't heard and was up and about, investigating. She could see the lamplight in her daughter's room filtering beneath the door, which, thankfully, remained closed. Likewise, when she reached the downstairs hallway, she could hear Marty snoring on the couch. *Marty . . . I love you!* She sent the silent refrain in advance of the disloyalty she was about to display.

Her heart beat so loudly in her ears she thought it must sound like a gong to the rest of the house. Yet miraculously no one stirred. With shaking fingers, she unlocked the kitchen door and turned the handle, staring out along the alleyway towards the gap at the end of the fence that had always been there. A space of twelve and a half inches where the fence ended and the wall of the Kelleways' carport started. How did she know it was a gap of twelve and a half inches? Because they'd once measured it. The side of their house was lit by the Kelleways' festoon of lights that hung artfully around their gazebo and barbecue area. It didn't bother her, having grown up in the shadow of the family who shone so brightly, festoon of lights or not.

She took a step outside and looked down at her bare feet on the concrete, noticing the dead autumn leaves still gathered in the corners of the path and clogging the small drain cover that sat at the bottom of the drainpipe. It only occurred to her as she trod the path that she was in pyjama bottoms and an oversized t-shirt with baked bean juice on the front. Not that there was a whole lot she could do about it at this point, and not that he was likely to notice, especially as he had been drinking.

The storm of emotions that swirled inside her were complex and multi-faceted. Rage certainly, at being summoned in such a fashion, as if she were still that sixteen-year-old who responded to a whistle. There was excitement, too, at the prospect of being in such close proximity to the man, and naked fear at what might pass. He was powerful and she was not and that sent a wave of nausea to lap inside her gut. The fact that he'd been drinking made him doubly unpredictable – she needed to be brave, face him, talk to him, and get the interaction over as quickly as she was able.

Don't worry about your greasy hair and the state of your t-shirt – what does it matter? He's seen you naked, touched your body, kept watch while you peed in a bush, lay next to you, bathed with you, swum with you, held you close, brushed your hair, put cream on your sunburn, had sex with you during your period, bleached your hair, read to you . . .

Yes, what did a smear of baked bean juice really matter in the grand scheme of things? Hesitating as she neared the gap, she placed her hand on the cool fence that felt rough, splintery and aged beneath her fingertips. She looked down again at her bare feet and saw the toes of her teen self, nails painted red, one toe sporting a silver ring, tanned, and running around at the whim of a heart so full of all it tried to contain. Bare feet that would run with energy along this very path, excitement jumping in her gut and desire in her loins, the moment her parents left for church. It was clichéd, it was sincere, and it was love.

Off to meet the boy next door. To put her hand through the gap where their fingers met, to give him the signal that the coast was clear. And not just any boy, but Lawrence Kelleway. Her Lawrie who was going to be a professional footballer and who would love her forever . . . not that she cared about his future job, not really. She only wanted him. Him for always, him forever no matter what . . . Knowing that each night she got to climb into bed naked next to him, to inhale the scent of his skin and to watch his face as he moved slowly above her was all she would ever need. He was like a drug, and she was addicted.

'Lee?'

She heard his call and her stomach folded. No one else called her that. It had been their thing. She called him Lawrie and he called her Lee – they had been studying *Cider with Rosie* at school and it felt fitting despite the difference in spelling.

'Shush! You need to be quiet,' she called, looking over her shoulder towards the back door in case Marty had stirred. Ironically, she knew it would be cider that ensured he slept soundly on the sofa.

Approaching the gap, she stood back, meaning she could only see him, and he her, in shadow. It felt safer that way and provided a distance that made her feel a little more comfortable. Sickness threatened and her limbs shook as if icy. She could see he had slimmed, narrower now across the shoulders and his face a little gaunt. This in stark contrast to the confident, muscled man who had been about to leave for a new life in Oz. To say she felt terrified was an understatement; this was her very worst nightmare come true.

'I needed to see you.' He spoke softly.

His words of longing tinged with desire were familiar and intoxicating and she hated the way it made her feel. She was married to Marty – lovely, kind, hardworking Marty who gave his all to keep his little family safe and provided for. A tolerant man, a man who loved her no matter what . . .

'You gave Daisy a big tip. She was very happy.' Her voice was raspy, not used to chitchat of any kind, and with a quiver to it that belied her nerves.

'I'm glad she was happy. She's a good kid.'

'You don't know her.' She looked up. 'But yes she is, a very good kid.'

'How are you?'

She heard the snap of a twig as he took a step closer so she took a step backwards, until she was pressed against the kitchen wall, as if aware in that moment of what he represented and, indeed, that the man himself was a very real and present danger. Her mouth was dry, her heart pounding and, screwing her eyes shut briefly, she hoped that when she opened them this whole encounter would be revealed to be no more than the ghastly dream she had often.

'How are you?' he repeated, forcing her to open her eyes. This was no dream.

How was she?

'Have you had a nice evening?' It felt safer to rebuff his question, to change the direction of the conversation.

'I needed to see you, needed to talk to you. I'm a mess, Lee.' He too ignored the direction, choosing to take his own line, putting his own needs/desires first. This should not have been a surprise.

She shook her head at his words. 'You and me both.'

'I know you said you didn't want to see me, didn't want to talk to me, and I do everything in my power to avoid you, trust me.'

'Trust you?' She laughed. 'Are you for real? I can't trust you. I could never trust you.' Words that had danced in her thoughts for the longest time trickled from her tongue.

'Please, Lee.' She saw his arm shoot through the gap. *His hand, those fingers, just there to be held, to knit with her own . . .* She coiled her hands into fists and kept them that way, stiffly by her sides and out of reach.

'There have been so many times, Lawrie, when I trusted you and you let me down. I'm done with it.' She folded her shaking arms across her chest, her clenched hands bunched under her arms. 'Entirely done with it.'

'I know.' Then came the unmistakeable sound of his crying. It was like a punch to her throat. 'I know.'

'I can't do this,' she breathed. 'I can't talk to you, I can't see you and I can't be near you. It's toxic. Damaging. Dangerous. You're like . . .' She struggled to find the words. 'You're like a weapon, something that causes destruction to my life, to me.' Her voice broke at this truth. 'You have had my beating heart in your hands so many times and you make it feel like the safest, warmest place to keep it, but then you throw it away, wipe your hands clean and move on, and I am left on the floor, trying to catch a breath, trying to understand that again my trust in you was misplaced and trying to pack my heart back into the place it should live. The disappointment is always overwhelming. I can't do it anymore. I won't do it anymore. It was okay when you were no more than a memory, to see you occasionally felt sweet, harmless, flirtatious. But to do what we did . . .' She shook her head, her hair falling over her face. 'It was anything but harmless. Marty loves me and I love him, and we have a wonderful family. You're poison, Lawrie, you're dangerous . . .'

'Please . . . please, Lee,' he begged.

'No, don't do that. Just go away! You have to leave me alone! You have to! I told you that three years ago and I'm telling you it again now.' Her words were harsh and yet no matter how well-intentioned, any casual observer would note that she stood still, unmoving, staring at the shadow of the boy next door instead of running as fast and as far as she was able.

'Everything's gone wrong!' he whispered.

'Again?' She couldn't help it, the word slipped from her thoughts straight out of her mouth.

'Yes, again.' He coughed to clear his throat.

'Money?'

She saw him nod.

'God, Lawrie.' She rubbed her face. Pity loosened the stays of her anger. 'Can't you ask your mum and dad if—'

'No! No, I can't.' He spoke sharply, a reminder of the hold they had on him, the spell of perfection he had woven that felt too hard to break, the consequences too great. 'I don't know what to do.' He sniffed and seemed to find a level of composure. 'I'm out of options.'

'This is what you do: you mess up your life and then you come and dump it on me. What am I, your therapist?'

'Kind of.' He took a step closer still and she could smell his cologne. It made her feel weak, sick, and was at the same time something she wanted to breathe in. His voice was lower now and she was thankful for it. 'Over the years, I've thought, what would Lee do, what would Lee say? And I imagine you standing in front of me, your sunny face, your optimism, your way of looking at the world in a way that I never could, the way you can always find solutions.'

'Oh yeah, that's me – a little ray of sunshine.' She rubbed her forehead.

'You're still mad at me.'

His words made her laugh. 'Still *mad* at you? You sound like a kid who's been found out. Mad at you doesn't come close. I could handle it. I could handle all of it with you on the other side of the world. It was easy. Like you didn't exist, like you'd just disappeared. I picked myself up and I carried on, Lawrie – I worked, danced in the kitchen sometimes, shopped, cooked, spent time with my family, watched telly on a Saturday night. I put you out of my head and I felt safe. And then *bam*! Back you came. No warning. No contact. No idea of the tsunami that your presence would create.'

'I'm sorry.'

'No, you're not.' She raised her voice, before checking her volume. 'Because I repeat: this is what you do! It's what you've always done. You pull people in with your tractor beam and then mess them up too, as if you need the company. You know, like those drunks at the bar who are always buying, and everyone thinks they're generous guys! The life and soul of the party, getting the drinks in, but they are paying for so much more than that. They're buying your time, your ear, your sympathy. That's you.'

'I . . .' He seemingly didn't know how to respond.

'It's true. Like coming to me before you went to Australia, telling me it was me and would always be me. That you and Julie were happy, but never, ever as happy as you knew you could have been with me. Your words were like putting a small pebble in my shoe, a cut on my thumb, a doubt in my mind. Marty and I were doing fine.' She cursed the tremor in her voice, and the tears that gathered at the back of her throat at the sound of her truth. 'And you pulled me in, you distracted me, you made me feel . . .'

'Made you feel what?' he asked softly.

'Made me feel like I was sixteen again with the whole wide world at my feet. Like anything was possible. And I liked it! I broke my marriage vows, and I did it so easily, so effortlessly that it felt right. But it wasn't right, it was wrong, and people got hurt. People who don't even know why or how they are being hurt. Marty . . .' Again she pictured her loyal husband, sleeping on the other side of the shabby brick wall who she had let down in the worst way. And sweet Julie who she knew held everything together. 'And it was starting to feel real, like we had turned back the clock, cheated time, like we were being given a second chance, starting out again on another incredible adventure, all underpinned by our wonderful history – as if we *deserved* it because of that history, as if we didn't have to worry about anyone else because *we* came first, you and I. Before Julie, before Marty, before anyone, it was just you and me, just like it had always been. If anything, *they* were the spare pieces of the puzzle, the ones who didn't fit!' She stuck out her tongue to catch the salty tears that fell over her lip.

'Just you and me,' he whispered. She ignored him.

'And just as it was starting to feel like a right, a habit and not a dirty secret, you upped and went. Just . . . disappeared! And I fell over.' To hear the words out loud made her want to crawl back to her bed and put her head under the cover.

'I had no choice; I owed money, things were getting . . .'

This was an inadequate, pathetic response, paying no heed to her emotional state, the damage he had caused.

'I don't care!' She almost ran at the fence, her teeth bared. 'I don't care! You never listen, and I don't fucking care! There is always a reason, always a problem, always money issues, and you bail, you jump ship, you just go!'

'What was I supposed to do? Come over, have a coffee with you and Marty, say my goodbyes?'

Anger flared in her veins. 'And you've always got a clever answer, a slippery response. But the simple truth is you don't give a damn who you hurt, who you let down, how it makes them feel or the shitstorm you leave behind. You're an unreliable human, Lawrence. You're unreliable. And that's dangerous, especially when people are counting on you. You let them down.'

'People *are* counting on me. Jules. The kids . . .' He paused. 'Things are bad, Lee. I've run out of options. I got into a building venture with some guys who have money to burn – footballers, ironically.' He gave a snort. 'Do you know Micky Tate? Big league, big money and I got carried away. I agreed to—'

'Listen to you! I don't think you've even heard me.' She straightened. 'I have just opened up, tried to explain to you that for the last three years, since the moment I knew you were back, something broke inside me. Something snapped and I stay in bed and I don't work. I keep the house dark and my kids and husband creep around like I'm a bear they would rather have sedated.' Her tears now fell freely. 'I'm swamped with guilt and fear, and it overwhelms me, paralyses me. Raw fear that Marty will find out what we did, what

I did. And all you can do is go straight back to talking about you and your problems.'

'I heard you,' he levelled, 'but just to get it straight, and so I understand it right, your sadness and your hiding is not because you cheated or because you still love me—'

'I don't,' she cut in, speaking emphatically, her fingers shaking with a shocking desire to hurt him. How dare he be so cool, so cruel? 'I truly don't.' This was the truth. She was able to recognise the heady mix of physical attraction and nostalgia for what it was and it was not to be confused with love like the pure, unconditional love she shared with Marty.

He ignored her. '—but because you're paralysed with fear about being found out and so you've taken to your bed and ruined your life through fear of having your life ruined, is that about right?'

There was no mistaking the hint of amusement in his voice.

It was more than she could stand. 'You're a piece of shit and that makes me immeasurably sad because I have wasted time thinking about you and I wasted my youth loving you. Remember that, Lawrie: you're nothing but a piece of shit.'

'You don't mean it, Lee! You're just mad at me.'

She heard the underlying note of glee, and it galled her. She took another step back towards the wall, just as his hand came through the gap, reaching for her, grasping in the darkness. With her arms by her side, she sidled along the wall, back to the door that led to her crappy kitchen, where her kids ate microwave meals alone and her husband pulled cold cans of cider from the depths of the fridge: his company and his solace.

'Please, Lee!' he begged. 'Please come back. I need to talk to you. I need you.'

'Goodbye, Lawrie,' she whispered. Caring little whether the words reached his ears or not, but knowing it was a phrase that was long, long overdue.

CHAPTER NINE

CASSIAN KELLEWAY

Cassian sat at the table in his grandparents' garden. He looked up into the inky June sky that still held warmth, his eyes drawn by the brightest stars. This kind of night, this kind of light, reminded him of Melbourne. Sitting now next to his grandad, who had fallen forward slightly, supporting his head in his hands and with his speech somewhat slurred, he felt more than a little uncomfortable. He didn't want to be babysitting his drunken grandpa tonight, or any night come to think of it. Bernie had started to waffle, as if his joy was now dimmed by the veil of melancholy alcohol liked to throw over you when its novelty wore off. This he knew, thinking about the early hours when after a night out the twin pincers of self-doubt and fear of the unknown held him in a vice. He wished it wasn't the case, he wished he had the confidence to stand up, arms wide and run towards his future, yelling to the world, 'THIS IS ME!' But even the thought made him quake with nerves.

'They'll take the tree, you know!' Bernie raised his voice to make the assertion. 'They'll take the bloody tree, and the truth is, I love that tree!' He nodded, eyes closed. 'I do, boy, I love it! I love them all and the thought of there only being three? It's crazy talk.

Winnie's right!' He slammed his hand on to the tabletop. 'But I know I need to keep calm and say it doesn't matter or your nan will get riled. That's my job, you see, to keep her calm, to be the steadying voice.'

'Yes, Mum's got that job in our house.' He thought of how she would let his dad rant, nodding quietly, sagely, as if she understood that he needed to get it all out of his system. He thought it must be wearing, having to be so placatory.

'It's not easy, son, none of it is easy,' his grandad babbled.

'What isn't?' It was hard to make out the words now directed towards the tabletop in a low mumble.

'Life. Life isn't easy!' He looked up. 'Where is everyone? Where did they go?' His eyes darted around the table, as if only just realising that the guests had thinned.

Cassian had watched the family dwindle. First Aunty Cleo and Georgie had left, and then Domino, off to study with her friend Ruby – yeah, right! He found it incredible how his little sister lied and his family just ate it up. It never occurred to them to question sweet Domino who never put a foot wrong. It was a joke.

This thought, however, was quickly buried under the weight of self-reproach. Who was he to talk? Quiet Cassian who liked to go chasing girls, play cricket, study and dream of the successful life that lay in wait for him. How could it not? Good-looking, polite, smart Cassian Kelleway, son of Lawrence . . . Plus there was no denying he felt in no small way responsible for Domino; she was his sister after all, although the idea of her listening to or taking advice from him was pretty laughable. She made her opinion of him very clear, her top lip curling almost involuntarily when he spoke to her. It mystified him and he wished she could at least be civil. Her hostility towards him had started when they arrived back in the UK after living in Australia, as if she resented him as much as she did their parents, blamed him, too, in some small way for how their new life was unfolding.

'I think they've gone home,' he finally answered.

'Who has gone home?' His grandad had clearly lost the thread.

'Cleo, Georgie, Dom – I think they've gone home. Nan and Mum are in the kitchen, and I don't know where Dad is. It's just you and me, Grandad. We're the survivors!'

'It's just you and me!' He banged the table again.

'Yes, just you and me.' Cassian had had more than his fill of sitting here in the back garden, trying to interact with the man who was in repetition mode. He reached for his phone and fired a text off to Jake.

You around? I'm going a little crazy here. #familyoverload

Yep.

His best friend's succinct reply. He felt his pulse settle a little. Jake was like an anchor that kept him steady while all around him was turbulent water. It wasn't enough that his home life was in chaos; Cassian had his own shit to deal with too.

Aware of his parents' situation, he had heard enough and seen enough over the last few months to figure that yet again they were in financial trouble. Mail whipped up from the floor the moment it plopped through the letterbox to be stashed away in drawers or shoved in the recycling bin. The phone left to ring, unanswered. The constant checking by his dad of messages and apps – detailing what, Cassian wasn't sure, but it reduced his dad's pupils to pinpricks and caused beads of sweat to form on his brow and top lip. The way his mum and dad argued, sniped, each harsh word they spat was a wounding to him, and it hurt. He lived with rising bile, swallowing the bitter taste of fear that yet again they would be forced to pack up and run. It had damaged him, leaving Australia like that, and he was only just starting to understand how much. It made no sense to him: why couldn't his dad just be open with Nan and Grandad? Closing his eyes he pinched his nose. *Easier said than done . . .*

'Secrets, eh, Cassie boy? Secrets.' His grandad tapped the side of his nose.

His unease was complete – secrets were the last thing he wanted to discuss with his sloshed relative.

'Just going to find Mum . . .' He let this trail as he sidled out from the wide wooden table and headed towards the house. He was startled by his dad coming up from the side garden and as he stepped up on to the deck, Cassian did a double take; it looked as if he'd been crying. It would have been hard to describe how the sight of the man in this state was simultaneously distressing and uplifting. Obviously, he didn't want his dad to be in tears, but to know his dad was more in touch with his feelings than he let on, to see first-hand that he too wrestled with all that was about to befall them as a family was a relief of sorts. It felt good to know that the choices his dad made weren't done flippantly and that there might actually be a plan after all.

'You okay, Dad?'

'Cass! Hey.' He seemed surprised to see him and ran his hand over his face. 'Am I okay?' He repeated the question as he ran his tongue up under his top lip, hands on hips, taking his time. His manner was as odd as it was unnerving. When he eventually spoke, it was not what Cassian had expected to hear. 'Do you think I'm a piece of shit?'

'What?' His dad's question was alarming and distressing in equal measure. It was an odd thing for anyone to say, let alone his dad. The random and strange nature of it unsettled him. 'No, of course I don't.'

'Right, thank you, thank you, son.' He sniffed. 'But I've let you down, haven't I? You and Mum and Dom, I've let you all down.'

It was odd to hear him talk this way, strange to be having this kind of conversation for the first time ever. He had to remind himself of all the awkward chats when his dad wanted to talk football, while Cassian craved interactions such as this: open and honest discussions that might actually help them get to know each other. God, how he wished they could all just talk! And not the casual chitchat they exchanged daily about nothing much in particular, but a real, no-holds-barred conversation without the padding of an event or celebration and the protection of the wider family to verbally joust and joke with. Just the four of them, really talking – now that would be something.

How to proceed? With caution, he decided. 'I don't think you've let us down, but . . .'

'But what?' Lawrence, unable to meet his gaze, urged, giving him permission of sorts.

'But I think if you spoke to us more, gave us a heads-up, let us understand what to expect, or just gave us fair warning, that'd be . . .' He felt the swell of nerves – this was, after all, his dad he was talking to. 'That'd be fairer.'

'Fairer, yes.' Lawrence nodded. 'I find it hard, to, erm, to open up to you and your mum and sister. It's like I need to be the one who deals with everything, keep it all in.'

'But you're not, Dad. You don't need to be that person. It's too much for you, too much for any one person. We're a family and keeping it all in isn't only hard on you, but it makes me feel excluded and nervous, like I don't know what's going to happen next.' *Like the ground might fall away from under me at any moment and so I need to stay on high alert . . .*

Cassian would never forget the day he got home from school in Melbourne to find his mum packing a case and sobbing so hard she found it difficult to take a breath.

'Where are you going?' he'd asked, worried of course, but also scared by her behaviour.

'Cass . . .' She had abandoned the packing and held the top of his arms tightly. 'Go . . . go get your things together – not much, just what you need. Do it now, Cass, please! Dom is getting her things together. We haven't much time.'

'But why? What's happening?' He remembered his mouth felt sticky with nerves, his spit thick, as he tried to fathom the panic and suppress the urge to cry, because if his mum, who was always calm and in control, was panicking, then how bad must it be?

'Please . . . please don't ask questions, not now, just go pack. We can talk later.'

'But what should I take? Where are we going? I don't know what you mean by "just what I need" – just what I need for what?'

'For God's sake, Cassian! Stop asking questions! How hard can it be? Just pack a bloody bag!' she had screamed at him, and it shocked them both. This behaviour new and all the more unnerving for it.

He had done what she asked, walking up the oak open-tread staircase to the galleried landing and into his dressing room, quietly unzipping the leather weekender he used for sleepovers and mini-breaks and into it he folded his pyjamas, toothbrush, schoolbooks, his sketchpad, a pair of jeans, two t-shirts, his cricket pullover, bathers, the photograph of him captaining the First Eleven and his phone charger. It was only when they arrived at the poky motel in Geelong, where they stayed for a week or so while his dad made the arrangements to travel, that he'd opened the bag and laughed at the absurd selection. No trainers, no underwear, not one complete outfit, no socks . . . The list was endless. His laughter had quickly turned to tears when he realised all that he had left behind.

When they had boarded the flight back to the UK in silence, he had stopped crying, but strangely the sensation carried on and he felt that he was weeping on the inside, coming to terms with the fact they were going home . . . *Home.* And to this day, Cassian had no idea where that was. He was wary of allowing complacency or even comfort to set in, knowing how much harder it would be if they had to uproot again. He now took solace from the thought that his next move would hopefully be to university, on his terms and a move of his choice.

His dad's words drew him from that painful memory into the present.

'When did you get so smart?'

He shrugged, wondering if this conversation was a gateway. Could it lead to more chats about other topics close to his heart? Was this how it started? He really hoped so, knowing that each day that passed without him being truthful was emotionally damaging and what he didn't need was any more emotional damage.

'Has it been hard for you, these last few months?' his dad asked again whilst looking at his feet, as if avoiding eye contact might make it easier to hear the answer.

The last few years, since we arrived here . . . Cassian swallowed the response. If his dad had already been crying, this was not the time to go in hard.

'I suppose, a bit. I think leaving Melbourne was difficult because it was a surprise, a shock. The way it was done, was . . .' Even now he found the words tricky. 'Kind of like we were at the best party on the planet and it was just getting going when the taxi arrived early, and we had to miss it, leave while everyone else was still dancing. And they were so busy dancing they didn't notice us leave so I didn't get a chance to say goodbye to my cricket team, my schoolfriends, or even process it.'

'It was one hell of a party, though, wasn't it? That house! The views! Day trips to St Kilda.' Lawrence smiled broadly, missing the point entirely and yet tears glinted in his eyes. 'I want . . .' He drew breath. 'I want to be more open, son. I want not to let you down, but sometimes it's like I'm in a sticky spider's web and the more I wriggle the more stuck I become. Do you know what that feels like?'

'Pretty shit, I should imagine.' It didn't feel good to hear his dad's description, putting Cassian at a loss as to what to say next, how he could help. And yet there was a small part of him that was grateful for his father's candour.

'Yes, it's pretty shit.' Lawrence smiled wryly.

'Time for a nightcap!' His grandad shouted loudly from the table, 'Make mine a large one, captain!' before slumping down again.

'Someone's going to have a headache in the morning.' Lawrence looked at his old man with obvious affection.

They both stared at Grandad Bernie. His dad reached out and squeezed Cassian's shoulder. He could vaguely detect the tremor in his grip. He guessed it was the equivalent of a good old-fashioned hug from the man who didn't really do physical displays of affection.

'I'd better . . .' Cassian pointed towards the house, quite unable to explain how the chat had caught him off guard and how uncomfortable he felt at the shoulder squeeze. What made it so hard for his dad to hold him?

Glancing back, he saw his grandad place his head on the cradle of his arms and lie very still. Finally, it seemed, he slept.

Cassian stepped into the house where his nan was wrapping large lumps of cheese in clingfilm and lobbing it into the wide, shiny American fridge that already groaned with cling-film-wrapped grub. His mum was nowhere to be seen.

'Do you need a hand with anything, Nan?'

She looked up at him and smiled. It took a second for her to focus, as if she didn't realise he was still around. He was used to this. Without the collective banter of a Kelleway gathering, without Domino looking pretty by his side, and his dad shouting and jibing at Georgie, he was quiet and despite being 'so very handsome' he faded into the background a little, and in truth he was glad of it.

'You're such a good boy, Cass. Any girl would be lucky to have you. Thank you for offering, but I'm fine, nearly done. My bed is calling. And who knows how much sleep I'll get if Cleo goes into labour? It's been quite a day.'

'Have you had a lovely anniversary?'

'Oh, I have, love, the best. Did you see the bouquet your grandad sent?'

'I did, yes.'

'And that speech with everyone in the restaurant listening. Quite a show. I must be doing something right to get such treatment after all these years, eh?'

'Yep.'

'Is he still outside?' she asked with the crinkle of fondness at her eyes.

'I think he's just fallen asleep at the table. Dad's out there with him.'

'Bless him. He's a wonderful son and a wonderful father, you don't know how lucky you are.' Closing the dishwasher door, she pressed a button to set it whirring. 'I'd better go and help my husband up the stairs.'

'Yep.' Cassian might only have been eighteen but knew enough to see that his grandparents idolised their son in the truest sense. It was both sweet and mystifying, as if they weren't aware that he was capable of any wrongdoing or even that he was an adult. He wondered for the first time whether his dad found this a little claustrophobic. 'Shall I help you take grandad up?'

'No, darling.' She reached out and ran her hand over his forearm. 'It isn't the first time and it won't be the last! Our bodies might be old, but our minds are still sixteen and I wouldn't have it any other way! Are you staying here tonight, love?'

'I might.' He was glad of the option, and as usual would see where he and Jake ended the night and where it was most convenient to crash out.

'Spare room is all made up for you.'

'Thank you, Nan.' He meant it, grateful for the bed, the love, the generous breakfast that he knew would be forthcoming if he stayed over.

'No, thank you, Cass, not only for offering to help but for making today so special. You make me so happy. You all do. My beautiful family. What would my life be without you all?' She walked slowly to the double French doors that led to the garden. 'Your mum went home. Don't know how your dad's going to get back. Maybe he'll stay too.'

He heard the note of hope in her tone, wanting her son under her roof.

'Maybe.' It worried him, his mum's tendency to slink off without a word. He hated how, recently, she seemed to live in her own bubble, her eyes brimming with all they tried to contain and her attention span brief. He knew that she too disliked the way his dad handled things, but was there a danger of her doing something similar? Of making her own plan, doing what was best for her and not thinking about him and Dom? He really hoped not. Secrets were harmful, the things they chose not to say and share seemingly just as damaging as those they did.

You can talk . . . his interior voice whispered.

'Thought I might have heard from my sister Pattie today, just a text or something to say happy anniversary, but no, nothing. Mean that, isn't it?'

'Maybe she forgot?'

'Maybe. She's an oddball that one, who knows where her mind's at. I think all that vegan food has addled her brain. Needs a good steak or a lump of cheese to put her right!' His nan ground her bottom teeth against the top ones and her eyes blazed briefly. He noted the anger she displayed. It obviously displeased her, having a sibling who was an oddball. He pictured Domino and wondered if she would be similarly angered in the future. He hoped not. He hoped they would find a middle ground, that she'd grow up and they'd be friends. He could wish . . .

'Well, you could always send her some – you've got more cheese than Sainsbury's.'

'I never want my family to go hungry. No one will ever say I didn't know how to feed my lot.'

'Don't think that's likely!' He laughed, and his nan's face softened.

'You go find Jake. Have a lovely evening the both of you.'

'We will.'

'If he comes in, show him my bouquet, won't you? It's in the sitting room.'

'I will. Night, Nan.'

'Night, darling. I'm one lucky, lucky lady.'

He wasn't sure how it would work out if Cleo went into labour, what with Grandad Bernie being drunk. He wondered if Cleo was scared, nervous or just excited. She always seemed a little outside of the inner circle, sitting quietly, watching proceedings, as if she was no more than an observer, only joining in when prompted. Not that dissimilar to his mum who, whenever she was with her in-laws, smiled so broadly he was sure her cheeks must hurt by the end of the evening. It was as if she was trying to convince them that everything was great.

It was all so predictable and wearing because of it. Was it even a family gathering unless his parents had fought en route to the venue, Grandad Bernie had cried, Cleo and Georgie had left early, and Nana Winnie had said how very proud she was of them all?

It was edging towards half past eleven. He wondered where Domino might have gone, guessing at Shiskas or The Race Club, and knowing that if he and Jake went out, they would avoid both of those places; the prospect of bumping into her was more than he could stand. It was one thing to hear the whispers of his sister's unsavoury behaviour, but quite another to have to witness it himself. He had to give it to her, though, she was smart, knew how to play the game. He envied her ability to sit smiling sweetly at everyone, quietly partaking just enough without drawing too much attention or overly engaging. Sometimes, he tried to emulate her but only appeared aloof, which as a Kelleway at a Kelleway gathering was not the done thing.

He hadn't wanted to come here after the restaurant, not really; he'd had enough of his family for one night, but it was, as his mum had reminded him earlier in the day, 'a very special occasion'. Besides, it was one step closer to seeing his best mate. It had been weird having Jake's little sister as their waitress. She'd done an okay job, although she was a bit vacant, which for someone who Jake described as the love child of Stephen Hawking and Marie Curie, was less than he had expected. He would never say as much to his best friend, but he found her to be a bit . . . dozy. Yes, that was the word: *dozy*. She was nice enough, but always looked as if her mind was on other things, and she was, sadly for her, without all the things that made Jake stand out: his athleticism, his humour, his energy. He pictured Domino, who spent her time scrolling her phone and giggling – and understood how it was possible to share parents and yet be very different people.

He took in his reflection in the kitchen window. Oh yes, it *had* been hard these last few months . . . his family living yet again on a greased tightrope. More than anything he wanted to make things okay for his mum, wishing he knew how to break the spiral of their rows that carried his parents round and round until tiredness or smashing something made one of them walk away. Tonight he had noticed the lines on her forehead which formed when she was quizzical or worried. She had them a lot recently.

'I'm okay,' she'd said when he'd asked and she'd smiled that smile that didn't quite reach her eyes.

He loved her so much. She was the person who made everything okay. The person who had *always* made everything okay. The person who painted on a happy face no matter what, even as they shut the front door of their East Melbourne home and threw their hastily packed luggage into the back of the rental car that would ferry them to Geelong, away from the life they all loved. He knew that he was coming close to talking to her openly, to sharing his secrets, it was all just a matter of timing. But what worried him most was that she might look at him differently. He couldn't stand the thought. What was it she always said? '*You are unique, beautiful and kind. The whole wide world is waiting for you, Cass . . .*'

He hoped it was true, knowing that as soon as he finished his education, he wanted to live in the countryside – anywhere that was quiet and uncomplicated. These two things he wanted more than anything. He knew Domino craved bright lights and fast cars, but he had his sights firmly on uncomplicated and peaceful. The word that currently best described his family life was 'turbulent' and he saw first-hand the stress that came with turbulence. Especially while they all had to pretend that everything was fine, keeping up the façade for Nanny Win and Grandad Bernie. Although this he kind of understood – the pretending. It had been good to hear his dad try to open up the conversation. He wondered what had made him cry.

It couldn't have been easy for him, having to give up his aspirations and dreams of becoming a footballer, and to hear it dragged up again in front of everyone tonight made him feel sorry for the man they had called Mr Moneybags. He knew what it felt like to be within touching distance of something and not be able to tell the world, and it felt like shit.

There was the sound of a light rapping on the front door. Opening it wide, Jake stood in the beam of the porch light. He looked golden. Cassian simultaneously felt his throat tighten and his gut grip. It was almost torturous to stand this close to him and not be able to touch him. He was unsure where his dad was and whether his grandparents had made it up the stairs yet.

He dug deep to find the persona, to recall the exact detail of the disguise he wore each and every time he saw Jake in public. He was well-schooled in suppressing the instinct to remove a stray lock of hair from his face, to reach for his hand so their fingers could entwine or to tell him in gushing tones about a dream where they had been together on a beach or bed, walking hand in hand, but always with Jake staring at him with a look of such intensity it caused Cassian's words to stutter in his throat and made him shiver with a longing that he carried with him for much of the following day. *Jake* . . . the boy he loved. And the boy who loved him in return. Theirs was a love of intensity, of loyalty, of promise for the future, and was a thing of pure joy! It made him happier than he had ever known was possible. And how Cassian treasured it.

They had started slowly, tentatively. Mates at first, each putting out feelers, testing the water, hoping they weren't misreading the sometimes subtle signals, and both utterly paralysed by the fear of rejection. But for the last six months, they had been open, letting love fill up all the empty spaces inside them, warming them from the inside out. Yes, his homelife might have been turbulent, but in the choppy waters, Jake was an island on which Cassian could feel safe, a place where he could not only be himself, but where he could breathe . . .

'Tell me you have beer. Lots of beer,' Jake said as he entered, leaving a trail of his scent in his wake, which Cassian inhaled as he nodded.

'Beer, vodka, cheese, you name it.'

'Yes, please!' Jake bared his teeth in a fake smile and Cassian could only think about his mouth and the urge to kiss it. 'In that case we need go nowhere else, although hold the cheese. All I need is enough booze to fell a wildebeest and I'll be happy. How was the party thing?'

'Fine. Boring. Just as you'd expect,' he whispered. 'Dom said she was going to study and left early – Ruby came and picked her up.'

Jake sprayed his laughter. How Cassian loved to see him laugh! The sound cracked the air around him like music. 'Only thing your sister studies is the form of the runners and riders at Kempton!'

'I know that. But she gets away with it.'

'For now. But it'll all come to light when she has to sit exams, or her report gets sent home.' Jake pointed out the obvious.

'I guess so.' He didn't like the thought of the fallout of that. Not only because he didn't want his little sister to have to deal with it, but also he knew that his mum and dad could do without another thing to fret over.

'It's true, Cass. People can live however they want but trying to cover up the truth is like putting leaves over a body – eventually the wind or an inquisitive dog comes along and exposes it. Things don't stay hidden.'

'Is that right? Wind or inquisitive dogs? Who knew?' He smiled, knowing Jake referred to them as a couple and how it was only a matter of time before the world knew . . . It was a thought that both terrified and delighted him. It was a conversation they revisited time after time, with him quite unable to put into words just how scared he was of opening up. How would his family react? But the idea of not having to pretend . . . well, that would be a dream.

Jake spoke softly. 'We need to tell people, Cass.' Reaching out, he ran his fingers over Cassian's forearm, a brief touch that was electric. 'I don't want to have to wait for an inquisitive dog to come along. I want to tell the world, tell our families. I don't want to have to hide anymore.'

'It's not that simple, things are—'

'It's never that simple!' Jake cut him off. 'Never. There will always be an event, a distraction, a reason, an excuse, an anniversary, an issue. There's no perfect time. Only now.'

'It's not easy.' He shook his head at the understatement.

'Nothing worth having is easy. But I love you and it's a good, good thing, Cass!'

'It is.' He smiled at the face of the man who made everything seem wonderful, wishing he shared his confidence when it came to telling the world. 'I will try. I'll take my lead from you.'

'Oh, I see how it is.' Jake mock sulked. 'You get me to shout it loud and then if there's no fallout you might put your hand up!'

'No.' Cassian shook his head and reached briefly for the hand of his boyfriend, glancing over his shoulder to check they were alone. 'I mean I'll try to be brave like you. I'll wait for the right moment, and I'll shout it loud if that's what you want.'

'It *is* what I want. Enough hiding.'

Cassian blinked hard, trying to swallow the white-hot fear that lanced his gut, wondering how his parents or, more specifically, his dad, might react. And that was before he considered Grandad Bernie and Nana Winnie. 'Let's grab some beers. I think the garden's empty; we can go sit out there.' He changed the topic.

'Hot tub!' Jake slammed his hands together loudly, his expression and tone bursting with enthusiasm for his idea. The very thought made Cassian's stomach fold with dread. The hot tub with Jake . . . if there were people around, it would be like putting a starving man at a feast-laden table and forbidding him to eat. And Cassian, who had not come out to anyone, let alone his family, and who was still processing the fact for himself, knew that for tonight and where Jake was concerned, he would have to stay hungry . . .

CHAPTER TEN

LAWRENCE KELLEWAY

Lawrence lay slumped on the sofa at his mum's house with his head on a silk cushion and his feet, minus shoes, dangling over the arm. He figured he might sleep for a bit, sober up enough to make the walk home, clear his head. This was the moment he disliked most in the drunk cycle – that point where the high was gone and reality had begun to edge out any distraction that alcohol provided. His mouth felt like it was littered with foul-tasting sawdust and his eyes were full of grit. He looked around at the clusters of artworks in heavy gilt frames and the pale blue and grey figurines placed on bookshelves. Fussy, is how he'd describe it and knew that slick and minimal was where the big bucks lay when it came to selling an upscale house. It was his business to know.

His watch nudged midnight. He took solace from the fact that it was late and much of the country slept – meaning he didn't, in that moment, need to fear his phone; during 'working hours' when anyone could call, make a demand, leave a message, he surely did.

There was nowhere on earth he relaxed like this, nowhere else he felt that the front door kept the whole world at bay. Safe. Hiding, if you like. When the world outside felt like it was against you, when you felt hunted, owed money, were chasing your tail and always, always in the life game of snakes and ladders, no matter how hard you tried, small moments of hiatus like this, being able to doze on his mum's sofa in a quiet, lamp-lit room were very much appreciated.

The truth was it had been quite a night in ways that he could never confide. What was it Lisa had said?

'*You're like a weapon, something that causes destruction . . .*'

It was a realisation that stunned him. Partly because he never would have thought this was how she viewed him, and partly because she was right. Reaching out, he placed the phone face down on the marble-topped coffee table and considered the names that lay at the bottom of his contact list, names that were gathered under the heading 'Blocked'. It was sometimes easier and often necessary to block the number of a creditor, an associate, a supplier or a customer, rather than try to field their calls. There were only so many times he could say, '*I was just about to call you!*' and '*It must have got lost in the post*' or '*The bank haven't got back to me*' and '*I'm on it, I'll get the money to you by . . .*' And worst of all: '*I swear . . . I swear I made that transaction – can I check the account number?*'

They gave up calling eventually, especially when word got out that he'd moved to the other side of the world, closed the company, changed the name of his venture, started over. Ghosting, wasn't that what they called it now? Yet ironically each time such an action was necessary, and it had been necessary a handful of times, it was he who became more ghost-like. Floating away from a situation unseen. Feeling so hollowed out by the failure he wouldn't have been surprised if he'd become transparent. That's certainly how he felt on the inside: like his guts, organs and everything of substance had turned to smoke – one long exhale and he could imagine the redundant shell of his body crumpling to the ground. To feel this empty was a horrible way to live and it wasn't what he had planned – not for him and certainly not for his family. He just couldn't seem to catch a break and it had always been this way.

His were always the best of intentions. Always. He had drive, initiative, vision and the gift of the gab. It was obvious to him that if he could align the right people with the right financial backing on the right piece of land, he could build great things. He could see it clearly in his head: ambitious building projects that couldn't help but make serious money.

His skill was knowing what people wanted: the feeling of space, a couple of mod cons to impress their visitors, wide front doors that gave the illusion of grandeur . . . It was all about that kerb appeal. People with money wanted gardens that were so much more than grotty green squares for the local cats to shit in. They wanted ornate spaces designed by Chelsea Flower Show gold-medal winner Penny Dommett – her name alone on a plan could add serious noughts. People wanted their outside space to be a room, somewhere to dine, entertain, drink wine under twinkling lights, and even though they might be within spitting distance of an arterial route, in those moments, and if the rain held off, they were on holiday where all their worries and the mundanity of life disappeared for a short while. They also wanted incredible, breathtaking kitchens; vast and shiny kitchens that spoke of a life of opulence and fine wine. Kitchens without the golden triangle and where no decent cook could comfortably operate, but if it had the power to make the neighbours salivate with envy at the Christmas drinks party, then that was the kind of kitchen that could sell a house. Yes, he knew what people wanted because it was what he wanted. Difference was, he knew how to build it.

His grand and elaborate business models always became complicated with so many moving parts, varied opinions, clashing ideas, and numerous administrative and legal hoops to jump through.

Time and again he lost his way; things got muddled, delays ensued, which inevitably led to finance being withdrawn, causing greater delays. Yet again he would find himself shifting money from one account to another, doing his best to pour oil on troubled waters, calming angry investors and customers, offering cast-iron reassurances and buying big lunches when what he was really buying was time. And all the while his dreams and plans for this latest venture slipped through his fingers, leaving him, once again, winded face down on the grass.

The word fraudster, thrown at him on occasion when communication with those who were angry and out of pocket was unavoidable, cut him to the quick. He was not a fraudster, not dishonest, and the suggestion caused him more offence than he knew he had any right to feel. He dreamed big! Was that such a crime?

Luck had never been on his side, and he cursed his lack of it. Lying in his bed at night as a teenager, he would run through the playbook in his head, studying form of the upcoming opposition and was able to predict how to get around even the most astute of defence. He could just do it. Never did he doubt his ability to win the tackle, get the ball, make the break, and score a goal. Never. His fitness was impeccable, his will iron, and his talent *'one of the best we've seen . . . He could go all the way . . .'* This was what the head coach had said to his dad, and he'd *heard* it. The words branded in his brain, motivating him when the alarm went off each morning before sunup, and while his classmates slumbered and dreamed of girls, he would lace up his trainers, set his watch and run. Run and run with his heart thumping and his vision laser focused as his feet pounded the streets. He was going all the way. He was unstoppable!

One particular image played over and over in his head like a movie. Him lifting the FA Cup with his teammates gathered around, faces lit with triumph, the crowd making a deafening roar.

He pictured it and he willed it. This was going to happen. He was Lawrence Kelleway: winner.

As far as he was concerned, when it came to his position in the team, there was no competition. He was polite to the rest of the squad but didn't foster the close relationships that some of his teammates did. He was young, without too much life experience, but knew enough to keep these boys at arm's length, because they might have all been one team, but they were still his competitors. To succeed, to get picked, required a certain ruthlessness that meant he only ever looked out for number one. Besides, he didn't need a ton of mates; he had Lisa.

It still foxed and confused him decades later that what put paid to his dreams was not a mighty foe of such skill, dexterity and power that he was powerless to defeat. No, what ended his career before it had started was a divot. A clod of earth, a dig in the grass, a tiny crater no bigger than the size of a matchbox. Yes, while he was busy envisioning his wins, running miles, eating right and staying focused, the universe – the very earth beneath his feet – conspired against him. One small unfortunate and perfectly positioned bump lay in wait on the turf to trip him up. Literally.

He often relived the moment in his head, waking with a start and in a cold sweat. Thinking of the almost infinite number of different moves/routes/steps/angles he could have chosen that would have avoided what happened. He liked to play it in slo-mo: it was a damp, grey day; he was running, his eye on the ball, space either side, aware of the goal but not focused on it; he planned on taking one more step, and then one more, and then he'd bring back his left foot and kick – in his mind's eye he envisioned smashing it into the top left. *Bang!*

But it didn't work out like that. He took one step and was about to take one more when his right foot clipped the divot, dipped a little, caught the grass, and his ankle tilted over at an odd angle.

He tumbled to the ground with his arms out to break the fall. The pain was instant and sharp, and he knew. Staring at the goal and the red and white ball trickling away in front of him, he knew. He didn't look down, couldn't bear to see his injury. He had felt it. He had heard it. A sickening, crunching, snapping sound. And in one second, everything he had planned, everything he thought he could count on and everything he thought he would become disappeared. Gone.

His parents, coaches and teammates had all smiled below eyes narrowed with concern. 'Bit of physio, maybe an operation, you'll be as good as new . . .' they lied, and it made it worse somehow that he wasn't able to howl his distress at what had happened. Instead, he too painted on a smile and pretended, pretended everything was going to be okay.

Maybe that was when it had started – the lying, the covering up of any failure, the pretence that everything was wonderful.

Lisa, however, had howled on his behalf. Great gulping tears that when he held her close, dampened his cheeks too and he was grateful for the feel of them.

'No!' She'd kissed his face. 'No, Lawrie! No!' Her head shaking with the sorrow that she could see and feel, because she loved him and he loved her. She knew enough, as did he, to recognise that as he hobbled on crutches with pins in his bones and a cast on his foot, his dreams had come to an end. Her honesty was a precious thing. It provided clarity, justification almost, for the deep, deep sadness that rolled inside him, filling him up.

He thought about her often, *his Lee*. More than he would ever admit and more often than made him comfortable. He couldn't explain why. It wasn't that he didn't love Julie or that he loved Lisa more – it wasn't like that. Rather she was a marker from his past that was wedged in his brain, a time splinter that he was unable to shift. Not that he'd tried, taking comfort from her memory as he drove alone, waited in a queue, showered, played golf, watched TV . . . On any given day, the smallest thing could remind him of her. The scent of tar – which they had once inhaled on the roadside, wondering if it might make them high. It had only made them sick and left him with a violent headache, but that was not the point. Peeling oranges: he would picture her small, neat fingers trying desperately not to break the peel, and revelling in the glory of the long, pitted snake that lay curled in her palm, a look of utter triumph on her face. And when that orange was prepped to her exacting standards, with all the white pith and pips removed, she'd pop a segment in his mouth and then one into her own, doing this alternately until the fruit was gone. She never asked if he wanted some, it was just what they did: split fruit, shared beers, bites of a sandwich.

It was these million small things that unified them, gave them a history, built their story. And there was more: the particular smell on his scalp when his hair needed washing, she often smelled a bit like that – a little irony and to most this might be considered unpleasant, but it put him so firmly in a place and moment where the sun shone and Lisa laughed, her long hair falling across his chest, and everything, *everything* felt possible.

Sometimes he would think of her when his thoughts were calm and in a break from worrying about money, a break from trying to mentally juggle all that he had to deal with: loans that left their monthly budget creaking at the seams; deadlines that he knew would come and go without progression or solution; and a ton of earnest promises, sealed with a handshake, made to associates, banks, financiers, developers and even his family that he knew would all be broken. It was a lot. Too much, in fact, for him to deal with. Thinking of Lisa and that undemanding time was like taking a mental holiday from the reality of his life.

Their affair hadn't surprised him, not nearly as much as it should. Not that he'd planned it or started it by design. It was far simpler than that, a visceral thing. The sight of her, the smell of her, one touch. That was all it had taken, one moment of reaching out and taking her hand into his and he had tumbled down the rabbit hole, back to the late nineties when they'd lain on the grass listening to The Verve and Radiohead, where lyrics were poetry written just for them. Each song had a meaning, speaking of how he felt and how he wanted to feel forever, but expressed with an elegance he could never have achieved. A time when he had little to worry about and he had felt special, convinced his life was going to be special too.

Guilt was a funny old thing. He felt guilty that the life he had always wanted to provide for his kids was as far out of reach as it ever was. Sure, they enjoyed the temporary bells and whistles of their rented lifestyle, but it was entirely without foundation. This bothered him, knowing that if he were to die today, they would have less than nothing.

He had always planned to leave them a nest egg, a trust fund, property; something that would mean they were set for life. It had been his dream. It was still his dream. He rubbed his hand over his face; his plan wasn't exactly on track. Right now, he had no more than the coins in his pocket and a credit card with a small amount of wriggle room. But where Lisa was concerned, guilt was in short supply. He had the knack of being able to compartmentalise the sex he had had with Lisa and the time he spent with his wife and kids. Entirely separate. Two different worlds that he had felt confident he could keep apart, convinced that even if Julie had found out, she would forgive him – she was that sort. Kind, loyal and unwilling to do anything that might fracture their little family. To him it was no different from keeping his office life and home life separate, holidays and workdays, being asleep and being awake, being dressed and being naked – all facets of his life that were distinct. And that was just how it was: Lisa and Julie, entirely unrelated.

Seeing her tonight over the fence hadn't been easy. The fact was he couldn't really give a shit about Marty. But to see her so timid, cowering against the wall, as if he really could or, worse, *had* caused her physical harm – that was hard. From the very start of their affair, there had been no manipulation on his part, no build-up or anticipation, no risk analysis of the pros and cons. Instead, he had seen her, and she had seen him, and with no more than a knowing look full of promise – exciting, illicit, and highly charged – it was as if the invisible thread of shared history that bound them pulled them tight, close together.

He had reached out to touch her hand, and as her fingers slipped against his, it was like diving into a warm pool on a still night. It was arriving at a place of safety after a long and arduous journey. It was restful sleep. It was coming home. It was igniting a spark that he believed to have long ago dwindled, and it felt good.

More than good, it felt like life! It was energy! It was joy! It was distracting and fulfilling and some kind of reward for all the low moments, the hard days, the days when he lost, the disappointments. When he held her hand, he was sixteen again: fit, happy, driven, and his life ahead looked golden. Touching Lisa, being with Lisa, was like entering a time-travelling portal that took him back to when life had been simpler, and who wouldn't want to do that, just for a short while?

He had known it was a transient thing, never for an instant had he thought it would last. Never would he have dismantled his wonderful family for a taste of his teenage life. Never. And yet right now, he felt the beginnings of sorrow, unsure what a life without Lisa as his mental escape hatch looked like. He wasn't sure it was a world he knew how to navigate. How could he ever explain *that* to his wife?

The answer was simple: he couldn't. It was yet another secret to be locked away, another aspect of his life not to be voiced, shared, dissected.

With his thoughts whirring and his rest disturbed, it was evident that sleep was not going to be forthcoming. He figured he might as well head off now, take a slow walk home, order his thoughts. He sat up straight and rubbed his eyes. Tonight, with the net closing around him, he had wanted nothing more than to talk to Lisa, to get her insight, to find comfort from her words if not her touch. That too hadn't exactly worked out. And here he was.

With a quick glance towards the stairs leading to the room where his mum and dad slept soundly, confident that life was good and on solid ground, he felt the familiar flicker of envy that he should be so lucky; envy and dismay that he had never figured out how to emulate their success, never lived up to their expectations. It made him feel sick. Quietly, he pulled the front door to his parents' house shut and put his arms into his leather jacket, liking the soft feel of it against his skin, the quality. He remembered the day he'd bought it *knowing* he couldn't afford it but feeling almost goaded by the cocky shop assistant who hadn't paid him much attention, as if she *assumed* he couldn't afford it. Her actions had caused a white-hot flash of rage inside him – who was she to dismiss him so summarily? He'd show her.

'I'll take it!' He'd strolled nonchalantly to the counter without even looking at the price tag. *Now* she was interested.

'Oh! Oh! Certainly, sir!' she had fawned, looking surprised, delighted, and he found it intoxicating.

'Actually, no, wait a minute.' He'd held up his finger and she'd stood still, staring as if he had the remote control and was keeping her this way. 'I'll take two, the brown and the black . . .' He'd swiped his fingers in the air and she had bustled into action, scurrying, bent over, flicking through the rails to find the item, make the sale, smiling, no doubt, at the thought of the commission she would earn. Yes, that had shown her.

Slipping out to the sound of Cassian and Jake laughing loudly from the hot tub, his heart swelled with love for his smart boy. They were no doubt discussing the antics of previous nights out, girls at school, conquests, making plans . . . He knew the score and felt a stab of something close to envy at the fact that the teenage life and all its wonderful revelations was so far behind him.

The fact that his boy, Julie, and Domino were going to have to leave their home again tore him to shreds. Where were they to go next? What was he going to do? Not that he was without a plan. There was a bloke – a friend of a friend – who worked as a high-end estate agent, and he, apparently, was in touch with some very, very well-connected people: the super-rich. People whose money was, how to put it, not acquired in the most standard way. Not necessarily illegally, but certainly without all the checks and balances that would keep HM Revenue and Customs happy. This, he was certain, was the kind of money that he could use to make his dreams come true and, more importantly, make all of his problems go away.

If he could secure the right amount, enough to pay off Micky Tate and his associates, and to bung some at the builders who had walked off site last month, enough to pay off the rent arrears, clear the backlog on the cars, settle the credit cards, reduce some of the overdrafts . . . And crucially it meant the kind of money that could open up new lines of credit. He could do it, he was sure of it, all he needed was time. Or, more specifically, all he needed was enough time to put all the cogs in place that would keep the whole shebang turning.

His heart suddenly raced, and it scared him. Slowing his pace, he placed his hand on his chest, going slowly, willing the panic to pass. This kind of nervous flare-up was nothing new and was therefore not as scary as it once had been. Experience had taught him that to clear his thoughts, he needed to breathe deeply, concentrate on breathing, go gently, make it all go away.

Not that it was easy. It felt as if he lived in quicksand, a large pit of which he had tumbled into a couple of decades ago and into which he had been slowly, slowly sinking ever since. At first just a little, so he had made no effort to try to escape, figuring he could shake it off his feet and run anytime he felt like it. Right now, it was up to his chin, which he jutted out and held high, but only to avoid slipping under altogether and disappearing for good. The truth was, he didn't know how much longer he could hold on. If the estate agent bloke didn't come good, if the super-rich contacts weren't made, if Micky called in his loans, if he ran out of time . . . He felt his heart race again and tried to think more mundane thoughts.

He was hungry, despite having been out for dinner where, he now realised, he should have eaten more and drunk less. He would be lying if he didn't admit that, on some days, the prospect of letting the quicksand wash over him entirely, pulling him down and sucking the air from his lungs until he was no more, well, let's just say it sounded almost like a solution. The big sleep. That's what they called it, wasn't it? And boy was he tired.

He ambled slowly along the streets, mostly quiet at this late hour. Looking up at bedroom windows where curtains were pulled shut, the occupants of these average properties no doubt sleeping soundly in their Ikea beds, thinking small thoughts about their small lives. Their biggest worry what to have for breakfast and whether they'd let the cat in. Average houses where crappy saloons were parked on angled driveways. It wasn't for him, never had been. He had always dreamed big.

'One of the best we've seen . . . He could go all the way . . .' That's what they'd said.

He took his time walking down Newman Road. Sober now, he took in the lilac bruise of night as darkness pulled rank on the warm day past, liking the halo of light around the top of the ornate lampposts lining his route. Looking to his left and right, he admired the neat, wide lawns, the pristine paintwork in a variety of Farrow and Ball shades, the clean windows, sports cars with personalised number plates, the electric-doored double garages, the expensive orangeries, the brass-plate house names, the winking burglar alarms that told anyone looking that these residents had something worth stealing. It made him happy, all of it, just walking down the road made him happy! He liked having keys in his pocket for a house just like the ones he admired.

This was the street that everyone in the area wanted to live in. The one with the biggest houses, the widest plots and the most swimming pools. A street the mention of which invoked a wide-eyed nod of acknowledgement and a shiver of envy. He liked to give the address loudly when asked, just to gauge the reaction of the person doing the asking. It made him feel important, like he had arrived. And since that day when his ankle snapped and he knew that the number ten shirt of a Premier League team was never going to be his, he had been waiting to arrive. Yes, he walked slowly, living the life. *Mr Moneybags* . . . He smiled at the irony.

He planned to hit the kitchen when he got home, to sit on a leather barstool at the counter and eat whatever leftovers his wife had put in the fridge. It was an indulgence, but one he could work off at the gym tomorrow. It was always a lottery, what he might find, and his mouth watered at the prospect. Cauliflower cheese, a single slice of pie – savoury or sweet, he didn't care. A nub of Brie, cold roasties, coleslaw, a well-cooked chop . . . He was suddenly ravenous, and his gut rolled with hunger. The walk home had only fired his appetite and he wished he'd eaten all that Daisy had served them.

Daisy, a good kid. Quite unlike her mum. She was without that fire in her eyes, that spark of joy that Lisa carried, which made you believe anything was possible. Correction, a spark of joy she used to carry. It was shocking to him how in three years she had unravelled. And yes, he had heard that she was low, the word 'depressed' might have been mentioned, but he had never thought it would be down to anything he had done. Why would he? When he had left her, just before going to Melbourne, she had been laughing hard, head thrown back, naked, happy, reaching for his hand, their legs entwined as if anything other than skin-to-skin contact was unacceptable. At memories such as this, he would ordinarily feel the flare of desire, but not tonight, and this was a new low for him. Again, her words came to him, clear and sharp, enough to make his throat dry.

'*This is what you do. It's what you've always done. You pull people in with your tractor beam and then mess them up too, as if you need the company.*'

'Maybe she's right,' he whispered into the dark. 'But, my God, I hate being so lonely . . .'

It was a little before one a.m. when he put his key in the front door. He'd expected to find the place quiet, with muted lamplight guiding him through the house. Peace, a seat at the kitchen counter and refrigerated leftovers was not, however, what lurked behind the front door.

It was a surprise to see activity in the house at this time of night, a surprise to see this level of activity at any time. His wife in her dressing gown – her face devoid of makeup, her hair mussed as if she'd been disturbed from her sleep – stood in the hallway outside the downstairs cloakroom, banging loudly, flat-palmed on the wooden door.

'There you are!' She cast the words in his direction, they were both accusatory and yet dripped with irritation – quite a skill.

'What the hell's going on?' He wanted to know who was in the bathroom and why his wife was angrily trying to rouse them. 'What have I missed?'

'What have you missed?' Julie shook her head, ignoring his question.

He watched her hammer on the door again, her tone now urgent.

'Are you okay, Dom?' She placed her ear to the wood, as if hoping for a clue. 'Dom? Talk to me!'

'Domino? What's going on? What's happened?' He felt his pulse increase at the mere mention of her name. The prospect of his little girl being hurt, sick or upset in any way was more than he could stand. It was the curse of having a daughter. He found it hard not to think of her as a toddler, a little girl who needed his guidance, protection and to take his hand when crossing a road, meeting a stranger, or trying something new. Why was she home? He thought she was staying the night at her friend's.

The door opened a crack and Ruby, his daughter's study buddy, poked her head out. How had they ended up here? Had something happened at Ruby's house?

'She's okay, Mrs Kelleway, she's . . .'

He listened to the pause and waited, wondering at what point to intervene, hesitating in case it was an issue of a personal nature. He had never been very good with periods. His daughter's periods even less so. As hard as it was to admit, he would rather not be reminded of her maturity, her journey towards womanhood. It was enough to make him shudder, the prospect of his sweet Domino having to deal with the details of adult life. He knew more than most how being a grown-up could take a scythe to all that was good and fun and cut right through it. Plus, she might be sixteen, but was only a baby really, naïve at best, and all the sweeter for it.

'She wanted to come home, insisted we come here, but . . . she's . . . she's got a bug.' Ruby bit her lip as her cheeks flamed.

Well-versed in lying, it didn't sound or feel to him like the truth. 'What's going on, Ruby?' he asked again with a little more force, taking a step closer until he stood by his wife's side. He saw Julie's nose wrinkle, as if his very presence was unwelcome. Well, that was just too bad. This was *his* house, *his* family. Again, he pictured Lisa's face, turning from him, dismissing him and now the same from Julie. It felt like shit.

'A bug?' There was no mistaking his wife's tone – sarcastic, disbelieving – and he was glad they were on the same page, not that this realisation did anything to untie the knot of concern in his gut.

'Yep – she wanted to come home. Our friend dropped us off because Dom had some bad, erm, some bad fish.'

There was a kerfuffle from inside the room and he and Julie exchanged a look. The tale was growing more preposterous. He knew from experience that was the trouble with lying – the devil was in the detail.

'I see. Well, thank you for explaining that, Ruby. I guess as long as you are with her, I shan't worry.'

'Okay, thank you, Mrs Kelleway.' The girl's words dripped with relief; she looked behind the door, clearly communicating with Domino who appeared to be hiding.

'Can I just ask you a question, darling?'

Ruby's reply was sincere and instant. 'Yes, of course!'

'Did Dom eat the bad fish before she got roaring drunk or after? And if you had to guess, is she being sick into the toilet bowl because of the bug/food poisoning/bad fish or the vodka, do you think?'

'I . . . I don't . . .' the girl stuttered, and he recognised the fight or flight panic that danced across her eyes. He knew what it felt like to be backed into a corner, to want to run, but seeing the path ahead blocked, to have to stand and front it out, not knowing whether it might be better to come clean or to keep going, hoping you could keep up the ruse for as long as it took to figure out your next move. His heart raced, but that was nothing new.

The door crept open an inch and a rather grey-skinned Domino poked her face around the door. His stomach clenched at the sour stench of vomit.

'Good God, Ruby, do you think I was born yesterday? Just open the bloody door!' Julie pushed in and he followed. Ruby leaned on the sink with her arms across her chest, her manner sheepish. They stood on the hand-painted Turkish tiles where their daughter lay, pale-faced and with her hair spread over the floor like a carpet of gold.

'At least she's been sick, got much of it out of her system.' Julie's words offered small comfort.

'Who did this to her?' He felt his heart hammer with anger and something else: sadness. He was sad because this was his little girl who liked to study and who had the whole wide world at her feet and if someone had hurt her, taken advantage of her . . . He flexed his fingers, breathing heavily through his nose, controlling the desire to punch the wall at the unwelcome and invasive images that filled his head.

'Who did this to her?' he repeated, addressing Ruby directly.

'Micky . . . Micky Tate.' Ruby spoke quietly and he thought he must have misheard.

'Say it again?' he asked, feeling as if the air had been sucked from the room and all he could hear were the two words that left Ruby's mouth.

'Micky Tate.' She held his eyeline.

'He got her drunk?' He could hear his heart beating in his ears, a drum that got faster and louder as his anger grew and his jaw clenched tighter and tighter.

'He . . . he bought her a couple of cocktails, I think, I'm not sure. Essie and me were on the dance floor—'

'Who?' he interrupted, trying to figure out who Essie was, and how and why they were on a dance floor. He thought she'd gone to

Ruby's house to study. Had Domino *lied* to him? Clearly she had, and the realisation was a slap in the face.

'Essie's our mate. She drove us to the club—'

'Go on.' It was Julie's turn to interrupt; she obviously wanted the detail as much as he.

Ruby looked at the floor, breathing fast. 'So, we were dancing, me and Essie, and then we realised that Ruby had left, she'd got in Micky's car, and—'

'Shutupruby!' Domino lifted her head, her words a little slurred, her head lolling as if her neck was spaghetti. 'Justshutup!'

Dropping to his knees, he ran his hand over the back of her head. 'It's okay, Dom, you can tell us what happened. Did Micky' – he looked at his wife, whose expression was as horror-stricken as his own – 'did Micky hurt you in any way? Did he make you do anything you didn't want to do? Did he . . . ?' He ran out of steam as his tongue lolled dryly in his mouth and panic flooded his veins.

'I wassick, I asked him to slow down, it was all going too fast, so fast, and then Iwassick . . .' Her words ran into each other.

'You asked him to slow down?' He cursed the crack in his voice. It was all he needed to hear. Jumping up, he marched from the bathroom and grabbed the car keys from the table in the hallway.

'Where are you going?' Julie ran after him, holding him by the arm and forcing him to concentrate on her. 'Don't do anything stupid!'

'I'll fucking kill him! I will! I'll fucking kill him!' He spoke through gritted teeth, taking comfort from the thought of exacting revenge with his fists.

'If you do anything stupid, you will only make our situation worse.' She spoke calmly, but he could see terror and hurt in her eyes that reflected his own. The irony wasn't lost on him that his wife had no idea just how fucked up the situation was, unaware of the amount of money he owed Micky Tate.

'How?' The tears that filled his eyes and trickled down his face were a release to the tension that had been building for the longest time. 'How, Jules? How could things be any worse?' He glanced to the cloakroom where the image of his daughter lying drunk on the floor would, he knew, never leave him.

'Whatever has happened, and we don't yet know what, will not be helped in any way by you beating someone up. Especially someone like Micky Tate. He's famous, you know. He's a footballer! Lives on a big farm just outside of town.'

'Oh, don't worry. I know who he is, and I know where he lives.' He spoke through gritted teeth. 'And what are you saying, that just because he's a somebody, we let him get away with it? Look at her!' He pointed towards the cloakroom. How could he explain that Micky had him over a barrel financially, and now this?

'Of course, I'm not!' she fired back. 'What a hideous thing to say! Jesus!' She covered her face with her hands.

'So, what then? Are you telling me this looks above board to you? Does it look like she's had a nice time? What the fuck!' He put his hands in his hair and paced.

'I don't know. I don't know what to think, Loz. I'm scared.' She folded her arms and her expression of pure sorrow was almost more than he could stand. 'I honestly don't know what to do next.'

'You seem very calm, considering,' he noted with an undercurrent of accusation that he couldn't hide.

'Calm?' She took a step closer. 'I am doing what I always do, Loz – trying to keep things together to make whatever shitstorm we are riding through the best it possibly can be for my kids! The one who can't lose it, who has to keep going.' She poked him in the chest. 'And we both know I've had some practice. We don't know what's happened tonight, and so yes, I'm calm. For now. And you need to follow my lead, but trust me, Loz, if that man has laid a finger on my daughter, you can do what you like to him, and I'll hold your coat. But until we have the full picture—'

'We don't need the full picture!' He pointed again to the room where his little girl lay.

'Loz, listen to me.' She took her time, and he didn't like it, getting the feeling that she was more than a little in the know, that she'd kept something from him. 'I am distraught, I am fuming, I am sick to my stomach' – her voice shook – 'but I also know that Dom might have a life that you and I know very little about.'

'What's that supposed to mean?' He resented the suggestion. It scared him. 'What kind of life?'

'I just mean that she's sixteen, she's not a baby, and I know she's been up to Shiskas in the past because Cass saw her there once. I thought it was a one-off, that she might be experimenting, dipping her toe in that grown-up world and I didn't think it was a big deal, she was with her friends . . .'

'What was she doing up there? And why didn't you tell me?'

Julie gave a small, exasperated laugh and looked skyward. 'You're never present. Even when you're here you're not present. When was I supposed to raise it? This is what I was talking about earlier, about you not knowing what is important! Being here for our kids, living the everyday, the small stuff, understanding what they are going through – this is what's important!'

'Oh, I might have known this would be my fault!' He couldn't believe she was using this as an excuse to give him another verbal kicking.

'Jesus! Not everything is about you!' She rubbed her fingers over her forehead, and he recognised the familiar pattern. How everything from the weekly shop, politics on TV, what route to drive and even the question, 'Has someone fed the cat?', descended into this exchange where voices were raised and teeth were bared. It was as if they couldn't help it, pre-programmed, locked in the cycle . . . He was mightily sick of it and judging from the slope of his wife's shoulders, so was she.

'Please don't go and find Micky.' Domino's voice drew them. The sight of her silenced him, two dark streaks of mascara ran down her cheeks and her eyes were swollen and smudged. Her shirt was undone, her bra visible. He could smell the pungent scent of booze and cigarettes, which was nauseating enough, but doubly so when it came from his daughter. His sixteen-year-old daughter. A child. Only she didn't look like a child, she looked like a teenager, a young woman and one who knew little of the world.

'You don't need to worry,' he began. 'Daddy will sort it out. Whatever has happened.'

'There's nothing to sort out!' she shouted, her arms stiff by her side, her words offered without censor, her truth aided by the liberal application of alcohol that clearly still swirled in her body. 'Micky hasn't done anything wrong, not really. I came on to him. I've been after him for weeks. We were heading off to his place for sex, he has a pool with a pool house and champagne. Not the cheap stuff, the really good stuff.' She gave a wry smile as her tears gathered. 'But I threw up when he took a bend too fast. I threw up all over the leather interior of his car. He's got a McLaren. Guess I fucked that up; he doesn't want to see me again!' She tucked her hair behind her ears, still a little unsteady on her legs.

'You're just . . .' He tried to speak, tried to shift the tangle of emotion that clogged his throat like fibres. 'You're just a kid,' he managed, unable to recognise the person in front of him, a clone of Domino, but her words alien, unthinkable.

'Am I, Dad?' she asked, as Julie rushed forward and took her daughter into her arms, cooing like Domino were still a baby.

'It'll all be okay, Dom. I've got you. It'll all be okay.'

It struck him, as he slammed the front door behind him, that he and Lisa had started when they were fifteen. That's when they'd fallen in love. So deeply in love that she was all he could think about. Lisa – the girl who still sat like a splinter in his thoughts.

He stood in the cool night air and fired off a text to Micky before jumping into the Merc that might be taken from him any day now, if he didn't sort out the deal with the estate agent's friends. He'd run out of money for the repayments. His standing orders had bounced and just like the house, it was a matter of when, not if, he would be forced to hand over the keys. Pulling out of the cul-de-sac, Mr Moneybags put his foot down and let the engine roar . . .

CHAPTER ELEVEN

Cleo Richardson

It was a little after one a.m. Thankfully, the pain in Cleo Richardson's abdomen seemed to have subsided, and she now soaked in a warm bubble bath, with a cup of tea Georgie had made her resting on the side, and a fragrant candle lit for good measure. She inhaled the warm scent of amber, finding it soothing. She wished her husband could find something similarly calming to distract him, as the sound of him pacing the living room below filtered up the stairs. His heavy tread on the laminate flooring, interspersed with the squeak of the loose board by the fireplace . . . it made her smile. He'd become the caricature she'd seen in movies, one they had mocked together: the pacing expectant father, hands wringing, prayers and wishes floating up to whoever might be listening, a tense look across a worried brow. In another era he'd have no doubt toked on a fat cigar. The thought made her laugh.

Still, the idea lingered that maybe they should move away, pack up their little home and go . . . anywhere. Start over, free from the clutches of her parents, the irritation of Lawrence, the inevitable comparison between her baby and its wealthy cousins . . . God, how she loved the thought!

She took deep, slow breaths, doing her very best to slow her pulse, knowing that to keep calm was the most important thing, aware that she would need to pull on all her reserves soon enough. They had read a book together when first pregnant, a book all about what to expect as first-time parents. She had read aloud the chapter on the importance for the person giving birth to feel in control and that their wishes were, as far as possible, adhered to at a time when they were most vulnerable. Yes, she remembered this clearly, knowing it would be in her husband's nature to want to take over, make plans, usher her this way and that, make suggestions, do what he thought best. She knew it would be killing him to hand over control.

'Did you call, love?' He poked his head around the door.

'No.' She shook her head and reached for her tea.

'Oh.' He bit his lip, as he did when he was nervous. 'Thought I might have heard you shout out. I yawned and was worried I'd missed it.'

'You didn't miss it. I didn't call. Come in, you dafty, come and sit with your wife.'

Lumbering in, he took up a seat on the loo and leaned forward with his large hands splayed on his knees.

'How are you doing, Georgie?' She spoke in the soothing voice that she used to greet him after a long day, knowing it helped ease his worries.

He considered his response. 'I've got to admit . . .'

She could see he was doing his best, choosing his words carefully, taking his time, as if he, too, might be thinking about that chapter in their book.

'. . . it's a bit alien to me that you want to be here at all. I thought you might be screaming in a state of panic for me to take you to the hospital!'

'This is real life, Georgie, not a movie. It's not always screaming and rushing. In fact, this bit is quite boring.'

'Well, I'm glad about the screaming, and I don't mind boring, but I wouldn't mind a bit of rushing.'

'Why would I want to sit in a strange room when I could be here instead, in my bath with my lovely candle and a cup of tea. This is better. Much better. Besides it won't take us long to get there when we set off.' She sipped her hot drink.

'I've done a few dummy runs.' He spoke quietly; it felt like a confession.

'What do you mean, "dummy runs"?'

'You know I like to be prepared' – he shifted on the loo – 'so I've gone out at all hours, in all weathers and all traffic to work out the best route for every eventuality. I've got the top four pro-grammed into the satnav, ready to guide me with no more than a single push of a button. I didn't want to leave anything to chance.'

'Oh darling, you already know every route! It's not that far!' She found his planning and concern sweet and typical of the man she loved.

'I know it's not far' – he held her gaze – 'the hospital, where they have machines that beep, drugs on tap and nurses who know what to do if and when anything goes wrong. The hospital where I want to take you sooner rather than later!'

She could sense his agitation. 'That's right. The hospital we will be at soon enough *when* we need to.'

He ran his palm over his face, his leg jumping against the lino-leum. 'The thing is, babe, I shan't rest until you're checked in and I can hand you over to the medical team.'

'Hand me over? You make it sound like dropping off a package or making one of your deliveries – are you going to ask someone to sign for me, and what will you do if there's no one there? Leave me in a safe place or shove me in the wheelie bin?'

Georgie sat stony faced, clearly in no mood for a joke. 'No, not like a package. Like my expectant wife who is in labour. It's not about shirking my duty of care as the father of this baby, far from it, but I know what I'm capable of in any medical emergency and what I'm not. When it comes to blown tyres, a burst water main, power cuts, then I'm your man, but when it comes to you, Cleo, my Cleo . . . no, you're far too important for me to take any risk.'

'I get it, love.'

'No, you don't!' he fired back. 'You don't, you can't because it's not me who is in labour. It's you – you, my wife. It's not just that I love you, although of course I do, with every fibre of my being. It's that you're my reason, my purpose, my meaning. Even now, after fourteen years married, to take your hand in mine . . . it fills me up.'

'Oh, Georgie.' She was no stranger to his lamentations of love, but tonight it felt more poignant, more special.

'You are fascinating to me. Everything about you! The way the sun picks out the highlights of your hair, the curve of your cheek, the little hollow at the base of your throat where your locket sits, all of it, just amazing to me.'

Her fingers went to the gold lozenge shape where a picture of her and Georgie on their wedding day lived, and a space, waiting for an image of their baby, who was on the way.

'I only have to close my eyes, Cleo, wherever I am, driving all over the country in my van, and nothing can touch me, nothing. People can yell insults about my driving, customers can scream at me when I'm late or because the order isn't right, and I take it all on the chin, because you make everything better. Knowing you're at home waiting for me, makes the early starts, driving rain, cramping leg muscles – it makes it all worth it. We might not have Lawrence and Julie's money, but I wouldn't swap the happiness we share for any number of fancy cars and designer labels. I'm content. You're everything. And so, forgive me, Cleo, if I would rather you were in the hands of a medical team who could take care of you better than me in this instance.'

Cleo felt the bloom of tears. Despite them never saying so directly, she knew her mum and dad would have preferred her to marry some flash Harry or someone with as much ambition as her dad, so that she too could have an extended patio, en-suite bathroom, and a shiny new piece of jewellery for each and every milestone, but Georgie was never going to be that person. She hoped in time they would come to see that he was genuine in his devotion to her, would fight until his last breath anyone whose intention was to hurt a single hair on her head. But at the same time, if they failed to recognise his true value, as they had after all this time, then that was just too bad.

'I love how you want to look after me, look after us.' She ran her hand over her bump. 'And you know that I wouldn't do anything to put either of us in danger. I'm not stupid.'

'I know, but this is my time. I might not be able to give birth, but I can step up. Our baby is on the way! I'm going to be a dad!' Removing his glasses, he wiped his teary eyes. 'Never, never in a million years did I think I would get this lucky . . . and I'm ready. I'm ready, Cleo.'

She watched him feel his shirt pocket and the reassuring lump of his car keys. 'You're going to do great; we're going to do great!' She yawned, blowing out from bloated cheeks, her movements languid. 'I'm glad you're here. I wanted a bit of company.'

'Of course.' He willed his heart to settle. 'I could eat another bowl of that tiramisu right now!'

'You and your puddings.' She rolled her eyes. 'I was thinking how funny it is really that Daisy, our waitress, is Lisa's girl, and you and Loz were only about her age when you all used to hang around together.' She pictured them in their teens; Lisa had been a knock-out. 'I thought you were so grown-up, a whole two years older than me. I remember the way Lisa and Loz were with each other – it was so intense. But when I looked at Daisy, no more than a little girl, really, I can see you were anything but. Just kids playing at being grown-ups, figuring it out as you went along. Poor old Lisa,' Cleo mused.

'Yeah. Depression is a horrible thing.'

'Thanks for that, doctor!'

He laughed. 'It's true though. It's hard to think of that vibrant woman not wanting to leave the house. He and Lisa were—'

'A disaster waiting to happen?' she interrupted.

'D'you think? I always liked her, and whilst I'm very fond of Julie, I wouldn't have been surprised if Loz and Lisa had gone all the way. Not that he's seen her for a couple of years now.'

'No way! There's no way he was that into her. I mean, yes, it was briefly intense, but Loz was living life with all guns blazing and she was this airy-fairy thing who always seemed quite fragile to me. I don't think he was that keen on her, not really, and I know my brother.'

'You do,' he agreed.

'I think maybe she was just someone to hang out with when he broke his ankle, a diversion. I know they haven't kept in touch or anything. And he never mentions her.' Cleo sat up in the water and splashed her face.

'Yes, that's probably true. It would have been weird, though, if things had worked out between them. Imagine him living in that grotty house next door; your mum would have a heart attack!'

'It wouldn't be grotty if Loz lived in it, would it? He's a bit different from Marty the lazy bones. No, Loz would have made it a palace to hand on to his kids. He'd have kept it tarted up and no doubt installed electric gates, a marble fountain, fancy kitchen, luxury bathrooms and then he'd have spent the next decade telling us how much it all cost and just how fabulous it was to live in.

And how lucky his kids were to be gifted such a haul when the time came!'

'Don't be mean.'

'I'm not,' she countered, 'I'm being truthful. And as for Mum having a heart attack, my God, Lawrence the golden boy living next door? I think she'd shit glitter for the rest of her life! Her Lawrence, next door? For my mother it would have been like winning the lottery on Christmas morning and discovering that chocolate was actually a weight-loss aid.'

He laughed out loud.

'It's odd how no one sees her, isn't it?' She thought again about the sunny girl who Lawrence had gone out with. 'I think she's a vampire.' Cleo pushed her teeth over her bottom lip, trying and failing to do an impression.

'You do?' He slid off the loo and came to rest on the floor where some spilled water soaked into his trousers. Not that he cared. She dangled her hand over the side of the bath, and he caught it in his own.

'It's the most obvious explanation, isn't it? I bet she only comes out at night, can't be seen in daylight. And now you come to mention it, that Daisy had a whiff of the underworld about her. She has very pale skin and dark hair and it's probably no coincidence that she works at the Italian restaurant with easy access to all that garlic.'

The two chuckled until they calmed. It was always like this, laughing, holding hands, silences that were far from awkward. Contentment. She ran her hand over her bump again, which stood proud of the bubbles, a foam-topped mountain inside which their baby lived.

'I can't stop thinking about moving away, Georgie, like, seriously thinking about it. Where could we go?' She held his gaze.

'I thought you were joking.'

She shook her head. 'Not really. Think how lovely it is when we go down to Ilfracombe, walk the harbour, eat fish and chips, watch the sunset from that bench on the hill up by the church . . . I can see us doing that.' *Away from the whole family* . . . her silent afterthought.

'Yes, but holidays are different, because they're a break from reality – you don't worry, you don't plan.'

'Exactly! We could live that every day.'

'It's a long way from your mum and dad.'

She let this settle. 'Yup.'

'To be honest, Cleo, I've got so much going on in my head right now, moving to Ilfracombe is going to have to take a bit of a back seat.'

He wore the expression she'd seen before when he felt a little overloaded. If the moment had been right, she'd have pushed the issue more, but with tension already high, she knew that this was not the moment. 'Just think, Georgie, in a day or a few hours, there'll be a little one right here with us! Outside not in!'

'Yep.'

Having been diverted by their chat, her words had seemingly brought him back to the reality of the moment and she saw beads of sweat form on his top lip. It was clear to her that every second they spent in the house and every second she got closer to giving birth felt like the most enormous risk to her husband. Maybe she should put him at ease and go in. He drummed his fingers on the bath, as if he could almost hear the clock ticking and again patted the car keys in his pocket, taking comfort from the fact that they were within reach. It made her feel anxious that he was ridiculously and illogically worried he might forget where he had put them.

'Do you think we should talk about names?' she asked calmly, loading up the bath sponge with warm water and squeezing it over her belly and chest.

'Are you kidding me? After all these months of me nagging you over names, you want to do that *now*?' He laughed nervously.

'Well, why not? We've got to call it something!'

It felt like as good a distraction as any.

'I still think Winnie if it's a girl—'

She cut him short. 'And I still think no bloody way!'

'It would make your mum's day – no, it would make her *life*! For her it would be like winning the lottery on Christmas morning, discovering that chocolate was actually a weight-loss aid *and* that Marty and Lisa had sold up and Michael Ball was moving in next door and was looking for someone to duet with at the WI summer ball!'

Cleo tipped her head back and roared her laughter. 'Stop! If I laugh too hard, I pee!'

'You can, you're in the bath, no one will ever know.'

She pictured giving her mother the news that their daughter was to be her namesake. 'It's a sweet idea, but if we named our daughter Winnie, she'd be forever in my mother's shadow. It might feel like a pressure. She'd be known as "Little Winnie"! Oh my God!' The thought horrified her. 'Can you imagine if, aged six, she started putting together over-elaborate cheeseboards, arranging flowers into ornate vases in every room and trying so desperately to be the perfect hostess! Every event would have to be "so much fun!"' She hoped she'd painted enough of a picture to put him off the idea.

'Okay, no. Definitely no! Not Little Winnie then,' he agreed.

'What about after your grandad, especially if it's a boy and he's born on his birthday tomorrow?' Her enthusiasm for the idea grew. It was staking a claim, it was announcing to her family that Georgie was not just some tag-along she was saddled with, he was her person, the father of her baby.

'Today,' he corrected. 'Tomorrow is now today and it's his birthday.'

'Oh! Happy birthday . . . What was his name?' She looked at him quizzically.

'Welland. Welland Thomas Richardson.'

'Sweet Jesus, please be a girl!' she yelled at the ceiling and again they laughed. 'I mean, can you imagine? "Welland, your tea's on the table!" "Clean your teeth, Welland!"'

'I rather like it!' He played devil's advocate.

'I don't. But I quite like Thomas. Tom, Tommy.'

'I quite like Thomas. Tom, Tommy.' He sounded out the names.

Cleo sat forward in the water and smiled at him.

'I don't think you have ever looked so beautiful, so serene. A goddess.'

His words were touching. And it was in that second that she felt a surge in her womb, a quickening in her veins and a throb of discomfort that was thrilling and terrifying in equal measure. 'This is it.' She spoke softly.

'Yes, my love.' He stroked her arm. 'This is it. We're having a baby; we are going to be a little family.'

'No' – she squeezed his fingers – 'I mean, this is it. It's time. Right now. It's happening. You can take me to the hospital.'

Georgie, who had heard her words, and apparently understood what she was saying, appeared quite unable to move. It was as if he were glued to the spot, while his brain tried desperately to goad his body into action.

'Georgie?'

'Yes?' He stared at his wife who now leaned over the bath, placing her forehead on his and speaking closely and quietly, her tone firm.

'We've got this. We can do anything, me and you. So, I'm going to get out of the bath, dry off, put on my comfies and you are going to drive us to the hospital, just like you practised, okay?'

'Okay.' He nodded and very slowly stood, feeling his way as he reached the bathroom door.

'Have you got the car keys?' she asked gently.

'Car keys? Erm . . . I think they're downstairs.'

She smiled at her man who had boasted how he was primed to assist, but in that moment, it appeared his mind had gone a little blank.

'Don't be scared, Georgie.' She whispered as she stood and reached for the large, soft bath sheet that was looped over the radiator.

'I'm . . . not scared . . . I'm . . .'

'Petrified?' she cut in.

He nodded. 'Yep, that's more accurate. I'm absolutely bloody petrified!'

CHAPTER TWELVE

Julie Kelleway

According to the bedside clock it was nearly three a.m. now. Julie had watched the hands going around for a while, finding it impossible to sleep, despite being so very tired. Her body was tense, thoughts wired, her brain on high alert. Her bedroom door was wide open, as was Domino's – on whom she had checked every ten minutes or so until she was convinced she wasn't going to choke on vomit in her sleep or leg it down the drainpipe to continue partying.

Cassian must have stayed at Winnie and Bernie's, as he sometimes did. Not that she minded. Her in-laws might drive her to distraction, but she was grateful for the way they loved her kids, knowing that when it came to parenting, you could never have too much support. She had made Ruby a bed on Domino's floor and was glad her friend was there to help keep an eye on her. She didn't blame Ruby for the whole fiasco – she wasn't one of those parents who instantly put misdemeanours and misadventures down to the company her children kept. Domino had a strong desire for fun and an even stronger will. That much she knew.

On her last venture along the hallway earlier, poking her head into the room, it had saddened and comforted her in equal measure to see the two girls sleeping under the duvets in shades of pink, hands curled under their chins, surrounded by unicorn rugs, sparkly handbags and furry slippers. They looked so young, childlike almost, and unrecognisable as the two who, reeking of cigarettes and booze, had barred the bathroom door while one of them threw up vodka into the toilet bowl. Just the memory of it was enough to make her shudder.

Having spent a quiet couple of hours searching local jobs on the internet, it had been a shock earlier to hear the beating on the front door as she readied for bed. With her heart pounding, wishing she wasn't alone in the house, she'd put on the chain and was about to take a peek when she heard her daughter shout loudly, 'For fuck's sake! Open the door!'

What in the world?

'Good evening, Mother!' Domino had tried to take a bow, but as she leaned forward she'd collapsed through the door, landing in a heap on the hallway floor.

She had looked at Ruby, who sucked in her cheeks, barely able to contain her laughter.

'My friend and I were wondering if you might have a room available in your fine establishment for two weary travellers?' Domino asked from the floor, using a voice that was part Bridgerton, part Downton. 'We have stabled our horses and would appreciate any snack that has bacon in it!'

This before she had crawled on all fours to the downstairs bathroom, leaving the stink of booze in her wake, closely followed by Ruby. And this was where Lawrence had come in.

It weighed heavily on her that she used to be close to her daughter: knew her friends, her likes, habits, sharing in-jokes as they spent time together socially. It had been easy in Melbourne when Domino was that little bit younger and Julie had had more time, money, and the mental capacity to invest in her kids. The school run twice a day had been far from a chore because it had meant they could catch up, talk.

Since they'd been back in the UK it felt as if their lives had slid to the side and this lopsided existence made everything feel like it was off-kilter, about to topple . . . With Lawrence largely absent, out and about working from his car/office, having various meetings, chats, and visits, it was left to her to hold the ropes, pulling furiously with every ounce of strength to keep them all upright. It was an impossible task for her alone. She was losing her grip, weakening, and they were, in that moment, tipping, tilting.

As a family, they had passed the point of no return and there was nothing more she could do to hold things in place. It wasn't that she had given up, but rather that her exhausted body and tired arms could no longer hold on. She existed, in that split second of realisation, between tripping and landing, and all she could do was hold her breath and wait. A small part of her wanted to feel the ground beneath her bones as she hit the deck, wanted to see the fragments of their lives shattered by the fall, as that would mean it was nearly over, because for her it was the waiting, bracing herself, that she found to be the most agonising.

It was the same pattern as before and one she knew well. It started with a feeling of safety and optimism – the good times when Lawrence started a project, secured funding, was high on all the possibilities of what this big win might mean for them. It was nearly impossible not to get swept up in it, to feel the joy that came off him in waves as he bounced around the kitchen. Difficult not to delight in his smiley face as he spoke with excitement, bought gifts, took them all out to dinner and showered her with affection behind closed doors, whispering promises of a rosy future. It would be hard *not* to love those times, even if she knew deep down they were not to last.

What came next was a partial withdrawing of that affection from him. He spoke with less volume, less energy when discussing his scheme, complained of minor grumbles over his plan, his grand idea now diminished in some way by events that were always, always beyond his control. And then came the final stage – where they were now. These were the dark times, when funds had dwindled and the pressure was so great her husband almost stooped under the weight of it. His moods threw a dark shadow over their house so that even to joke or sing felt like a contravention of the rules, putting them all on edge. And in this murky half-light, with voices low and everyone under the roof wired and waiting, they would retreat alone into spaces trying to find solace, a little peace.

For the kids it was their bedrooms, for her the bathroom where she could lock the door and close her eyes or howl at the moon through the wide Velux window. It was a debilitating way to live and this before she considered the big smiles they painted on for any family gathering, accidental performers in the drama Lawrence had been starring in since he was a boy, with her and the kids consigned to the wings, bit players called upon to prop up and endorse the impression of the perfect world he had created.

As ever, her head thumped with a stress-induced headache. It was always this way when her tangle of thoughts kept her awake.

'Micky Tate,' Julie whispered the name into the darkness. What on earth was Domino thinking getting involved with a man like that? He had a frightful reputation. She'd seen numerous articles in the magazines she grazed while in the supermarket queue, all detailing his penchant for fast cars, lavish spending, with alleged rumours of drugs. He was always, always pictured within reach of a beautiful woman. And this before they addressed the fact that he was at least ten years older than her daughter. Not so much of an issue if Domino were thirty, forty, fifty, but at sixteen she was barely fully formed, without the experience or knowledge to back up the demands her hormonal teenage body might be making.

The girl couldn't work the washing machine or make a decent cup of tea; she wasn't even allowed to vote! What did a man of that age see in a young girl like Domino? What on earth did he think they might have in common? The answer offered her very little comfort and again she shuddered at the unsavoury possibilities that filled her already busy head.

Julie planned on talking to her daughter during the day, when tempers, emotions and alcohol levels had all calmed. She made the decision not to get angry. She would not rage but would talk to her softly about her fears and all that she hoped and planned for her daughter's future, explaining that while their home life might be in a state of flux, staying true to her future self had never been more important – she needed to have enough self-respect not to make decisions she might regret. She prayed that would be enough to make her little girl rethink her actions, her choices.

The fact that Lawrence had left in such a state and wasn't answering his phone did nothing to help her insomnia. She hoped he wasn't going to do something stupid. Closing her eyes, she imagined how much worse their situation would be if he was facing a charge for GBH on top of everything else. Not that she thought it likely; he was not and never had been a violent man, but she had never seen the rage in his eyes before, reminding her of a man who had very little to lose, and it scared her.

It was as she was wondering whether to try his phone again that she heard the sound of the front door closing, and without hesitation threw back the coverlet, grabbing her dressing gown from the back of the door as she went, unsure if it was Cassian or Lawrence, but knowing her son was unlikely to venture home at this ungodly hour and was more than likely tucked up safe and sound at his nan's house.

She felt a little sick as she stood on the bottom stair, taking in her husband who still looked distressed, dishevelled but certainly more contained than when he'd left. Her sickness was no surprise – she was full of anxiety, sleep deprived and still with vast amounts of the Brie she'd felt obliged to eat riddling through her system.

'Where have you been?' she asked softly, not wanting to wake the sleeping girls.

He put his car keys on the narrow console table where a matching pair of lamps sat at either end. The table where they placed keys, parcels, letters, all part of the comings and goings of family life, the little shared rituals of the house and the people who lived in it.

'I just drove around.' His voice carried the huskiness of fatigue.

'I see.' It was an inadequate answer, but right now it was relief enough that he was home; she could probe further later. 'Would you like a cup of tea?'

'Yes, please.'

His politeness, his reticence, fired a familiar bolt of empathy for the man who, though he was flawed, troubled and his own worst enemy, was still her husband, the father of her children. And they had come this far . . . These were the ties that bound her to both the man and her marriage. That and the background hum of hope that things would get better, because that was what he promised: a better life, a calmer life, happiness.

He followed her into the kitchen and took a seat at the breakfast bar, staring out across the garden while she filled the kettle. She followed his gaze, still mulling over how to intervene, how to have the conversation that things needed to change – that moment in the shop when her cards were refused now lurking behind the horror of Domino's return, but still there, nonetheless.

'I love this time of night – or is it morning? I never know what to call it when I haven't slept.'

'It's morning,' he confirmed. 'Saturday morning.'

'I can picture different times in my life when to be up and about in the early hours felt like a gift, a wonderful and exciting thing.' She popped teabags into two mugs set on the countertop. 'I remember when we started dating and we'd sit talking and laughing for hours and hours, and before we knew it, it was nearly the dawn of a new day and I remember the light being breathtaking. It was this same beautiful mauve shade.' She pointed at the sky. 'The whole world seemed still and everything felt possible. I'd never met anyone like you, Loz, never met anyone who didn't seem to see any obstacles in the way of his dreams, someone who just believed and went for it. I thought that was brave and exciting. I still do.'

This felt like a good place to start, a reminder to both her and him of the essence of the man and what had made life good, an anchor point.

He nodded, his emotions clearly still hovering near the surface.

'Then when Cass was born . . .'

'Just after midnight,' he chipped in with a small smile, as if he too could readily recall that moment their lives had changed forever.

'Yes. And you'd fallen asleep in the chair in my room. I was holding him and time slipped by until the darkness gave way to light. It felt so precious: his very first day on the planet and I got to hold him through his first dawn. That feels like yesterday, and here he is nearly grown-up, chasing girls, heading off to uni. A mere blink from that moment when I was cradling him, watching the sun come up with you snoozing in the corner.'

He rubbed his unshaven face.

'I guess I want to remind you that we have a wonderful history, Lawrence, and that I know you have always tried your best. But I also think it's good to know when to quit.' The last sentence she almost whispered, knowing it would be as hard for him to hear as it was for her to say. 'You need to take a step back and see the bigger picture, understand how your actions have consequences for us all.'

He nodded and stared at her, unblinking. 'Yes, I've been thinking about that this evening.'

She wanted him to open up to her, knowing this would make the next phase of communication easier, unsure of how he would react to her requests that he get a regular job, that they live simply, move somewhere affordable, tell his parents . . . she knew it was a lot.

'So, you just drove around tonight?'

'Yes.' He coughed. 'I wanted to get away from the house, from the . . . the situation with Dom, but also I wanted to spend time in my car.'

'I think Dom and I might have needed you to spend time with us.' She didn't know why she said it, having in truth preferred him out of the way while she'd ferried her girl up the stairs, into the shower, finding her clean pyjamas while letting the fractious air settle. It would, however, have been nice if he'd not stayed out so late without word.

'I know that.' He held her eyeline. 'But sometimes if I need to think or get something straight in my head; I can only do it when I'm on my own, and driving helps. No music, not going fast, I just put the window down and see where I end up. Never far away, but after a while, I kind of come to, if that makes any sense, and a bit of the fog lifts and I know it's time to come home.'

'I understand that need for quiet and to have some time alone.'

'I wasn't alone all of the time; I went to see Micky Tate.' He blinked up at her like a child who thought he might be in trouble.

'You did? You went to his house?' Her voice went up an octave, shocked that he would pitch up at the footballer's house and equally worried of what he might have done or said in his riled state.

'I've . . . I've been there before.' He spoke quite matter-of-factly.

'You have?' This was news. 'Why? How do you know him?' Her stomach jumped. What else didn't she know?

He spoke slowly. 'He's one of the investors in the new build.'

'One of your investors?'

'Yes.'

'Micky Tate?'

'Yes.'

'What did he say about Dom? What did *you* say?' She gave him her full attention, wanting the detail, hoping to dispel some of the unpleasant images that had filled her head earlier, but in truth, the peeling away of another layer only made his business dealings seem more troubling.

He closed his eyes and gave a wry laugh. 'Where to begin . . .'

She waited, holding her breath.

'He's a nasty piece of work. And the upshot is, he's sending me a bill – a hefty bill – to have the leather of his car interior replaced and some other work. I think the end amount will be more than my actual car is worth.'

'God, Lawrence!' She shielded her eyes from view, wanting to hide just for a second and envying him his earlier moments of solitude and escape.

'Yep. Domino threw up all over the inside.' His nose wrinkled. 'It's a mess. He said nothing else happened; he was shady, defensive. I told him how old she was and he went pale. I could have hurt him, Jules, but I didn't. I believe him that nothing happened, but I don't doubt it would have done.' He visibly shuddered. 'He was far more concerned about his car. He's not a liar. He's absolute scum, but he's not a liar.'

'Scum you now owe even more money to,' she concluded, beginning to understand that her husband might be incapable of sorting their dire situation, of making the necessary changes.

Maybe it was down to her to take the reins, maybe it was *all* down to her to figure it out, find a way forward.

'That's about the size of it.' He again looked close to tears, and she felt a flash of pity for the man who had gone to sort things but only succeeded in making them worse. 'Micky can get in the queue, wait like everyone else, and the funny thing is, Jules, if my new investors don't come up with the goods, then everyone who's already invested, Micky included, will be waiting for a slice of a pie that doesn't exist. There is no money! So, what can I do?'

'I don't know, Lawrence.' Her gut gripped with anxiety. 'What can you do? Because we need to do something.' She ran her fingers over the marble countertop, wondering how long before she would be closing the front door for good. Feeling a ridiculous flash of concern for food in the freezer that needed using up – a couple of quiches she'd made, tubs of ice cream and an apple crumble. It was odd that this low-value worry took precedence in her thoughts when there were so many bigger things to worry about. A diversion, if you like, from the daunting task ahead – that of fixing her family and digging their way out of the hole they found themselves in.

'Yes, we need to do something,' he echoed. 'I am trying to get my thoughts straight, driving helped. I parked up, calmed down.'

'Where did you park?'

'By the river, opposite those flats they built a little while back. Some had their lights on and in one a young couple were sat on the balcony having a drink, looking out over the water. They looked really happy, and I was trying to figure out how you had a life like that.'

'What do you mean?'

'A life where you live in one of those flats, which are nice enough and probably don't have too many outgoings. They're not flash, but they seemed happy enough. And I want to know, Jules, how do you get to live a life like that where the middle of the road is enough?'

He looked at her quizzically, and her heart soared, wondering if, finally, he was coming around to her way of thinking: that to live a simpler life, a less expensive life, would give them the freedom and security she so craved. It was, considering the most terrible night they'd spent, entirely hopeful. This in turn the perfect segue into the conversation they needed to have.

'I guess by not overstretching yourself financially, by being content with less. That's how I grew up. I can recommend it.' She looked at her handbag, still on the chair but soon to be emptied, packed up and shipped off to its new owner for a fraction of its real worth. 'I went to buy the chocolates for your mum earlier . . .'

'Yes, I know. Thank you for doing that, I—'

'No,' she cut him off. 'I don't want thanks. I want to tell you that I tried to pay with our bank card, which got refused. My credit card too.'

'Shit!' He reached for the mug of hot tea and held it in both palms, his gaze downcast.

'And it makes me feel awkward, uncomfortable having to say it, having to mention it, but it shouldn't. It really shouldn't.' She paused. 'And this sums up how hard I find it to talk to you about money and the debt.' It was true, it was a topic that he avoided and made awkward, and it coloured the whole issue for all of them. But no more. She was putting herself in the driving seat, she was going to take control.

Enough was enough, she never again wanted to feel as she had in that store, staring into her empty purse as if she could magic some cash into her hand.

'It's ludicrous because it affects all our lives. Debt and dishonesty are the worst bedfellows, and they operate like a tag team, elbowing me in the ribs to stop me sleeping, stop me from thinking straight – they don't give me a moment's peace! And I'm so tired of it, Loz! I'm so tired of it all. And I know you must be too.' She tucked her long hair behind her ears and sipped her tea, hoping it might give her the energy to continue the conversation, as exhaustion lapped at her heels. 'I think . . . I think we need to come clean about it all. We need to be able to talk about it, be open about it and try to plan what comes next. For our sake and the kids' sake too. We need to be honest. To face it.' This she knew would give them the best shot of going forward, of seeking help and turning things around.

He gave a single nod but said nothing, kind of confirming her point about the awkwardness. It felt a little easier to continue now that the topic had been broached.

'I kept some cash in a small purse inside my handbag, a few notes that I've managed to squirrel away over the weeks. It gave me comfort knowing that, no matter what, I had that tiny amount to buy food or whatever we might need in an emergency, and I know it wasn't enough to make a huge difference, but it was just enough to make a difference to me, for me to feel a little happier – a little safer, if you like.' As she spoke, she could feel anger bookending her words, recalling exactly what he had done and how it had impacted her.

'I know what you're going to say.' He held her eyes and took a deep, slow breath as his shoulders slumped.

'Yes.' She held her breath, waiting for him to tell her why he'd felt justified in taking the last of her cash, the last of their cash.

'Everyone around the table was calling me Mr Moneybags, joking about me picking up the tab, as if they expected me to and then, if I didn't, I was going to look tight or broke—'

'You are broke.' Her tone was steady.

'Thank you, yes.' And just like that any suggested contrition was diluted, leaving her feeling hollow inside. 'Dad gave his speech, and I looked up and Daisy was stood by the bar just watching, staring, waiting.'

'Daisy?'

'Yes, the waitress!'

'Jake's sister? I thought her name was Darcy, anyway, carry on.' She failed to see how him taking the money and the odd girl staring at them were connected, and she needed him to get to the point so she could go to bed, because right now she felt about ready to collapse.

'I knew you had some cash, saw you pop it in your purse a few days ago, and so I borrowed it for tonight, in case anything came up.'

'You *borrowed* it?' She couldn't help her disbelieving tone, knowing it was most unlikely he would have taken the money with the intention of returning it to her. And recognising that this was how he could justify most things: with an elaborate reason or plan as to how the situation was a) reasonable, b) going to get resolved. His excuses, like her tolerance, were wearing thin, causing her harm and they sat like a woodpecker beak inside her thoughts, tap, tapping away until she couldn't stand it anymore.

'Yes, you're my wife.' He stared at her, as if it was her who just didn't get it. 'I borrowed some cash from your purse – it's not a big deal.' She watched him wipe the sweat from his top lip with his index finger.

The fact that he just didn't get it fired fury into her veins. 'What did you need it for? What came up?'

'I had to give it to Daisy!' His voice was now a little raised, his tone a little fraught, his blink fast, as if he knew it was bullshit, but also that he had to tell the truth.

'Sorry, I . . .' Maybe it was a lack of sleep, but she was failing to make the connection. 'What do you mean you had to give it to Daisy?'

'For a tip, for looking after us all. Georgie was watching, everyone was, and I know that the restaurant owners talk to other customers. Word gets around. Mum and Dad were shelling out for the whole meal, and it felt like the right thing to do. It was the least I could do.' His fingers drummed the countertop. 'I felt backed into a corner, Jules. It's not easy for a man like me to have to admit that I had to go begging to my wife for scraps!'

This was typical: his need to show off, to be seen to be flash, to sustain the illusion. It was true to form but no less gut wrenching because of that.

'But you didn't come begging to me! You quietly, secretly *borrowed* it.'

He ignored the implication. 'It was only a hundred and fifty quid.' He shook his head as if the amount made the difference.

'So, how much of it did you give her?' Biting her lip, she did her best to keep her rage at bay.

'How much?' He licked his lips. 'All of it. I gave her all of it.'

Julie let out a laugh that was part raspberry. The news was bizarre and typical! And his announcement left her breathless. She spoke now with her hand on her chest. 'Are you serious? You gave the waitress my last hundred and fifty quid? You gave it to the *waitress*, just so the owners might tell another customer, who has probably never heard of you, that you gave a big tip?'

'You don't get it—' he began.

'No, Loz, *you* don't get it! I stood in that shop with three things in my hands: a box of bloody cereal, some milk and chocolates for your mother, and I couldn't pay for them, and all the while Daisy or Darcy or whatever her bloody name is, gets to roll around in her hundred-and-fifty-quid tip, no doubt trying to work out how many new lipsticks it'll buy her! Jesus Christ!'

'I have a reputation—'

'And I have near empty cupboards and an almost empty bloody fridge!' She cut him short. 'I was so humiliated! Standing there with three measly items that I couldn't pay for, and I thought I was being smart, thought I'd put enough away in that little purse for moments just like that.'

She hadn't meant to yell, but it was as if a force greater than her was pulling the strings, a force that had lain dormant for the longest time. She watched him slink back in his seat. It was unusual for her to shout. But now, she figured, was the time for shouting. She downed the rest of her tea. The facts raced around her head: he had given their money to Daisy! It was unfathomable to her, but then no more so than taking out such huge loans, lying about his income to secure their vast mortgages, fudging the figures, wasting cash on cars and shit, and then having to pack in haste to run away. All the times she had heard his garbled excuses with a rising sense of panic, too afraid to speak up, to knock his confidence with the words of proof that she knew he was talking rubbish! How she wished she'd had the confidence sooner to smash the glass, start the difficult conversation. Now was the time. Right now!

'I'd have thought that after what happened earlier, you'd want to talk about Dom.' His voice shook with nerves. His suggestion a diversionary tactic at best, if she'd had to guess, and a rather shitty one.

'I do. I do want to talk about Dom. The thing is, there's so much I want to talk about, it's hard to know where to start. But start we must, for all our sakes.'

'It's a mess, Jules. It's all a big mess.'

'Ain't that the truth.' She took a seat opposite him. They were quiet for a moment, and she was glad of the chance to let her anger settle, knowing this needed a calm approach if she was to make any headway, if she was ever going to understand the true size of the shit mountain they were trying to dig their way out of.

'We are in a mess,' she asserted, 'and we can't go backwards, only forwards. And we need to find a way to do that. It's time for some straight talking.'

'When you say "we", you mean we'll do it together?' It appeared he couldn't contain the tremble to his bottom lip or the tears that pooled in his eyes; it was hard to witness.

She nodded, knowing that to throw in the towel would be the easy thing to do, but life with Lawrence Kelleway had never been easy and she figured they weren't quite done yet.

'Yes, we'll do it together, Loz, like we always do. But things need to change, and this isn't some idle chat. I mean it – things *really* need to change. Everything needs to change. You need help, we need help. I crave the kind of stability of the lives you mock; it's what I need, what we as a family need if we are going to thrive.'

'I know, I know.' The breath caught in his throat. 'I want things to be different. I do.'

'Okay.' She took her time, working out how to phrase what needed to happen. 'Okay then. The first thing we need to do is come clean. We need to tell everyone, including your parents, that we are broke and that we are in trouble. We need to stop the lies, the performance. I can't do it anymore, Loz. I love you, God knows I love you, and I know you can't help it in a way, but it has to stop. All of it . . . We're living a lie! It's like we're a tanker whose coordinates were a little out, but every mile we travel we are heading further and further away from where we need to be. And everyone we know and everyone we love is standing on the dock, flag in hand, waiting to wave us in, but we are way off course! And even thinking about it makes me want to vomit.'

'Where is it we need to be, Melbourne?' His voice broke.

She shook her head. 'No, not Melbourne, that's done. And it's not a place we need to arrive at, it's a way of living. A way of being. I meant what I said: a simple, quiet way of life where you go out and earn what you can, and I do the same. We need to structure our debt, ask for help, do what it takes, live within our means and without being scared of it all being taken away. I want us to live without worrying about every phone call, every piece of mail and the fear of having to run.' Just the thought of a life like that was soothing. 'I can't and I won't do it anymore.'

'I hate that you and my kids are going to have to live a life like that.'

'What do you mean a life like that? It would be blissful! Sleeping soundly and not having the worry, which is exhausting. That would be success, not failure! I envy people who live like that. I envy Georgie in his granny car!'

'I wanted so much more, Jules. I wanted to be a footballer. It was so close; I could touch it!' He spoke through gritted teeth. 'They said I could go all the way, they said that to my dad, I heard them.' It was a familiar lament that tonight only served to irritate.

'Oh God, that again! Yes, I know! I know! And I wanted to be a pop star! I'd sing every night into my hairbrush. I thought I was the next Madonna, but I wasn't. I am not. I am Cassian and Domino's mum, your wife, and I would like the opportunity to like my life instead of being made to hanker after the one we can't and will never have. You're never going to be Pelé!' She rubbed her forehead.

'Pelé? I wanted to be Gazza.'

'Course you did.' She shook her head. He still had the power to do that, to make light, throw in a funny; this was how he had hooked her in, this was the man she had fallen in love with, one with humour as his weapon, but it was wearing a little thin. 'I sold the bag you bought me. My Mulberry. For grocery money. I didn't get nearly what it was worth but when it hits my account it'll help. I'm selling other stuff too: shoes, clothes, bits of jewellery, anything I can think of that will bring some cash in.'

'I can get you another bag, a better bag, a bag with—'

'God, Loz! You just don't get it, do you?' His response was a sharp reminder that words were easy and they had a long way to go before their simple life could come to fruition. His suggestion was disappointing to say the least. It required change at a fundamental level. 'I couldn't give a damn about the label on the bag or what you paid for it. It was the bag you gave me for my birthday, on the day Cassian and Domino started their new school. We got fish and chips and sat on that hill overlooking the city and you promised me it was a new start. You said that no matter where we lived or what we lived in, it was you and me against the world, that we were the gold, you and me, and that nothing else mattered.' She wiped her tears on the sleeve of her dressing gown. 'And I wanted so badly to believe you. I did believe you. I missed my mum, my family, missed a lot of things, but I would have stayed happily on the other side of the world because I believed you. I thought we were done running. I am so ashamed of not asking the right questions, of not going straight back to work when we arrived here in the UK, of giving you control and coming along for the ride!'

'I never wanted . . .' His voice cracked.

'You never wanted what?' She kept her voice low.

'I never wanted to be ordinary,' he managed, as tears spilled from his eyes. 'Mum and Dad were on cloud nine when I got given my Spurs kit – they told everyone! Showed everyone! They kept looking at me and shaking their heads like they couldn't believe it. So bloody proud! And I've spent every day since it all went tits up trying to match that feeling of success, feeling like I was someone.'

'But you are someone, Loz! You're my husband and the kids' dad and that should be enough! You need to not give a flying fuck what your parents think. You're an adult and this is your life – *our* life – not theirs.'

His whole body seemed to sag as he sank down on to the counter. 'I'm tired, Jules. I'm so tired. You know, I don't sleep either.

I lie awake for most of the night, trying to find solutions to not having enough money, trying to work out how to shuffle my debt around, robbing Peter to pay Paul and loading up credit cards to keep going, but I'm so tired . . .'

'So give it up. All of it. We need to take control, make it stop.'

'What would our life look like then?' He stared at her with red-rimmed eyes.

She laughed, a short burst of ironic laughter that she had to explain. 'Like everyone else's. The life I grew up with, which was enough. My mum and dad were happy, we were happy. In fact, I can tell you even now about the treats, the meals out, the presents because they were few and far between and therefore meant more. I see how spoiled Dom is and I know it's our fault, but things need to be different, for all our sakes.'

'I'm lucky to have you. So lucky.' His tears came again. 'And Georgie. He's a good mate. He's good for Cleo.'

'Georgie with his old lady car?' she whispered, hoping to remind him that his cruel barbs had no place in their lives.

'I can get used to driving an old lady car.'

'You'll have to,' she pointed out. 'We need to sell the house before it's taken from us, settle our debts, hand the cars back, give up the timeshare and the gym membership, stop buying all the shit we don't need, and we need to refocus. And do what we can. We need to be proactive, take back control, work hard to get straight – I don't care what job I do. I know you've never wanted me to work, and I agreed so readily! But I'm going to, I have to.'

He didn't object. Didn't rail against it or mention how he didn't want people to think he couldn't look after his family, as she had suspected he might, but instead nodded and reached for her hand.

For the first time in as long as she could remember, she felt like she could breathe, knowing this was what it would feel like, she guessed, not to live on the knife edge of worry, waiting and dreading the knock on the door. It gave her hope for the kind of future she had outlined, and it was tinged with sweet relief.

'I love you, Loz.' She climbed from her seat and walked around to his side of the breakfast bar, holding his head against her chest, liking the feel of him holding her close in return. It had been months since they had shared this kind of closeness, as if his edginess and her worry covered them both in spikes.

'I love you too.' He sniffed. 'You're right. We need to talk. I want to get it all off my chest, all of it. I want to tell you everything and I want us to put it all behind us and move on, Jules.' There was a quake to his words that told her how sincere he was.

She closed her eyes, thankful that he had come around. Feeling, if anything, a little excited about the new shape of their lives. Looking out of the window, this felt like a new dawn in every sense.

'Yes. I think that's what needs to happen.' It was about time she fully understood exactly how much trouble they were in financially. She wanted him to open up about the borrowing, the deals, the business plans, the hands shaken on schemes with the likes of Micky Tate, and promises that bubbled away in the background, all built on the most fragile of foundations. It felt about time he trusted her with the information and allowed her to help him find solutions. Because that's what families did: they stuck together and they helped each other.

'This isn't easy for me to say,' he began, his voice uncharacteristically quiet.

'I know, babe, but it needs to happen and then with nothing unknown between us we can move on, rebuild, start over and be happy with our lot in life. That's all I've ever wanted.' Her smile now was genuine and wide. This could be the start for them, a new beginning.

His fingers dug into her hips, as if he was clinging on, and she ran her palm over his scalp, as he took a deep breath. If anything, she admired him, felt proud, knowing this was a pivotal moment.

'When things were bad, when the kids were younger, and my creditors were just about to pull the plug, just before we decided to go to Oz, I was in a bad place. A really bad place.'

'I remember.' And she did: he used to prowl like a caged animal until the early hours, almost in a trance, running through numbers in his head, he explained, like trying to solve a maths riddle.

Question: if Julie has one hundred and fifty pounds and Lawrence gives one hundred and fifty pounds away, how much does Julie have left to buy her family food?

Answer: the square root of sweet Fanny Adams.

'I felt so alone,' he murmured.

'Me too.' Again, the truth. And it was on a day of sweet reconnection, with the sun breaking through the clouds, a shared bag of fish and chips, sitting on a hill overlooking the city of Melbourne in the country they had chosen to make their home that he gave her the bag. A lovely thing, a gift for their cherished new start.

'I went to see my mum and dad one night, a few months before we left, and bumped into Lisa next door.'

Daisy's mum, Lisa Harrop, poor girl . . . Julie didn't know her, not really. Knew of her, of course, but by all accounts, she was a bit of a troubled one, depression or something, she wasn't sure.

'I cheated on you, Jules.'

She moved her arms so she could see his face and stared at him, convinced she must have misheard. It made no sense; she'd thought he said . . .

'What?' It felt as if her legs belonged to someone else as they trembled. Her heart raced and her fingers shook. 'What?' She could only repeat. The room suddenly felt airless.

'I . . . I cheated on you. I cheated on you.'

She took a step backwards.

'Oh!'

It was a lament, a moment of impact, the crashing down of the emotional fortress that she thought she lived within. Infidelity was not something she had felt concerned with. Never. It was a thought that hadn't troubled her, not ever. Not with Lawrence. Her Lawrence who was rubbish with money, who made bad choices about careers and who had ideas and plans far bigger than he could ever deliver, but the fact that he tried at all was, for her, something to be admired. He wasn't a bad person, just a trusting one; a man with issues that meant he didn't know when to quit, to say no, to come clean . . . But cheating on her, having sex with someone else? No. Not him. She would have staked the last bank note in her purse that he would never, ever do that to her. That was if he hadn't taken her last bank note and given it as a tip to Daisy.

Her stomach felt like it dropped to her feet. Light-headed, she staggered backwards until she hit the wall and slid down it, sitting with her knees raised and her head falling forward. She couldn't look at him. It felt like the room was spinning. She closed her eyes.

'I don't believe it. I don't. Not you. You cheated on me?' She needed it confirmed, because despite understanding what he had said, it made no sense! She had never thought – never – that he could . . . that he might . . . She felt her breath come in shallow bursts.

'I'm sorry! And if I could turn back time—'

'Who . . . who with?' she interrupted him; to hear his apology was like lighting the touchpaper.

Lawrence blinked quickly and his lip stuck to his teeth; he was nervous, she could tell, but that was just too bloody bad. Anger wrapped in humiliation had started to edge out her shock.

'Lisa,' he whispered.

'Lisa next door to Winnie? Daisy's mum?' She of course knew which Lisa he meant, there was only one Lisa, but still it felt so impossible she needed to hear it confirmed.

He nodded.

She placed her hand over her mouth to stop the vomit reaching her lips.

'No!' She shook her head. 'No. I can't believe it, Loz, I can't. It's like a bad dream. I never, ever thought . . . I can't believe it!' She was well aware of her repetition, but no other words seemed fitting.

He got down from the chair and came to where she sat on the floor, crouching, imploring. 'Listen to me, Jules.' He grabbed her arms and fixed his gaze on her face, his tone urgent. This wasn't the first time he'd done this: physically held her as if this might make his words more earnest, his determination more keenly felt, his spiel more believable.

'*Listen to me, Jules, we can start over – we can go to Australia! Leave our worries here and go live in the sunshine! It will be paradise!*'

'*Listen to me, Jules, we can start over – go back to the UK, and leave our worries here, go live a quiet life! It will be paradise!*'

She grimaced at the thought of what he might say and how many times he might think they could crisscross the globe, running, reinventing, with the same high expectations, the same lies, only for it all to come crashing down when the one common denominator that they couldn't outrun or hide from messed up yet again. And that common denominator was him. *Him.*

Armed with the knowledge of what he had done and with these thoughts, her desire to move forward together, as a couple, began to slip from her. Replaced with a cold, hard resolution that enough was actually enough. Looking towards the door as he held her fast, she couldn't wait to be away from him, so she could breathe, think, plan . . .

'And I know this sounds harsh, but it was no big deal,' he began, and she smarted at the disservice he did them both. The flippant way he discarded the issue and the fact that he must think she was very stupid. It was clear he now wanted to talk, wanted to get it all off his chest and maybe for him it was cathartic. But his words were like smoke, twisting and twirling high above them, filling her lungs and throat with their essence and leaving her a little breathless.

He gabbled on. 'We used to have a thing when we were at school. Lisa and me. We'd meet up when our parents were out – it was just sex really.'

Lisa and me . . . Lisa and me . . . Lisa and me . . .

She stayed silent, letting him spill the words that spewed from him, each one incriminating, each one like a scythe to the delicate stays that had held her fast for so long but which in recent times had been slowly fraying. Each one a blade to sever the excuses that had kept her tethered to him.

'It was just sex then and it was just sex when I cheated. That's all,' he repeated, and his naivety made her cringe. It seemed he couldn't stop talking, filling the quiet space with admissions and confessions as if they might counter her silence. Each word a rock hurled at her head.

'I went over that night to see Mum and Dad and tell them we were going to emigrate, and she was on the path where we used to meet at the side of the garden, and I was confused, lost, scared, and we just . . . it just . . .'

'How long?' She coughed to clear the distress from her throat. 'How long were you seeing her before we went away?'

'Not long, two months, three . . .'

Months! Not just one time, but months . . . She thought she might vomit.

'When was the last time you slept with her? How long before we left for Australia?'

'Why does that matter?'

'When Lawrence?' She wanted – no, needed – the detail.

'I don't know, ten days . . .'

Ten days! She thought about that frantic yet exciting time before they boarded the plane for their new lives down under. Packing bags, saying her goodbyes, placating the kids, reassuring her parents, thinking about the journey. And every night longing to feel the arms of the man she loved around her, telling her that everything was going to be okay, because this was their fresh start, this was the new beginning they had been waiting for. And all the while he was having sex with Lisa, the girl next door. She felt the rise of bile in her throat.

'It meant nothing. She's nothing! When I got to the airport, just before we flew, I deleted her number from my phone and I went into the Mulberry shop and bought you that bag. I kept it for your birthday. I knew I wanted to get you something nice, wanted to give you a gift that you'd carry every day, a reminder of how much I love you, our new life . . .'

Julie opened her mouth to speak, but nothing came out. She was mute. Struck dumb with the shock of his admission. She had never suspected in a million years, of all his crimes – his lies, his deceit – infidelity had not entered her mind. And because it never entered hers, naïvely, she had thought they were the same. Honouring the vows they took while Winnie sobbed, and her own parents beamed at the great catch she had landed. What a farce.

'And then when we were away, I put her out of my head, forgot about it completely. In my mind, it made sense – it was like, because we'd been together as teenagers, it didn't really feel like cheating. I managed to forget about it.'

None of it makes sense . . . Poor Lisa . . . Poor me . . .

'And then at Mum and Dad's after the dinner last night, I saw her again.'

Julie exhaled as if she'd been punched in the gut. It was the sound of a woman winded and wounded.

'You . . . you slept with her again last night?' She closed her eyes as if this might prevent her seeing and hearing more.

'No, of course not! But she was blabbing about letting it out, after all this time, how she thought it might fuck up both our families, and how worried she'd been about her husband finding out.'

Julie pictured the bearded man she'd seen shuffling in and out of the house next door to Winnie, always in his work clothes. Working hard to live his ordinary life, a life made dishonest, a lie, by his wife's deceit. Her heart went out to him.

'Is she going to tell him?' Her voice was small, reed thin and brittle with emotion. She felt unbelievably sad for Jake, Daisy, and the man with the heavy tread in the red polo shirt.

'I don't think so.' He cried again but this time his tears repulsed her. Staring at the man she didn't know at all, she felt numb; sick and numb.

'Do you love her?' She could barely stand to ask, the words like glass on her tongue.

He shook his head, snot and tears snaking into his mouth. 'No! I love you!'

'My God.' She felt her body sink until her cheek lay on the oak flooring. This was where she needed to be, flat and horizontal so she couldn't fall. His words echoed.

'I promise you, Jules, I promise you that it all means nothing to me – not the sex, not Lisa, not any of it. I love you! I love our family! If I could turn back time and wipe it all out, I would; if I could do things differently, I would. But I can't, so all we can do is go forward, like you said. We go forward together, start over, lead a happy life.'

'Do Winnie and Bernie know?' she managed.

'No. No one knows, just Lisa and me, and now you.'

Cassian and Jake were the very best of friends and all the while their parents . . . The thought was more than she could process.

'There's no need for anyone else to know; what would it serve? No need to upset the kids or her family or Mum or Dad, no need for any of that.' He wiped his face and took a deep breath.

His words confirmation of another lie, another topic over which they would put their heads in the sand. He slunk down beside her and wrapped his arms around her and there they lay, with him breathing into her hair, crying, begging for forgiveness, and rocking her like she was a child . . . a child who was supposed to absorb this latest subterfuge. A scheme of a different kind, but this time not one with money at its heart, but sex.

It was pathetic, so clichéd and easy, she was repulsed. She pictured Daisy, the gangly girl, only a year older than Domino, whose mother had had sex with Lawrence. Daisy, a girl who looked like a rabbit caught in the headlights, as if life was a bit more than she could handle, and this Julie Kelleway more than understood.

Lawrence's phone pinged in his pocket. Letting go of her, he reached for it and sat up, before reading the text out loud.

'Cleo's had a little boy. Mother and baby doing well.' His lip trembled as if more tears were imminent.

She stared at him, thinking about the child who had been born into the Kelleway clan. She was pleased for Cleo and Georgie but felt already that this news might be nothing to do with her and it therefore might be preferable to keep a certain distance.

'How lovely.' She stood, wanting to shower, to wash away his touch, his scent and to clear her thoughts. Because she might be fuddle-brained with shock, but one thing was for sure: when it came to Lawrence and his fucking parents, their golden veneer was most definitely dulled to reveal the true colour, and it was dark. Very dark.

CHAPTER THIRTEEN

WINNIE KELLEWAY

Winnie stood at the kitchen counter, still tingling with euphoria from the previous day's celebrations and pleased she had bothered to get everything cleaned up and shipshape last night before bed. It had been a faff, but there was nothing worse than coming down to a messy kitchen. To see the shiny surfaces and clean sink gave her a feeling of wellbeing. Bernie was still snoring, the little love, so she'd let him be and take him up a decent coffee with a frothy top and a biscuit when she heard him stir. He'd had more than a skinful last night, and why not? It wasn't every day they were going to hit a milestone like forty years! Not that her sister had chosen to acknowledge it. Jealousy was, she reminded herself, a terrible thing.

Winnie's requirements for sleep seemed to lessen as she aged. Not that she minded. It was in those early hours when the rest of the house slumbered and the world seemed quiet that she achieved the most: dusting in awkward places, polishing her ornaments, sweeping the patio free of leaves. The quiet hours she called them; just her, birdsong, the purr of the coffee machine and her phone to scroll through while she stood at the French doors and looked out over the garden. Bliss.

Wondering if anything was happening with Cleo, she checked her messages. But there was nothing from either her or Georgie. No harm, she figured, in firing off a quick text – nothing too pushy or invasive, just a quick reminder that she was on standby.

ANYTHING TO REPORT? X

She guessed not. Georgie might be hapless, but at least he was a good communicator. An over-communicator, if anything; he was always texting, emailing, calling, dropping in. Jeez, didn't he have his own family to irritate? She knew that was mean, but it made her laugh a little anyway.

Tightening her cotton kimono dressing gown around her waist, she checked her hair in the hallway mirror. Her blow dry was holding strong, and this too made her happy. It was important to her, her appearance. Opening the front door, she stood on the step and breathed in the fresh morning air. Glancing along the street towards the four oaks that stood in all their magnificence, she decided to call Mr Portland. He'd have a better idea of what to do about the whole fiasco, because presumably it was in his interest to make sure areas like this retained their value, their prestige . . . Plus it would be a good excuse to engage with him, even introduce him to Cleo . . . This thought seemed to ignite the sparks of excitement that lingered in her gut, as memories of the previous night danced in her thoughts.

How beautiful had Cass and Dom looked? Such stunning kids . . .

Lawrence was so funny! What was it he said? 'You get less for murder!' How they'd laughed! He was so witty!

And the cake! Everyone had loved it.

Bernie's speech – Bernie's very public speech – there'd not been a dry eye in the house . . . it had been perfect. Absolutely perfect. It was important that everyone present see and hear how happy, how lucky, she and Bernie were, and they had.

Sidling down by the old garage between the wall and the fence where spiders lurked, she found it hard to lift the recycling bin. Huffing and puffing she dragged it along the passageway by the side of the house, hating the scraping noise of its plastic corners on the path. It was three parts full and heavy. There was no denying this was a rigmarole, but it was worth the effort to have the bins stashed out of sight. How she hated to see them abandoned and grubby, lids flapping, food leaching from the sides – and all right there on the pavement for the world to see – or worse, shoved in front of a house, spoiling the view. It didn't take much effort to pop them away. She couldn't understand why other people didn't take as much pride in their homes as she did. It wasn't hard, was it? Mow grass, pick up litter, grab a paintbrush . . . she was thankful her thoughts were not words when a voice called over the driveway, alerting her to his presence.

'Do you need a hand there, Mrs Kelleway?'

He was, as usual, in heavy work boots, grey slacks and a red polo shirt, either off out to work early or else he'd slept in his clothes. She watched as he ground the butt of a cigarette under his heel into the path and exhaled the bluish smoke to taint the glorious morning air.

Smoking, eugh! It made her shudder.

'Oh, bless you, Marty. No, I'm fine, I'm fine. I'm stronger than I look!' She flexed her slender muscles inside her dressing gown and smiled at the man who lived next door.

He nodded, his expression one of relief.

'Did you hear about the tree?' She pointed in their general direction.

'Yes, I read the letter. Not sure what we're supposed to do about it though? A dead tree is a dead tree, right? If it's a danger, I'd rather they took it down than let it fall.'

'Well, I'm not going to admit defeat. I'll be speaking to Mr Portland – do you know him? Drives a blue Porsche?'

Marty shook his head as if he didn't have the first clue what she was talking about. She decided to change the subject.

'Lisa all right?' she asked as she positioned the bin in front of their garden office, ready to receive the bottles and cans from last night's celebrations, which lay in a bucket in the back garden.

'She's great.'

'Good! Give her my love.'

He nodded and went inside. It made her think about how time flew. There was Lisa, his wife, mother to two grown-up kids, when Winnie recalled, like it was only yesterday, how Lisa's mother, Mrs Knowles, had near yelled the house down when her labour became a little more than she could bear, and Lisa had popped into the world. But that was Mrs Knowles all over: dramatic. *God rest her soul* . . .

Lawrence and Lisa were about the same age – the same year at school, certainly – but the girl was never . . . what was the word? Never really the sort of person that Lawrence would be interested in. She wasn't nasty or dumb, nothing like that, but a boy like Lawrence was always going places and a girl like Lisa . . . well, Winnie didn't want to say she knew best, but proof of the pudding was in the fact that the girl still lived next door in her mother's house with the lovely but unambitious Marty. Marty, who worked at the sorting office and who, in her humble opinion, needed a good shave and a decent haircut. Enough said.

Not that she had anything against manual labour – good Lord no! Physical work was something she respected and understood. It just wasn't for someone like her. And look at how far she'd come. She smiled, stooping to retrieve a wisp of grass that dared poke its head through the gravel, thinking again about the scene of extravagance in the restaurant last night, and Bernie's speech which everyone had heard. *Everyone.* It was about as far from a life of manual labour as she could imagine. A wonderful life.

Her own father had dug ditches for a living. Yes! Ditches! Going out in all weathers with the wooden handle of a shovel in his palm that over the years wore the skin where it touched shiny and hard, until it was not like skin at all, but more a glove into which the spade fitted. As if he had evolved to accommodate the tool and not the other way around. Making him and his shovel one and the same. She'd watch him walk the front path each morning, usually before sunup, stopping at the gate to wave to her as she knelt on her bed, alerted by the sound of the front door opening, with a thick wool blanket, issued in wartime, about her shoulders to ward off the chill. She'd wipe the condensation, frost, or ice from the inside of the window and wave back, believing it might give him a lift to his day. His grey, hollow face would break into a smile as if that little wave was all the fuel he needed. Far better than any warm grub that might line his gut and help stave off the cold.

When he died young, no doubt worn out from all that digging, she'd stared at his pyjama-clad body, noticing, possibly for the first time, the frailty of it: the stoop of his spine, as if the years on the job had worn him down so much that his body had finally acquiesced and moulded itself to the shape of his temperament; the tight, hard knots of muscle sitting under his translucent skin; and the lack of fat making him look sicker than he'd felt. He was buried not a day when her mother grabbed the damn implement from the front hallway and carried it outside.

'What are you doing?' Patricia had asked as their mother held the spade out in front of her as if it were contaminated, dirty or both.

'I'm going to burn it! I'm going to burn the bloody thing!'

Usually a quiet, contained woman, it was the only time they'd heard their mother cuss. At the time Winnie put it down to grief, but as the years passed, she wondered if it was nothing of the sort, but a futile hatred of the implement that had robbed her of the kind man she loved. The kind man who without the confidence to use his wits, gave his body in service of mud, so that they could eat, put coal on the fire once a day, and, at Christmas, feast on a goose so fat and a plum pudding so vast they felt like queens!

Winnie understood her mother's hatred of that shovel, knew what it felt like to fixate on one thing that felt to blame for spoiling what should and could have been the most lovely life.

Her dad had died aged forty, but with the bones and defeated manner of a man double that age. At his funeral, Winnie could only think about two things: first, the way he'd waved to her each morning, digging just for her, her sister, and the woman he loved. And second: she was determined to make a success of her life, determined to have goose and plum pudding any day she wanted, because when you were poor, life was tough, harsh and she was not going to see any man she loved put into an early grave with the effort of it.

Turning, she took in the façade of the house next door. 'Shabby' was the word.

It had been a relief to hear that Lisa was well; she couldn't remember the last time she'd seen her. A bit of a hermit in recent times by all accounts. Cleo had mentioned she thought the girl might have depression, and that would be rotten. Winnie had read an article saying that a good walk and plenty of spinach cured depression. Maybe she'd look it up and put it in an envelope – just in case anyone might need it. Would it be too obvious to pop it next door? She only wanted to help. Plus, if Lisa's depression got cured then maybe, just maybe, she'd find the inclination to smarten up the house – something from which they could all only benefit.

It seemed to her, though, that things like depression ran in families. Thank goodness hers was not afflicted. Not that it was a surprise; what did they have to be depressed about? They all had wonderful, happy lives. Last night and the glorious evening just spent was proof of that. Her cheese board had been a resounding success, even if Julie had returned without the chocolates that would have made serving coffee perfect. Not that she'd ever say anything, but she was fairly certain her daughter-in-law had deliberately tried to put a dent in her celebrations. Who in the world goes out to buy chocolates and then returns saying they couldn't find a parking space or some other odd excuse? The whole thing was most peculiar. Winnie was sure Julie had been lying. But no, she wouldn't say anything, wouldn't give Julie the satisfaction, and besides, she would never embarrass Lawrence by troubling him with it. She didn't want to sound petty.

Making her way back inside, she let her eyes linger over the elaborate display of roses – *lucky, lucky me . . .*

With her phone in her hand and paying no heed to the early hour she fired off a text to Mr Portland.

Good morning Mr Portland, Winnifred Kelleway here. We live in Four Oaks, you might remember me as the lady whose son lives on Newman Road? I'd be most grateful if you could give me a call or drop by on a most urgent matter about which I need your sage advice. Many thanks, Mrs Kelleway.

She added her address for good measure.

Her phone pinged with the sound of a text; she was delighted by the man's prompt reply, but closer inspection revealed it was not from Mr Portland. It was in fact a message from Georgie – it took a while for her eyes to register that it was an image.

'Oh, my goodness! Oh, will you look at that!'

Her heart flexed at the sight of the tiny baby in a little blue knitted hat that graced her screen. Underneath was written:

Hello Grandma Winnie – here I am, your new grandson! Looking forward to meeting you when Mummy and I come home later! Born just after 3 a.m. I weigh 7lb 2oz and I'm very handsome!

Feeling more than a little overcome with emotion, she leaned on the table in the hallway. Again, she studied the image of a baby boy with a squashed face and tiny, tiny fingers. He was beautiful! The newest member of the family. Instinctively she held the locket at her neck and swallowed the tears that gathered at the back of her throat. *Little Louis . . .* how she missed him still.

'Morning, Nan.'

Spinning around towards the stairs she had almost forgotten that Cassian had stayed over.

'Morning, darling! And what a morning it is, look at this! Look who's arrived!'

She held out her phone and watched as Cassian took the phone into his hands and smiled.

'Ah, that's lovely. What's he called?'

'I don't know! Probably not got a name yet or I think Georgie would have said.'

'When was he born?' her grandson asked, as he made his way to the kitchen and reached for a glass from the shelf.

'Three a.m. apparently.' She gave a small laugh to mask her embarrassment. It bothered her that this was the first she knew of her grandson's birth – a picture of him, freshly arrived. The deal had been that Georgie would make contact when Cleo went into labour, so she and Bernie could be on standby, or at least be able to share the excitement of what was about to happen. They had agreed this several times! What did he think? That they might turn up at the hospital with a balloon? The more she considered this exclusion the angrier she felt about it. They had agreed!

'I just got a text from Dad.' Cassian held up his phone. 'To tell me Auntie Cleo has had the baby; I guess it's doing the rounds!'

'I was going to call him and let him know,' she added curtly. 'I wonder who else knows? Oh, I do hope they haven't put it on Facebook or anything like that. Not that it would surprise me.'

'I think everyone puts everything on Facebook nowadays.' Her grandson offered the depressing view.

'Mmm.' The only way she could express her disapproval without being explicit. It upset her that she didn't know how Cleo was, what kind of birth she'd had and, as Cassian had pointed out, whether this new addition even had a name! Why was she being left out like this? What had she done to deserve it? Christ, hadn't she and Bernie bought the cot, the pram, the bloody car seat?

I bet Georgie has filled in his parents with all the details. What a mean thing to do. Oh God! They might have even seen the baby already, how is that fair? Cleo is my daughter, the mother of this child!

Her phone rang, it was Cleo!

'Darling!'

'Hey, Mum.'

'Oh, darling girl! How are you?'

'I'm . . .' Winnie recognised the faint, slow speech of someone either in a state of euphoria, shock or still a little drug-addled, possibly all three. 'I'm brilliant. He's here, I can't believe it, but he's here.'

'Congratulations, I'm so proud of you, so proud! And I can't wait to meet him.'

'I'm coming home today!'

'You are? You didn't have to have a caesarean? I know there was talk . . .'

'Nope. All very straightforward and a little quick once we got going. We didn't even call you, didn't call anyone, quite swept up in the moment. Just arrived at the hospital, straight in and whoosh, here he is. I mean, not *whoosh*, but you know what I mean.'

'I do know what you mean and don't worry about letting us know; I didn't give it a second thought. You just did what you needed to do and now he's here! That's all that matters. Does he have a name?'

'Not yet. Well, we're almost there. Anyway, look, better go as I promised to call Georgie's mum too. She still doesn't know. We'll come straight to you, Mum, if that's okay?'

'Oh, it's more than okay! Of course, I can't wait. Take care, my darling. And well done, Cleo, well done, my girl.'

'All okay?' Cassian asked from the sink where he sipped water.

'Yes! I'm the first gran to know; they haven't told Georgie's mother yet.' She liked the fact she had been chosen to know before Georgie's mother, feeling it gave her a certain status. 'They're going to come straight here from the hospital. Isn't that wonderful? Cleo will be tired, but we can all rally around, welcome the little chap and make him feel at home.' It was satisfying to know it was her side of the family that the little chap would meet first.

'That'll be good. I'm going home first though, Nan. I want to have a shower and get changed.'

'Of course, darling, see you in a bit. I'm going to take your grandad a nice coffee and break the wonderful news.'

'A new little Richardson!' Cassian raised his glass as if in a toast.

'Well' – Winnie studied the image of her grandson – 'technically, I suppose, but his mother is a Kelleway, and he certainly *looks* like a Kelleway.' She turned the picture so Cassian could see it. 'Don't you think?'

CHAPTER FOURTEEN

MARTY HARROP

'*Give her my love!*' Marty Harrop parroted as he shut the back door, imitating the woman next door and her fake, slightly nasal tone that got right on his goat. There was something about her, the way she looked at him, the way she let her eyes dart behind him as if checking out the house, while trying not to; what did she want, a guided tour? And the way she spoke with a tone that reminded him of someone who'd arrived at the scene of an accident and was trying to keep the situation calm. He couldn't help it; she irritated the shit out of him. It bothered him, the way she smiled while unable to hide her judgement. He could well imagine the kind of slurs that passed back and forth across their breakfast table.

He still hasn't shaved . . .

Would it kill him to pick up a paintbrush?

What would old Mrs Knowles say if she could see the place?

Well, what would Mrs Knowles, his mother-in-law, say? He often wondered this himself and hoped that she'd thank him for keeping her family safe, for doing his very best for her daughter, for loving her without judgement or pressure, and for working his hardest to ensure his children would have choices he hadn't.

Not that it was always easy, and this last week, with tiredness lapping at his heels, he was finding things tough. In the past, when the kids were small, no matter how hard his day, with the support of Lisa, the love of Lisa, the *joy* of Lisa to come home to, it had made everything feel better. He missed it.

He closed the front door behind him quietly, not wanting to wake the kids. Jake who he knew would have been out with Cassian or on his computer until late, gaming no doubt. And Daisy who had worked her shift at the Italian restaurant in town. He loved her work ethic, knowing it would be the key to her success. He was so very proud of them both. Jake was kind with a whip-smart sense of humour that could defuse any situation. And what he lacked in confidence, he more than made up for in initiative. Not for the first time Marty closed his eyes and hoped that the grades his son needed to take up his apprenticeship would be forthcoming. Electrical engineering . . . that was to be Jake's calling and oh how proud he would be to tell whoever asked what his son was up to. For Marty it was simple: he could toil all day every day in that big old warehouse, with aching knees, a twinging back, and failing eyesight, sorting mail, pressing buttons, shifting blockages on the line, putting up with his moaning colleagues, moving canvas trolleys that bulged with all kinds of packages, ferrying them from one place to another, stopping for two breaks and one lunch, digitally clocking in and clocking out, counting the hours, calculating his bonus, doing overtime and putting in the grind because he saw himself as no more than a conduit that would allow his children to be whatever they wanted to be. Some might disapprove of his role in life as a sacrificial lamb, working hard and saving so his kids could benefit, but he saw it more as a privilege. The thought of their glorious future is what drove him.

And Daisy . . . where to begin. Sweet, funny Daisy. He had known she was smart when not yet aged two she had picked up a book and turned the pages, making gobbledygook noises and pointing at the words, as if she knew it should be read, understood enough to turn the pages and scan the images, but was unaware of how to link it all together, to sound out the words. Not that it took her long and by the age of six she was reading Harry Potter, the weighty volumes that some adults shied away from. By eight she was studying maths for fun and asking questions at the dinner table that neither he nor his wife had any hope of answering to her satisfaction.

'So how do we actually measure space?' she'd asked with a speared piece of fishfinger on her fork, her little nose wrinkled, waiting and wanting someone to help her figure it all out. 'I mean, how do we know how much space there is out there? Where does it start and where does it end? I can't hold it in my head!' She'd closed her eyes briefly as if even the thought was frustrating.

He and Lisa had looked at each other and laughed, not mockingly, but more that they were so full of joy at their daughter's smarts, and equally just as flummoxed as how to best answer.

Her grades were matched only by her industry as year after year she pocketed science awards, certificates and prizes that each spoke of and confirmed her promise. She had her sights firmly set on Cambridge and he was determined to help her get there. For her to be given such talent, it would feel nothing short of negligent for him not to do everything in his power to turn that promise into a life she would love. And while he may not, on his rather crappy wage, have been able to provide new shoes, fancy holidays and designer brands, he figured his dedication to her life goals was the best gift of all.

He had been deep in thought when Winnie next door had spied him, thinking about how it was time – time to get Lisa help whether she wanted it or not. He had made enquiries, had uncomfortable, covert, guilt-inducing conversations with helplines and their own GP, trying to understand what assistance was available and how much of it required his wife's approval. The issue was, whilst he would always, always respect her autonomy, her very illness made her an unreliable decision-maker. It was a quandary.

Marty firmly believed, however, that to do nothing was not an option, not anymore. Things had deteriorated too far for that. They needed to find a way out of the dark forest that entombed them because if things didn't change, he feared Lisa might not be the first to reach absolute breaking point. Unwilling to admit to the feelings of hopelessness that had made him on more than one occasion look at the whisky bottle in the wee small hours and wonder if there were any pills lurking in drawers that he could wash down with the warm liquor . . . to slip away, to find peace. He could certainly, when the night was long and lonely, see the attraction in it. Any thought of his kids, however, was enough to snap him out of it, not that it had been any less scary for that.

It was as he mulled over the uncomfortable next steps that he stopped short in the doorway. It was a surprise and shock to see Lisa sitting at the kitchen table at this early hour; in fact, a surprise to see her sitting there at all. Hers was a horizontal life, spent wrapped in a blanket on the sagging sofa, or wrapped in a blanket on their sagging bed. It was a shock, too, that the blind was up and the window open, a fresh breeze whipping around the walls. This one small act was enough to lighten the stagnant air that usually filled his lungs with a lurking weight of anxiety. *How were they going to get through the day? How was Lisa's illness and distance going to affect their kids? Had he remembered to get milk? What time did his shift start?*

'Morning.' He settled on this as his greeting, rejecting, '*You're up!*' and, '*Well, hello stranger!*' because she might mistake them as something adversarial or goading and the last thing he wanted to do was hurt her feelings or fight.

It was wonderful! His wife was up, dressed, awake and present – in every sense, present. The damp hair about her shoulders told him she'd showered and this he knew was real progress. There had been days and days that had gone by without her washing, lifting her head from the pillow or cleaning her teeth. The sour smell of her in the bedroom so strong that he preferred to sleep on the couch. He hoped she didn't know this, hoped she never knew this, aware that for the woman he loved, personal hygiene was cruelly relegated in the face of her illness, and equally just how hurt she would be to hear it.

It had not always been this way, far from it. Only four years ago, she was the fuel that kept the engine of their lives turning, the one who knew stuff – like the Wi-Fi password, the due dates for insurance policies and dental appointments, what food lurked in the cupboards and exactly what everyone needed or wanted by way of a birthday or Christmas gift. She had been fun: the brightness on a gloomy day, the voice of enthusiasm for any task or suggestion. She had been wonderful! That was unfair, she was still wonderful, but was now wonderful with the veil of melancholy thrown over her. Despite his very best efforts and so many suggestions of how she might seek help, he felt powerless to assist her.

But here she was!

He felt optimism flare in his gut at the sight of her, reminding himself not to expect too much, that lucid moments, engaged conversations, even whole good days had come and gone before. But in a place where gloom and despondency had been unwanted houseguests, he'd take the small signs of hope and hold them fast.

'Morning.' Her voice was clearer than he'd heard for a while and again the joy he felt at this one simple thing, which most would take for granted, threw him with the strength of it.

'You look great.'

'I washed my hair.' She held his eyeline as she tucked her long, beautiful hair behind her ears.

'Ah, that'll be it.' He smiled and pulled up the chair opposite her at the table.

'You're not off to work today?' she asked, her gaze narrowed, as if she'd forgotten it was Saturday or was thrown by the fact he was still in his clothes.

'No, not today. But I fell asleep and then when I got up it felt easier to stay in these.' He plucked at the polo shirt. 'It's the height of laziness, but also the comfiest thing imaginable when your clothes are soft from wear and you're already warm and you can go outside to smoke without fear of being seen by Old Lady Kelleway lugging the bins out . . .'

She laughed, a real laugh, a small laugh, but enough to put a great big chunk of sunshine into his mood. He knew she liked it when he called their neighbour this.

'I hear ya!' She tapped the tabletop, and it took all of his strength not to grab her pale hand, crush her fingers to his mouth with kisses, to howl his relief that for this moment at least, he felt whole and not cleaved apart by having to witness the shell of the woman he married, hidden beneath a blanket in all weathers.

'The kids still asleep?' He knew they were, but wanted to keep the conversation light, easy and untaxing.

'I think so.' She looked up towards the ceiling. 'Did you hear about Daisy's tip?'

'No.' He leaned forward, elbows on the table. 'What tip?'

'At work last night it was Winnie and Bernie's ruby wedding anniversary dinner. They had a big table and a big old supper.'

'Of course they did!' He rolled his eyes. 'Biggest table in the house, the most wine drunk. I can only imagine.'

'Well, save your judgement, because they gave Daisy a whopping tip.'

'How much?' He cut to the chase, thinking it must be around the fifty quid mark to have made such an impact on his wife.

'One hundred and fifty pounds.' She stared at him. 'One hundred and fifty pounds!'

'Jesus!' He put his hand over his mouth as emotion flared, partly in delight and a little overwhelmed by the generous gift his girl had received, but also because anyone looking in through the window would see a normal scene: a husband and wife at the kitchen table, chatting, catching up . . . He had dreamed of mornings like this.

'She said she might get her bike fixed up. I know she's been hankering after a basket for a while now.'

'I'm so pleased for her!' He meant it, caring less that the cash had come from Old Lady Kelleway – money was money. 'She deserves it.'

'I love you, Marty.'

Her words were like nectar for his soul! They warmed him and filled him right up. Placing her mug on the tabletop, she let her fingers move slowly towards his hand until they came to rest on the back of his. He placed his other hand on top and loved the feeling, the contact, skin to skin, which had been missing for the longest time. She was trembling and it tore at his heart; his beautiful, wounded wife.

'It's important you know it, Marty, and how much . . . how much I value you. Appreciate you.'

'And I . . .' He coughed to clear the emotion that pulled his words taut. 'I love you too, Lis, I really do.'

'Don't cry.' She scooted her chair until it was next to his and laid her arm across his back. 'Don't cry, my Marty.'

'I miss you!' He hadn't meant to let it out, hadn't meant to give in to the emotion he kept in check most of the time, but that was of little consideration now as the tsunami of feelings erupted from him. It was as if for the last three years, he'd had the taps that kept his feelings at bay turned tightly off and now they'd been loosened there was nothing he could do to stop the torrent of his inner thoughts, hurts and worries cascading from him.

'I miss me too and I hate that you're holding the fort, doing it all.'

'I don't care about that.' He spoke the truth, wiping his nose. 'I just wish I could make things better for you, make you happy.'

'It's not about me being happy.' She spoke slowly, and he could see by her pained expression that to say this out loud was a big deal. 'It's about me being less sad. Less . . .'

'Less what, love?' This opportunity to talk was rare and he wanted to extract every drop from it.

'Less preoccupied with the things that drag me down, that drown me. Because that's what it feels like. It's like drowning every day, and waking each morning knowing this is what is waiting for me is exhausting, depressing.' She gave a wry smile at her choice of words.

'I can imagine. Tell me what I can do to make it easier, make it better, help you stay afloat?' He grabbed her analogy and went with it.

'You do it all already. You take the running of the house on board, the everyday stuff – like the laundry, making supper – all of that, and just knowing I don't have to think about it, that's huge, it frees my mind to . . .'

'Frees it to concentrate on not drowning.'

'Yes.' She looked into his eyes and he saw her sadness. 'But something happened to me last night.'

'What?' He felt a knot of anxiety flare at what she may have been through. 'What happened?'

'I think the only way to describe it is that the scales were removed from my eyes. Something that has jump-started my recovery, made me want to get better.'

'Okay.' He had no idea what she meant but was simply glad that they were talking at all and that she was opening up. He could mine for the detail another time.

'And it was like I realised that all good things come to an end. And that's that!' She shrugged her shoulders. 'All good things come to an end, and it doesn't make them any less wonderful to experience, it just makes them part of your journey, something that shapes you, but you have to find a life after. And you have to learn how to forgive. You have to learn how to forgive yourself, don't you think?'

'I do.' He paused, again treading carefully in both tone and content. 'And this . . . this realisation has made you feel better?'

'I didn't wake up feeling depressed, Marty. It isn't an overnight thing and I know I won't wake up tomorrow feeling full of the joys of spring, but I know that wanting to change how I live, how I think, how I feel, is a huge step towards recovery and I'm determined. So determined to really work at it. Just the fact that I feel able is a huge breakthrough.'

He could barely contain his joy at hearing her thoughts. 'That is . . . the best thing you could say. I can't tell you how proud I am of you right now, but I don't want to pressure you or set any unrealistic timescales or expectations; just the idea that you are getting back on track, that things might change, could change, it's wonderful, Lis, it's wonderful!'

'It is wonderful, and when I'm feeling better, when I've sorted out my messed-up head, when I'm feeling stronger, there are things I need to tell you, things we need to discuss, that I hope will help us start over. It will be a fresh start, or a clean end, whichever you choose.' She caught her breath. 'But I hope, I really, really hope that you can learn forgiveness too, because I love you, Marty. I just love you.'

Oh God! This was it! This was the moment he had been both dreading and rehearsing for the longest time. His mouth felt dry with nerves and his leg jumped under the table.

'Are you going to tell me about your affair with Lawrence?' He spoke softly, slowly.

It felt odd, to say out loud the words that had rattled around in his head for the longest time, the words that wrenched him from sleep and had the power to sap him of joy on the sunniest of days. A mental lesion that never fully healed. He watched as she opened her mouth to speak, but it seemed *her* words were in short supply as shock only allowed a squeak from her mouth.

'I know, Lis. I've always known.' He nodded and looked at their joined hands on the tabletop, feeling the cold creep of inadequacy that she had chosen that Kelleway prick to sleep with over him. It hurt then. It hurt now. It would always hurt. But was it enough to shatter their family into fragments? To smash the life they had so carefully and lovingly crafted? Did he want to walk out on this little collective of humans that he so loved? He had given this more thought than he dared to admit over the years, but his conclusion was always the same. No. No, he wasn't going anywhere. This decision based not on weakness or indifference, but on strength. Lisa might pick Lawrence over him on any given day, but he would not allow her actions to separate him from his kids. Not ever.

Not that he hadn't come close to throwing in the towel, packing up his rucksack and disappearing. In the immediate aftermath of discovery, he had come closer than he cared to admit.

The passing years, however, had given him a different perspective, a rounded and forward-thinking view where he could see that to leave served no one and would have surely broken his heart.

Even though it was a matter of such angst-ridden agony to him, he was still a fair man, one who believed that his marriage was worth fighting for and that his wife's indiscretion should not, could not, be allowed to destroy his family unit. He had grown up without a mum and the thought of grabbing his kids and taking them away from her love, away from the only home they knew, was more than he could consider. If that were to happen, it would feel a lot like Kelleway had won and he was not going to let him win. His job, as he saw it, was to stay, to mitigate the harm done to his children by their mother's mental absence and to patch up the holes of their lives where and when he could. No, he would not leave, he would instead do what he had always done and find a way to navigate the heartache and sense of betrayal, harnessing the memories of their life before and believing that the happiness they had shared would return. One day.

'How . . . how do you . . .' she managed. Her wide-eyed stare was one of shock and yet also something else – relief, maybe?

He took a deep breath and sat back in the chair, a little surprised how even after all this time it was still almost too painful to recall.

'It was a Wednesday afternoon about six years ago, just before they went to Australia. The kids were at school, I'd finished my shift early and I remember I was in a really good mood. Happy. I thought I'd come and get you, see if you fancied a walk in the park to get an ice cream. I let myself in and I could just . . .' He swallowed as the memory of that day caused his tears to swell. He cuffed them on to his arm. 'I could just sense that something wasn't right. I started to feel anxious, wondering why my sixth sense was tingling; my thoughts ran riot. I wondered if there might be a burglar in the house or something similar. I was looking around the hallway to see what I could grab to use in self-defence, when I heard you laugh.' He paused, remembering the sound that had spoken volumes; the memory of it still made him shiver. 'It was the kind of big-mouthed laugh that you don't do when you're alone, as if someone was making you laugh in that way. I took a step into the hallway and could see you both through the gap in the sitting room door. You had your . . .' He took his time, recalling the detail was hard and his heart hammered in his chest now as it had then. 'You had your head on his shoulder and he had his arm across your back, and I remember thinking that it looked like you fitted there, right next to him.'

'Marty—' she began, her face pale, eyes wide.

He held up his hand, knowing that if he stopped talking about it now, he might never start again. 'No, just let me . . .' He closed his eyes and steadied his voice. 'I knew you'd been a thing when you were kids, but we've all got that, right? All got that someone. I never thought . . .'

'I love you. I love you.' She spoke as her tears fell. 'I do, I love *you.*'

'I know.' And he did, understanding how a physical indiscretion could happen, despite wishing with his whole being that it had not.

'The thought of you finding out.' Her voice, he noted, was small. 'I thought you might at any time over the last three years when he came back from Australia; it made me scared, so scared! I just . . . I just stopped functioning. I shut down, too afraid to breathe, too nervous to look you in the eye in case you could tell. I hate it, I hate that it happened, and I hate that I let you down. I am sorry. I am so, so sorry, Marty. You deserved better from me – the kids too. How could I do that to my kids? It was like it was happening to someone else – I got swept up, carried away and it was surreal. But the moment I came to, realised what I had done, I hated myself. I have wished day and night that I could go back and never go near him!'

227

He stared at her now, as she spoke with fists clenched, her words like a flame to the ice that sat in his gut. 'I thought . . .'

'What did you think?' she asked through her distress, her tone imploring.

'I thought . . . I thought you were broken because he'd come back, but not come back to you. I thought you were sad to have got me, the consolation prize.' To say the words out loud was like exorcising poison and his hands shook against the tabletop. 'And so I thought if I kept small, kept busy, kept quiet, we might get away with it because the last thing I wanted to do was break up our family. I didn't want that. I don't want that. Not at any cost. It's a price too high to pay for one mistake, Lis.'

He watched as his wife stood and slowly walked behind him, putting her arms around his chest, and laying her head on his back. It offered a particular closeness, warmth that went through to his very bones.

'You are not and never have been any consolation prize. You are my love, my *love* and my husband. And I'm sorry. Oh my God, I will spend the rest of my days trying to show you that I am so very sorry.'

He nodded, taking a moment to feel the warmth of her holding him fast, just as he had remembered her doing in the time before Lawrence Kelleway took a bite out of his family.

'I'm so sorry, Marty,' she repeated.

'I don't want you to live in regret. I want us to work, get back to happy. I want us to figure it out.' This was the truth. 'You and the kids, you're everything. But you need to get help, Lis, you need to talk to someone, a professional. You have to.'

She held him tighter. 'I will, I will. That's all I want, to get back to happy. It'll be wonderful. Hard work but wonderful. God, how I have missed you!' she breathed against him.

'What's wonderful?' Daisy asked as she made her way to the sink for a glass of water. Lisa let go of him and slipped back into the chair.

'The possibilities of life!' He beamed at her, feeling quite overwhelmed by the developments and simultaneously like he could punch the sky!

'Okay, Little Mr Sunshine – where's my dad and what have you done with him?' She turned to stare at her mother. 'Come to think of it, where's my mum and what have *you* done with *her*?'

'It's true, Daisy.'

He watched as Lisa spoke to her daughter with caution, hesitant, as if she wanted to make amends but not really knowing how. Not that she needed to feel so guilty – yes, she had made a mistake, but her failing mental health had seen an opportunity and swooped in, holding her fast. She had been poorly, she *was* poorly, and he was aware more than most, having lived with her shoulder to shoulder in recent years, that one good day did not make her fixed.

'There are so many possibilities. You have your whole brilliant life to look forward to.'

'Thank you, Mum.'

He noticed how Daisy never let her eyes leave her mother's face and it told him how precious this moment was and how much they would all thrive with regular interactions such as this. His gut folded at the thought that it might only be a temporary reprieve and he wondered how long she might be present before slinking up the stairs to seek out the feel of her fleecy blanket. Rather than let this thought rob them of the moment, he banished it, deciding to make the most of whatever time she was 'present', hoping it was forever, but fearing it might be much less . . .

'Gia said something similar to me last night. Is there something going on I don't know about? Should I be scared? Like, "You have your whole brilliant life to look forward to . . . but you've only got three weeks to live!" Because I'm kind of getting that vibe. Plus, I have a stack of library books that need to go back. I'd hate you guys to have to deal with a fine as well as my passing.'

Even Lisa raised a smile and in that split second, it felt like they all had a lot to look forward to.

'We should tell her.' Lisa held his gaze.

He felt a tight band of panic across his chest; what on earth was she thinking? To come clean about her and Lawrence, to shatter the frail security that he had created for them . . . the thought was horrific and he would do whatever necessary to stop her telling the kids, to help keep the illusion, to allow them peace. He stood, with sweat pooling on his back and face, prepared to manhandle his wife out of the room if necessary, no matter how frail. Whatever it took, he was not about to sit back and watch her smash to smithereens all that he had tended and held dear in the years she had been absent. No way!

Lisa looked up at him and it was as if a penny dropped and she subtly shook her head. It seemed he had got the wrong end of the stick. He exhaled, unaware that he had been holding his breath.

'About her nest egg,' she clarified.

He had heard the expression 'sweet relief', but never really understood it until that moment, as something cool and, yes, sweet, flooded his veins and his breathing was restored to a normal rhythm. *Her nest egg . . .*

'Oh!' The suggestion caught him by surprise. He retook his seat at the table. Not only was it unexpected but flew in the face of what they had agreed when her mother had died.

'Ooh, I like the sound of a nest egg! Is it ostrich? They're huge. Knowing my luck, it'll be more quail – tiny and frail. Unless it's chocolate! I do love an Easter egg – yes, I think that'd be my preferred nest egg of choice; I can eat the whole thing in one sitting.'

He barely gave Daisy's rambling any notice. This was huge; they had agreed not to say a word, not yet, but maybe Lisa, like he, was aware that her presence and participation might be temporary, or at best sporadic, and so wasn't this exactly what he had settled on, to make the most of every second? To help lay a foundation for those times when maybe he and the kids were again consigned to a quiet house where they lived gently behind closed doors, aching for joy, for hope and for interactions such as this?

'If you think so.' He held her eyeline, speaking cautiously.

'I do.' Lisa closed her eyes briefly. 'I really do.'

'Shouldn't we grab Jake?' he suggested, feeling the rise in his gut of a potent combination of excitement and nerves. 'I mean, if you want to tell them then we should tell them both.'

Lisa nodded. 'Daisy, can you go call your brother?'

He watched his daughter, who moved with hesitation, suddenly quiet. 'I feel a bit scared.' She placed her hand at her throat.

'Don't be scared.' He felt the enormity of what they had to say rise in his chest like a bubble.

Daisy left the room and hollered up the stairs from the hallway.

'Jake! Mum and Dad want you in the kitchen right now!'

Despite what was going on around them, he and Lisa exchanged an amused look. What was it with teenagers and their ability to yell so loudly? Middle age seemed to have given them an awareness that to shout out like this was not only painful to hear but also no more effective than a mid-range call.

Daisy leaned on the sink and Jake eventually loped into the room.

'What's going on? I can't believe I'm up this early on a Saturday! I still had a lot of good sleeping to do. Can you make it quick?' He yawned, scratching his hair, which stood up at all angles.

The way Jake stole glances at his mother as if shocked at the sight of her was another powerful reminder of how rare and wonderful it was to all be together. Marty hated that this wasn't their everyday lives, but hoped, prayed, it might be the start of just that.

'You okay, Mum?' Jake asked Lisa directly.

She nodded, a little overcome. Her tears pooled and Marty more than understood.

He took the lead, as Jake sat at the table.

'We wanted to talk to you about something.' At the sight of his kids' pained expressions, he hurried his speech and cut to the chase. 'Don't worry, it's a good thing, something to feel excited about, we hope.' He felt nervous. It felt like a big deal – it *was* a big deal! So great had been the decision, so hard the work to make it all happen. 'Mum and I, as you know, are not really into material stuff.'

'No shit!' Jake leaned back on the squeaky, ancient wooden chair, as if to prove the point. It lightened the atmosphere.

'Well, actually that's not true,' Lisa cut in and to hear her voice, to see her so engaged was groundbreaking. 'It's not that we aren't into material stuff, I mean, there are things I would like, certainly . . .'

'Like what, Mum? What would you like?' Daisy asked so sweetly Marty felt a firebolt of love and pride shoot right through him for the beautiful, considerate young woman they had raised.

'Oh, well, I can't think right now.' Lisa took her time. 'Maybe new loo seats, erm, a decent range to cook on.'

'You mean you might start cooking?' It was as if the words slipped from their son with unbridled hope.

'I used to love cooking.' Lisa looked down into her lap.

'And we loved you doing it. I remember your apple crumble.' Jake's words were edged in sadness for such a simple pleasure denied them for the last three years. It was also unspoken recognition that it was these little things that made them a family: communal eating, chatting at the table . . .

Marty felt a familiar spike of hatred for the man next door who had robbed his son of apple crumble and he of so much more. And it would be a lie to say that he didn't in some small way resent Lisa for her part in it, but still, his love for her and the thought of all that he stood to lose diluted that resentment, watered it down until he was able to swallow it.

'I'm going to try, Jake. I'm going to fight to feel better.'

'And we'll help you every step of the way, we will help you.' Marty wanted her to know this, that they were united. He and the kids were her safety net.

She nodded and for the second time he reached for her hand, holding it tightly, almost lost to the novelty of it.

'Anyway, I interrupted you, you were saying that we're not into material things,' Lisa quietly prompted.

'Apart from loo seats and ranges,' Daisy quipped.

Marty sat up straight; he had played this moment over in his mind many times and now that it was here for real, it felt both flatter and more nerve-wracking than he had imagined.

'When your gran died, she left Mum the house, obviously, which was the most incredible thing, and it gave us a foundation we could only have dreamed of. A house in which we could raise our family.' He paused. 'She also left us nearly a hundred thousand pounds.'

'Wow!' Daisy mouthed.

'Well, yes, wow. It's a lot of money, that's for sure, and it was even more money back then. Your mum and I thought long and hard what to do with it. We had plans drawn up for an extension, and then we considered a new bathroom with a fancy shower and whatnot.'

'That gets my vote!' Jake pulled a face – the hours he spent in the bathroom and in front of his bedroom mirror were legendary.

'I fancied a new car,' Lisa cut in.

'So why didn't you do all of it or some of it or any of it?' Jake asked.

'One hundred thousand is a huge sum, but it's amazing how quickly those numbers got eaten up when we started doing the maths and deciding which project to put the money into. We decided to be careful and go slow and spend it wisely.'

'Tell me you didn't buy magic beans.' Jake made them all chuckle.

'No.' Marty looked at his wife: this was the moment, this was it. 'But we did use it as a deposit on a flat. Two flats, in fact. New builds at the time, which are now just over fourteen years old.'

'You've got two flats?' Daisy's tone suggested she didn't believe a word of it.

'No. No, we don't.' Marty exchanged a knowing look with Lisa, whose expression was full of love and which he returned to her tenfold. 'But you guys do. You two have a flat each.'

He watched the kids stare at each other.

'Is this a joke?' Jake had gone a little pale.

'No, love,' Lisa confirmed. 'We decided that it was more important to give you both the start we could only have dreamed of. We know that you, Daisy, want to go off to Cambridge and if that's what you decide or *whatever* you decide, you will have the flat to sell, rent out, live in, whatever works for you. And for you too, Jake. You can live in it, sell it, rent it out – it's yours.'

'Where . . . where are the flats?' he asked.

'You know the ones they built overlooking the river and the park?'

'Yes.'

'Yep.'

The kids echoed.

'We bought a couple of those. With lovely big balconies and two bedrooms.'

'Are you *joking*?' For Jake, it seemed, it just wouldn't sink in.

'No, son. We've rented them out to pay the mortgages on them. Only another ten years and they'll be mortgage-free. They've gone up considerably in value, too, since we bought them.'

'I don't believe it,' Daisy whispered. 'My head won't let me think it's true.'

'It's true.' He felt the emotion of the moment, delighted still at the choices he and Lisa had made to provide for their kids in this way.

'Thank you.' Daisy looked a little overwhelmed. 'Just, thank you!' She ran over and hugged first him then her mother. 'I can't believe it!' she repeated.

'This changes so much for me, my whole future.' Jake shook his head. 'I don't know what to say.' His voice faltered, overcome with emotion as he placed his hand over the lower half of his face.

It was the reaction Marty had dreamed of – his kids' appreciation of this act that would give them so much freedom. It felt as good as he had always imagined it might.

'You could have spent the money on this house.' Daisy blinked.

'We could, but we're safe, warm and happy, and besides, if we tarted this house up, what would all the neighbours have to talk and complain about?' He winked.

'I own a flat!' Daisy swiped at the tears that trickled down her face.

'You do, love,' Lisa confirmed. 'We should do some work here though.' She looked around the kitchen like she was seeing it for the first time. 'A lick of paint.'

'I'd love to make the garden nice!' Daisy spoke up.

'That would be great.' Lisa smiled at her. 'Maybe later we can go into the garden and pull up some of those weeds. Maybe we could plant some of the flowers you talk about?'

'We can.' Daisy looked like she might burst. 'I'd love that, Mum. I'd love it so much! And maybe we could write that letter to the council about the tree.'

It didn't surprise him that their daughter might want to adopt this cause.

'We could.' Lisa held her daughter's gaze and there was promise in the exchange; he just hoped it was made in earnest.

'We can certainly get started.' Marty felt motivated by the momentum. 'I've let things slide over the last three years, given up a little on the house, but we owe it more than to let it decline like this. So I promise to get going, watch less telly of a weekend, drink less cider of an evening, and I'll dust off my paintbrushes.'

'I can help you,' Jake piped up, his eagerness confirming that it was a good idea.

'I own a flat!' Daisy shouted suddenly, the air around her crackling. 'I own a flat!'

'I own a flat!' Jake matched her, rising from his chair and he lifted his sister up and the two danced on the spot, spinning and twirling with infectious joy.

Marty knew he would never forget the moment, the look on their faces or the feeling that he and Lisa had done something incredible for their children. It made it all worth it: the early starts, the extra shifts, the cold mornings, the tiredness . . . it was all worth it.

'I love you,' his wife whispered.

The words hovered below the din and landed in his chest. 'And I love you, always have, always will.'

'I guess' – Jake put his sister down and leaned next to her by the sink – 'I guess that as we're having this heart to heart, it's as good a time as any to share something with you guys.'

Marty stared at his son, who had gone a little pale.

'What is it, mate? You know there's nothing you can't say to us. We love you.'

Jake nodded. 'And I . . .' He looked at his feet and exhaled, as if the words were hard to sound. 'I love you guys.'

Daisy looked quizzically at him and pulled a face, as if to let him know that she was clueless as to the big news.

'I'm gay.' Jake bit his bottom lip, his voice quavering. 'I'm gay! That's it.'

Marty stared at his son, his heart fit to burst. 'Is that your news?'

'Yep.' Jake nodded, his chest rose and fell in an exaggerated fashion, as if he might be close to panic.

'Oh, love, we've known that for a long time. I mean, I don't want to burst your bubble or spoil your moment, but we just thought you assumed we knew, and we assumed you knew we knew.' He spoke the truth; having thought how he might respond if ever Jake decided to clarify what to him and Lisa was a given.

'You're confusing me!' Jake put his hands out.

'I guess what your dad is saying, love, is that he didn't realise you were going to have to tell us; he figured, *we* figured, that you knew we knew.'

'*I* didn't know,' Daisy piped up. 'I mean, I don't care, of course I don't care, why would it matter? I love you. That's it, but I didn't know!'

Marty stared at his kids, his brilliant, brilliant kids. 'All I want for you, Jake, all I want for you both, is that you find someone who makes you happy, like your mum does me. And not happy all the time because that's impossible, but happy enough – "supported" is probably more accurate. Yes. Someone who will emotionally invest in you and support you, that's what you should look for. Someone with whom you can weather the storm. Find someone you can build a life with, a good life, with friendship, love and understanding at the heart of it.'

Lisa again wiped tears that fell down her cheeks.

'That's the thing – I have, Dad.' Jake's voice was small but his face beaming. 'I have found someone I want to build a life with. I love him and he loves me.'

Daisy threw her arms around her brother's waist. 'I am so happy for you! So happy for you, Jake!'

'What's his name?' Lisa asked. Her eyes lit at the prospect of the detail.

'It's Cassian.' Jake spoke his name in a sigh. 'Cass and I, we . . . we just work!' He laughed.

Marty watched as Daisy's arms slipped from her brother's waist and fell by her sides before she staggered backwards and seemed to lose her footing, stumbling until she sat on the kitchen floor, almost like she had fainted.

'Daisy!' He jumped up and ran to her. Lisa followed suit. 'What happened, love? Get her some water, Jake!' he barked, trying to take control and calm his own sense of rising panic. 'Open the door, let the air in! Daisy? What happened love? What happened?'

'I can't breathe . . .' She clutched at her throat. 'I can't breathe . . .'

CHAPTER FIFTEEN

BERNIE KELLEWAY

It was bright and beautiful on this fine Saturday. At a little before midday, Bernie Kelleway parked and locked his Audi and pushed his sunglasses up on to the bridge of his nose, cursing his lingering headache. He was, as he approached his twilight years, confident that he was still in good shape. His long legs were one of his best features and he couldn't deny that to be sporting a full head of hair set him apart, he felt, from most of his follically challenged peers.

Headaches like this were one aspect of ageing he found hardest to handle. Not for him the creak of sciatica, the swell of arthritis or the foggy memory of increasing senility, and thank the good lord above his plumbing was in tip-top condition. Nope, his biggest and most frustrating age-related affliction was his inability to handle his hangovers. He used to be a master. Knocking back plonk in the early evening, before switching to port in the winter and gin in the summer – both helped to lubricate his stories, which he happily retold into the early hours. The following morning, he'd wake, shower, eat the bacon and eggs Winnie had prepared, washed down with fresh, sharp, cold orange juice. A couple of coffees, a quick gander at the newspaper while he made his morning visit, and he was raring to go! But these days, after overindulging, his sight was a little grainy, his tongue coated, his gait sluggish and there was the unmistakable and unwelcome hint of sickness.

Not that he had time for any of it; today was one of celebration! He had become a grandfather again! He couldn't wait to see the little fella and hoped Cleo was doing well. Not that he had to worry too much; Georgie was about as devoted a husband as he had ever seen and he, unlike his wife, was thankful for him. Bernie was confident that his precious daughter and new grandson would always be in the very best of hands.

'Two birds with one stone . . .' he muttered under his breath, a reminder of why he was here and what he needed to say, to do.

He slowed, walking now with a hesitancy to his step as nerves rippled through him. Or maybe nerves was too strong – an edginess might be more accurate. He formed a fist, before flexing his fingers, but took his time approaching the building and peering inside. Eventually, he rapped on the closed door of the Italian restaurant where only the previous evening they had dined in celebration of his ruby wedding anniversary, and now here he was, only a matter of hours later, Grandad to a new little boy. His life was an ever-changing and wondrous thing.

Gianna came to the door and looked behind her before opening it. He watched her do a double-take and bite her nail, as if considering whether to open up or not. He sincerely hoped she would. He was a man on a mission. He was relieved when she turned the key, opened the door and stood in the doorway, her arms folded.

'We don't open for another hour and a half. My husband is still at the cash and carry.'

He pushed his sunglasses up on to his head, nodded and stepped forward until his toes rested on the brass lip of the step. His breathing came heavily, and he was aware of a slight sweat covering his tanned, unshaven face.

'My daughter.'

'Cleo.' She stared at him.

'Cleo, yes, she gave birth in the early hours to a little boy. I have a new grandson!'

'Congratulations,' she offered flatly, clearly sharing none of his enthusiasm for the event. Not that he was surprised – the woman had never struck him as maternal.

'He's beautiful, perfect.' He had only seen the one picture Georgie had texted, but it was enough to convince him that the latest addition to the Kelleway clan was a little superstar.

'Of course he is.' Gianna gave a wry smile.

'They've not named him yet and I've only seen a photograph.' He drew a sharp breath, aware that he was babbling a little. 'But he looks a gorgeous, sturdy little thing.'

'Mr Kelleway' – she spoke over his head – 'this is all very interesting, and I'm happy for you and your lovely family, but are you going around the neighbourhood telling everyone in person all the details or is it a special honour for me? I don't wish to appear rude, but it might be quicker to send a group email. It's just that I have arancini to prep, salad to wash and pasta to make.' She pointed over her shoulder towards the kitchen.

His face fell. Her tone was cold and he understood. He swallowed, his mouth dry and when he spoke, his voice had an unfamiliar falter to it.

'Cleo has become a mother for the first time. She's done a marvellous job, and it was a long time coming. She is a warrior, tired, victorious, elated, and all she wants to eat is some of your Fettuccini Alfredo.' He smiled now. 'I thought you'd take it as a compliment. Her husband has offered her the best steak, sushi, sweet desserts, anything she wants! Turns out the only thing she wants is a bowl of your Fettuccini Alfredo.'

Gianna hesitated, as if weighing up whether to agree to his request, before nodding and opening the door wide to allow him entry.

'I can make a batch and put it in a plastic box for her.'

'Thank you! Thank you!' He raised his hands in praise, his tone dripping with gratitude.

'You'll take it straight to the hospital?' She walked towards the kitchen.

'No need. She's coming home already.' He spoke softly. 'I wouldn't have asked, only—'

'Don't explain.'

Darting around to face him, she briefly held his gaze and the way her eyes searched his face made him look away. He swallowed the hard ball of guilt that sat at the base of his throat. Following her into the kitchen with a growing feeling of unease in his gut, he stood by the wall, marvelling at her artistry as she pulled one of the heavy blackened frying pans from the shelf above the stove and set it down on top of the flame.

'I am making this for your daughter because she has become a mother and that's an incredible thing. I also know how hard she fought to become a mother and to that I can relate, and I respect her for it.'

Her words made him rethink the assumption that she was not maternal.

'Gia . . .' He stepped forward and raised his hand.

'Don't touch me! Don't you dare!'

To see her recoil was like a punch to his throat.

'I mean it, Bernie, do not touch me. Not here in Carlo's restaurant, not ever again. You understand?' Her stance was steady; her voice, however, wobbled.

'I understand you're upset—' he began.

242

'Upset?' She spun around and he now noticed the tremble of her hand. 'I am not upset! I am furious! I am fuming from the depths of my shoes to the tips of my hair! I am so angry!' She clenched her fist.

Bernie had known the speech he made to his wife would impact his lover; he wished he'd drunk a little less as that might mean he was able to remember exactly what he had said. It was as if she read his thoughts.

'The things you said, Bernie!' Just the memory of these words was seemingly enough to distress her. He hated to see the slip of tears over her cheeks, which left her eyes raw.

'Gia . . . Gia . . . what was I supposed to do?' He tried to remember the words he had rehearsed in the car, the ones that might pour calming oil on to the troubled waters. 'The kids wanted me to give a speech, they insisted on it. I had to say something! I had no choice; I was backed into a corner. I even suggested you both leave, gave you an opportunity to make a hasty retreat, but your husband was having none of it!'

'First you let your wife book *my* restaurant when there are a hundred other places you could have gone to celebrate your perfect marriage.'

'She loves it here, we all do – that's how you and I met, don't forget.'

'I never forget!' she yelled, and he looked towards the back door, as if her volume might have invited unwanted attention. 'I never forget! It's not me with the memory loss! It's you! All the promises you have made me, all the things you have told me about your nagging wife, your demanding wife . . . My God! To hear you last night you'd think you were on a first date – so much love! So much passion!'

He felt his pulse race; he didn't want to fight with her. Didn't want to fight with anyone – confrontation had never been his

243

strong suit. This one trait, he was convinced, was the reason for his long and 'perfect' marriage. He had figured early on it was easier to go with the flow, agree with whatever suggestion, and do exactly as he pleased rather than try to stand his ground with a woman like Winnifred Wallace. It was easy. Keep her happy with shiny baubles, home improvements, extravagant bouquets, and a week or two in the sun, and the rest of his time was his own.

'I didn't want to rock the boat by asking her to cancel and find somewhere else. What would I have said? How could I have justified that? And by the time I found out she'd booked it, she'd invited all the family and they'd made plans . . .' It was almost the truth. That and a small part of him liked the idea of having the two women in his life in such proximity. Mischief at its most thrilling. And at his age, such thrills were sadly few and far between.

Gianna shook her head as she threw heavy cream, butter and cornflour into the pan, no measuring needed. She cooked by eye and by instinct and he found it most alluring, always had. There was something about a woman like Gianna who was the embodiment of generosity, not only physically, but in her very nature. The way she revelled in the experience of food, wanting to create the rich, tasty, satisfying, flavoursome dishes to show love, and this she achieved with every mouthful. It was no surprise to him that Cleo, with her energy and reserves depleted but filled to the brim with the emotion of new motherhood, wanted only to taste Gianna's food.

It had been a favoured thing for them, after sex, to lie on the makeshift bed in the storeroom at the back and talk about food: the source of food, the harvesting of food, the preparation, her likes, dislikes, and always with a bowl of fat olives to hand, some thrice-cooked chips with a strong dipping aioli or one of her rich baked cheesecakes and a glass or two of red . . . He was in awe of how, after so many years of cooking, she still loved what she did, loved the sounds, sights and smells of the kitchen and still felt the thrill of produce being delivered early in the morning. He was as attracted to her passion as he was her nature and her body.

He recalled one conversation in particular, in the early days of their affair. 'Seriously, Bernie.' She had sat up, unabashed by her nakedness in a way that was intoxicating and in stark contrast to Winnie, who was always willing to indulge but favoured the drape of a robe or the corner of a sheet to preserve her modesty. Not that he compared the two, never that. But how he loved when Gianna would lean forward, eyes wide, hands expressive and her tone enthused. 'There is still something so awe-inspiring about running my hand over the silvery skin of a fat salmon, inhaling the scent of the sea on a sprawling glossy octopus or cutting a fresh lemon and breathing in the smell of summer. It shouldn't bring me so much joy, but it does, Bernie! To handle wide artichokes, gaze at that particular hue of a ripe blackberry, set dough to rest, peel weighty onions, bite salty olives, taste the sweet, earthy notes of a ripe, young tomato, or inhale the peppery scent of a fine olive oil – it takes me to my happy place!'

'I can see that.' He'd laughed. 'Look at your face!' He had never seen such contentment.

'You can laugh, but it's true! No matter the weather outside, even on the greyest of days in the suburbs, the produce takes me back to my nonna's garden, where the heat of the Tuscan sun warmed every stone of her Montepulciano home. God, I love that place! My childhood was the stuff of fairy tales.'

He had listened rapt, envying her, and picturing his own young life of thrift and hardship, the stuff of nightmares.

'I would wake and start cooking early in the morning with my nonna; she'd trust me with a sharp paring knife and let me help prepare food on a long wooden table with a thin plastic tablecloth nailed to the wood underneath. I can picture the floral print, which faded year on year, bleached by the sun's rays.'

'It sounds idyllic.' He meant it.

'Oh, it was!' She'd leaned forward and kissed his forehead. 'I'd spend the day running wild with my cousins. Laughing and singing! We'd play among the vineyards, idle in the piazzas, and eat sweet soft gelato before returning home as the sinking sun set the sky on fire. *Home*, to sit at that same long wooden table where politics, art, farming, music, local gossip, taxes, opera, love and loss were heatedly discussed by my extended family!'

'I would have loved to have seen it.' He'd felt almost melancholy for the life she described; a life devoid of dust-free surfaces, crystal serving bowls and accent lamps in shades of teal. A life where he could wander bare chested in the sun, wearing battered espadrilles and letting his stubble grow into a beard if he felt like it, completely unconcerned with 'standards'. 'I like the sound of the freedom of it all,' he'd confided, only willing to give away this small hint that he sometimes found his life to be a little constricting, no matter how blessed.

'It was certainly that.' She had run her finger over his shoulder, her touch enough to make him shiver with want. 'The conversation, no matter how loud, only ever the background to the main event – eating. We'd roll up our sleeves, secure a napkin at our necks, lift the spoon and tuck into vast bowls full of garlicky, homemade pasta with soft bread to dab up the remnants of the complex tomato sauces. God, Bernie, I can still taste them now! Those sauces made to Nonna's exacting standards. They were beyond compare, multi-dimensional and, like the finest wines, carried high and low notes, sweet and savoury aspects, varied textures that made my tongue sing! These sauces are my food heritage and I have to confess, despite all my years in the kitchen, I can only dream of replicating them. It was all about the food, yes, but it was more than that; love floated around us, bound us and held us fast in a nest that was safe, warm and comforting. I still dream of it – those moments, the smells, the sounds, the taste of that fairy-tale life.'

'I'd like to go back with you one day,' he'd confessed, a moment of honesty before the complexities of their situation and the realities of life caught up with his tongue. A moment when he'd let himself imagine the Tuscan heat on his skin, the feel of her skin next to his with the scent of olives and lemons filling a stone-floored room with a grand bed and shutters drawn, putting the room in shadow while they lay and laughed and loved . . .

These were the days, the memories, that filled his dreams, his quieter moments. Her voice, now firm, brought him back into the present, as she slammed another pan on to the range.

'I get that you had to give a speech, Bernie. Of course, you did. I was prepared for it. I imagined it. I settled on something touching, funny even, and then a clink of glasses as you cut the cake. But that's not what happened, the words you used . . .'

Bernie felt a flutter of nerves as he tried in vain to remember exactly what he had said. Unluckily for him, Gianna was about to remind him. It made him cringe.

'"You had faith in me. You loved me." That's what you said. That's what you said to her in front of everyone. In front of *me*!' The crack to her voice was hard to hear.

'Yes, I know, I . . .' His thoughts whirred as he tried to come up with something that might placate the voluptuous woman he so adored and at whose bosom he found warmth and comfort.

'Those words haven't left me, Bernie. I haven't slept, chasing them around my head like a movie on a loop.'

He watched as she reached for a large ceramic bowl and into it she grated a soft, pillowy mountain of Parmesan, before adding a long grind of coarse black pepper. His mouth watered. She pulled fresh fettucine from a wooden rack where it hung in pale strips and set it to boil in salted water.

'I have cut and diced your words every which way, trying to figure out why they lodged in my heart like daggers, and I got it. Last night, just before the sun came up, in the darkness, I lay there, and I figured out why.'

'Why, Gia?' He felt the rush of adrenaline, wary of what she might say next and knowing it would be hard to hear. Her tone so cool, her hand out of reach, it felt like the beginning of the end and that thought was almost more than he could stand. He very much liked his life with her in it. He had come here with the explicit intention of getting the food and to apologise. Ending their affair had not been on his mind.

'Because I have had faith in *you* for the last seven years. Faith that you would keep your word and that the future was ours. That we would be together, somewhere new. A fresh start. I never doubted that you meant it and I have thought of it every moment we have been apart. Standing here at this stove, lost entirely to dreams of you and me, together. I believed you. And as for love . . .' She paused and transferred the pasta from the boiling water into the cream and butter mixture bubbling on the stovetop before scooping up the grated, peppery Parmesan and sprinkling it generously over the top. Gently, with a spatula, she folded the mixture together before adding a heavy splash of the pasta cooking water. She stirred and stirred until what lay in the pan was a glossy, cheesy sauce-coated pasta that he could have dived into, mouth open wide. 'I can see, Bernie, that to say "I love you" is something that's easy for you. I thought you were sincere. I thought you loved me as I love you.'

'I do! I spend every minute I can in the driveway at the side of the house, making out to prune that damn climbing rose bush, calling you, texting you, listening to your voice. Those moments when I stand in all weathers, making even the smallest amount of contact with you are the very best part of my day.' He felt a rising sense of panic at the thought of losing this woman whose affection sustained him, nurtured him and made him happy! 'I do love you, Gia and we *can* be together, we can! I'll do it. I'll tell Winnie and you tell Carlo, and we can just pack a bag and go!'

'Go where?' she snickered, as she loaded the hot, steaming pasta into a container and sprinkled it with fresh, rough-chopped, flat-leaf parsley, sealing it tight.

'I . . . I don't know. I . . .' He floundered, thinking of the hurt it would cause Winnie, the pain he would be inflicting on Lawrence and Cleo, on Cassian and Domino, all of whom looked up to him, the head of the family. And he pictured the little red face of his baby grandson, the newest member of the Kelleway clan. 'I don't know,' he repeated and was stunned to realise he was close to tears. He couldn't remember the last time he had felt like this – not tearful, tears came often – but never this lost, alone, bereft at what was to come. 'I don't know.' It was both an admission and a realisation that this was their ending.

'I don't know either.' Gianna handed him the box. 'I hope your daughter enjoys this and please tell her congratulations.'

He put the box on the counter and grabbed at her, pulling her into him. He closed his eyes, committing to memory the feel of her soft form against him, her scent, a drawing feeling in his gut for all he was going to miss, all he was going to be denied.

'We can't do this, Bernie, not anymore.' Gianna spoke with her eyes closed as if this might make it easier. 'I mean it. My mind is made up.'

'How? How do we just stop? Seriously,' he breathed against her neck, holding her against him, 'you do something to me . . .'

'We've been lucky, Bernie. After all these years for us to still feel the same level of attraction, but enough now, enough . . .' She let the thought trail, her smile forced as if this were inevitable. Never before had she spoken these exact words and certainly not with such resolution.

'I don't know what I'll do without you, Gia.'

'You'll figure it out.' She kissed his cheek. He could feel her tears on his skin.

He caught her wrist. 'When the woman you love is in distress or pain, you feel so helpless.' He shook his head.

'I'll be okay. It's just going to take time for me to adjust. But I survived before you and I will survive after. It will help that I know you are a fraud, Bernie, a big old fraud.'

Her accusation bothered him. 'I do love you, Gia! I love you! And if things were different . . .'

'Things are not different.' She pressed her fingers into his back, and he felt the flame of desire as was usual when he was within touching distance of this woman who had taught him the meaning of love and all that it could be. If life with Winnie was brittle, with Gianna it was yielding. If Winnie was ice, she was fire. And in her arms, he had slept like never before, as if the world were a wondrous, ever-blue-sky place where he could finally rest, knowing he would wake with an abundance of pleasure at his fingertips.

'You want a speech? You want a speech, Gia?' His throat felt tight and there was the unmistakeable irritation of a twitch beneath his left eye. Without prior thought or having to draw on lines he may have rehearsed en route or in a state of panic, he spoke firmly and loudly.

'I am entering that time in my life when I will wither – when I will become no more than the snap of ashy bone. And in this withering time I will miss the grape, grain and fat that have made these last seven years glorious! That is a gift you gave me and one I will never forget. You, Gia – you are like rain on my face after drought. You are warm food on a cold, cold day. You have been my comfort and rest when the road ahead looked long and lonely. That's the speech I give you.'

The sound she made was part whimper, part sob and this, too, he knew he would never forget. It was the sound of a person wounded, a soul damaged and a body, like his, understanding that this was the end.

'Mr Kelleway!' Carlo yelled heartily from the back entrance of the kitchen. 'How lovely to see you! I hope you enjoyed your meal last night. Everyone seemed to have a great time!'

Bernie felt his cheeks flame scarlet and his stomach drop with fear as he and Gianna darted apart. He was unsure how long the man had been standing there. His bowel spasmed with fear as he scrabbled for the box, grateful for the prop, as he raised it high. 'Your wife has very kindly made pasta for my daughter, for . . . for Cleo who has just become a mother for the first time! It's a big day!' He smiled. 'A big day for us all!'

'A big day indeed! My sincere congratulations!' Carlo boomed. Bernie felt the man's large hand on his back, as he guided him towards the front door. 'And did Mrs Bianchi tell you my news?'

'Your news? N-no . . . no, she didn't,' he stuttered, looking over his shoulder to where Gianna stood with her hands knitted at her chest, almost in prayer and with a tortured expression that cut him.

'Yes, big news.' He opened the front door and Bernie took a step outside. 'I'm going home! I'm returning to Tuscany to sit in the sun, grow my own food and take slow walks. I can't wait.'

'It sounds . . .' Bernie looked at the ground, trying to sort the competing emotions as distress, envy and loss fought for pole position.

'We are?' Gianna asked with her chest heaving and her face breaking into an expression of joy, replacing the look of fear. 'We are going home?' She placed her hand over her mouth as if it was almost more than she dared believe.

'No, no, Gia, *amore mio. We* are not going home; *I* am going home.'

Gianna looked like she might fall as, reaching out, she placed her hand on the countertop to steady herself. Bernie felt conflicted, keen to be gone from the man's restaurant as well as not show any familiarity towards Gianna in front of him, but also wary and a little ashamed of not being there to catch his lover if she fell.

Carlo took a step closer until he and Bernie were almost nose to nose. He leaned in closely, so close that Bernie could smell the coffee on his breath. To be in such proximity to the man made him feel deeply uncomfortable.

Gianna's husband whispered softly into his ear. 'If I see you again – here, or anywhere else – I will kill you. And I don't mean figuratively, my friend. I mean that I will *kill* you. And they will never find your body. Do you understand me?' His words so gently spoken, were all the more chilling for that.

Bernie nodded, fear quaking in his limbs.

'Now fuck off and never, ever come near me again.'

Bernie turned on trembling legs and caught the way Carlo stared at his wife with his top lip curled in an expression of pure disgust. Gianna seemed to shrink under his gaze. She looked suddenly older and . . . afraid. Yes, she looked afraid, and he more than understood, remembering well what it had felt like to stand at the bus stop and not know where his next penny was coming from or even how he was going to get out of the blocks.

He walked briskly towards the car. Juggling the hot pasta box, he fumbled in his pocket for the car keys. Climbing onto the soft leather, he placed the food on the front seat and pulled his sunglasses over his eyes before starting the engine and driving away as quickly as he was able.

Despite the gut-churning terror he had felt at Carlo's threat, there was also no small amount of relief. Fear of discovery had lurked in the background of their dalliance, a minor detraction from the joy of his infidelity but a detraction nonetheless, and now he didn't have to worry about that. He didn't have to worry about any of it. It was, he decided, probably a good thing that Mr Bianchi was leaving the area. And as for Gianna? He knew it was best to close that chapter in his life, best for everyone. The aroma of the freshly made piping-hot Fettuccini Alfredo filled his car and made his mouth water. Yes, it was probably all for the best. But my God how he would miss her and how he would miss her pasta . . .

CHAPTER SIXTEEN

Julie Kelleway

Julie stood in the bedroom and listened as Lawrence showered. He'd made clear his intention to go straight to his mum's to be part of the new baby celebration. His mood she could best describe as ebullient, which, when she considered the dagger-like pain that split her chest in two, only served to irritate and distress her. If there were a better metaphor for how he caused such pain, such disruption and then sauntered on as if nothing was amiss, she was hard pushed to think of it. She could hear him whistling now, and it made the hair on her arms bristle. She stared at the wall. How to explain this numbness – was she in shock? Quite possibly. *Lisa . . . Lisa next door . . . Depressed Lisa . . .*

This, however, wasn't her first time at the rodeo. This feeling in her gut, the nervous anticipation bookended with naked fear, topped with pure sorrow, took her back to that day she got the call, just over three years ago now. She'd never forget it and still relived the horror of it in her quieter moments.

It had been a sunny day in their East Melbourne home. She'd folded the laundry with the radio playing, had a cup of coffee and placed the mug in the dishwasher. Sun diamonds sparkled on the surface of their swimming pool and the muslin curtains of the day room wafted in on the breeze. The way they skirted the dark wood floor was pleasing and, as ever, she felt delighted that this was her home, her beautiful home. She wondered if she would always feel like the girl from the Merrigo estate and that she had no right to be here.

The thought was without prophecy, no more than a consideration, and yet within minutes her phone rang. It was Lawrence who sounded . . . How did he sound? Angry? Flustered? Agitated? Yes, all the above, but something else too and it was this final realisation that meant he held her attention, paying heed to every word he rattled off. He sounded scared. Yes, he sounded scared, and this alone was enough to frighten her.

'Pack a bag, just . . . just take what you need. I'll be there as soon as I can.'

His words were odd, bizarre, alarming.

'What?' she'd laughed, waiting for the punchline.

'Listen to me. No time to explain. Get the kids to pack too, but not too much, just one bag.'

'What do you mean, "pack a bag"? Why? What's happening? You're scaring me. Why do I need to pack a bag?' Her voice was high and anxious.

'No time.' He breathed heavily. 'No time to discuss it, Jules, just please, *please* do as I ask, no questions, just pack and get the kids to do the same.'

'Is this a joke? I honestly don't know what to think – you're being weird! Where are we going? How long are we going for?' Mentally she ran through her muddled thoughts, trying to remember what clothes were clean or dirty, where she'd put her holdall, where she'd left the novel she was reading . . .

'Please, Jules, no more questions, I've got to go. I need to make some calls.'

'No, Loz, you can't just call and say this, make my heart pound and leave it at that! What shall I say to the kids?'

'Fuck!' he screamed, whether in response to her or to someone else she wasn't sure, but her whole body jumped just the same. 'Tell them we need to leave. Tell them their dad has royally fucked up. Tell them he borrowed money from some people who he thought were reasonable, and tell them those people now want their money back and are being very unreasonable. Tell them those same people are getting very close to knowing where he lives and therefore where they live and that they will stop at nothing to get their hands on their cash or anything else they think might be of value. Tell them we are going home because we have no fucking choice! Tell them—' She heard his sharp intake of breath and then the sound of him crying. 'Tell them their dad is very sorry. And I'll be with you as soon as I can.'

This panic, this hysteria, was very different to when they'd left the UK, heading out to make their new life. That time he had calmly stressed two things: first, that this would be the only move they were going to make, and second, there was no urgency, but to avoid the incurrence of huge costs, to make their new life possible, it was better they left sooner rather than later. And she had believed him, but then she had believed lots of things.

Like when he said he was working late, tying up loose ends, when what he actually meant was that he was sneaking grubby sex with Lisa next door while she boxed up their home, tried to placate the kids that it was all going to be okay and had last cups of tea with her bereft mum who kept shaking her head at how far away Australia was. These thoughts sent a fresh batch of tears down her face.

On the day they left their East Melbourne home, even though she knew time was of the essence and that she had to hurry, it was as if her brain and body were out of sync. Her thoughts continued to race around her head like fireworks in a confined space and yet her hands moved slowly, her legs felt leaden. It was akin to that dream where you have to run to stay safe, but find yourself stuck in one spot, unable to move. Caught. This was similar, although hindsight would reveal it was no dream, but instead the start of a living nightmare. A living nightmare that was still rolling and one only she knew how to make stop, to wake up from, and the answer was to remove herself from the situation.

Three years ago, she had done as he asked: packed a bag, corralled the kids, answered their questions as best she could, watched as their few belongings were bundled into the trunk of the car. She had then tried to keep the mood light, still in the dark as to exactly what they were running from and why, as her husband drove them a little erratically along the coast to Geelong. It felt like hiding out and his jumpiness was infectious. She'd cooked supper on the inadequate stove of the rented motel apartment, taken Cassian and then Domino for long walks to stretch their legs and to change their scenery. She'd listened as Lawrence used a burner phone to book flights, preparing for them to come home. Her heart sank at the prospect, not because she didn't miss her family and her UK life, she did, but things in Australia had been so perfect – or so she had thought.

But it was all an illusion. Like it or not, she was part of a crazy arse world that she could not even imagine. A dangerous world that was like nothing she had known, and one that filled her with a fear so real that even consideration of it made it hard to sleep and impossible to eat. Compliant, she had done his bidding. He hadn't had the decency to consult or discuss the move with her and his implicit instruction left her feeling diminished, like an employee – or worse, his charge.

He had almost beamed when he'd said, '*We're going home . . .*' Like a con artist, a confidence trickster who employed simple tactics to make you believe it was what was intended all along, nothing but a good thing, selling the idea with such conviction it was easy to get swept up in it. *Home . . .* a curious word and one that now mystified her, realising the last time she had felt at home was in her childhood bedroom at her parents' small house on the Merrigo. The place she had been so desperate to escape.

'Right, that's me ready.' Lawrence spoke from the dressing room and pulled her into the present. She could smell his strong cologne, undercut with minty mouthwash. 'I'll see you at Mum and Dad's. I'll take the Mini so you can drive comfortably with the kids. Cass is on his way back, apparently, wants to get showered.'

They had a Mini, a runaround for Cassian and the car Domino would drive when she passed her test, although it was Julie's car, supposedly. This, too, she now had no doubt was either rented or defaulted on – potato potarto.

'Sure.' She managed a small smile.

'I feel good, Jules! Like, really good!' He exhaled, rolling his shoulders, breathing deeply. He looked like a man without a care in the world. 'I feel relieved, like this is our new start, our new beginning, nothing left unsaid between us. That's what we agreed, right?'

'Yes, a new start. Nothing left unsaid, only the truth from now on.' She accepted his tight hug – and heard him whistle as he took the stairs quickly in the manner of someone who was loving life – knowing that the truth might be that she had had enough.

Staring now at the suitcase on the bed, she looked from it to the wardrobe and back again, wondering how much time she had. The family would, she knew, be busy welcoming Cleo and Georgie's little bundle, preoccupied and no doubt being force-fed leftover cheese by a highly agitated Winnie. She could just imagine the fuss, and quite right too – a new baby was a wonderful thing for any family.

What to pack? She wasn't sure where she was heading or for how long, but one thing she knew with complete certainty: she needed time alone to think. Time out of the eye of the storm where it took all her energy just to remain upright. She needed to go somewhere, anywhere she could take a breath and view the situation with some clarity. If they were to find any way forward, it was entirely necessary to walk away and look at things from the outside in. Her jaw tensed every time she thought about her husband's parting words. '*I feel good, Jules! Like, really good!*' Lawrence, the man who had plunged her life into this chaos in the first place. The man who was unreliable, a liar. She had always been willing to concede that maybe he lied with the best of intentions, that his actions were all about trying to build the very best life for her and the kids, the people he loved, but what if this had only been her putting a spin on things to justify her own inaction, her cowardice? It was a jarring thought. He was a cheat – had had an affair, and this was a whole other thing.

She pulled a cool cotton maxi dress from the hanger and rolled it tightly, as she'd been taught, popping it into the corner of the case. She remembered packing her one case to leave their East Melbourne home – she'd thrown in a pair of jeans and a navy blouse before rummaging under the pillow for her pyjamas. It had been quite unlike filling a case for a holiday where you could predict the weather – sunny on the beach, cool on the slopes. It was instead packing for a new life, starting over, reminding herself that no matter what, she would embrace all the good things that lay ahead, and they would face whatever came next as a family, together. Yet now she knew that while she willingly did her husband's bidding, loyal to him and whatever their future held, he had been sleeping with Lisa. *He had been sleeping with Lisa!* Even the mental reckoning of this made her cry. Fat tears that stung her eyes and trickled down her cheeks.

'What are you doing?' Cassian's voice from the doorway drew her attention.

'Cass!' She couldn't hide her distress. 'I . . . I didn't know you were back.'

'What are you doing?' he repeated.

She saw his breathing coming fast, and his obvious agitation.

'I just . . .' Her sadness wrapped and weakened her and she sank down on to the bed.

'Mum, what on earth's going on?' He pointed to the case, the flash of distress on his face telling her that he too remembered that dark day in Melbourne when the world they had thought was safe and secure crumbled under their feet. When they had thrown bags into the car, buckled up and headed out. She had smiled at them through the gap in the seats, smiling so hard as if this one facial expression could wipe away the worry, the hurt. It had made her complicit, enabling Lawrence to ride roughshod over the routine and life they had built and the glorious future that had felt within reach.

Keeping her eyes low, she found it easier to talk to the pale wool carpet, avoiding his gaze and any judgement that might lurk there.

'I just need a little bit of time to get my head straight. I'm not sure I can do it anymore.'

'Do what?'

She hated the tone of concern from her sweet boy. 'Pretend. Prop up your dad and all his—' 'Lies', that was the word she wanted to say. *Lies*. But even at this juncture she was intent on doing her best to preserve his reputation for his son, to smooth the path, to keep things civil. 'His schemes.'

Cassian looked deflated, as if the strength had left his legs, and it tore at her heart to know she was the cause, understanding how words could be weapons. What was it Lawrence had said? *It meant nothing. She's nothing!*

'I love you, Cass, I love you so much. You and Dom, you are my whole heart. Half each.' She tried to find a bright tone. 'But I am so tired of visiting Winnie and Bernie and listening to their bullshit, eating cake, cheese, whatever, knowing that we're a gnat's fart away from total collapse. It's madness!' She put her hands in the air. 'He won't talk to them. Your dad thinks it's better to keep up the façade, splash out, drive that big old car, and jangle his watch to whoever is looking rather than say out loud that we're broke. Flat broke. And I'm so tired.'

'So, you're leaving us?' His words were like knives, spoken as his lip trembled at the prospect that overwhelmed them both.

'No! No, I'm not leaving, not running, not hiding, but I am moving out briefly, or thinking of it, just taking a beat to gather my thoughts.'

'Don't do that, Mum, please!'

It was all it took – her son's distress enough to put a big dent in her confidence that she had made the right decision.

'I just don't know if I can live like this anymore, Cass. I don't know if I can do it.' It was as if the voicing of her feelings was enough to affect her physically. It took all her strength to hold her head up high. 'And it won't be forever and probably not for long. You and Dom can stay here or come with me or split your time; whatever works best. I would never ask you to choose between your dad and me, never. I would never want you to. He loves you so much, he loves us all, but I swear, Cass, I need a break, need a pause, because I'm almost beaten. I want a moment of peace. And I think . . . I think . . .' Sorrow swamped her as she heard his words, his admission that he had had an affair with the girl next door, and that he had shoved their shopping money at the woman's daughter. 'I think I deserve a moment of peace.'

'He won't survive without you.' The sight of her son's tears was like swords through her gut. 'He won't be able to do it, Mum. Even if you only go for a short while. He'll sink. And' – he wiped his nose – 'and you do deserve peace, you do. You're the best, you're the best mum I could ever have asked for.' His words were like balm, they healed and soothed in equal measure. 'And if you don't love him then I get it and I think you should do what you need to . . . need to do . . .' he stuttered. 'But if you do love him then please, please don't abandon him. He is literally only held up by the perception of other people and you. That's it. We all know it – he knows it!'

She shook her head, knowing she would never share her husband's betrayal, wanting to leave him as shiny as was possible in her son's mind. Despite his many and obvious flaws, her job was not to sully or put a hole in their relationship, but rather to steer Cassian calmly and be there for him to answer all and any questions: his mentor, his cheerleader, his mum . . .

'I do love your dad. I do.' Again, her tears fell, and she sniffed. 'But right now, Cass, I need a bit of space. I need him to think about what happens next, and I need to breathe! To sleep a night without the worry lying on me like a heavy blanket. I need to figure out what I need, because I count too.' Again, she looked skyward, feeling dogged by exhaustion at the effort of it all.

He came to rest on the edge of her bed, sitting with his back to her. She watched him hunched over and wished there were another way. Another way to make Lawrence wake up and speak the truth, to make him understand just how much he had hurt her and that there was no going back from it. How could they? He had slept with Lisa, had an affair, been unfaithful, broken their vows – he had hurt her. She was cut so deeply by the fact, she looked down at her middle, expecting to see light coming through.

'I know loving someone is hard, but it means loving them no matter what – that's what you always said!'

'It's not always that straightforward, Cass. Sometimes self-preservation has to come before love or there's a danger you might *both* sink.'

'I guess I just don't want this to be how it is. I don't cope very well with change. It scares me a bit. And I worry that you might go for a short while but never come back. You might like wherever you go more than being here.'

'That won't happen. The place I like best is wherever you are. And change scares us all, love, that's the truth.'

'I've . . . I've met someone, Mum. I suppose I'm in love.' He sounded coy yet was clearly keen to share it with her. His admission drew her focus and blew hope on the flickering embers of joy that lay within her, almost extinguished, but not quite.

His words were a surprise. She knew they were cause for celebration, a milestone, a joyous thing, and guilt flooded her veins that the news was not delivered in the way she had always envisaged: over coffee, around the kitchen table, idling at the edge of the pool in Melbourne . . .

'Cass! That's wonderful! I'm happy for you! I'm so happy for you! Oh, that's great. Who is she? Does she make you happy?' Her voice broke, remembering what it felt like to be in the first throes of love, to carry that joyous bubble of all the wonderful possibilities that lay ahead. First love, when joy felt infinite, happiness unbridled and no matter what the future held, the prospect of being by the side of the person who made the world a better place meant anything was possible.

Her son nodded. 'I am happy. Happier than I have ever been. It's Jake.'

She had lost the thread. 'What's Jake, darling?' She wondered at what point they had changed topic and how she had missed it.

'It's Jake who makes me happy.' He turned to face her and delivered his words slowly. 'It's Jake that I love. And he loves me back.'

'Cassian!' She placed her hand over her mouth. 'I'm . . . I'm . . . I don't know what to say.'

'Just say something, say what you are feeling, what you think!' He swallowed, his skin dotted with nervous sweat. 'Jake said we should tell people and I've wanted to, kind of. Not as much as him . . . I don't know what Dad will say. Tell me how you're feeling!'

She stared at her beautiful son and felt her heart swell. 'I guess I feel sad.'

'Oh my God!' He shook his head. 'Not you, Mum! That's not what I thought, no way. I—' His chest heaved.

'No! No, Cass. Oh, my baby boy, no!' Scooting forward, she reached for her son, pulling him towards her, holding him fast and cradling him like he was a baby, as she kissed the top of his sweet head. 'No, not sad because it's Jake, not at all, but sad that you haven't spoken to me sooner, couldn't tell me how you felt.'

She felt him relax in her arms, with what she guessed was relief.

'I needed to figure it out in my head first.'

'I get that, I do. But you must have had so many questions, been so scared. I don't know, I just can't stand the thought of you having to figure anything out without my support.'

'I need your support right now,' he whispered.

'And you've got it, darling, one hundred per cent you've got it.' They sat quietly for a second or two, letting the new world settle around them. 'I often wondered how it would feel losing you to someone you loved more than me, and of course I wanted it to happen. I want you to fly, Cass, I want you to live your best life! And here we are, and it's strange, because I am so happy for you, happy for Jake, but it means I lose a little bit of you, don't I?'

'Only a little bit.' She could tell he was smiling.

'Oh shit!' she cursed, realising in that moment as her mind caught up that Jake was Daisy's brother, and Daisy was the daughter of the woman her husband had slept with.

'What's wrong?' He pulled away from her and she noticed how he had, in such a short space of time, leapfrogged from boy to man.

'Nothing, darling. Nothing.'

'So, what do you think Dad'll say, and Nan and Grandad?' He bit his lip.

'I think it doesn't matter what anyone says or thinks. It only matters what you and Jake think.'

'We think the world's a better place when we're together.' He laughed softly and she knew it was at a memory and that he had lied to her: she had lost more than a little bit of him, but that was just the way it had to be. 'I don't know if I'm ready to tell them all yet, especially with the new baby and everything; I think they have enough going on.'

'It's no one's business but yours and Jake's, tell or don't tell. Just live your own true life and don't let anyone push you off course.' *Like they did me . . . I have been running for too long . . .*

'Where are you going to go, Mum?' He ran his finger over the rim of her suitcase.

'Well, if I went anywhere, it'd be back to Nanny and Pop's on the Merrigo. And you and Dom would have a bed there too, of course. Nanny and Pops would love it. But I'm not going anywhere. I'll put the case away.'

She watched as Cassian wiped the beginning of tears from his eyes; she knew that right now she needed to be by the side of her kids.

'Thank you, Mum.'

'You don't have to thank me. I love you. I love you all. It will be okay; we'll make it okay.' Sighing, she looked out of the window, over the manicured garden that a man came weekly to keep

265

in order; a man who would soon enough be losing his job as the whole deck of cards fell.

'How can you make things better with Dad? Make your life easier?'

She looked away, hearing the words come from his sweet toddler mouth, and it tore at her breast as she considered how best to answer.

'I need him to come clean, open up, tell his parents exactly what's going on and the mess we're in. I think that would ease the pressure, start the conversation, but that needs to be the minimum. He said it's how he wants to live too, to be more honest, nothing left unsaid.' Again she blinked away the image of Lisa. 'Yes, that's it in a nutshell: nothing left unsaid, nothing but the truth.'

'What shall we do now, Mum?' His breath came fast.

'Right now, we shall go downstairs, put the kettle on. I want to hear all about Jake. I mean not the Jake I know, but the Jake you know. The Jake you *love*.'

'I do love him, Mum.' He wiped his tears with his delicate long fingers.

'Well, now I also know that he's the luckiest boy in the world because you're fabulous. So fabulous.'

'I'm worried about Dom,' he said as he stood.

'Me too. I want to say the way she behaves is because of the crowd she hangs around with, bad influences, but I don't really buy that. Ruby seems like a nice girl.' She pictured how she'd tried to cover up for her drunk daughter in the early hours. 'But I do worry about the path my little girl is walking. She used to talk to me, used to confide in me, but in recent months it feels like I'm the enemy. I'm scared for her, that's the truth, and I get it, I do. Her whole life uprooted from Melbourne, a place she loved.'

'My whole life too.'

'Of course.' She reached out and squeezed his arm, swamped with self-recrimination, wondering how different things might now be for them all if she'd had the courage to rail against them leaving, to find a way to stay put.

'But I met Jake and so for me it's working out, kinda.'

'I don't know what to do, Cass. Sometimes it feels like I don't know what to do about anything!' She cursed the pull of more tears.

'Do you want me to speak to Domino?'

'Yes, she might listen to you.' She felt a wave of gratitude for this sweet, caring human who was such a wonderful son and brother.

The front doorbell rang. Julie made her way down the wide, sweeping staircase and opened the front door, Cassian close behind her.

'Mrs Kelleway?' the man with the clipboard asked.

'Yes.'

'We're here from Walker and Sons. We've been appointed on behalf of the company who you have a car finance agreement with.' She felt her limbs go rigid with fear. Knowing this was going to happen and it actually happening were two very different things. He held out an ID card with his photograph and some laminated stamp. It could have said anything. His tone was overly officious, and she reminded herself that he was only doing his job. 'You have failed to keep up the payments for the black Mercedes-AMG GT 4-door Coupé. And in that regard, I am required today to either take payment in full for the outstanding debt plus any interest accrued on the debt, and our fee, or I will be repossessing the vehicle.'

Julie pictured her purse on the kitchen table devoid of cash yet stuffed full of credit cards and bank cards that all groaned with how much was owed on them; each one might very well see a similar representative turn up with a clipboard at any moment. This was the way it would be until, piece by piece, their whole life would be dismantled, reclaimed, confiscated, carved up, recouped, and handed back. She hadn't intended to laugh, but a small titter left her mouth.

'I'm so sorry,' she managed, knowing she wouldn't be able to explain how she was laughing at the futility and desperation of it all.

'That's quite all right.' The man was stern, cool and yet not unsympathetic.

Cassian began to snicker behind her and before she knew it, they were roaring their laughter, leaning on the wall of their debt-ridden home of which they didn't own so much as a doorknob.

'What the fucking hell's going on?'

She and Cassian turned to see Domino, who stood at the top of the stairs in her dressing gown, an eye mask had been pulled up on to her forehead and her expression was one of fury at having her hangover disturbed.

'Dom! There you are! This man's come for the car. We'll have to get a taxi to your nan's, if either of you have any cash.' she managed to say before the next bout of laughter robbed her breath of its rhythm and she folded over, trying to gain control, as her laughter turned very quickly to tears and her son, her beautiful, beautiful son held her upright.

CHAPTER SEVENTEEN

Daisy Harrop

Daisy parked her bike behind the bench and took a seat. She had stopped crying, thankfully, quite sure she must have run out of tears. Her eyes were sore and her throat raw. The feeling in the base of her gut would have been hard to describe, but shame – shame laced with acute embarrassment – came close. Thankfully her parents had no clue as to the root of her sadness, assuming she was a little overwhelmed by the rather fraught morning where not only did her mum appear to be present and correct for the first time in a very long time, even making promises not only to write to the council about the tree and help her transform the neglected garden, but also the news that she and Jake were far from skint. It was a shocker! They owned flats. In fact, two of these flats opposite where she now sat. She wondered which ones. Looking over the wide sweep of river to the low-rise block where the glass windows looked shiny, the window boxes well-tended and the whole place, for want of a better word, rather fancy.

Any happiness, however, at this wonderful, life-changing news was a little tainted. It was hard to find the joy when she was nursing a freshly broken heart. And not just broken, not cracked, or in need of a slick of glue, but a heart that was shattered – splintered into a million million pieces that she was certain would be impossible to restore. It would be like trying to remake a shell from sand. Where to start? It wasn't only that she had loved Cassian for the longest time, had dreamed explicitly of Cassian, vividly enough to make her blush in his presence, but also that she loved Jake and wanted to be happy for him. But how could she when he had inadvertently stolen her first crush and when her first crush had picked her brother over her? The news had even made the one-hundred-and-fifty-pound tip given to her by Cassian's father feel a little grubby.

Worst of all was the pure, sour-tasting jealousy that sat in her mouth like poison. To be jealous of her own lovely brother was, she knew, a terrible thing. Her lovely brother who had found the confidence to speak out, and for the first time ever, had looked and sounded happy. Her face broke into a smile at this fact. Her envy was a dark thorn she wanted to pluck from her skin but she knew it might take time. It wasn't only that he would get to hold Cassian, be with Cassian, stare into his beautiful face and hear reciprocal words of love, but also that if it worked out between them, Jake would be part of the Kelleway clan. And this had always been her secret dream.

Jake, who was already a regular visitor, would be able to set foot on the hallowed grounds of next door where he'd no doubt be welcomed with open arms and a cold drink in a tall, ice-filled glass. She did her best to tamp down the green-eyed monster that rose in her throat. How she would love to walk into that house, a place she had only visited briefly twice. Once to get a tennis ball that she had been throwing against the wall, counting each bounce until it hit a small rock and ricocheted over the fence and into the Kelleways' back garden. Her mum had told her not to bother the neighbours and that they'd lob the ball back when they came across it, but she was not about to see an opportunity like this slip through her fingers. Instead, she had rocketed around the fence like a terrier with the scent of a rat, and run into the driveway – just the crunch of the immaculate gravel underfoot was like a treat.

'Hello there, Daisy!' Bernie had called out from the side wall where, with his left hand, he snipped at a clambering rose with a small pair of scissors which, in her inexpert opinion, didn't really look up to the job, and in his right hand he held his phone to his ear, breaking off the conversation when she got close. 'What can I do for you today?' he asked, smiling.

'I came to get my ball back.' She pointed over his shoulder. 'It went into your back garden.' She hoped and prayed that he might open the front door and lead her through the house and out the back, giving her a glimpse of the interior, which she had only seen lit by lamps from the outside, but it was enough to tell her it was very upmarket. He might even offer her a glass of squash! Much to her disappointment, he had held up his finger, as if to say, *one sec*, turned and opened the side gate, before returning mere seconds later with her ball.

And the second time was a week later when she figured if she lobbed the ball a bit further into the garden, it might take longer to retrieve or the Kelleways might be inside and be forced to open the front door and invite her in. She wanted so badly to peek inside . . . But no, yet again he was out cutting that damn rose bush and again she left feeling just as frustrated as she had the first time. What was it about him and the need to prune morning, noon and night – surely nothing grew that fast?

Not that it mattered now, any of it, and she hated how on the day when Jake had made this huge announcement, her mum and dad had told her of the most extraordinary gift, here she was, sitting on the bench feeling torn in two over the boy who would never be hers. It seemed crazy that only last night she had ridden her bike to work and been filled with dread at the prospect of waitressing for the family she held in such high regard, and yet here she was on this Saturday lunchtime, with a big fat wad of cash in her pocket, a flat of her own, her mum more awake than she'd been asleep, and Jake having found happiness – surely she could dig deep and find joy! Closing her eyes, she let her head fall back against the bench and steadied her breathing.

'Come on, universe, give me a break!' she whispered.

'Hey, Daisy!'

She turned at the sound of her name to see Dylan Roper a little way down the path and lifted her hand in a wave. He cycled over and jumped off his bike, propping it next to hers, before taking a seat on the bench. His actions were confident, slick, as if they had arranged to meet and it wasn't a coincidence, such was his ease.

'What did you put for 4B?' His opener.

'Erm, 4B.' She tried to remember what question 4B had asked on the chemistry sheet she had to do for homework.

'Yeah.' He pushed his glasses up his nose. 'It wanted to know is NH or OH more polar?'

'It's OH.' She didn't have to think about it. 'Duh!'

'That's what I thought.' He sniffed.

They sat for a moment or two, quietly but not awkwardly. This was quite standard; very often he would sit next to her in the lunch hall or find her on the school field and plop down next to her and their chat was always easy, natural. It was nice. The river burbled over stone and reed, the sound a pleasant one, and one she wouldn't mind lulling her to sleep from a bedroom in the flat across the way. She drew breath to tell Dylan but decided against it; she didn't want to brag and was still digesting the news for herself.

'Have you been crying?' He was, if nothing else, direct.

'A bit.' She rubbed at her eyes, which she had no doubt were red and swollen.

'Anything I can help with, or anything you want to talk about?'

His kindness was sweet, and she was grateful for it. 'No and no.'

'Thank God for that!' His unexpected response made her laugh. 'I mean, no offence, Daisy, but I find the whole tears and emotion thing a bit tricky to deal with.'

'Who doesn't?' She glanced sideways at the nerd who sat next to her in chemistry, maths, and physics. 'Did you hear they are going to take one of the four oaks down?' She shook her head at the horror of it.

'Yeah, but it's just one oak tree. Don't forget they were once part of a wide wood, a forest, and these four are all that remains after they felled them over the years, culling the majority in the nineteen thirties to build houses.'

'That's heartbreaking!' She tried to picture the expanse of green where tarmac and wheelie bins now stood.

'Yes, but it's progress. We need housing, we need roads, yada yada . . .' He shrugged. 'The constant dichotomy of providing for a species who destroy their very habitat to thrive.'

'So, these four oaks are the survivors; it makes me want to fight harder for them,' she reasoned.

'But what about the others long gone? It's only your place in time that makes these four special. They were all special once, but someone came along and—' He mimed swinging an axe.

'I think they're my grandparents,' she blurted.

'You think what are your grandparents?' He looked a little confused.

'The . . . the trees, the oaks. I guess because there's four of them. I talk to them. And I can't bear the idea of one of them being taken away!' Damn those tears that came at the most inconvenient of moments.

'Please don't cry, like, seriously – it freaks me out!'

She half laughed through her sadness. 'I worry about there only being three trees; it's like we need four to keep everything supported, keep everything as it should be, keep everything upright!'

'Well, that's a crazy notion, but no more than thinking the trees are your wrinkly relatives. A triangular structure can be just as supportive, as can a circle. You need to rethink your square.'

She glanced at him again. Maybe he was right. She needed to rethink her square . . .

'It's bloody hot!' He exhaled. 'Scary, really. Recent data shows methane warms the atmosphere eighty times more than carbon dioxide in its first twenty years of emission. And you think people are worried about cow farts, just wait till the permafrost melts. Bloody worrying.'

'It is bloody worrying,' she echoed. 'And that's before we even get on to albedo feedback.'

'Yep, absolutely: less ice equals more warming, which equals less ice.' He rolled his hand to indicate the never-ending, depressing loop of decline.

There was a moment of silence while each pondered the issue.

'I might go for a swim.' He jumped up, changing the topic entirely.

'In the river?' She felt simultaneously horrified and attracted by the idea.

'Why not?'

She watched as he slowly slipped off his socks and trainers, before peeling off his long-sleeved t-shirt and his jeans and folding them neatly into a pile on the bench; his glasses he placed on top of his clothes and there he stood in his snug, cotton boxers.

Daisy felt the spread of crimson over her chest and neck. Dylan was . . . Dylan was quite beautiful. His muscled back rippled as he moved his arms above his head, treading cautiously along the riverbank. His legs were wide, and his chest smooth and defined.

He put one leg forward and placed his fingers on his hips, elbows out, looking straight ahead. 'Who am I, Daisy?' His face was pensive.

'What?' She tore her eyes from his chest.

'Come on, who am I?' He exaggerated his pose.

'I-I don't know!' She admitted defeat.

'The Bather – I'm The Bather! Cézanne – you know it, right?' He relaxed his arms and held her stare.

'Yes.' She swallowed. *Cézanne . . . of course.* 'Yes, I know it.'

'Are you coming in?' He waded into the river and dropped down among the weeds, letting the clear water rush over his shoulders as he shivered.

Daisy looked around, making sure the coast was clear before stepping out of her dungarees and t-shirt, wishing she'd worn her one decent bra. It felt rash, daring and illicit, and gloriously life-affirming to be standing here in her knickers and bra on this fine Saturday afternoon. Especially with her knees on display. The knees she kept firmly under wraps in all weathers. Dylan didn't seem too offended by the sight of them, in fact, he looked quite delighted as, tentatively, she put her foot in the cool water, going deeper until it lapped her skinny ankle. A step further and the grassy bank gave way to soft mud.

'I'm scared I'm going to stand on a frog or a fish!' She giggled as she made the claim.

'It'd have to be a tiny fish.' He laughed, making the minute size apparent with his thumb and forefinger.

'I've never even seen a fish that small!' she protested.

'Have you never fished for tiddlers with a net and an old jam jar?'

'No, I've never fished for a tiddler. Not even sure I know exactly what a tiddler is?'

'Oh, Daisy!' She liked when he used her name. 'If you've never caught a tiddler you haven't lived! It's the most brilliant thing!'

She loved his enthusiasm for something so simple. 'Wading bare-foot with your jeans rolled up, it stirs the silt into muddy clouds around your ankles so you never quite know what you are going to stand on next – it's a footfall lottery!' He leaned towards her as his enthusiasm for the topic grew, pawing the air with his fingers as if sculpting the image in front of him. 'It might be a mound of mud that squishes between your toes, but equally it could be the sharp bite of a rock or the tickle of a darting minnow or a stickleback. How does that sound?'

'Scary! Horrible!' She shivered, suddenly feeling very doubtful about what might lurk on the riverbed, concerned about not being able to see what was around her feet, while knowing there were fish, pebbles and weeds to navigate by touch alone.

'You can't let it put you off.' He took a step forward until his face felt very close to hers, his eyes bright, his shoulder-length hair tucked behind his ears, his skin a little tanned, and she could smell his savoury scent – it was very attractive. 'To catch a tiddler in a net and then place it in the jam jar feels like a triumph, and to briefly see a creature like that close up is amazing.' He looked skyward and seemed older than his years. 'We can come back here, if you like, and I'll show you how to catch a minnow, a little stickleback, we'll take a picture and set it free.'

She found both his presumptuousness and kindness endearing.

'I might be a bit of a scaredy cat; not sure I'd like to catch a living thing. In fact, I might be too scared to come any further – you've put me off swimming!'

'Don't be a scaredy cat. It's just life, Daisy.'

He was right: it was just life. She liked Dylan. Gianna's words came back to her. '*Find someone who gets you, who likes you and who you like in return . . .*'

Daisy smiled as he stood in the water with his muscled arms wide open, ready to catch her. As she made her way cautiously towards him, she glanced up at the flats and found herself looking through an open set of French doors, through which she could see the widest, deepest sofa she had ever seen! She imagined falling into it and knew it would be blissfully comfortable. Unlike her family, she'd never been one for daytime napping, but my goodness with a sofa like that to tumble on to, maybe she'd give it a go . . .

Her own flat! It still hadn't sunk in. She owned a property. She had an apartment! Her heart sang as the fact settled. She knew that one day she would sit in that very spot, looking out over the river and she would remember this day, this moment, when she did something daring, stripped down to her underwear and walked into the arms of this boy. A boy who, she felt sure, was capable of taking an eraser to the images of Cassian Kelleway that she carried in her brain.

'I've got you.' He held out his hand. 'Come on, don't be scared!' She walked forward and put her fingers against his where they knitted with ease. 'I've got you.'

Wheeling her bike slowly, ambling from one side to the other, Daisy walked home with damp clothes clinging to her wet skin, and a lightness to her spirit. She pulled the scarf from around her neck and removed her beret, stuffing them into the canvas pannier, which had a hole in it. Turning her face towards the sun, she pictured the moment she and Dylan had parted, and he had given her a wide smile that spoke of promise . . . A smile that filled her with something that felt a lot like hope. And the fact he was happy to discuss topics that fascinated her and was also hoping to head off to Cambridge was no bad thing.

Approaching the four oak trees at the top of the road, she stared at the one with yellow tape around it and it struck her as almost comical. What on earth did anyone think yellow tape was going to do in terms of protection if this mighty tree decided to topple? Abandoning her bike on the pavement, she crept close to the tree that was so cruelly adorned, marked out as different. Gently, she lifted her hand to the gnarled bark and rested her palm on it. Taking a step closer, she stood as near to it as she could and placed her other hand on the rough exterior.

'I'm sorry, Gramps. Sorry we chopped down your forest and sorry that I might not be able to save you.'

After a quick sweep of the area to make sure no one was watching, she planted a kiss on the tree and said her goodbyes.

Arriving home, she looked up at the front of their house, the only one on the street where paint clung in thin strips of pale lemon, where the front door let wind and leaves whistle through a gap at the bottom and the original wooden garage doors listed to the right. And it made her smile, knowing that every spare penny went on securing a future for her and Jake. It was the most incredible gift and one that she would never, ever take for granted or stop feeling thankful for. She was lucky, so very lucky to be a Harrop. It was as if she felt elevated, her self-esteem increased, just knowing how very loved she was and how much her mum and dad had sacrificed for her. Who knew, if she worked hard, got to Cambridge, made the success of her life that Gianna and her parents felt she was capable of, one day in the future, she too might have a family like the Kelleways . . .

With her key in her hand, she was about to open the front door when a sound from the back garden drew her attention. It was the scrape of a shovel on the path, digging.

'What's going on?' she asked, at the sight of her mum who was very much up and about, turning over soil and sorting through it with her fingers to remove the weeds.

'I'm weeding so that we can plant daffodil bulbs.'

'Oh! Okay, great!' She couldn't disguise her delight, both at the prospect of the flowers that would bloom in the spring or the fact that her mother was doing the very thing she had dreamed of.

Lisa straightened and with both hands on the shovel she smiled at her. 'They'll be beautiful, Daisy. Not immediately, I mean they'll take a while to figure out which way is up, to bed in, they might need to rest, to learn what comes next, but when they do, they will shine and our garden will be beautiful.'

'It will, Mum.' Daisy smiled at her – her wonderful, wonderful mum. 'It will be perfect . . .'

'I thought we could do this bed today and then, tomorrow, you can give me a hand.'

Her mum's enthusiasm felt like the most glorious reprieve. 'What do you need a hand with?'

Lisa pointed to the small gap between the fence and the wall that ran along the boundary between their house and the Kelleways'.

'I'm going to put some stakes in and plant a climber, fill that space, block it off.'

She looked determined, motivated and Daisy felt nothing but pride for the corner her mother seemed to have turned.

'I can help you in the morning, but I won't be here in the afternoon.'

'Oh, where are you off to? Not working extra shifts, are you? I don't want you working too hard, love.'

'No, not working. I'm going fishing.'

'Fishing? I didn't know you were into fishing! But then I didn't know Jake was into Cassian, so what do I know?'

'He seems happy, Mum.' This a reminder that it was a happy thing – Jake had found love! No matter her heart still flexed at the thought of her brother's beau. She looked forward to the day this ceased to be the case.

'He really does. I'm so proud of him, proud of you both.' Her mum squeezed her hand.

'And I'm proud of you.' She meant it.

'So, should I get the chips on tomorrow? Are you going to come home with a big fat fish for supper?'

'No.' Daisy shook her head. 'I'm not going to catch myself a fish. I'm going to catch myself a nerd.'

'You'll need a big net.' Lisa laughed and in that moment with the sun shining and her mum laughing, everything felt possible.

CHAPTER EIGHTEEN

Cleo Richardson

'Can I really go home?' Cleo asked the nurse who had just taken her temperature and blood pressure.

'Yep, you've had the all-clear from the doctor, you've showered, been to the loo and the little one's doing well. You're all set.'

'Do you think I should maybe stay a bit longer, just to make sure everything is okay?' She was aware of the nervous edge to her voice.

'Everything *is* okay. There's no reason to keep you here. Take your baby home and rest!'

'It feels a bit quick.' She felt conflicted, wanting to get out of the place and show her son off to the family and also to get him back to their house in Swallow Drive so their life as a little family of three could begin. Yet simultaneously, she felt the flickering flame of fear rise in her gut at the thought of taking her son out of this building, being responsible for him without a clutch of capable medics just the other side of her door for any eventuality.

'It would be odd if you didn't feel a bit nervous,' the kindly woman placated her.

'I still feel like I'm catching my breath,' she confided. 'And I know it sounds ridiculous, but even though I had nine months to get used to the idea of having a baby, it's still a bit of a shock! One minute I was on the old gas and air, pushing when instructed, and now I'm going home and, like I said, it feels a bit quick.'

The nurse laughed. 'Again, all quite normal. Motherhood is a shock. I still feel that way.'

'How old are yours?' Cleo was keen to know when this feeling might subside.

'Thirty-four and thirty-six.' She winked.

Cleo laughed. 'I also feel a bit . . .' She tried to think of the word.

'A bit what, love?' The nurse drew the curtains, letting the daylight flood the room and turned to give Cleo her full attention.

'A bit, I don't know, like my body doesn't belong to me. My boobs are so sore.' She placed her hand on her chest, feeling the sting of where her little one had chomped with his gums on her nipples for what felt like hours.

'Everything, every single aspect of your life will require small adjustments, or sometimes big adjustments. It can make you feel panicked: what happens if he gets sick? Supposing I drop him? Is he hungry? Too hot, too cold? How can I go to the loo with a baby, make a cup of tea with a baby? How will I remember it all – the feeding, the bum-changing, the bathing, the sleep routine? All of it can seem overwhelming, but you *will* remember it all and you do get through it, and he'll help you.' She looked towards the little boy who slept soundly in the bassinet by the side of the bed. 'He'll give you clues, make noises, pull faces, and steer you. And if you forget to change his bum one time or he doesn't feed for long enough, or he cries a lot one day, or sleeps a lot the next, that's okay. It's all okay. You'll figure it out together, but you *will* figure it out and one day you'll wake up without that feeling of panic, without worrying about getting it right, without rushing to check on him if he hasn't murmured. You won't fret about making a mistake or worrying what you've missed, you'll just mother him, and it will all feel like second nature. But it takes a while.'

'Thank you.' Cleo meant it. The nurse's words had helped. She couldn't wait for that day when it all felt like second nature.

'All set?' Georgie loped in with the car seat in his hand.

'Nearly.' She smiled.

'I told Bernie when I called earlier that I was worried about putting the baby in the car seat, I don't want to squash him or pinch his skin.' He pulled a face. 'He said, "Be brave, son." He called me *son*!'

'That's nice.' She knew how a crumb of acceptance from her parents could make you glow, and it bothered her, noting how her family also held her husband in their palm, handing out compliments that felt like gold. Did she really want her little one to grow up like this too? The thought of moving to Ilfracombe again flew into her head. She pictured walking the harbour with their baby boy, away from it all . . . It was what she wanted, no doubt. A new start, a new life, a whole new world at the seaside. 'And don't worry, it's normal to feel a bit overwhelmed, Georgie. Every aspect of our life will require small adjustments or big adjustments, but we'll figure it out.' Cleo smiled at the nurse who bustled out of the room.

'I guess so. This is it, Cleo, his first day on the planet! And we're off to introduce him to his family! I'm so excited. Scared, but excited too.'

'Me too.'

'And did they say when we could, you know?' He winked. 'When it would be okay to—'

'Georgie, are you seriously asking me about sex when we haven't even left the hospital?'

'No!' He shook his head. 'Not at all. No way.' He tutted. 'But if you had to guess . . .'

She reached over and batted him with her hand. 'Don't listen to your daddy! He's paying no heed to what is best for me and only thinking of his own selfish needs.' She spoke mockingly to their son who slept soundly.

'I'm a daddy!' George shook his head.

'You are, my darling.' Joy burst from her, as she packed up her bag ready to go home.

◆ ◆ ◆

Georgie drove like a man delivering fresh eggs over cobbles, but finally, he pulled up in front of her parents' house. It was odd to think it would be full of the people who, only the night before, she had eaten dinner with in the Italian restaurant. Incredible how much life could change in just a few short hours. Now parked on the driveway, she took her time unbuckling her seatbelt. It was a small disappointment that her stomach still looked as if she was yet to give birth. She'd seen enough social media posts of women posing in skinny jeans and whipping up a carrot cake only minutes after the umbilical cord had been cut to figure it might at least have gone down a little. Not that she really cared if she carried this tummy for the rest of her days – her incredible body had grown her a baby and she would forever feel indebted to it.

Her bones felt soft, her muscles tired, her thoughts a little fuddled, but her heart was twice the size and bursting with more love than she knew it could contain for the little boy who was hers. For the thousandth time she stared at his tiny face, sleeping soundly in the carry chair, right next to her on the back seat of Georgie's car, the one with chicken nuggets nestling under the front seat, still quite unable to believe that he was for keeps. The prospect thrilled and petrified her in equal measure. Yes, it was going to be just as much fun as she'd planned, but where was the manual? Sweet Jesus, she'd spent the best part of a month getting to grips with the new carpet steamer, studying the instructions, testing it, dismantling it, and pondering over the attachments, some of which she'd still not been brave enough to try out. There had even been online tutorials! Yet here she was with a tiny human, a tiny human with needs and she didn't really have the first clue.

'We can do this, baby. We'll figure it out together.'

'Are you okay?' Georgie opened the back door and ran his hand over her face. It might have been her imagination, but she was sure the way he looked at her was a little different; his expressions had always been ones of love, but now he gazed at her as if he had seen an angel. And she understood, knowing that how she felt about him was also magnified: they had done something wondrous together, created this little life. This achievement seemed to amplify their love.

'I'm fine.' She smiled her widest to reassure him. 'Just a bit sore, bit achy, bit like my bones are made of chalk and my muscles glass – tired, but fine!'

'Oh, mate, you did so well. I can't believe he's ours!' He blinked away the tears that he'd been crying since their son had been placed in his arms for the first time.

'Remember the plan, Georgie.' She needed him to focus. 'We have a quick cup of tea, we let everyone meet the little fella and then we go home, unplug the phone, board up the windows, triple lock the door and keep the world out for a few days, got it?'

'Got it!' he agreed, before kissing her hard on the mouth.

'And who knows, in those few days, we may decide to pack up and make a break for north Devon, never to return!'

Georgie laughed as if she were joking and she wondered how to press the idea as it grew, quite fancying the thought of starting over, away from the Kelleway shadow, to live in the sun . . .

'I love you. I can't believe what you just did, you're bloody Wonder Woman!'

'I know and I love you. And yes, I am bloody Wonder Woman, although I might need a month or two to get back in my costume. Now, go get the baby out of the other side, I think they know we're here.'

No sooner had she spoken than the sound of squealing could be heard. Instantly she doubted the wisdom of making this detour on the way home, but it was far too late to do anything about it now. Bracing herself for the attention, she looked towards the house as her parents and Lawrence came out on to the driveway. She had already clocked her sister-in-law's Mini parked out front, glad that Julie was here to meet her new nephew.

'Oh my goodness, oh my!' Her mum was crying, her dad too, as they clung to each other. Lawrence looked somewhat bewildered and unusually a little heavy around the eyes, like he hadn't slept. Still, he presented his usual suave, slick, coordinated and groomed exterior that told the world he was living his best life, although he was unshaven and his happy expression was, she noted, a little forced. She figured he must have hit the sauce after they'd left for the evening.

She watched as Georgie slowly lifted their newborn from the car and her parents crowded around. The expression on her mum's face was one that she hadn't seen for the longest time. It was the same look Winnie had given Lawrence at the end of the school day, her whole demeanour lit up, her face beaming. It made her feel powerful, excited, and accepted. *So this is what it feels like . . .* She couldn't deny it felt good!

'Look at him! Just look!' Winnie shook her head at the utter delight of her grandson, and this Cleo more than understood. Slowly she climbed from the back seat, tensing and leaning on the open door until she felt steady on her feet. As Georgie spirited their son inside, flanked by Lawrence and her dad, she felt a strange gripping anxiety ripple through her as her baby was taken out of sight. A sensation that was both new and unexpected.

'Cleo! Oh, my clever girl!' Her mother raced over and held her fast in a warm embrace, kissing her face and running her hand over her back. Cleo struggled to recall a time she had received such a physical welcome. It felt as if finally, finally she had earned her place at the Kelleway table, and her new baby was the ticket that got her there. It saddened her that this was what it had taken and she thought of how different things might have been if she'd not conceived. But she knew better than to raise this today of all days, deciding instead to simply revel in the moment.

'Well done, my clever girl!'

'He's perfect, Mum,' she whispered.

'Of course, he is,' her mother responded without the faintest whiff of irony, as, arm in arm, they made their way into the house.

Cleo was glad to sit. Even the short walk from the car to the sofa had taken more effort than she would have imagined.

With the baby seat positioned securely on the wide sofa, Lawrence hung back a little, which again was unlike him, and there was no sign of Julie. She watched as he clapped Georgie on the back, before pulling him in for a hug. This, she knew, would make her husband happy and she wished he wasn't so accommodating, wished he too was starting to see that the Kelleway love was conditional, judgemental, tarnished.

'Are you hungry, darling?' her dad asked. 'When I spoke to Georgie earlier, he said you fancied some pasta from the place on the high street, I can't remember its name.' He clicked his fingers, as if this might be an aide memoire.

'You were only there last night, Dad. Please don't let me get old if that's how quickly your memory goes!' Lawrence jested with their old man.

'You can laugh, but it comes to us all, Loz!' Bernie chuckled and, without waiting for her response, ambled off to the kitchen.

'Pasta, how lovely. Thank you.' She was touched by the gesture, only having commented in passing how she could murder a plate of it. 'As I said on the phone, we're not staying long, Mum,' she reminded her mother's back.

Winnie ignored her, crouching down on the rug, and staring into the car seat at the face of her new grandson. 'Look at you. You little poppet!' her mother cooed, stroking his cheek with her fingertip. 'You gorgeous boy, I'm your nana, yes, I am! I'm your nana!'

'I thought it'd be easier to come here as you've got more space, and everyone can see him and then we're going straight home to sleep. Where are Jules and the kids? I saw her car.'

No one seemed to have heard her.

'If you think you have a lack of space now, just wait until this little one starts collecting toys and wanting bikes and running around. You'll have to think about getting a bigger place. I know' – her mother twisted to face her – 'I could have a word with Mr Portland. Do you know him? He co-owns the estate agent on the high street, drives a blue Porsche. I'd go so far as to call him a friend of the family. Maybe I could ask him to pop over and go through your options with you.' Winnie turned her attention back to the baby.

'Flippin' 'eck, I think we've got enough going on right now, Winnie, without a house move to contend with. Besides, don't think he covers Ilfracombe.' Georgie mumbled the last sentence, and it made her laugh. He spoke for them both and pulled a face at her behind her mum's back.

'Well, the offer's there. He's got very long legs, hasn't he?'

'Who, Mr Portland?' Lawrence quipped.

This time everyone ignored *him*.

Cleo, caught up in the moment and with no small amount of drugs still in her system, felt a swell of pride at her mother's observation. She knew leg length was not something she could take credit for, but the fact that it implied she was likely to have a tall boy and tall teen, in a house where such a thing was prized, made her feel like she was winning.

'Cassian always had long legs.' Lawrence gave a single sage nod, as if this boded well.

'Georgie's tall.' She looked over at the man she loved, the father of her baby, who stuffed a croissant into his mouth, taken from a tray on the coffee table, and brushed the resulting crumbs on to the carpet. 'He takes after his dad.'

'Mmm, no, I think he takes after his grandad,' Winnie chimed. 'He's got long legs like his Grandad Bernie. Your grandad has got great legs and so have you, little one. Haven't you, darling?' She addressed the sleeping child who ignored her.

'If you say so.' Cleo knew it was easier to agree than rail against her mother.

'I do say so! In fact, that's what I'm going to call him, Little B, short for "Little Bernie", that's what your nana is going to call you!' She bent low and gently kissed his tiny foot. 'Hello, Little B! Hello, darling boy!'

'He's not going to be called Little B!' Cleo hadn't meant to raise her voice, but in that moment, having been so adamant that if they'd had a girl she would not be called Winnie after her mother, this felt like a small kick in the tits. She was beginning to regret the decision to come here first. Maybe a few days' grace, alone with her boys, pottering about in her slippers might have been the better option.

'Everything all right, love?' Georgie managed through a mouth full of buttery pastry, spraying croissant dust as he spoke.

She nodded and found a tight smile. 'I was just thinking that it's about time we gave him his proper name.' It was timely that her dad reappeared with a bowl in his hands, as the eyes of the assembled fell upon her. A hush came over the room as they waited with bated breath. 'He shares his birthday with Georgie's grandad and so we are going to name him after him.'

Looking up, she caught the open-mouthed look of disdain her mother shot her father, but that was just too bloody bad.

'His name is Thomas.' She spoke with confidence. 'Thomas Welland Richardson, Tommy for short.'

Georgie's face lit up and he held her gaze, full of love that she felt in return. 'Tommy.' He beamed. 'Thomas Welland Richardson.'

There was a second of collective silence while she, and she suspected all present, waited to hear Winnie's view on their choice.

Instead, she shouted, 'Dad got you the pasta you wanted!' Leaping up she grabbed the bowl from his hands.

This was her mother's way: rather than comment, discuss or let the idea settle, like a footballer with her eye on the goal, she tackled, sprinted, spun and deployed the verbal equivalent of fancy footwork to distract and confuse the opposing team, meaning she would always, one way or another, get a shot at the target. And Cleo knew in that moment it wasn't how she wanted to raise her baby.

'Are you hungry, Cleo?' Her mother pushed. 'He went all the way up the high street to get it for you. Didn't you, darling?' she called to her husband.

The rumble in her stomach confirmed that she was indeed hungry and she figured food could only help quell the feeling of light-headedness that weakened her. In truth, all she wanted to do was pack up her baby and go home and she knew the key to leaving quickly was to get that pasta down her neck. Plus, the scent coming from the hot bowl of Fettucine Alfredo was enough to encourage her to stay just a little bit longer. This aside from the fact that her sweet dad, who was now staring out of the window looking thoughtful, had gone to so much trouble.

'Are you okay, Dad?'

'Oh, more than okay, my love, more than okay. It's a daunting thought, isn't it, the withering time . . .'

She caught Georgie's eyeline and they both pulled faces; what on earth was her dad on about?

'Just standing here trying to take it all in: a new grandson, new beginnings, it really is something. He's certainly a smasher, like his mum.'

It must have been her hormones but to hear her dad say something so lovely was like touchpaper to kindling and her tears bloomed.

'Oh dear! You want to keep an eye out for the baby blues.' Her mother spoke firmly as she handed her the large white dish full of steaming pasta, which looked and smelled incredible.

'I'm teary because it's an emotional time!' She took the bowl into her hands. 'I only gave birth like five minutes ago. I have pushed something the size of a melon through a very narrow gap and it bloody hurt!'

'Yes, we all know how much it hurts,' her mother whispered to her. 'But there are only two sorts of women, darling: those who moan about it, dine out on it, and think they are unique – and those of us who just get on with it.'

For some reason the woman's lack of empathy made her laugh. It was typical, and Cleo couldn't wait to get home, pull up the drawbridge and get on Rightmove to seek out cottages in Ilfracombe.

'But I mean what I say.' Her mother wasn't done. 'Look out for baby blues. Keep your boobs clean, rested and empty, and eat well. Oh, and sleep when the baby sleeps, that's the key. Ask *Georgie* if he wouldn't mind pitching in and letting you rest a bit.'

Choosing to ignore her mother's words and without the energy to explain how *Georgie* did more than his fair share around the house – he cleaned the bathrooms, vacuumed the floors, did laundry, washed dishes, almost as if he were a functioning adult living as her equal! The irony wasn't lost on her that her own father did very little, other than man the barbecue and the odd spot of gardening.

'Hello?' a male voice called from the hallway.

'Come through, we're in here!' Winnie yelled without knowing who it was and this was enough to send a protective jolt right through Cleo, who considered retrieving her baby from the seat and holding him close.

A man in a neat blue linen blazer, tight chinos and tan loafers stepped into the room.

'Mr Portland! How wonderful!' Winnie gushed. Jumping up, she ran over to him and stood very close to his side, as if presenting him to the wider family. 'This is Mr Portland!' She grinned.

Mr Portland looked more than a little uncomfortable. 'I don't want to intrude,' he began.

'Oh, not at all, you're welcome any time! This is my daughter, Cleo.' Winnie pointed in her direction. Cleo raised her hand.

'Lovely to meet you.' The man blushed and looked most awkward. 'I can't stay but was passing and was a little worried about your message earlier, Mrs Kelleway.'

'Winnie, please!' she trilled.

'W-Winnie, yes. I didn't know you had family around you and thought you might need help or be in difficulty. You said it was urgent and so . . .' He sucked air through his teeth. His discomfort was excruciating.

'What message?' Lawrence asked what they were all thinking.

'Oh!' Her mother batted her hand. 'I only wanted to ask Mr Portland for advice on the oak they want to take down. I thought with his connections at the council he might be able to have a word with someone about it.'

'Oh, I see!' The man looked from Winnie to the floor. 'I don't really . . . I was only checking in on you; we like to keep an eye on the elderly members of our community. All part of the Portland and Portland customer service!'

Cleo winced. The word elderly, when used in association with her mother, was, she knew, never going to go down well. Georgie smirked. Her mother however laughed loudly, as if he was joking.

'You are funny, Mr Portland. And may I say it must be so lovely working with your older brother. I would love my children to all work together. Family is so important, don't you think? This is our newest addition.' She pointed to Tommy.

'Ah, he's lovely – congratulations!'

Cleo smiled her thanks.

'And, actually, I don't work with my older brother.'

'Oh, well, I've put my foot in it, haven't I? Are you the oldest?' Winnie pushed.

'No, no, he's not my brother. He's my husband.' Mr Portland held up his left hand that sported a shiny gold band on the third finger.

'Well.' Her mother's smile never faltered, but she spoke as if all the air had left her lungs. 'That's lovely.'

'I'd better make a move, we're off to the garden centre. I'm afraid we're at that age where we appreciate a wander around the hardy annuals and a good garden centre lunch!' Mr Portland pointed towards the driveway and made his hasty exit.

Winnie showed him out, returning to the kitchen where she loudly clattered cups and saucers.

Cleo and Lawrence exchanged looks of bewilderment and amusement at the rather random visit.

'Where's Jules?' Cleo asked again, using the question as a diversion, but also wishing she were here as she sucked the warm pasta up into her mouth.

'Logistical issues with the kids as usual,' Lawrence explained. 'So I came ahead, but she'll be here any minute in the Merc. She needed to wait for Cass to get showered. God only knows what he got up to last night. I think he and Jake probably went on the prowl after I'd left.'

Cleo noticed his double blink and wondered what had put him so on edge.

'Dom's home, though, fresh from hitting the books with her friend Ruby. I know she can't wait to meet her new cousin.'

'She's such a wonderful girl!' Winnie said, in case anyone hadn't got the memo on just how fabulous her grandchildren were, as she swept into the room, gathered an empty glass and swept out again, back into the open-plan kitchen.

Cleo forked a heap of the garlicky, parmesan-scented ribbons, finding she didn't care about much in that second, other than filling her face with the glorious pasta; she couldn't eat it quickly enough, greedily scooping it into her mouth like it was going to be taken away from her. Her hand, it seemed, was motored by her famished body.

'Oh my God, thank you for getting me this, Dad. I love this woman's cooking so much!' It was true, and Cleo knew that she would forever associate this dish with the day she gave birth, the Friday evening spent at the restaurant immediately before going into labour and all that this incredible food represented. 'She's like a magician, a witch, casting a spell with the silkiest pasta, the richest sauce; it must be easy to make someone fall in love with you when you can cook like this! It's saucery! See what I did there?' She tittered through her mouthful. No one laughed at her joke, which she felt deserved more. Bernie smiled and, as was his MO, looked a little close to tears.

'I fell in love with you, and you can barely heat up beans.' Georgie beamed at his wife.

'Give her a break, Georgie Porgie, she's just had a bloody baby! You can get your own food!' Lawrence shot his words at the man who shrugged, as if nothing, not even the snarky tone of his brother-in-law, could put a dent in his happiness. And just like that normal service was resumed.

'Hell-oo?'

'Jules.' She smiled in anticipation of showing off Thomas Welland . . . he had a name! It felt like he had properly arrived, a citizen of the planet, a proper person. *Thomas Welland Richardson*. And he sounded wonderful! Lawrence folded his arms across his chest and again she picked up on his uncharacteristic nerves. Something was definitely up, but she had no idea what – a tiff with Jules maybe?

'What time do you call this? We were about to send out a search party!' Winnie joked with typical lack of awareness from the kitchen. It was her way of reprimanding their tardiness without seeming to do so.

Julie, Cassian and Domino walked in. They looked a little less than enthused for such a huge event, their shoulders somewhat rounded, eyes a tad downcast, and it rankled a little; surely today it could just be all about Tommy.

'Can you believe he's here? Our Little B!' Her mother's words, yelled across the hallway, would have irritated were it not for the fact that her energy in the face of Julie's lukewarm entrance was welcome – that and Thomas made a small mewling sound. Opening his mouth to reveal tiny gums, he screwed up his eyes and his arms moved a little. Cleo wondered if the sight of him waking, the sound that came from his mouth, would always have this effect: that of battling an entirely immersive wave of unconditional love. Then just like that he went straight back to sleep.

Julie bent low and kissed her. 'How're you doing?'

'I'm good.'

'You look it.'

'Do I?' She wiped the pasta sauce from her chin.

'You do, you look . . .' It was actually touching to see her friend so wrapped in emotion that her words were gentle, her eyes misty. 'You look like someone who has that air of contentment that all is right in the world.'

Cleo reached out and briefly took her friend's hand, which to her surprise was shaking. 'It is really.'

Cassian was clearly drawn to the baby wrapped in a white crocheted blanket and knelt down in front of the car seat to get a closer look. The whole family stared at Tommy, whose little sleeping face peeped out from inside the soft wool.

'Isn't he something?' Her dad shook his head, as if unable to believe that this new addition was here. 'And a boy, Cass! How lucky did we get, a boy!' he boomed.

Domino caught Cleo's eye and the two shared a look that was one part bemusement and two parts despair. *A boy!* Those two words heralded with such joy and confidence as if any other result would have been second best, a failure. Cleo smiled at her, and Domino, despite her tender years, shook her head with a maturity and understanding that made Cleo realise that her niece was growing up.

'He's called Tommy boy!' Georgie announced.

'Well, just Tommy,' she corrected, although quietly enough so as not to put a dent in her husband's pride.

'Hello, Tommy boy!' Cassian cooed and Cleo bit her lip.

'So, Cass, you're now the oldest grandson, so you're going to need to take this little fella under your wing. He's going to be a footballer, I can tell!' Lawrence stared at the now sleeping baby with an obvious lump in his throat. 'What do you reckon, centre forward?'

Cleo knew that it was vital to get this little boy away from their constant commentary, best to take him somewhere he could grow up away from their influence, free to be whoever and whatever he wanted. Yes, her mind was made up.

'Maybe.' Her nephew sighed with obvious irritation.

'Who's hungry?!' Winnie laughed, walking into the sitting room and placing a crystal tray loaded up with tiny crustless sandwiches on to the coffee table. 'There's also cheese and crackers on the counter in the kitchen, help yourselves. Although the Brie is a little depleted.' Cleo saw her mother's eyes dart briefly towards Julie. 'Well, Domino, what do you think of your new cousin?'

'He's very cute, Nan.' Again, she looked at Cleo as if at a loss at what else she was supposed to say. Sixteen, that awkward age between child and woman. Cleo winked at her, remembering what it felt like in the time before she had grown into herself, when the world of boys and babies was alien and extreme self-consciousness cloaked her. She hoped Domino would find her feet soon enough, come out of her shell a little.

'We got you a small gift.' Julie stepped forward and handed her a pretty box. 'It's a bubble bath for you. I think those little moments like taking a bath become so precious when you're a new mum.'

'Oh, Jules, thank you, that's lovely!'

'I know that when I had mine, the babies got lots of presents and yet it was me who had done all the hard work.'

'Are we doing gifts now? I'll go grab mine!' Winnie said with enthusiasm.

'No, Mum, I don't think so, not now. We'll be off in a mo.' Cleo put the gift by her feet. 'As I said, we're not staying long, just popped in really and then I got tempted by this.' She lifted the empty bowl before setting it on the coffee table next to the sandwiches, which only Cassian seemed to be eating. 'But we couldn't wait to let you all meet Tommy.' She couldn't help but enunciate his name. 'But I'm honestly knackered and I want to get home and get settled so I can feed him – still navigating the whole sore nipple, leaky boob, baby's little gob thing.' Her mother winced, although she suspected it was more at her turn of phrase than the topic in hand. 'So, we'll push off if that's okay.' She edged to the corner of her seat. 'But I promise, give us a couple of days to get straight and then all come over to ours or, better still, we'll all come over here and you can cuddle him to your heart's content and we can do gifts and whatever – not that we expect gifts or anything! I mean, I'm not haggling for a Daisy-sized tip!'

'What do you mean a Daisy-sized tip?' her mum echoed loudly enough for Lawrence to look up and Julie to visibly bristle.

'Lawrence gave Daisy a whacking great tip last night after dinner.' She thought it was common knowledge.

'Course he did!' Winnie smiled at her son. 'Such a generous boy.'

'Yes, course he did!' Julie echoed, but there was no mistaking her sarcasm.

Cassian stopped eating sandwiches and stared at his mum. The atmosphere was suddenly a little weighted and Cleo tried to catch Georgie's eye, signalling with a jerk of her head towards the door that it was time to go.

Her mum did her best to steer them back to calmer waters. 'I find it hard to know what to buy for babies. In my day we used to make blankets and knit matinée jackets, but nowadays it's all baby monitors, organic facecloths, whale music and mini sleeping bags – another world.' She clapped with delight. 'Anyway, I've decided that for this little fella, we are going to plant a tree or a shrub, something to signify new growth, new life.'

'That's a lovely idea, Winnie!'

'Glad you approve, Georgie, although it won't be me caring for it, it's my darling husband who has the green fingers.' She smiled at Bernie and it warmed Cleo to be here in the thick of it, witnessing the great love her parents still shared, knowing that despite their flaws, this was the family who would help raise Thomas Welland. Although they would do so from afar, with the occasional visit, the odd phone call, even holidays where they might join her by the sea . . .

'Flattery will get you everywhere!' Bernie walked over and kissed his wife on the forehead.

'I think it'll be lovely to all get together in a few days. I'll send out invites, do it properly.' Her mother, she could tell, was already in planning mode.

'Of course, you will!' Cleo, despite her ever-growing tiredness, chuckled at the idea. *Ilfracombe . . . fish and chips and choppy seas, real fires, great pubs, sailing boats, beach walks, shell collecting, surfing when he's older . . .* She couldn't wait to lay her plans bare to Georgie, knowing he would love it as much as her once he got his toes in the sand.

'It'll be a "Welcome to the world" party. I'll get a cake made!' And just like that her mum was up and running. 'I'll call the lady who did one for *Gardeners' World*. It was all over the local paper – she presented it to Monty Don and he ate it with his soil-covered hands. I remember at the time thinking a quick whizz with a nail-brush wouldn't have done any harm. Anyway, a famous cakemaker for our Little B! It'll be fabulous.'

Cleo felt the rise of irritation and reminded herself that this was a day for thanks and celebration, not for verbally jousting with her mother over a nickname that was likely to be quickly forgotten. At least she bloody hoped so. Besides, it wouldn't matter what Winnie called him if they were in north Devon. Her mum was loud, but not that loud . . .

'Where have you parked the Merc?' Lawrence looked out over the driveway.

'I'll tell you later,' Julie replied a little curtly, her smile tight.

'What do you mean you'll tell me later? That sounds ominous! You haven't bashed it, have you?' Lawrence cupped his chin, as if this might be the very worst thing he could imagine. 'Please tell me you haven't damaged that paintwork?'

'No, Loz, I haven't bashed it or damaged the paintwork. But *Mr Walker's* associate dropped by and so we took the bus . . .' Julie's tone was deliberate, paced.

Cleo wondered who Mr Walker was. First Mr Portland, now Mr Walker, it was all very mysterious. Any thought of humour, however, vanished as she watched the colour ebb from her brother's face. It was hard to gauge the atmosphere, but 'tense' would come close.

Julie continued, 'But you know what they say' – she clicked her fingers – 'easy come, easy go.'

Cleo looked towards Georgie who gave a subtle shrug; he too was clearly wondering what the hell was going on. Lawrence looked grey, as if his blood had run down into his boots. Everyone turned to stare at him. Cassian stood tall, his fingers flexing by his sides. Domino curled into the chair and put her arms around her knees.

'Would anyone like me to bring the cheese in?' Winnie trilled.

'So that's that, Loz.' Julie ignored her mother-in-law and stared at her husband. 'That's that.'

'Well.' Georgie, her beloved Georgie stepped forward to try to defuse the situation, remind them all why they were there. 'This is Tommy's first day and I'm sure he has loved meeting you all, but . . .'

'The truth is . . .' Her brother ignored Georgie and began in a faltering tone that changed his demeanour. 'The truth is . . .' He closed his eyes and there was a second when no one moved, still unsure if this was part of some elaborate pantomime or whether the couple were mid-row; either way it was more than awkward. 'Things are about to change.'

'What's going on? What's going to change?' Winnie asked with her hand at her throat. All thoughts of cheese seemingly now fled.

'We're thinking of moving.' Addressing the room, he shook his wrist, as was his habit, suggesting the feel and movement of his weighty Rolex was a thing of comfort.

Cleo felt her mouth drop open as he stole her, as yet unannounced, thunder. *Please God don't say you're thinking of north Devon too . . .*

'Moving? Moving where, for goodness' sake? I don't understand. You have that beautiful house; you don't mean out of the area, do you? You don't mean . . .'

Her mother, it seemed, ran out of words and Cleo more than understood, feeling an awkward cloak of embarrassment settle over the room. She was certain that everyone, like her, was thinking about the last time they had upped sticks and gone to Australia. And how Winnie had crumbled. She wondered now if her departure would have a similar effect, but doubted it.

'Course not out of the area, Winnie! How could they? The kids are in school, it's where their friends are, it's where we are! And Loz has got big projects here, the new builds, the . . . the . . .' Bernie sounded similarly stunned, as he voiced what they were all thinking.

Lawrence wiped his face and turned to look at his wife. There was a pause when he stared at Julie and she stared back, her expression fixed, her stance assertive, until eventually, he spoke with his hands on his hips, as if this power pose might help him finish.

'You're right, Dad, you are absolutely right! Lots of big projects going on, but sometimes moving is positive. A change of scenery can be good for you, gives you a new perspective.' He banged his hands together and immediately Cleo looked towards Tommy, who thankfully hadn't stirred at the loud crack. 'The new houses are going to be something else; I've got such plans. They're huge, with beautiful wide front doors, ornate gardens, incredible, breathtaking kitchens and so much more. I know what people want and what's more, I know how to build them!'

'You do, son,' Bernie echoed. 'So, where's the Merc?' he asked with a look of confusion, reminding them all that this was how the topic had started.

Cleo looked on as Domino rose from the armchair and stood with Cassian, flanking their mum, who now stared at her husband with what looked to be a mixture of loving and loathing. Thomas slept soundly and she was glad; this was hardly the induction she had envisaged into his new family.

'I'm getting it resprayed.' He nodded.

'Oh, how lovely!' Winnie clapped her hands. 'What colour? Mr Portland the estate agent has a Porsche 911 and it's a beautiful blue. He was here earlier, you just missed him, Jules. He's married to a man! I must admit I was quite surprised; he doesn't look gay.'

'What does gay look like?' Cassian asked.

'Not like Mr Portland,' Winnie fired. 'Anyway, would you like me to ask him what the exact shade is, Loz? I think any car would look smashing in it.'

'Yes, yes, that'd be great, Mum, thanks, and I can pass it on to the garage. They're specialists. High-end specialists, they'll do a good job. I'm sure.' He swallowed.

Cleo watched as Jules's face fell; she looked close to tears. It was hard to fathom what was going on, but she got the feeling all was not well between her brother and sister-in-law and from the

302

way the kids stood close to their mum, it was clear which side of the fence they stood. Her heart flexed in anguish for them all. It made her feel thankful for the simple, uncomplicated love that she and Georgie shared.

'It'll be okay, Dad.' Domino's words of support were both curious and heart-rending, and as Jules sniffed, Cleo felt the pull of tears herself.

'Of course it will all be okay!' Bernie did his best to jolly the atmosphere. 'Of course it will! We are the Kelleways, everything is always okay! We have so much to look forward to, and so much to celebrate – all good things! Not least the arrival of little Tommy boy!'

'You're right, Dad.' Lawrence looked his father in the eye. 'We have a lot to look forward to, we really do. I mean, look at my kids, my brilliant kids.' He spoke with a crack to his voice as he pointed at Cassian and Domino who took a step closer to their mother. 'Domino is going to go far – she's smart, beautiful. And you, Cass,' he addressed his son directly, 'you have the whole world at your feet, off to university, one big party. Just think of it, all those girls yet to meet.'

'I'm not interested in meeting girls, Dad.' Cass's voice cracked.

'Of course you are! Good God, is it only me who knows how to look on the bright side?' Lawrence raised his voice. 'Look at us all sat around with faces like a wet weekend! We should be celebrating the arrival of this little one!'

Cleo smiled as he and everyone else turned their attention to her baby boy.

Georgie stared at her wide-eyed, as if, like her, he was trying to figure out what exactly was going on here.

'So, Loz, where do you think you might move next?' Georgie asked his friend with a tone of concern. Cleo knew how much he had hated it when Loz had been so far out of reach in Australia.

'Not far, Georgie, not far,' her brother replied.

'Not far at all.' Julie spoke up, her voice more commanding than her slightly stooped posture and look of dejection might have suggested. 'You'll find *me* back up the Merrigo. The kids too. And I'll be living quietly. I'm done.' Her tears trickled over her cheeks. 'I am absolutely done.'

Cassian looked a little overwhelmed. He leaned against his mum in an act so loving, Cleo could only hope that she and Thomas might share a similar closeness. She and Julie shared a knowing look, as if they had both come to conclusions, as if they were both moving on. Finally, done.

'The Merrigo!' Winnie laughed loudly. 'Oh my goodness, can you imagine?'

But no one else saw the funny side.

This exchange was not what Cleo had imagined when they arrived earlier, and it was yet another unexpected layer to spoon on this already fraught gathering, which was supposed to be no more than a pop-in for a quick cuppa.

Winnie walked backwards until her calves met the smaller sofa and sat down.

'I quite like the Merrigo.' Georgie winked at their nephew. 'Got some smashing customers up there.'

'Thank you, Georgie.' Cassian spoke with affection to his uncle.

She had never, ever loved her husband more.

Domino reached out and took her brother's hand and Cleo hoped the siblings would always take comfort from the love of each other, love that would see them through the darkest of days. The kind of relationship she had always longed for between her and Lawrence.

'We'd better get Thomas home.' Cleo rose slowly, feeling a fragility to her body of bone and muscle that was still a little raw. 'We've already been here far longer than I planned. I want to be home when he needs a feed.' She looked around the room. 'We love you, Cass, Dom, you know that, right? And we are so proud of you both. I reckon Tommy is very lucky to have cousins and role models like you two. You too, Jules, my wonderful mate.' She turned to her brother. 'And we love you, Loz, because of our history and our ties, and, just for the record, not because of the car you drive or the house you live in. You're my brother, you're Tommy's uncle!' She smiled, hoping he understood that her words were the truth.

'Thank you,' he whispered, his mouth twisted with emotion.

'Well, this isn't getting the chores done, is it, all this navel gazing?' Winnie stood up and coughed, pulling her shoulders back.

Cleo's phone beeped. She fished for it out of her bag and read the message aloud.

'Ah, it's from Aunty Pattie. "Congratulations on the birth of your precious baby boy!" That's nice.'

'Isn't it just?' Her mum's response a little cool, a little clipped. 'Come on, Cass, you can help me get my jobs done.' She smiled at Cassian. 'Right now I need a bit of help in the garden.'

'Sorry, Nan, but I'm going with Mum.' His tone was resolute.

'I see.' Winnie took a deep, calming breath, her tone a little resigned, her demeanour calm, as if taking it all in.

'I'd love to help you.' Bernie stepped in.

'Good.' Her mum straightened. 'Because the first thing we are going to do is cut down that climbing rose and put Little B's new shrub there instead.'

Cleo saw the look of anguish on her dad's face at the suggestion, and she understood! She knew the hours and hours he put into caring for it, tending it in all weathers, day and night.

'Really, Mum? You're going to chop it down?' she asked.

'Yes! Really, Cleo!' Winnie spoke loudly, laughing suddenly. 'I absolutely hate the fucking thing!'

'Mum!'

'Winnie!'

'Whoa, language!'

Cleo, Bernie and Georgie simultaneously expressed their shock. Only Lawrence laughed, and Domino, the poor little mouse, didn't know where to look or what to do. The whole atmosphere was suddenly a little charged, and more than a little awkward.

'Well, it's true, I do!' Winnie was unrepentant.

It was after a silent pause that her dad spoke softly. 'I'm done with caring for it, Winnie. I really don't care if it grows wild or falls over.'

'Really?' her mother asked with eyes full of tears in a rare show of emotion.

'Really. But just so there's no doubt, my sweet' – Bernie coughed and, walking over to his wife, he held her arm – 'I will chop it down. I'll do it right now, in fact. It sounds like a way to herald new life, new beginnings; the perfect plan.'

'I think so.' Winnie Kelleway kissed her husband lightly on the face, wiping the stray tears that escaped down her cheek as she did so. 'And you do know how I love a plan.'

ABOUT THE AUTHOR

Photo © 2023 Paul Smith @paulsmithpics

Amanda Prowse is an international bestselling author of twenty-nine novels published in dozens of languages. Her chart-topping titles *What Have I Done?*, *Perfect Daughter*, *My Husband's Wife*, *The Coordinates of Loss*, *The Girl in the Corner* and *The Things I Know* have sold millions of copies around the world. Other novels by Amanda Prowse include *A Mother's Story*, which won the coveted Sainsbury's eBook of the Year Award. *Perfect Daughter* was selected as a World Book Night title in 2016, and *The Boy Between* (a memoir written with her son, Josiah Hartley) was selected in 2022. She has been described by the *Daily Mail* as 'the queen of family drama'.

Amanda is one of the most prolific writers of bestselling contemporary fiction in the UK today. Her titles consistently score the highest online review approval ratings across several genres.

A popular TV and radio personality, Amanda is a regular panellist on numerous daytime ITV programmes. She also makes countless guest appearances on national and independent radio stations, including LBC and talkRADIO, where she is well known for her insightful observations and infectious humour.

Amanda's ambition is to create stories that keep people from turning off the bedside lamp at night, that ensure you walk every step with her great characters, and fill your head so you can't possibly read another book until the memory fades . . .

Follow the Author on Amazon

If you enjoyed this book, follow Amanda Prowse on Amazon to
be notified when the author releases a new book!
To do this, please follow these instructions:

Desktop:

1) Search for the author's name on Amazon or in the Amazon App.
2) Click on the author's name to arrive on their Amazon page.
3) Click the 'Follow' button.

Mobile and Tablet:

1) Search for the author's name on Amazon or in the Amazon App.
2) Click on one of the author's books.
3) Click on the author's name to arrive on their Amazon page.
4) Click the 'Follow' button.

Kindle eReader and Kindle App:

If you enjoyed this book on a Kindle eReader or in the Kindle
App, you will find the author 'Follow' button after the last page.